Wicked Fantasy

Nina Bangs

BERKLEY SENSATION, NEW YORK

THE BERKLEY PUBLISHING GROUP
Published by the Penguin Group
Penguin Group (USA) Inc.
375 Hudson Street, New York, New York 10014, USA
Penguin Group (Canada), 90 Eglinton Avenue East, Suite 700, Toronto, Ontario M4P 2Y3, Canada
(a division of Pearson Penguin Canada Inc.)
Penguin Books Ltd., 80 Strand, London WC2R 0RL, England
Penguin Group Ireland, 25 St. Stephen's Green, Dublin 2, Ireland (a division of Penguin Books Ltd.)
Penguin Group (Australia), 250 Camberwell Road, Camberwell, Victoria 3124, Australia
(a division of Pearson Australia Group Pty. Ltd.)
Penguin Books India Pvt. Ltd., 11 Community Centre, Panchsheel Park, New Delhi—110 017, India
Penguin Group (NZ), 67 Apollo Drive, Rosedale, North Shore 0745, Auckland, New Zealand
(a division of Pearson New Zealand Ltd.)
Penguin Books (South Africa) (Pty.) Ltd., 24 Sturdee Avenue, Rosebank, Johannesburg 2196,
South Africa

Penguin Books Ltd., Registered Offices: 80 Strand, London WC2R 0RL, England

This is a work of fiction. Names, characters, places, and incidents either are the product of the author's imagination or are used fictitiously, and any resemblance to actual persons, living or dead, business establishments, events, or locales is entirely coincidental. The publisher does not have any control over and does not assume any responsibility for author or third-party websites or their content.

WICKED FANTASY

A Berkley Sensation Book / published by arrangement with the author

PRINTING HISTORY
Berkley Sensation mass-market edition / May 2007

Copyright © 2007 by Nina Bangs.
Cover illustration by Danny O'Leary.
Cover handlettering by Iskra Johnson.
Cover design by Lesley Worrell.

ISBN: 978-0-425-20995-0

BERKLEY SENSATION®
Berkley Sensation Books are published by The Berkley Publishing Group,
a division of Penguin Group (USA) Inc.,
375 Hudson Street, New York, New York 10014.
BERKLEY SENSATION is a registered trademark of Penguin Group (USA) Inc.
The "B" design is a trademark belonging to Penguin Group (USA) Inc.

PRINTED IN THE UNITED STATES OF AMERICA

10   9   8   7   6   5   4   3   2   1

Wicked Fantasy

Prologue

"You are *so* burnt toast without butter, hot bod." Sparkle Stardust aimed her most ferocious-but-still-sexy glare at the man leaning his hip against her candy counter. And a spectacular hip it was, attached to an equally yummy torso topped off by broad muscular shoulders beneath his white T-shirt.

The grim reaper tattoo on his right bicep was a cool touch that added to his whole dangerous-dude image. Sparkle loved dangerous men.

Too bad he had scrambled eggs for brains. "Question to self: Who in their right mind would *dare* insult me to my face?" Sparkle tapped her chin with one perfect nail, rolled her eyes to the top of her head, and pursed her lips in fake thought. "Um, no one with the sense of a beetle."

"You have no idea who I am." His glance was dark defiance.

"Damn right. I don't have a *clue* who you are. I just know the Big Boss sent you here to learn at the totally perfect knee of the best. That would be me, the *undisputed* number one at creating sexual chaos throughout all of humanity." Why the hell had the Big Boss sent her someone with a big, fat attitude? Deimos might have been a little immature, but he'd at least been malleable.

Stupid Guy's smile was slow and sensual, almost as sexy as hers. But beneath the smile something shadowy lurked, something that chilled her. Sparkle frowned.

"I've been a cosmic troublemaker for a lot of years, lady, and I don't need anyone to teach me about erotic energy." He leaned closer. "Or its uses." His amber eyes set off little squiggles inside her that usually only did their thing with Mede. "I sort of resent that the Big Boss sent me here for training. How hard can messing with humans' sex lives be?"

Rage darkened his eyes. He might sound almost playful, but the eyes didn't lie. This guy was trouble. What a waste. His lips were made for kissing every inch of a female body, and his thick tawny hair begged for a woman's fingers. He had a lot to live for, but he was definitely working on a death wish.

"So beautiful . . ." Huge fake sigh. Sparkle did regretful sighs well. Okay, so she did everything well. "So dumb. Let's get things straight. You were sent here to take the place of Deimos—who had an unfortunate obsession with action heroes—because I'm simply the best at creating wicked sexual situations. So are you up for being mentored or not?"

"I'm up for lots of things, but being mentored isn't one of them." He lowered his thick lashes and gripped that luscious lower lip between perfect white teeth. He glanced down in case she couldn't figure out what part of him was "up" for lots of things.

"Then you can leave." Where did he get off thinking he could compete with her, the woman who'd reigned as the queen of sex, sin, and seduction in the cosmic troublemaker world for thousands of years?

His gaze turned thoughtful. "You think you're so great, then how about a little contest, hmm? I bet you're working on a project right now."

"Contest?" The whole concept of "contest" was foreign to Sparkle. She'd been at the top of the sexual heap for so long that it never occurred to her there might be other troublemakers who thought they were good enough to take her place. Well, beating up on this jerk might be amusing. "What're the stakes?"

His shrug was casual, but Sparkle didn't miss the gleam of battle in his eyes. He'd probably cheat. She certainly intended to. Not that she *needed* to. Ever. But cheating was fun.

"Here's the deal. Whichever one of us hooks up a happy couple first gets to mentor the loser. And this can't be one night of sex and out. Too easy. To win, you have to prove your couple is having an ongoing sexual relationship." His smile promised she'd enjoy any lessons he taught her.

Under different circumstances, she'd be tempted to explore possibilities with him. Not this time, though. He probably thought he was manipulating her, but he'd learn soon enough that you didn't bait Sparkle Stardust and survive to brag about it. "Sure. Why not?" She allowed herself a small secret smile. "In fact, I have the perfect twosome for you. I was going to tackle them myself once I hooked up the people I'm working on now. But hey, if you're as good as you think, you won't even break a sweat."

"Uh-huh. Details?" He looked suspicious, as well he should.

"A wereshark is working in the Castle of Dark Dreams. Banan . . . Remind me to find out his last name when I see him. Anyway, he doesn't have a mate." Sparkle hoped her smile didn't look as sinister as it felt. "He's just a good old boy looking for some love. And lucky Banan, Destiny Moya just checked in. She's into fish. They're perfect for each other."

His expression said he figured there were a few things she wasn't telling him.

Sparkle jumped in with a question before he could ask for more info about Banan and fish-woman. "So what should I call you, Mr. Tall, Delish, and Delusional?"

It was his turn to frown. "Didn't the Big Boss send my résumé to you?"

"Nope." Now why would the Big Boss choose to keep things from her? Sparkle didn't think for a minute that he'd forgotten about the résumé, because the Big Boss remembered everything, including how many times each trouble-maker cursed him each day. "Tell me about yourself."

"Edge. No last name. Guess you don't need to know who I was, just what I'm going to be—the mentor to Sparkle Stardust." Grinning, he pushed away from the counter and walked to the door. "By the way, you have a nice setup here. With the candy store right next to a theme park dedicated to adult fantasies, you must get lots of . . . business."

"Edge? What's with the über alpha name? And yes, Live the Fantasy supplies me with lots of customers." All so sadly lacking in satisfying sex lives. "I just expanded my operation. I opened a small club in the park's most popular attraction, the Castle of Dark Dreams. Stop by for a drink when you need something to dull the agony of defeat."

His quick smile acknowledged her hit. "You have no idea how much of an über alpha guy I am. Don't underestimate me. I sure won't underestimate you, even with the Sparkle Stardust thing going on." His smile widened. "By the way, the nail color's chipped on your big toe."

Sparkle didn't even notice when he left because she was staring down in horror at the toe exposed for all to see by her strappy Jimmy Choo sandals. Damn. She'd just put that color on last night.

When she finally dragged her gaze from the offending

toenail, she stared at the door Edge had left ajar. Her instinctive shiver had nothing to do with the cool breeze drifting over her bare arms—weird, because Galveston in September didn't have any cool breezes. He *knew* her. He'd understood that chipped nail color would upset her. She, on the other hand, knew squat about him.

Then she took a deep, steadying breath. She'd find out all there was to know about Mr. Sexy and Mysterious right away. Yeah, something about him set off warning signals, but she chose to ignore them. No one could beat her in head-to-head, mouth-to-mouth, or any other matching body part competition. Certainly not a nobody named Edge.

Choosing a chocolate cream from her display case, she slid her tongue across all that sensual sweetness and then sucked the cream slowly into her mouth, savoring the almost orgasmic pleasure. Mmm, yes. Chocolate always put things in perspective.

She wondered what Edge would do when he found out that Destiny Moya was a shark hunter?

I

"Heard from the bitch goddess tonight." Conall threw back a shot of whiskey and then placed the empty glass firmly on the counter. He ignored the words of seduction in every language known to man—and some probably *not* known to man—carved into the wood. "The curse lives."

What Conall really wanted to do was fling the glass through the mirror at the back of the bar. The mirror with all the erotic scenes etched into it. But then he'd be facing seven years of bad luck. He'd already lived through centuries of hell, and he didn't need any extra years tacked on. "Morrigan paid me a visit in her crow form. She perched on the edge of the sink while I was shaving. Where're all the cats when I need them?"

"Let me guess. She figured you'd enjoyed life too much lately, so she found another Kavanagh for you to serve and protect." Eric's smile showed fang, a sure sign he didn't like the goddess.

Who did? Morrigan wasn't a lovable kind of deity. "She stopped by to tell me the last living Kavanagh would be here tonight. Not married and no kids." And if Conall had his way, there wouldn't be a next generation of his hated enemies.

Eric frowned. "You should've called me. I might not be able to take down a goddess, but I could sure let her know you have friends in high places." He pushed his untouched glass around on the bar as he transferred his bad temper to the painting on the wall opposite him. The one with the almost-naked men and women doing what almost-naked men and women usually do when they hook up. "What was Sparkle thinking when she decorated this place?"

Distracted for a moment from his anger at Morrigan, Conall glanced at the painting. "She was thinking about sex. You don't name a club Wicked Fantasy and then put cherubs on the walls. But if she gets any more explicit, Galveston's finest will be knocking on her door."

Eric nodded and then shifted back to the main topic. "No chance Morrigan will reduce your sentence for good behavior?"

"Nope." Conall felt Eric's anger at Morrigan as waves of outrage. Eric's friendship warmed him, as much as he could be warmed after interacting with the Irish goddess of war. Too bad Morrigan trumped even the power of an ancient vampire. "Thanks for the support, but there's not much you can do. I pissed her off eight hundred years ago, and she's got the memory of an immortal elephant."

Eric shifted his body a little to the right, making sure he wasn't in line with the bar's mirror. Most of the club's customers were too into their partners or drinks to notice that one of the guys at the bar was a no-show in the reflection department, but Eric couldn't take a chance. Mortals stampeding from the club screaming "Vampire!" might cut into Sparkle's profits. And next to sex and shoes, Sparkle was all about profits. Conall smiled grimly at the thought of a ticked-off Sparkle Stardust. She might be a pain in the ass, but she was also dangerous.

"Maybe if all the nonhuman entities in the castle united,

we could chase Morrigan's vindictive butt back to Ireland."
Eric grinned. "I'd pay hard cash to see Sparkle go a round
with her. And what about Asima? Snooty messenger of
Bast or not, she's got a goddess in her corner."

Conall shook his head even as he scanned the shiny new
club Sparkle Stardust had opened in the hotel lobby of the
Castle of Dark Dreams. He ignored the darkly lush sexual
décor in favor of searching out the reason for both the
whiskey and his depression. "Even if we got rid of Morrigan, it wouldn't end my curse."

Eric followed his gaze. "Will you know this Kavanagh
when you see him?"

"Yeah. All of the rotten, lousy, cheating, thieving"—
pause for deep breath so he could continue his list—"con-
niving, manipulating, arrogant, lecherous bastards look the
same. I'll know him." Conall just hoped this Kavanagh
stayed in Galveston so he wouldn't have to leave the
friends he'd made at the castle.

"Think he's here yet?" Eric was staring at a small table
tucked into a corner of the intimate club. "You said all the
Kavanaghs you'd served were men. Wonder why?"

Conall glanced at the door where a couple had just entered. "Nah, no sign of him. I'm always assigned to protect
the oldest of the jerks, and the Kavanagh men live longer
than the women. They're too mean to die." He looked to
see what had caught Eric's attention.

A woman sat at the table talking to Sparkle, a woman
who sucked the breath right out of him. Conall leaned forward so he could see better in the club's dim interior.

"Want me to describe her? I have enhanced vampire vision, remember?" Eric didn't try to hide his amusement.

"I can see just fine. And you're married. Don't look."
The anticipatory tightening of his body surprised him.
He'd thought he was too focused tonight on Morrigan and
the curse to notice a woman. Evidently his body didn't
give a flip about evil goddesses or curses.

Eric slapped him on the back. "Go over and meet her. Maybe this Kavanagh won't even turn up tonight. Don't waste your time drinking with me." He glanced at his watch. "Besides, I have to go. Promised Donna we'd walk on the beach tonight." He slipped off the stool. "I'll have my cell with me. Give a shout if this guy shows."

"Walking on the beach?" Conall grinned. "You're so whipped."

Eric offered him a glare before stalking away.

Conall felt his smile fade. He wouldn't call Eric. He'd handled his curse for eight hundred years, and he'd keep on keeping on. He got off the stool and headed toward the woman at the table.

Gerry Kavanagh had come here to catch a snake, but she'd caught a Sparkle Stardust instead. She preferred the snake. Who had a name like Sparkle Stardust anyway? Gerry rubbed the spot between her eyes where a headache would've been forming if she could still get them.

"Look, Sparkle, I love your club, and I appreciate that you sat down to keep me company. And huge thanks for the heads-up on what I need to do to make my outfit more sensual. But I'm here on business, so I'd better get on with it." She glanced at the nearby tables. Whoever had e-mailed the anonymous tip had promised that Jinx would be here tonight. "Uh, have you seen a guy that sort of looks like a snake?" Did that sound dumb or what? Besides, Jinx in human form looked more like a happy ferret.

Sparkle raised one perfectly arched brow. "Snake? Why? I mean, if you're going to hit on a guy, pick one who's decadently gorgeous and built for sex. Like him." She pointed toward the bar so Gerry wouldn't mistake exactly which "him" she meant.

"I'm not here to hit . . ." Gerry glanced at the bar. Whoa!

Would you look at that. There were a bunch of men at the bar, but only one worthy of a "whoa!"

He was a visual hot fudge sundae and a major wow on her personal sizzle meter. Not only was he tall—hard to judge sitting, but he had to be six-four or six-five—he had the broad shoulders and muscular body to make that height seem formidable. Dark, shaggy hair and a hard, uncompromisingly male face pushed every one of her buttons from her neck all the way down to . . . wherever. She was totally unbuttoned.

She coughed to clear her heart out of her throat. Snake. She was after a snake. That's all she needed to concentrate on right now. Play wasn't on her agenda tonight. "Yeah, he's spectacular, but I don't mix business with pleasure." She fixed her gaze on Sparkle. Absolutely no pleasure allowed. Damn.

Sparkle made a small moue of disappointment. "How shortsighted. And your business would be?"

Okay, important decision here. She had to find out if Sparkle knew anything about Jinx without—

"Hi there, sweetie. We were just talking about you." Sparkle reached up to grab the arm of the man who'd walked up silently behind Gerry and was now hovering over their table. "Sit for a while." She urged him into the seat between them.

Gerry met his intense stare. Gray eyes. Hard, like the rest of him, but softened by a thick fringe of dark lashes. Uh-oh. Business and pleasure were about to collide with enough force to rain down pieces of her good intentions onto her hapless head. How could she concentrate on Jinx when Mr. Whoa was only inches away? She firmed her lips; she'd find a way.

Sparkle leaned toward him and slid her fingers the length of his arm. Gerry lived the moment vicariously—the feel of the smooth silky shirt over flexed muscles and warm flesh.

"Gerry and I were talking men. She was looking for some guy who looked like a snake, and I thought that was pretty pathetic. So I pointed you out as an alternative to the snake." Sparkle's smile was a sly lifting of her lips. "She thinks you're hot."

Gerry forced herself to glance around the club again. If she didn't look at him, maybe . . . Hot? "I didn't say he was hot." Okay, so she'd used the word *spectacular*. But spectacular didn't have the same sexual connotation as hot. Fine, so he *was* hot, but Sparkle didn't need to put words in her mouth.

"Meet Conall McNair. He helps run the Castle of Dark Dreams. So if you wake up in the middle of the night with an insatiable appetite for something sweet, make sure you call Conall." Just in case Gerry didn't "get it," Sparkle slid her tongue across her lower lip while her strange amber eyes gleamed with the joy of her wicked suggestion. "He'll cure any woman's craving for sweets."

Sparkle was so outrageous that Gerry couldn't help herself. She grinned. Then she made a major mistake. She looked at Conall. He returned her smile, but his was a lot more effective. It was slow heat set for long, leisurely loving until she was fork tender.

Gerry swallowed hard. *Snakesnakesnake.*

"Sweet?" He looked offended. "I might be a lot of things, but sweet isn't one of them."

He was right. Conall's overwhelming physicality—a smooth-muscled body that was so there it screamed sexual animal—combined with the hard eyes of a man who'd seen too much violence and the sensual mouth of a man who'd seduced too many women, delivered a one-two punch of erotic desire.

Violence? Her imagination was officially out of control. She broke eye contact to sweep the room again. No Jinx. Stiffening her spine, or whatever part of her body needed stiffening, she looked back at . . . Sparkle. *Coward.* "It's been great meeting you and Conall, but I really have to find this guy—"

"Why?" Conall leaned forward, his large hands resting open on the table.

Body language? Leaning forward, aggressive. Open hands, nonthreatening. Which signal to believe? "Because it's my job." There, she'd said it. Now how to explain what she did in a way that wouldn't have them making a call to the nearest mental health facility.

"Not to repeat myself, but your job would be . . . ?" Sparkle tapped one perfect nail on the table. Definitely threatening.

"I'm like a cop, but I work for the private sector." The private sector as in all those entities that officially went bump, grind, or boo in the night.

"You mean you're a PI?" Conall looked confused.

"Uh, not exactly." She glanced at the floor for inspiration . . . and spotted Jinx slithering along the baseboard in his little green snake form. He was wearing a megawatt diamond ring around said sneaky form. Well, hell. "Oops, gotta go."

Gerry pushed away from the table and rushed in pursuit of the snake. She didn't know whose ring he'd snatched, but she wanted to catch him before the victim discovered it was missing. Hysterical shrieks and confusion would only aid Jinx in his escape. Humans rarely looked down when they were pursuing a thief.

As Gerry wound around tables, trying to keep her attention totally on the snake, Jinx spotted her and slithered faster. He was heading for the restrooms. Gerry grinned. She had the little bling bandit. He'd probably stashed his clothes in the men's room. As long as the room didn't have an open window, Jinx had nowhere to go. Besides, he'd need a few seconds to change back to human form. She'd pounce on him as soon as he changed forms.

But fate intervened, as fate had a way of doing. No one

came out of the men's room so that Jinx could slither inside, but someone did leave the ladies' room. Jinx didn't
have time to be choosy. He slithered inside just as the
woman let the door swing shut.

Gerry charged in after him . . . and came to a skidding
halt. Five women jockeyed for position in front of the
mirror.

"Ugh, I can't stand it. Look at these lines in my forehead. Good thing I have my plastic surgeon on speed dial.
I feel a Botox moment coming on." The woman leaned
closer to the mirror, the better to view the horror.

"God, I hate these lights. They show up every little
thing. Look at these grooves next to my mouth. I look like
Pinocchio."

Gerry coughed to get their attention. "Umm, has anyone
seen my pet snake? He slipped in here—"

Oomph. The women shoved her against the wall as they
all stampeded from the restroom like the wrinkle fairy was
in hot pursuit. The two women still in the stalls screeched
as they lifted their feet off the floor.

"Is it poisonous?" This from the stall nearest the exit.
Sounded terrified. "If I tiptoe, can I slip out the door?"

"Who the hell would bring a snake into a club anyway?" The middle stall. Sounded really cranky. "I bet it's
illegal. Where's my cell phone? I'll ask my lawyer."
Rooting-around-in-purse noises.

Uh-oh. Gerry had to keep them there until she cornered
Jinx. He'd be waiting for the first woman to open the door
so he could slither out. "Leaving is so not a good idea. Jinx
attacks anything that moves. Stay still. And keep your feet
off the floor. He loves ankles. Can we say bloodthirsty
predator? He enjoyed the last ankle he bit so much that he
left his little fang embedded in it. Don't worry, though, the
fang grew back."

Silence. Okay, that had worked out semi-nicely. Gerry
figured it wouldn't take her long to locate Jinx and then—

Someone flung the restroom door open. Damn. Jinx's body was a green blur as he made a break for freedom. "Stop him!" If she didn't catch Jinx, she may as well flush her budding career down any one of the room's toilets. What were her chances, though, that any woman walking through the door would collar Jinx?

But the hand that reached down with blinding speed to scoop Jinx up was very male. And very familiar. "I think you have some explaining to do." Conall's sexy mouth was drawn into a grim line.

He glanced at the stalls. "I have the snake, ladies. You can come out when I leave. Be sure to talk to Sparkle Stardust. The club will want to make up for all your mental anguish."

"Mental anguish? Give me a break." Gerry blinked to keep from rolling her eyes.

"Mmm. Every club should have a sexy guy in the ladies' room for little . . . emergencies that come along." Eyes peered at Conall through the cracks in the stall doors. The middle stall was in a better mood now.

Conall held Jinx by his tail. The ring slid from the snake's body and into Conall's open hand. He studied the ring before handing it to Gerry. Then without speaking, he pulled open the door and waited for her to walk past him.

Once in the hallway, he studied the little green snake still dangling from his fingers and then speared Gerry with a tell-all-or-die glare. "Talk."

Urp. Gerry stared up at Conall. Way up. Good Lord, he filled the whole doorway. And he looked determined. *Really* determined. She didn't blame Jinx for not trying to change back to human form. This guy would make green Jell-O out of him.

There'd be no escaping without feeding Conall some kind of story. Possibilities raced through her mind, all completely implausible. If she couldn't think of a believable lie, she may as well tell him the truth. He'd think she was crazy, but that was fine with her. As long as he gave Jinx back.

She nodded at the snake. "Jinx is a thief. He's also a shape-shifter. I work for a group dedicated to making sure that nonhuman entities obey Texas laws." There. He'd gaze at her blankly and then either laugh or shake his head in disbelief. "Now if you'll give Jinx to me, I'll see that he doesn't visit the Castle of Dark Dreams again." She held out her hand.

Jinx turned his beady little eyes toward her, and Gerry didn't have any trouble reading his intention. He'd wait until Conall was gone and then he'd return to human form, counting on his speed and strength to escape from the rookie cop. Was he in for a surprise.

Conall raised his hand, moving Jinx out of her reach. Jinx looked a little panicky as the floor grew more distant.

"Uh-uh. Don't touch. Thieves don't slither in and then just slither out. I figure Jinx came in this direction because he left his clothes in the men's room. I'll go get them and then we'll meet you outside the castle. Jinx and I need to have a man-to-snake talk." Conall smiled at her, but the humor didn't reach those cold gray eyes. "So you police the paranormal world? A cool but strange job for a human."

"Uh, right."

"Give the ring to Sparkle. She'll get it back to the owner."

Gerry stared wide-eyed as he turned and walked into the men's room, leaving her standing there. Not only did he believe her, but he'd kept Jinx. She was screwed.

Anger roiled, and she thought about racing after him, using her superior strength to body-slam him to the floor, and then ripping Jinx away from his grasp. What a satisfying thought.

Of course, she'd have to do this in the men's room. In front of men performing necessary bodily functions. Not the low-key approach Payton favored. Maybe Payton was right about not calling attention to her . . . uniqueness.

Okay, she could handle this. First she'd get rid of the ring, and then she'd retrieve her prisoner.

It didn't take long to find Sparkle. She was waiting for Gerry at the end of the hall. "A mob of women almost knocked me down a few minutes ago, and I just saw Conall go into the men's room holding a snake. Dare I hope for an explanation?" Her eyes were bright with curiosity as she led Gerry back to her table.

"No." Gerry didn't have time for idle chitchat. She held the ring out to Sparkle. "I found this in the restroom. Someone must've taken it off when they washed their hands." The lie didn't matter since she'd never see Sparkle again.

Sparkle took the ring and stared down at it. "So glittery, so beautiful." She sounded mesmerized.

Weird. Gerry half expected her to fly off to her nest with the shiny bauble, cawing happily. "Well, it was great meeting you, but—"

"You should answer your phone." Sparkle never once glanced away from the ring.

Gerry frowned. "Why? I turned it off when I—" Her phone rang. What the . . . ? She pulled the phone from her pocket. Yeah, it was definitely ringing. She moved away from the table to take the call.

"Gerry, this is your supreme leader. I assume no one is listening."

Gerry sighed. Supreme leader? God save her from old vamps who'd once been dictators of small third-world countries. "I hear you, Payton. What do you have?" She knew her boss wasn't calling about Jinx. Little pissant thieves didn't warrant a call from Payton the Pompous.

"I just received a tip from a reliable but anonymous source that one of the most dangerous entities on earth is staying at the Castle of Dark Dreams." Payton oozed self-importance. "Unfortunately, you're the only one we have on the spot."

She could almost hear his frown. Gerry grinned. Tough shit. This was her chance to prove she could handle more dangerous criminals than Jinx. "Name and description?"

"Mmm." Payton would be studying his computer screen right now. "He has many aliases. I'll e-mail you a list. Usually only uses a first name. No last name on record. Tall, sandy-colored hair, amber eyes, and irresistible to women. Oh, and he has a grim reaper tattoo on his right arm. Do not, I repeat, *do not* try to apprehend. If you locate him, simply observe whom he meets and what he does. I've recalled Burke from his assignment. He'll be down to take over as soon as possible."

Gerry narrowed her eyes. Not if she had anything to say about it. She was ultracompetitive. Always had been. This was *her* man. "What type of entity is he, and what's he wanted for?"

She spoke quietly as she glanced at Sparkle. Sparkle offered her a finger wave before turning to the two angry-looking women bearing down on her. Gerry guessed these were the "mentally anguished" women from the restroom.

"It doesn't specify what type of entity, but he's wanted for marrying, fleecing, and then permanently disposing of five hundred wealthy women."

Five hundred? Wow. If she handled this case right, she would advance right up the paranormal police ranks. "So he's offed a bunch of wives. Definitely a creepy criminal. But he's just dangerous to his wives, right? I mean, he's not a whoever-gets-in-my-damn-way serial killer?"

"The report says he murdered three hundred twenty-one husbands and one hundred fifty nosy neighbors who 'got in the way' of his marriages." Payton was starting to sound a little bored.

Too bad. This was her butt on the line. "So that's it, right? Just his wives, their husbands, and their neighbors?"

"Along with ten pizza delivery guys, four meter readers, three pool boys, and two carriage drivers who saw too much."

Gulp. "Carriage drivers?"

"He's been around for a while." Payton coughed, his signal that the briefing was over. "Good luck. Oh, did you catch Jinx?"

"Yes." Kind of.

"Good, good. I'll let you know when Burke is on his way." Payton hung up before she could involve him in a chat about a few minor details.

Like how the hell was she supposed to catch a nonhuman killing machine when she'd only been on the force for a few months? Yeah, she'd wanted to move up from tracking the Jinxes of the world, but this guy sounded seriously homicidal.

Okay, choices. She could hang around until Burke rode to her rescue. Not a choice at all. Her extreme drive for success had paid high dividends in her sales career before she became vampire. She intended to parlay that same drive into a great career at PUFF. To do that, she had to ID this murderer and then bring him down.

Right now, though, she had a snake to arrest. She'd worry about Hell's Husband afterward. She turned to smile at Sparkle, who'd made short work of her two outraged customers. "I think I'll be staying in the castle for a few days. Hope they have a free room."

Sparkle looked way too pleased. "Oh, yesss. I'll have time to expand your sensual universe beyond your wildest dreams. That's assuming you have any wild dreams." She almost purred at the possibilities. "September is busy, but talk to Holgarth and he'll get you a room. You'll find him in the great hall organizing the nightly fantasies."

Fantasies? Oh, right. The Castle of Dark Dreams was part of Live the Fantasy, an adult theme park where people could role-play until they dropped. Good thing she didn't have any desire to act out strange and scary scenarios. Been there, done that. Besides, she had work to do. A killer was on the loose and probably scoping out another rich wife even as they spoke.

"Will do. Now I've got to go out and collect my snake." She winced as she realized what she'd just said. Sparkle would bury her under a deluge of questions.

Sparkle merely smiled as she slipped the ring onto her finger and held it up so she could admire it some more. "Enjoy your stay in the castle. And don't forget to water the plant."

Plant? What the . . . ? Gerry didn't get it. Where was the curiosity and anger over the snake? Well, she wasn't going to hang around to find out. "See you." Then she hurried from the club and out of the castle to where Conall waited in the shadows with Jinx.

Gerry paused to let the darkness wrap around her. She loved the humid warmth of the Galveston air. No more freezing her buns off during Chicago winters. Although it wasn't the cold winds that blew her out of her hometown. Too many life-altering events happened there, and some memories weren't all warm and fuzzy.

She glanced up at the looming castle, which was spot-lighted for effect, and then down at the shadowed figure of Conall. For whatever reason, both sent an unwelcome chill down her spine.

The huge keep with its four square towers along with a moat, curtain wall, and drawbridge had a sort of savage beauty. But even though it was white, no one would ever mistake it for a fairy-tale castle.

Almost the same could be said for Conall. Savage beauty was a perfect description. But she didn't understand her frisson of fear as he watched her approach. Sure, he was big, buff, and really scary. But he was human. That should cancel out any worry on her part. It didn't.

Oh, what the hey, she was letting the castle's brooding

atmosphere get to her. She pasted on a smile as she reached the two men. "So, Jinx, had a busy night?" Gerry put off meeting Conall's stare, but she could feel it.

"That was a great ring. I coulda fenced it for big bucks. You got no heart, lady. I have a mortgage and car payment to make in three days." He twisted his narrow face into an expression of pitiful desperation.

Gerry sighed and ignored Conall's restless movements. Jinx wasn't a big man, but Conall made him look even smaller and more nondescript. And that's what Jinx wanted. A thief no one remembered was a successful thief.

"Gonna tell me about your starving wife and children now?" She kept her expression neutral.

She watched Jinx calculate his chances with that story. He must've seen something in her eyes because he shook his head. "No wife and children." His expression brightened. "But I do have an old, feeble mother who—"

"Shut up." Conall had spoken.

Everyone shut up. Gerry swallowed hard and searched for her missing voice. God, the man was walking intimidation. She wondered if she'd have that kind of presence after a few more years of experience. Nah. That talent was natural. You either had it or you didn't.

"Your prisoner bit me." He held up his thumb. Sure enough there were tiny twin fang marks on it.

"Yes, well, I'm sorry for that. I'll take him off your hands now and—"

"No."

The deep resonance of the word bounced around in her head for a few seconds before triggering her anger. "I don't think you have a say in the matter, Mr. McNair. I represent the Paranormal Undercover Field Force and . . ." Oops, she hadn't meant to blurt that out.

Conall stared at her for a moment, and she could almost hear his mind click-clicking over the name. She knew the exact moment he "got it" because a flare of amusement lit those gray eyes. "So you work for PUFF?" He allowed himself a soft chuckle.

"Don't blame it on me. They already had that name when I joined them. It's a point of contention within the force, I guarantee." In other words, Payton loved the name and everyone else hated it.

His amusement over, he crossed his arms over that wide chest and once again became Mr. Immovable. "He owes the castle."

Good, he'd reminded her of why she was mad at him. "You're interfering with my sworn duty. Now get out of my way." She put her hand in her shirt pocket, palmed her Securer, and then slapped Jinx on his bare arm.

"Ow! What the hell was that?" Jinx twisted his arm to get a look.

Of course there was nothing to see. "I have to stay at the castle a few days, so I've just made sure you'll stick around until I leave." Gerry grinned. She loved telling him about this part. "The research section of the force developed a chip that ensures you won't wander far from me. If you try to escape the park, you'll get a headache that'll put you on the ground until you crawl back to where the Securer can monitor you. I just inserted the chip into your arm. And don't even try to dig it out. It has ways of punishing that kind of behavior. I'm the only one who can take it out."

Jinx bared his teeth, making his resemblance to an angry ferret more obvious. "Bitch."

She smiled. "I try."

Jinx turned and raced toward the park's entrance. Gerry watched him go. He was in for a nasty surprise when he reached the Securer's limits. Once the pain hit him, it wouldn't take Jinx long to stagger back toward the castle. Once within the Securer's designated parameters, the pain would disappear.

"He's mine." Conall's angry rumble didn't brook argument. "He stole from the castle, so he has to work to make up for his insult."

Gerry frowned. Good grief, he sounded like Medieval Guy. She finally focused her full attention on Conall. Fine, so he looked like Medieval Guy, too. "He's my prisoner, and I'll pay for his room until I'm ready to take him away."

Without warning, Conall moved into her space and leaned down until they were almost nose to nose . . . and lips to lips. Wonderful, full, sexy lips. He was all angry male and sensual heat. The sensual heat made her almost forget the angry male part.

"Since I only have your word for who you are, I'd like to see some kind of ID and badge." His breath moved warm across her forehead.

Mmm. Felt good. She widened her eyes as she realized where her thoughts were headed. She was *so* not thinking tough and kick-butt. Reaching into her jeans pocket, she pulled out her badge and her ID. There. Let him argue with that.

And as he stared at her ID, she once again wondered at his easy acceptance of Jinx as a shape-shifter and her as part of some paranormal police force. A normal person would've called her crazy and walked away. What was with this guy?

When he finally looked up, his thunderous expression pushed her back a step. His scary index soared.

"Your name is Gerry *Kavanagh*?" He wore the same expression she'd always gotten when she tried to eat anchovies. Really grossed out.

"Uh, yeah." Maybe she shouldn't have admitted that. He looked seriously steamed. But then she remembered what she was. Conall couldn't hurt her.

His smile was the most terrifying thing she'd seen in a long time. It was bitterness, anger, and loathing all wrapped into one twist of his expressive lips.

"Take care of your prisoner. I'll come to your room later. We have to talk." He walked away into the darkness without giving her a chance to respond.

Gerry stared after him. Her intuition shouted an unnecessary warning.

This was bad. Very bad.

2

Conall stood outside the service door of the castle's restaurant while he took deep, calming breaths. He was counting on the routine of doing what he always did at this time of night to restore his common sense, because Morrigan would go ballistic if he strangled the last living descendant of Sean Kavanagh.

Three stray cats wound around his legs and meowed their demands that he feed them faster. While he filled their dishes, he tried to figure out why his temper was flaring out of control. Other Kavanaghs had earned his contempt, but this anger felt kind of personal.

As he'd stared at Gerry's ID, his first reaction was denial. This had to be some other Kavanagh. There were plenty of them around who weren't descendants of Sean.

Then he'd really looked at her—a small, curvy woman with long black hair, a sexy, pouty mouth, and eyes as green as Ireland itself. And in those incredible eyes he'd seen the shadow of Sean Kavanagh. All of Sean's descendants had those eyes. Conall would've recognized them sooner, but she'd distracted him with the aforementioned curves, hair, and mouth.

Besides, he wasn't expecting a woman. He'd *never* had to serve a female Kavanagh. Didn't want to serve *this* one. Why not? He wasn't sure yet, but he'd sort it all out as soon as he started thinking straight.

"Are you still feeding the riffraff? Face it, they're free-loaders. They could be earning their keep by catching mice, but why bother when they have the great enabler filling their bowls every night." Asima sat down beside him, wrapped her tail around her elegant Siamese body, and sniffed her disgust of the local tomcats. *"I get propositioned every time I come out here."*

"Then don't come out here." He didn't need the castle's resident messenger of Bast talking in his head right now. "Look, I have some heavy stuff coming down. I'm not up for a friendly chat."

"I come out here because every woman wants a little male admiration once in a while." She lifted one slim paw and licked it. *"I listen to them go on about my delicate ears, my beautiful legs, and my hot tail. Then I go back inside. I'm a tease, and I'm fine with that."* She sighed. *"It'll feel good to get back to human form."*

"And that'll be when?" Cat form or human form, it didn't make any difference. She'd be a pain in the ass either way.

"When I've finished my assignment for the goddess. Of course, I can't tell you what it is because it's a secret." She blinked huge blue eyes as she stared up at him. *"What heavy stuff is coming down?"*

He shouldn't tell her, but he needed to say something or explode. "The last Kavanagh is in the castle. Her name's Gerry."

The worst part? The first time he saw Gerry Kavanagh he wanted to strip every piece of clothing from her lush body, lay her down in the middle of Wicked Fantasy, and then try out with her all the erotic acts he'd ever imagined. If anyone had told him he could feel that way about a Kavanagh, Conall would've lopped off the liar's head and kicked it into the nearest ditch.

But that was before he found out she traced her lineage back to the Great Bastard. Knowing she was related to Sean should cool down all that lust real fast.

Something in Asima's gaze sharpened, became focused, expectant. *"And the significance of this Gerry person is . . . ?"*

Jeez, he should've kept his mouth closed. Asima had an unhealthy interest in everything having to do with his life. Maybe she was fixated on him because he liked cats, but whatever her reason, she got on his nerves.

"You've been sneaking around the castle long enough to have heard everything there was to hear about Eric, Brynn, and me. So don't pretend you don't know about Morrigan's curse. I'm not repeating the story to amuse you. Gerry is the last of Sean Kavanagh's descendants. I have to protect her and just hope she doesn't have any kids before she passes on." Somehow the thought of Gerry "passing on" didn't give him the pleasure he'd expected. "If she dies without leaving any little Kavanaghs behind, then Morrigan will free me from the curse."

"If she marries and has kids, they won't have the Kavanagh name."

Something in Asima's voice made him uneasy. Besides, he didn't want to think about Gerry marrying. "Yeah, but they'll still be Sean's descendants. Morrigan doesn't split hairs."

"I see."

Conall didn't have any trouble interpreting the grim determination in Asima's eyes.

"So it would be in your best interest if Gerry Kavanagh died young, correct?" She narrowed her eyes to dangerous slits.

Oh, crap. "Don't even think about it, cat. That's not how

the game's played." He offered Asima the glare that had sent grown men fleeing from the battlefield.

Asima didn't look impressed. *"I'll never understand the human mind. Everything's clear to me. If you have a problem, you make it go away. Preferably sooner than later."*

Conall studied her. She'd always been a pain, but she'd also amused him with her attempts at bringing culture to the castle. There was nothing amusing about this side of her character. "Cold, Asima. Really cold."

She gave him a cat shrug and then stood. *"I work for Bast, and the goddess is goal oriented. If a few puny human lives have to be sacrificed to achieve that goal, so be it."* Asima started to pad away from him.

"No, you don't." Reaching down, he scooped her into his arms. "You can take care of Bast's business any way you want, but my life doesn't concern the goddess. Here's the deal. Morrigan won't let me go unless this Kavanagh dies without my help. If Morrigan thinks I gave Gerry a shove into the hereafter, she'll punish me. And I've had eight hundred years of Morrigan's crappy temper. So don't mess things up for me. I can wait a few more years."

He was a hypocrite. He'd spent a few sleepless nights trying to figure out how to hurry the last Kavanagh on to his final reward without Morrigan knowing about it. So what was different now? He firmed his resolve. Nothing. He'd do what needed doing. Without Asima's help. Without *anyone's* help.

Asima sniffed. *"I like my way better."* Unblinking, she stared at him until he set her down.

Conall hoped he wouldn't have to protect Gerry from Asima. He'd seen the cat's power, and stopping Asima would be a bitch. "If you want to be helpful, keep an eye out for any men who look interested in her. I don't want her falling in love with some guy, marrying him, and then procreating all over the place."

"Hmm. A challenge. Interesting." With a swish of her tail, she stalked away from him.

The toms watched her leave and then went back to their food. Smart cats. Conall raked his fingers through his hair. He wanted to go up to Gerry's room now so he could get the whole revelation thing over with, but he knew it would take her a while to register and settle in. Besides, he needed to work off his mad first.

Wandering back inside, he went in search of Holgarth. The wizard was never a fun guy to talk to, but he seemed to know more about everything than anyone else in the castle. If nothing else, Holgarth would be an irritating distraction.

He found Holgarth in the great hall overseeing fantasies. Good thing Conall had Mondays and Tuesdays off. No way would he be able to concentrate on fulfilling other people's fantasies when Morrigan was trucking his life off to the local landfill. Granted he'd lived through this lots of times before, but it never got easier.

"Everything going okay tonight?" Conall scanned the hall. Nope, Gerry was nowhere in sight.

Holgarth took a moment to center his tall conical hat before answering. "Dealing with the masses is always taxing. One has to herd them like overeager lemmings." Stroking his long pointed beard, he studied Conall with piercing gray eyes. "Sparkle called. I'm to expect a Gerry Kavanagh, who'll want a room for a few nights. We have none at the moment, but Sparkle felt it was important that I find one for her. I assume this is the Kavanagh you've been waiting for?"

"Yeah." What else was there to say, and what the hell could Holgarth do to help? "I took the job here originally because Morrigan said the last Kavanagh lived in Galveston. The goddess likes playing games. She tells me where to go, and then I wait. I'm not allowed to pick up a phone book and find the bastard myself. Morrigan wants to manipulate the first meeting. I've just been hanging around until the goddess gave the word."

Damn, he still couldn't believe this last Kavanagh was a woman. "Morrigan visited me again tonight to let me know the last Kavanagh would be at Wicked Fantasy. Gerry's a—"

Holgarth held up a hand to stop him. Imperious. That's the only word that could describe the gesture. He swirled his long blue robe with its gold suns, moons, and stars around his thin body for effect. Holgarth was all about perception. And Conall's perception of the wizard was of a shrewd, powerful, and overbearing old fart who didn't give a damn what anyone thought of him.

Holgarth's thin lips lifted just a fraction, the equivalent of a belly laugh for him. "This overbearing old fart knows everything there is to know about Gerry Kavanagh. Leave her to me." With a dismissive wave of his hand, he turned to the next unlucky customer waiting to buy a ticket.

The fantasies were great once you got past Holgarth's poisoned tongue, but Conall never understood why people kept coming back once they'd gotten a dose of the wizard's snarky insults. Holgarth had given him exactly what he'd expected. Nothing. Maybe he'd go to his room and watch some football for his last half hour of freedom.

Conall turned to leave and then paused. "Are you ever going to stop rooting around in my mind without my permission?"

Holgarth raised one brow. "Of course not. Why ever would I? Your brain is such a treasure trove of amusing thoughts. They keep me laughing for hours. I'm so glad you're human and can't keep me from my nightly entertainment."

Conall exhaled sharply. "Don't underestimate me, old man." If he concentrated, Conall could probably lock the wizard out of his mind, but it'd never seemed worth the effort. He headed toward the stairs and his football game with visions of taking out his frustration on Holgarth's pointy head.

Gerry worked her way toward the pointy blue hat someone had told her belonged to Holgarth, while a grumbling Jinx trailed behind her. The only thing any worse for wear after Jinx's initial experience with the Securer was his temper. But she could deal with it for a few days.

"So if I shift will the chip stay in me?" He sounded sulky.

"You betcha," she countered with unflagging good humor. Why not? She'd caught her man and maybe had a shot at something bigger if she got a bead on this supercriminal before Burke arrived.

When she finally reached Holgarth she couldn't say anything for a moment because the complete cheesiness of his outfit took her breath away. Sure, he needed the outfit for the fantasies, but a black outfit would've lent a dark dignity to the whole thing. Blue with gold suns, moons, and stars was so Magic Kingdom.

Taking a deep breath, she pasted a smile on her face and approached him. "Hi, I'm—"

"Gerry Kavanagh. I know." He wasn't a lot taller than she was, but his gaze slid forever down his ski slope of a nose as he studied her. His expression said he was considering calling in the exterminators. "You have a secret that makes you feel, dare I say it, invulnerable." Holgarth's eyes looked cynical and very, very old. "Perhaps the Castle of Dark Dreams has its own secrets." His gaze hardened. "Always remember that the castle protects its own."

Enough. She'd had all the weirdness she could stand for one night. "I'll keep your cryptic warning in mind. But right now I need a room for a few nights." She glanced back at the glowering Jinx. "He'll need one, too."

Holgarth's lips twitched. A smile? Seemed unlikely. She didn't think a laugh line would dare form around his grim mouth.

"Ah, Jinx. A thief who lacks even the rudiments of cleverness. You allowed an inexperienced officer to trap you in the ladies' room." Holgarth was an equal opportunity insulter.

Gerry frowned. He knew a lot about what had happened tonight. Sparkle and Conall must've talked to him already, but just like those other two, he was taking the paranormal stuff in stride. Not normal behavior.

Jinx transferred his bad temper to Holgarth. "Hey, wizard dude, I do the best I can. Make yourself useful and convince Terminator Chick here to let me go." He paused to consider what Holgarth had said. "Got any suggestions I can use?"

Something wasn't right about the castle. Gerry would never claim to be a person overly sensitive to inner vibes, but she was getting a bad feel about this place. She owed it to her career to stay here, though. "News sure travels fast. And how'd you find out about this secret I'm supposed to have?"

Holgarth pursed his lips. "I can read everything in your very open mind. You really should make some effort to shield your thoughts." He turned away from her to speak to Jinx. "I wouldn't dream of interfering with an officer of the law, even one who has never experienced real evil."

"You don't have to experience evil to recognize it. So cut the patronizing drivel, wizard." Gerry's temper was so frayed that if Holgarth pulled the wrong string she'd unravel right in front of all his precious customers.

"That would definitely dim the gloriously happy atmosphere, so please, save any tantrums until you're snug in your room." Without even glancing her way, Holgarth continued speaking to Jinx.

"And if you wish to be more successful in the thievery trade, you should expand your repertoire of shapes. For example, a mouse could've moved a lot faster with that ring. Perhaps a tarantula would be best for escaping with a bracelet. You could carry it on your hairy back." Holgarth seemed to be really into his take on how to be the perfect thief.

Hero worship shone in Jinx's beady eyes. "Yeah, I get what you're saying."

"Hate to break up the Robbery 101 class, but I've had a long night." And it was getting longer by the minute. "Can we get two rooms, please?" Maybe after she relaxed for a few hours, all this wouldn't seem so bizarre. Besides, she was getting hungry.

Holgarth nodded. "Of course." He waved someone over to take his place and then guided them to an authentic-looking stone stairway. "Do you have luggage, Ms. Kavanagh?"

"Nope. I live at the west end of Galveston, so I didn't think I'd be spending the night here." She anticipated his next question. "I'm staying because I feel like it. And why are we going down?" Gerry peered into the blackness. Didn't look promising.

One puny wall sconce lit the bottom of the stairs. What lay beyond its small circle of light remained in darkness. Holgarth turned to look at her, and something in the play of shadows across his narrow face chilled her.

"The only rooms left are down here. The dungeon is to your right and all the other rooms belong to the vampires." He moved into the darkness.

Vampires? Gerry hurried to stay with him. She was afraid of the dark, had always been afraid of the dark. Which was a big, fat, honking laugh considering her present lifestyle. But the habits of a lifetime didn't die after two years.

She filled the scary blackness with words. "I chase non-human bad guys every day, so paranormal entities don't freak me out. So far I've met you, Sparkle, and Conall. Can you separate the humans from nonhumans for me?" Gerry tried to look only casually interested. All fake.

She couldn't sense nonhuman entities, so it made her job harder. Up till now, her work hadn't taken her to places where the paranormal activity went beyond the criminal she was tracking. But she got the feeling that Jinx and the serial wife killer might not be the only nonhumans hanging around the castle.

Holgarth didn't answer as he stopped in front of a door. The door swung open.

Major clue. No key. "Are you human?" She was pretty sure of the answer.

"Jeez, I can't see my hand in front of my face." Jinx bumped into her back when she stopped.

Holgarth waved his hand, and the lights came on in the room. "This is where you'll stay, Jinx. I put you right next to Gerry's room. I knew you'd want that."

"Yeah. Right." Jinx pushed past Gerry and Holgarth to get into the room. "See you tomorrow." He closed the door in their faces.

Holgarth moved on to the next room. He paused before opening the door. "Human? In a superficial way, I suppose." The door swung open, and he waved to turn on the light. "I'm simply a very old wizard. You can pick up a key to the room at the registration desk."

She refused to let it go. "How old?"

"Napoleon used my services in many of his more successful military campaigns." Holgarth started to turn away. "He should never have let me go."

Gerry remembered to close her mouth. She'd never met any human or nonhuman that old. Time to play it cool, though. Holgarth would enjoy her shock too much.

Once again he honored her with a small lift of his lips. "I'm enjoying your shock immensely. Your mind? Learn to close it or else your thoughts will be the main attraction at every party. That's if you play in the paranormal world very long." His brief attempt at a smile disappeared. "Or you'll be dead. On that cheery note, I'll warn you to leave

Conall alone and then take my leave." He faded into the darkness. She didn't even hear his footsteps on the stairs. And her hearing was very good.

Leave Conall alone? What was that about? She might have incipient lust for the guy, but she wasn't about to jump him any time soon.

Closing the door, she leaned her back against it and allowed the virtual breath she'd been holding to escape in a relieved whoosh. Blessed solitude. She kicked off her sandals before collapsing onto the nearest chair. Closing her eyes for a moment, she tried to plan ahead. Thank heaven Mom had a key to her house. She could bring some of Gerry's clothes to the castle. Gerry didn't dare leave to get her stuff. First off, she'd have to drag Jinx with her. Besides that little inconvenience, Payton had ordered her to stay at the castle.

Opening her eyes, she made the call and then looked around the room. Massive four-poster bed, sitting area with couch and two chairs, several antique-type pieces of furniture. The rich dark wood of the furniture, hardwood floors, and jewel-toned area rugs gave an opulent feel to the room. And then there was *the plant*. It was more stick than anything else. A few sickly-looking leaves clung stubbornly to the stick. What had Sparkle said about the plant? Oh, yeah, she had to water it. Why would a hotel put something like that in a guest's room anyway?

Her brain could use a few minutes of downtime before tackling problems like: Was Conall human, how was she going to keep Jinx out of trouble, was Conall human, and would she get a crack at collaring Mr. Murder before Burke arrived to do it for her? Oh, and was Conall human? So she stood and headed for stick-plant. A few minutes of mindless watering were just what she needed.

She was bending down to lift the plant when the door swung open with so much force it bounced off the wall. With a startled yelp, she straightened and turned around.

The object of her conjecture filled the doorway. All of it. And he looked really ticked off. "I love a man who knows where he wants to go and goes there with authority. Applause, applause." Gerry hoped her snarky comment took his attention from her shaking hands. He was a primitive male force that two years ago would've backed her flat against the wall. She concentrated on stilling her hands. It didn't matter if he was a tower of testosterone, because he couldn't hurt her.

"I wanted to get this over with. Sit." He gestured toward the chair.

"No." She remembered how well he did looming. She'd stand.

He practically thrummed with angry tension. "If I'd told you to stand?"

"I'd sit." And she also enjoyed poking sticks at big, fat wasps' nests.

He grunted at her before flinging himself across her couch. "Suit yourself."

Since the challenge was gone, she sat on the chair and tried to look relaxed. "Talk."

He raked his fingers—long, well-shaped fingers as opposed to the blunt fingers she'd have expected—through all that thick mane of hair.

"My last name isn't McNair. For publicity reasons and to guard our identities, Live the Fantasy advertises Eric, Brynn, and me as the three McNair brothers. We act in the fantasies as well as running the castle. Eric's a Mackenzie and Brynn doesn't remember what his original name was."

She didn't need any extraordinary powers to sense there was something definitely wrong with this whole picture. "Why can't Brynn remember his name?"

"The memory of his life before he became a demon of sensual desire was taken from him." Conall frowned. "Guess that sounds pretty weird."

"You think?" Two years ago she would've labeled Conall as whacked-out crazy. Now? Not so much.

"Brynn thought he was a demon until he discovered that a powerful but twisted being had manipulated him."

"Twisted being. Got it." What are *you*?

"Eric belongs to the Mackenzie vampire clan. He's one of the most powerful vamps I've ever met."

"Powerful vamp. Uh-huh." But what *are* you?

"And I'm Conall O'Rourke." He waited expectantly.

"I get that I'm supposed to react to that news, but I haven't a clue why." She sort of liked the way he tightened his spectacular mouth as he got all grim and gorgeous.

He looked disbelieving. "Don't you know a thing about your family's history?"

What did her family's history have to do with anything? Okay, so his last name was important. Nothing on Mom's side rang a bell. Her father? "Wait, I do remember something. My dad died when I was young, and Mom saved a diary he gave her. She showed it to me when I was a kid. I read it, but since I've never met anyone from his side of the family, I haven't looked at it in years."

"And?"

She thought about it. "Yes, I do remember the name O'Rourke. A bunch of slimeballs according to the diary." Oops, he might take offense at that. "Not you, of course. It's all ancient history. The chief slimeball was someone named . . ."

He waited silently.

"Um, Conall O'Rourke." Gerry stifled her nervous giggle. Strong kick-butt officers of the law didn't giggle. "What a coincidence. This Conall O'Rourke killed a Kavanagh ancestor, a really brave and great all-around guy named Sean. Well, isn't that . . . interesting." Something bad was coming. She could feel it.

"The damn Kavanaghs couldn't even do a decent job of

passing down the stupid curse to their descendants." He looked like that was just one of many Kavanagh sins. "Now I'll have to explain everything from the beginning."

Don't ask. She asked. "Curse?"

"Meet the chief slimeball. I'm the original Conall O'Rourke. Sean was in tight with the Irish war goddess, Morrigan. The bitch goddess was really pissed when I killed her favorite, so she cursed me to serve and protect his descendants until they were all gone." His smile was slow, wicked, and promised his next words would *not* be words of friendship and joy. "You won the lottery, Gerry Kavanagh. I've waited eight hundred years, but you're the last living descendant of Sean Kavanagh. I get to serve and protect you until the day you die."

Her heart pounded out a rhythm of disbelief. This wasn't happening. She couldn't take two life-altering events within two years. After all, there were people out there who'd never even had one. She'd share with them. "How do I know you're not just a guy with a crazy delusion?"

"Go back and read your family's history. The curse is in there. If that doesn't convince you, look up the family of Mick Kavanagh in San Diego. I'll give you their address. They can identify me." For just a moment, his gaze seemed to soften. "I'm real, Gerry. Guess we're stuck with each other for the duration."

Her mind raced back and forth in a random pattern of complete panic. It paused for a moment at a minor detail. "You don't sound Irish. What happened to your accent?"

Gerry thought she saw a flicker of sadness in those eyes. Then it was gone. "I lost it a long time ago."

She got the feeling he was talking about a lot more than just his accent.

"I haven't seen Ireland in seven centuries. None of the Kavanaghs I served cared about revisiting the past."

Great. Just freaking great. Stuck for the rest of her existence with a spectacular man who hated her and wanted her dead. "So if I die without having kids, you'll be free of the curse?"

"Yeah, that's how it shakes out."

Oh, shit. "About the dying part. Uh, that could be a problem."

"Why?" His expression said she wouldn't dare not die after her allotted years on this earth.

She smiled, exposing her fangs.

"I'm a vampire."

3

"Vampire." A sense of inevitability settled over Conall. Only the self-discipline of 800 years kept him from tearing the room apart in his fury. He'd probably be following her around until the earth exploded. No, it wouldn't end even then. They'd have space travel by that time, and she'd escape to another planet. He was doomed.

"Don't feel any obligation to go into serve and protect mode. I mean, I pretty much take care of myself." Her glance skittered around the room. "Maybe when I entered Live the Fantasy I crossed over into an alternate universe, because what's happened tonight is bizarre even by my standards." She met his gaze. "If Morrigan drops in for a report, I'll just tell her I gave you a few centuries off, so everything's cool."

And that was supposed to make him happy? "It doesn't work that way. I *have* to serve and protect you. I'll move a bed in here so I—"

"Nope. Not going to happen. I don't need you to protect me. I'm a vampire for crying out loud." She looked desperate. "You can't possibly expect to hang around messing with my life for the rest of my existence."

"I can, and I will." He hoped she read stubborn in his expression. "This isn't open to negotiation. If I don't follow through with Morrigan's plan, she'll make me pay. I can't escape the curse, so I'll damn well make it as comfortable as possible."

Curiosity warred with panic in her eyes. "What will she do if you just say no?"

"When men and women go to war, Morrigan chooses who'll live and who'll die. She has a low tolerance for people who cross her, and I ticked her off big-time when I killed Sean. If I 'just say no,' she'll kill my descendants who're in the military one at a time. And after eight hundred years I have lots of descendants."

"In the military?"

"She's a war goddess. She has power over anyone who picks up a weapon to fight for their country."

"I see." A line formed between her eyes as she thought. Cute. No, not cute. *Definitely* not cute. Nothing about a Kavanagh could ever be cute.

She frowned. "Wait. If you have tons of descendants, how could I be the last of the Kavanaghs? Common sense says that Sean's descendants would increase rather than decrease."

Conall shrugged. "Don't know. Over the years, they just disappeared. I only have to protect the oldest one. The Kavanaghs I served died of old age. Morrigan thought I might be getting rid of the others, but she could never find any proof. Hey, it was all good to me." He knew his grin was unrepentant.

"They disappeared?" As she thought about that, she gripped her lower lip with her teeth. When she released her lip, the wet sheen of it distracted him. "That sounds suspicious."

"I guess." Who cared what happened to them? "Your ancestors did some stupid stuff. Took after Sean."

She narrowed her eyes. "I've had it with you insulting my ancestors. From the little I remember, *you* were the super-jerk in this whole family saga."

That did it. To hell with her tempting lips and curvy little ass. "We'll talk about it tomorrow when you're more rational." He strode to the door and left before she could launch a counterassault. Once in the dark hallway, he paused to think.

Maybe he should be thankful all the previous Kavanaghs he'd had to protect were men. The Kavanagh men instantly saw the benefit to them. A Kavanagh man would've told him to sleep on the couch while he figured out how Conall could make him money or kill his enemies. Not that he'd done any enemy killing lately. The last time he got to use his sword was when he'd cut Mick Kavanagh's wedding cake. Mick Kavanagh had been a boring man. But at least he'd had the decency to die childless.

Conall eyed the room next to Gerry's, the one on the other side from Jinx's. It had a connecting door. It would have to do for now. He didn't intend to sleep on the floor outside her door like a lethal Not Welcome mat. He'd put a stop to that kind of crap centuries ago.

The room was occupied, so he'd have to get rid of the guest first. If he went upstairs to Holgarth, the wizard would give him a hard time. Conall didn't have the patience for that tonight. He knocked on the door.

A male vampire answered. Conall offered him an apologetic smile. "Hate to disturb you, but we just found out that a group of insane vampire-hating scientists sabotaged your room. You're not going to believe this, but the damn crazies sprayed the room with spores."

The vampire looked outraged. "See, I knew there was a reason why my allergies were acting up." Then he seemed to think about how that sounded. "Sure, we're not supposed to have allergies, but that's a crock. Good thing I brought my nasal spray."

Okay, so nutty humans made nutty vamps. "Problem is, when these spores touch a vampire's cock . . ." Conall shrugged and tried to look regretful. "They dig in and start growing."

"*Dig* in? Start *growing*?" The guy's eyes widened. "I brought antibacterial spray. Will that help?"

Good grief. "Don't think so. They're spray resistant. The crappy part is they live off your cock until one day you look down and its gone. The last vamp that stayed here has two inches left, and it's shrinking fast."

"*Two inches?*" His voice was a horrified squeak.

Conall paused for effect. "And it doesn't grow back." Then he softened it with an encouraging smile. "It's not all bad, though. The spores have little pink flowers. Pretty. The castle takes complete responsibility, of course."

The vamp slapped a protective hand over the area in question.

Conall hoped to God the guy didn't have a spray to make cocks grow back. He put on his really concerned expression. "You just checked in tonight, so unless you ran around naked, you're probably okay. I'll move you to another room so we can kill any spores still in there."

Conall leaned against the doorjamb as the vamp rushed back into his room and started throwing clothes into his suitcase. Within minutes he was out in the hallway again.

Conall didn't have to bother settling the guy into a new room, though, because once in the hallway, the vamp kept on going. He raced up the stairs, and before Conall could even remind him to check out, he was gone. Oh well. Maybe he wouldn't mention this to Holgarth. Conall transferred what he needed from his old space. Then he tried to relax with his football game.

A short time later he gave up on the game. He couldn't keep his thoughts from the damn Kavanagh next door— without her jeans, without her top, with only that luscious bare body pressing against his . . . He let his head fall back against the couch and closed his eyes. *Hell.*

How do I hunger? Let me count the ways. What do you know, her poetry class in college hadn't been wasted. Gerry spent two hours just sitting on her bed trying to come to terms with Conall O'Rourke. What would she do with him?

Fine, so she knew what she'd *like* to do with him. She wanted that muscular chest bared so she could skim her fingers across his nipples, slide her palm over smooth warm male flesh, and slip her hand beneath the edge of his pants to discover . . . Uh-uh, couldn't and wouldn't go there.

Better to concentrate on the other hunger. She'd perfected the sip-and-run technique. She'd sidle up to her pick on the menu—always a great-looking guy; if you were going to dine, dine well—lean into his neck, and bite.

Gerry didn't recall too much about the vampire who'd made her, but thank heavens she'd evidently inherited his ability to wipe away a human's memory of any neck nips just by the act of biting. It must be a chemical in her saliva or something. A big, fat yuck, but it came in handy. Besides, it was sort of cool to have a forget-me power.

And because she still had the whole human conscience thing going on, she only fed a little from each person. Ergo, she had to hit an appetizer, entrée, and dessert before she was satisfied. At least she didn't have to feed every night anymore. Twice a week kept her happy. Maybe as she grew older, she could stretch it to once a week. A vampire could hope.

Sighing, she gave in to her need and headed for the door. Too bad she had to stay near Jinx. That meant she'd have to feed from several someones in Live the Fantasy.

She was lucky the park stayed open all night. There would still be people around.

Once in the hallway, she hurried toward the stairs and light. Sure, with her enhanced senses she could see a lot better than when she'd been human, but dark was still dark. As a child, she'd pulled the covers over her head to escape the ghosts, goblins, and ghouls who came out to play at night. She'd chosen to believe the monsters couldn't yank off the blankets to get to her. Now, even as a bona fide night-scary herself, she feared the darkness. Dumb, dumb, dumb.

Gerry was so intent on reaching the stairs she almost didn't hear the footsteps behind her. She whirled just in time to see Conall grab Jinx by his shirt and lift him into the air, where he dangled helplessly. Jinx still gripped the lamp base he'd hoped to use to bash in her head.

Conall ignored Jinx's useless flailing as he stared at Gerry. "This is why you need me. I can't believe you let him sneak up on you. Any experienced vampire would . . ." He narrowed his eyes as a thought struck him. "When were you made?"

She *hated* telling him. "Two years ago." Now he'd use the information as a weapon.

Conall didn't disappoint. "Two freaking years?" He laughed derisively. "You'll be lucky if you survive another year."

He paused. Gerry read the open conflict in his eyes. Her survival wasn't a desired goal of the Conall who wanted the curse to end. But he was also committed to protecting her Kavanagh behind. Her sudden deep sadness surprised Gerry. It wasn't fun knowing someone wanted you dead.

The moment ended as he continued to point out her stupidity. "The problem with young vamps is they feel invulnerable. They don't realize that once they turn, every crazy in the universe will be out to get them. And taking a head isn't too tough for a dedicated wacko. Wake up and smell the danger, lady."

She tried to ignore her voice of reason that thought he had a good point. "Give me a break, O'Rourke. Jinx wasn't going to kill me with a lamp. He just would've made me mad." She turned her anger on the unfortunate shifter. "That was really stupid, Jinx. What was the purpose?"

Conall finally set the shape-shifter down, but kept hold of his shirt. The glance Jinx threw Conall said he thought this guy was one scary dude.

Then Jinx glared at Gerry. She evidently wasn't about to share scary status with Conall anytime soon. "I wanted to knock you out so I could search you for the remote, or whatever thing controls this damned chip in me."

Gerry sighed. This was going to be a long few days. "You would've knocked me out for nothing. The key is up here." She tapped her head. "The 'remote' is my brain. Each chip is calibrated to be in sync with the brain waves of the officer using it. I'd have to think you free. Not going to happen until we get to Hobby Airport."

"What's at Hobby Airport?" Conall released Jinx and then stared him back into his room. He waited until Jinx slammed his door shut before turning back to Gerry.

"A plane to take us to the middle of nowhere in west Texas where the prison for paranormal entities is." Damn Jinx for giving Conall the ammunition he needed to pro-claim her the witless wonder of the vampire world. Now he could justify tagging along with her for the rest of the night. "It's below ground, so no one is likely to spot it."

Conall looked dutifully impressed. "I've never heard of a prison for nonhumans."

She couldn't help her twinge of pride. "It's the first of its kind. Out-of-control beings give all of us a bad name."

"Sure." His gaze sharpened. "Where're you headed?"

"To feed." Would that gross him out? Would he leave her alone?

He nodded. "I'll go with you. Make sure you pick a woman. A man could hurt you."

Okay, this wasn't going to work. "Look, I'll say this really slow. I. Am. A. Vampire. Men can't hurt me unless they have big swords with them. And I feed alone. Go away."

"No." He set his sensual mouth in a grim make-me line. "And I have the big sword to keep you safe."

I bet you do.

To prove his point, he drew a sword from a back scabbard she hadn't noticed in the dark.

"That's it. I'm not doing dinner while some guy trails me with a blasted sword." Gerry didn't have any fancy vampire skills, just the basics: enhanced senses, increased physical strength, and preternatural speed. She used the speed now.

Within the blink of an eye, she was outside the castle and headed toward the nearest Live the Fantasy attraction, a pirate ship. Once on the ship, she relaxed a little. Conall couldn't reach her until the ship returned to shore. The man-made lake it floated on was perfect for losing pesky immortal warriors. She looked around for an appetizer. Thank heaven the ship wasn't crowded, so she'd have some privacy.

A man stood at the bow of the ship watching her. When she met his gaze, he grinned. For just a moment, something about his face reminded her of pictures she'd seen of her uncle Ray, who'd died before she was born. Then the moment was gone. This guy really didn't look that much like her uncle. They both had red hair, that's all.

Gerry studied the menu. Nice face, athletic body, *food*. She returned his smile and walked toward him. Perfect. He was the only one there, and the bow was in shadows.

When she reached his side, she leaned against the railing to gaze across the water.

"Beautiful night to be on a ship." He sounded friendly.

She turned to look at him. "Yes. All kinds of fantasies are possible on a night like this." Gerry leaned toward him.

He smiled again, revealing straight white teeth. "I'm Dell."

"Gerry." It didn't matter if she told him her name, because he wouldn't remember her.

He had short red hair and eyes that were so pale they almost looked colorless. An unfortunate combination. But he had a great smile, and all blood tasted the same in the dark.

"So are you just here for the night, or are you staying at the castle?" He edged closer to her.

Mmm. She imagined the hypnotic rhythm of his heart pumping all that wonderful blood through his veins. "I'm staying at the castle for a few days."

"Look at me, Gerry." Something in his voice had changed, become more intense.

"Hmm?" She leaned close, picking out the exact spot on his neck where she'd place her mouth.

He shifted a little away from her, and she raised her gaze to his eyes. Without warning, she felt dizzy. What the . . . ? She groped for something to hold on to, and Dell put his arms around her.

He was saying something, but she didn't pay attention because it felt like all the atoms in her body were drifting apart. Any second now her body would be gone. She'd just be a fading memory in the Texas night.

As quickly as the sensation began, it ended. She straightened away from him, and he let her go. His gaze was fixed over her shoulder. She turned to see what he was watching.

Well, hell. Conall stood waiting on the dock. He speared her with a stare that should've left a smoking hole in the middle of her forehead. Beside him stood a woman, beautiful with long blond hair. The woman waved at her when she saw Gerry staring. And for just a nanosecond, something that felt suspiciously like jealousy stabbed her.

Of course, it wasn't. Beautiful-and-blond was welcome to him.

The ship was moving toward the dock. They hadn't been out very long, but from the look on Conall's face she'd bet he'd ordered the ship back to shore. She hadn't had a chance to get a drop to drink.

She turned toward Dell. "Thanks for catching me. I . . ." He was gone. Gerry frowned and glanced around. He must've joined the crowd waiting to get off the ship. Huh, so much for her vampire allures. Guess she didn't have any. But there was no more time to think about Dell as the ship reached the dock. She took a deep, fortifying breath. Even though breathing wasn't a necessity now, she'd never lost the reflex action.

Conall didn't give her a chance to open her mouth before going on the offensive. "Look, I have a job to do, and you're making it tough, lady."

He raked his fingers through his hair, and for a moment she allowed herself to imagine how those silky strands would feel sliding over her breasts. She blinked away the thought. Better not to imagine any part of him touching any part of her.

"You interrupted dinner, O'Rourke. Now get out of my way." She attempted to push past him, using her strength to enforce her demand.

He didn't budge. "Your vampire strength won't work on me."

She looked up at him with wide, startled eyes. "Why not? I thought you were immortal, nothing else."

Nothing else? The rage of 800 freaking years blotted out all his good intentions to stay calm. He leaned close, letting her see all he was and all he'd been. "Wrong. I'm so much more. I've crawled through the mud and filth of ancient battlefields. I've slain brave men at the command of your ancestors. And in recent years I've longed for those battlefields just to feel alive again. Hate for the Kavanaghs and Morrigan have fueled every minute of those eight hundred years."

"Oh." For just a moment, he thought he saw regret in her eyes.

Too bad. Regret wouldn't bring back all those lost years. "Yes." The word was a harsh expletive on his tongue.

She backed up a step, her eyes still wide. "Fine, so I'll walk around you. I mean, it's no big deal. Have you considered counseling or maybe some help with anger management?"

He growled low in his throat. *Downshift and stay in control, O'Rourke.* After all these years, he couldn't let a Kavanagh with big green eyes, a smart mouth, and too much attitude make him lose it. "Morrigan gave me the strength to save Kavanagh butts." He crowded her, invading her space, and if he just moved a little closer he could feel the texture of those sexy lips. Then he'd cup that tempting behind in his hands and pull her close. For the first time in eight centuries he'd find joy in a Kavanagh ass. "Morrigan also gave me the skill to track a Kavanagh she-vamp who won't let me do my damn job."

A pointed cough behind him reminded Conall he wasn't alone. Exhaling deeply, he tried to draw the tatters of his lost temper around him. Then he glanced at Donna. She was Eric's wife and light to Conall's darkness. Maybe she could talk some sense into Gerry.

Donna stepped to his side and smiled at Gerry. "Now that all the roaring is done, we can talk. I'm Donna Mackenzie, Eric's wife." Her long blond hair lifted in the light breeze blowing off the gulf, and her brown eyes were soft with understanding.

Conall backed away from Gerry, leaving Donna to do her thing.

Gerry nodded as she cast Conall a wary glance. "You need to learn some coping skills, O'Rourke, because if you get bent out of shape every time I make an independent move, you won't last eight minutes let alone eight centuries."

Donna's laughter seemed to be Gerry's signal to relax. She offered Donna a tentative smile. "I'd like to talk, but it'll have to be later. I'm starving, and I didn't get a chance to feed on the ship because we came back to the dock too soon."

Left unsaid was that it was all *his* fault. He frowned. "Feed? I saw you from the moment the ship left the dock, and all you did was stand by yourself at the bow."

Gerry looked puzzled. "No, you couldn't have seen me, because I was talking to a guy named Dell." Her voice trailed off as she studied his face. "You really didn't see him?" She glanced at Donna.

Donna shrugged. "Didn't see anyone." She cast him a pointed glance. "Look, why don't you stay here while Gerry and I hunt up dinner." Then she focused on Gerry. "I've only been vampire for a short while, but I've learned from the best. You'll meet Eric soon."

Gerry looked startled. "You're vampire?"

Conall tensed. Oh, shit. "Don't tell me you can't sense other vampires?"

"I can't sense *any* entities." She shrugged. "So what? Hey, I still do my job. My boss gives me a description or picture of the bad guy, and I go get him. I found Jinx, didn't I?" Her expression dared him to deny her success with the thief.

"Don't mean to rain on your parade." Sure he did. "But it would be hard to miss a snake slithering across the floor with a ring around its body."

Donna looked confused. "Okay, I know this probably makes some kind of sense, so why don't you explain everything to me while we hunt?" She urged Gerry toward some benches set in the shadows where a few people sat by themselves. The look she threw at Conall when Gerry wasn't looking said, "Sit. Stay."

Stubbornness warred with common sense. For once common sense won. Conall took off his sword before easing himself onto the nearest bench. Hell, old Mick Kavanagh was looking damn good right now.

"Oh goody, I found you alone." Sparkle Stardust's voice was low and husky, a sexual purr honed to perfection over thousands of years. But Conall knew the sensual persona was a useful front few saw past. He'd seen what she could do, and he'd *never* underestimate her. She skimmed her fingers across the back of his neck, and he tensed at the tingle of power she left behind.

Sparkle sat down next to him, and he watched all the guys within staring distance fix their gazes on the glide of her short black skirt up her bare thighs as she crossed her legs. She leaned toward him, and every man's attention snapped to the front of her black top as it gaped open. Way open.

She slid her gaze to the staring men and then offered Conall a sly lift of her lips. "Men have such simple needs. What about you, Conall? What do you need?"

Sparkle was working the room right now, but he wasn't in the mood to amuse her. "I need to be left alone. Why don't you get your kicks by playing to your audience? Cross your legs again. Pick up that penny from the ground."

"Mmm. Are we grouchy tonight? An angry male animal has a sexy primitive aura that excites me." She watched him from those strange amber eyes.

"All men excite you, Sparkle." She wasn't going to leave him alone.

She smiled. "That's what Mede always says." Her smile faded. "I miss him."

I miss him, too. Ganymede was a cosmic troublemaker of such immense power that Conall didn't doubt he could destroy the planet or help the Texans win the Super Bowl if he so chose. He was also the "twisted being" who'd made Brynn's life a misery for so many centuries. Ganymede had sort of redeemed himself with that one, but Conall didn't trust him. Ganymede lusted after the dark side too much.

Right now, though? Conall wished Ganymede was here to distract Sparkle from him. "I hear you got a new guy to help you. What's he like?"

She stopped smiling. "I don't want to talk about Edge. He's not what I was hoping for." She took a deep breath, and her male audience took a breath along with her. "So what do you think of Gerry? With someone to tweak her wardrobe, she'd be spectacular."

"I didn't notice."

Sparkle patted his knee and then let her hand rest there. "Of course you did. I can feel that you're conflicted. The scale right now is perfectly balanced: attraction to a beautiful woman versus hatred for all Kavanaghs." She studied him. "I wonder what it will take to tip that scale?"

"There won't be any tipping going on. I'll do my job for as long as it takes, and that's it." He scowled. "If she'll let me." Okay, a moment of self-honesty. He *was* attracted. And he hated it.

Sparkle shook her head. "You're so not getting it, Conall. I don't even have to root around in your mind to know you'd like to have sex with her. And right now she's looking at my hand on your knee. She's fighting the jealousy, but she's losing." Sparkle grinned. "Yeah, I am rooting around in *her* head."

Conall closed his eyes and fought against the pictures trying to form behind his closed lids—placing his mouth on Gerry's breasts, teasing her nipples with his tongue, spreading her legs and thrusting deep inside her. He shook his head to clear it and opened his eyes. "What's your point, Sparkle?"

She shrugged. "Sex is my thing. It's powerful, provocative, *perfect*. So I see this really hot guy who's going to be stuck with this woman for hundreds of years, and I say to myself, 'Self, why wouldn't this man get it on with this woman?' It sure would make the centuries go past faster."

"She's a Kavanagh, Sparkle." Jeez, he must have some kind of repetitive-message syndrome. Said and thought it all before. But he couldn't help it. No way could he lose the hate and contempt built up over eight centuries in one night. He didn't think he'd ever be able to look past her name and his curse. "Besides, the way things are going, I won't be getting that close to her. She's fighting me on the serving and protecting thing."

Sparkle sighed as she studied her nails. Eye-poppingly purple. "You haven't given her a good reason to accept you. Gerry needs to see a benefit to having you around." She slid her gaze the length of his body before lifting her gaze to his face. "I, of course, immediately saw the benefit of that gorgeous body." She glanced to where Gerry and Donna were heading back toward them. "She's hunting criminals alone. You're big and powerful. The two of you could catch criminals a lot faster than she could alone."

Sparkle had something there. Gerry couldn't even sense nonhumans—not that he could either. She wasn't old enough to have any advanced powers, so his strength and experience might help balance out her weaknesses. "Good idea. Thanks."

Sparkle started to say something, but suddenly froze. She was staring past the ship to the beginning of the Wild West section of the park. Conall followed her gaze.

"That bastard." She glared at a guy talking with three women.

Wow, and what women they were. Tall, blond, and beautiful. Walking clichés. Conall was impressed. "So who's the guy?"

"Edge." Sparkle spoke through gritted teeth.

"Do you know the women?" He was already losing interest as Gerry drew closer. He'd have to find a way to offer his help without making it sound like he didn't think she could do her job by herself.

"Oh, yeah. I know them." She sounded a little scary.

"Not friends, huh?"

"They're going to complicate things." She stood.

Conall watched her curl her fingers into claws. Uh-oh, Edge and the ladies had trouble heading their way. "So who are they?"

She glanced at him, and her amber eyes actually glowed. "They're demonic vestal virgins." Then she strode toward the group.

4

Sparkle forced herself to slow down, look more uncon-
cerned, and put more sway into her swagger as she drew
nearer Edge and his twisted-sister trio. She wouldn't give
him the satisfaction of knowing how pissed off she was.
Where the hell had he gotten the power to interest *them*?
Because the virgins were all about power, lots of it.

Edge smiled as she reached his group. "Having any luck
hooking up your immortal warrior and the sexy little vampire? Gotta hand it to you. Trying to match up the last of
the Kavanaghs with a guy Morrigan loves to hate takes
guts. The goddess doesn't want Conall having fun with any
part of his curse."

"And I should care why?" Once again, Sparkle sensed
darkness behind that I'm-just-an-ordinary-guy persona. His
black T-shirt, khaki cargo shorts, sandals, along with that
bland smile couldn't quite camouflage what lay beneath.

"You've found out a lot about my project in a short
time. I wonder how?" She'd discover who leaked info to
Edge. And when she did? The responsible party would be

visiting a proctologist, because it was kind of hard to remove your head from your ass.

And why was she having so much trouble tracking down any useful details about *him*? The Big Boss wasn't returning her calls, and no one she'd contacted recognized his name.

He shrugged. "I've been around long enough to have lots of sources."

Suspicion touched her. "How long?"

He slanted her a sly look. "I'd like you to meet my friends."

Sparkle allowed herself to be distracted. For the moment. "We've met before. And friends? I don't think so. Unless you make a habit of cozying up to scorpions." She turned her gaze on the women. "Fulvia, Tullia, and Varinia. The demonic eye color is so you. Having any trouble adjusting to the hot climate?"

They looked stunning. Damn it. Their white I'm-so-pure swirly dresses were a lie, but the color looked great on them. Wow, would you look at Tullia's man-killer stilettos? Incredible. Sparkle hoped they really hurt. *Keep your mind on business.* "So what brings you to this little corner of Texas?" She *wouldn't* ask about the shoes.

Tullia licked her bottom lip and cast Sparkle a sideways glance from her pale demon eyes. "Once a virgin, always a virgin. Edge called the Castle of Dark Dreams to our attention. It's a hotbed of sexual excess. My sisters and I are here to make it stop." She shifted her feet to better display her awesome shoes.

Where did she *find* those shoes? Metallic shine, soft, smooth leather . . . Sparkle took a deep breath to refocus her attention. "Give me a break. You're vestal virgins who broke your vows. And to top it off, you kicked the shit out of the other virgins who threatened to rat you out." She smiled and hoped it looked as nasty as it felt. "How's hell treating you, girls?"

Fulvia snarled, exposing sharp white demon teeth.
"We got thrown into hell just for breaking a few dumb
vows. Yeah, so we kicked some virgin ass, too. So what?"
She waved her hands around to emphasize the unfairness
of it all.

Sparkle narrowed her gaze on Fulvia's nails. The nail
color was so red, so rich, so *perfect*. What color was that?
She had to know. Uh-oh, wandering off course again. She
did a few mental head slaps to reshuffle her priorities. "I
totally sympathize with you." Not. "Back to the reason for
you being here. Is Edge going to help you stop the sex?"
What *was* that color?

Varinia blinked. "Duh. *He* called us out of hell, so I'd
say that was a yes. We don't need him, though. The three
of us can make sex a nonissue whenever we want. It's what
we do. The Big Bad who heads up the underworld con-
demned us to eternal virginity. So if *we* can't have sex,
damned if anyone else will." She glanced at her sisters for
support and then back to Sparkle. "And you can't stop us."

"Okay, I get it." An eternity of virginity? Sparkle shuddered. She tried to glare at Edge, but her gaze kept sliding
back to those shoes, those nails. "You brought them here
so they could help you keep Conall and Gerry apart." The
shoes and nails were *not* important. "By the way, Tullia,
where'd you buy those shoes?"

"You like them? An old Italian man makes them by
hand for me." Tullia's smile was knowing.

Sparkle forced her gaze back to Edge. "If cheating is
your game, two can play." She'd meant to anyway. "You
called in more power, so I guess I'll make my own power
call." Those shoes were making her all shivery. Yeah, she
was shallow. So? "What's this old man's name, Tullia?"

Tullia shook her head and looked serious. "If I even
breathed his name he'd never make another pair for me."

Rats. Sparkle intended to get that old guy's name even
if she had to pull Tullia's fingernails out one at a time.

Speaking of fingernails . . . "Uh, what nail color is that, Fulvia?"

Edge frowned at her. "Look, I brought in the virgins so I could cheat and humiliate you. So where's the fury, the threats, the gnashing of teeth?" He looked mildly ticked off.

"Huh?" Sparkle pulled her attention back from the grip of nail-color fever. "Why should I be mad?" She *was* mad, but shoe and nail-color lust diluted it. "I expected you to cheat. You did. And if you think you've cut a deal with them to spare your two favorites, Banan and Destiny, forget it. They're not good at honoring vows or deals. The virgins will try to shut down all sex in the castle. They can't. As long as I'm in charge, sex will happen."

Sparkle decided that sounded like a great walk-off line. Besides, if she stayed one more minute, she'd grab Fulvia's wrist and twist it until the bitch told her the name of that sexy nail color.

Sparkle didn't look back, and she didn't stop walking until she reached her candy store, Sweet Indulgence. Edge was supposed to be watching the place for her, but he'd closed it down so he'd be free to plot behind her back with the Sisters Sinister. She slammed the door shut behind her and then turned on the lights. A closed store didn't make money.

She perched on the tall stool she kept behind her counter and reached for her phone. First she'd call Mede. Then she'd call the Big Boss to ask, okay, beg him to take Edge back and drop him in the primordial swamp where he belonged.

Sparkle punched in Mede's number and waited for that sexy voice.

"Yeah? Talk fast, my ice cream's melting."

"I need you."

"On my way, babe."

*   *   *

Gerry usually woke to silence. This time was different. As she lay in bed with eyes closed, drifting in that peaceful place between sleep and waking, she tried to make sense of the voice whispering in her head. It was telling her something important. Well, if it was so important, why wasn't the voice yelling? Hmm. And what was that smell?

She tipped over into complete wakefulness with a hard thud. The smell was burning cloth. Ohmigod!

"Yoohoo, Gerry? Uh, wake up, wake up. Your bed is on fire. Well, not technically on fire yet, but . . ."

Her eyes popped open and then widened in horror as she watched flames leaping and dancing from a burning candle across the upholstered bench at the foot of her bed. Any second the bed would be ablaze. Candle? Frantically, she scanned the room. What? Who?

A Siamese cat sat on the bureau watching her. *"Oh, goody. You woke up."* The voice in her head sounded disappointed.

Gerry's preternatural speed was on automatic as she leaped from the bed and made a grab for the phone. Just then, the sprinkler system kicked in.

Spitting and hissing, the cat jumped from the bureau and scurried under the couch from where it glared at her.

She clutched the receiver to her ear and waited for a dial tone. Nothing. What the hell . . . ? And where was the ear-piercing shriek of the smoke detector?

Before she could drop the phone and run for safety, the connecting door to the room next to hers exploded inward, followed closely by a very large, very naked male body.

Conall stood, strong legs spread wide, holding a fire extinguisher. Some women might lust after Superman. Gerry decided she'd take a naked warrior clutching a fire extinguisher every time.

He didn't say a word as he made short work of the flames, then he reached for the phone.

"It's dead." Just like she almost was.

Gerry reined in her panicked thoughts long enough to form a logical string of events. Fell asleep. Hadn't seen a lit candle before conking out. She wouldn't have missed that. Vampires tended to notice open flames. Glancing at the smoldering remains, she assured herself that, yes, there was a candle. Ergo, someone had wanted her dead, and they'd wanted it to look like carelessness on her part.

What was the point? Who'd want to destroy her . . . other than Jinx and Conall? Okay, so maybe that sarcastic wizard and the wife killer, if he'd found out she was hunting him.

Conall followed the phone line to the wall. "It's unplugged." He bent over to plug the cord back into the jack.

Be still my undead heart. If she wasn't freaked out by someone's attempt to barbecue her while she slept, she might be more affected by the most spectacular male butt she'd ever seen. It was smooth, tight, and compact. It begged for a woman's fingers to explore its masculine curves. But of course she *was* freaked out, so she didn't pay much attention.

"It was fine when I went to sleep." She frowned. Was it? She hadn't actually used the phone. "I think."

He reached up to press the test button on the room's smoke detector. Nothing. "Someone will check this out." Conall walked back to the phone. "I'll get someone to shut off the sprinklers."

While he was on the phone, Gerry couldn't have moved if she wanted to. She stood frozen, dripping water, trying to ignore the stench of soggy, burned fabric. Fact: Someone had put a candle on the bench, lit it, and then put something flammable close enough to catch fire and spread the flames to the bench.

She looked closer at the charred lump next to the candle. Damn it, the jerkwad arsonist had used her extra nightshirt as a fire starter. Memo to self: Send outraged note to manufacturer suggesting they use fire-retardant material for their nightshirts. Right now, though, she had to come to terms with the reality that someone had homicidal designs on her.

Which seemed pretty weird. She was a good friend, kind to animals and senior citizens, and pretty much an all-around likable person. Good grief, in high school she'd been voted Miss Nice.

Maybe it was the vampire thing. "Nice" wasn't a defining vampire characteristic. When had she started the deadly slide into ruthless and evil? She'd used the Securer on Jinx without a twinge of conscience. She loved tracking down paranormal nut jobs. And she hadn't watered that poor plant. Would she eventually morph into the queen of mean?

Get a grip, Kavanagh. She closed her eyes, hit her mental delete button to clear her mind, and then opened her eyes.

Glancing around, she spotted the cat still crouched under the sofa. How did it get in? How . . . ?

"I opened the door and walked in." The sprinklers suddenly shut off, and the cat crawled from its shelter. *"I don't have to actually open doors to get inside, but seeing a cat materialize in front of some people upsets them. Of course, once inside I could've changed to human form, but my job description stipulates that I remain a cat until I complete my assignment."*

Gerry narrowed her eyes on the cat. "You're a telepathic shape-shifter with the power to teleport. Impressive. Why're you here? And did you set the fire?"

"Setting fire to someone's bed is beneath me." The cat's narrow elegant face managed to convey outrage. *"I'm Asima, messenger of Bast, the Egyptian goddess of cats, the moon, sexuality, physical—"*

"I'll give you time to change into dry clothes and pack your stuff, then I'll get you into another room." Conall had moved to her side, still naked. The force of his presence felt like the hard shove of a hand against Gerry's chest. She almost reached up to rub it.

Conall was at ease with his body. Gerry wasn't. She glanced at that broad muscular expanse of wonderful male body, let her gaze dip to between those powerful thighs, and found it all . . . hard to ignore.

She forced herself to blink and then looked back at Asima. The cat avoided her gaze. "Why didn't you warn me?"

Asima tried for a hurt expression and failed. Or maybe she wasn't trying for any expression. A cat's facial muscles didn't lend themselves to deep emotion. *"I did warn you. I sat right on that bureau and yelled, 'Fire! Save yourself.' "*

"Uh-uh. Not true. You *whispered* in my head. Luckily, it was time for me to wake up anyway." Gerry heard Conall move closer, could feel the heat of his body. The temptation to stare at him was like the compulsion she felt when she stood at the top of a tall building. She wanted to look. She was afraid to look. Fear mixed with an unreasoning urge to jump. She wouldn't do it, but the desire was there.

"Don't mess with me, Asima. Did you set the fire?" Conall took deadly to a whole new level.

"No." A direct answer. Asima was no dummy.

"But you didn't overwork your vocal cords trying to warn Gerry." His voice was cold and quiet.

"Why would I?" Asima's tone said she was the only rational being in the room. *"If Gerry was stupid enough to leave a lit candle near her bed . . ."* She let the insinuation that stupidity deserved to be punished hang in the air. And then she said what Gerry sensed was the cat's true feeling. *"She would've caused her own death. Morrigan couldn't blame you. End of curse."*

"Gerry didn't leave that candle lit."

Thank you, Conall. But then he ruined it.

"Even a Kavanagh wouldn't be that stupid."

Conclusion? If neither Conall nor Asima had left the candle there, that meant . . . "Is there anyone in this castle who *doesn't* want me dead?" She held up one hand. "No, don't answer that. I'm overreacting. I'm sure there're a few—the guests, the maids, and oh, probably three or four others."

Conall ignored her comment while he studied Asima. "What were you doing here anyway?"

Asima did a cat shrug. *"Curiosity. A weakness of my species. I wanted to see her wardrobe."* She glanced at Gerry. *"Your clothes are extraordinarily unremarkable. Can we say boring? You're like a ball of clay waiting to be molded. Beware if the slut queen takes an interest in what you're wearing. Do* not *listen to her. I'll be around to help you pick out a few tasteful outfits once you settle into your new room."*

"Slut queen?" Too late. Asima disappeared.

"Sparkle Stardust. The two of them together is a scary happening." He raked his fingers through his damp hair. Then he looked at her. "You're wet. I like it. Change."

"You're naked. I like it. Put something on."

His sudden smile heated her all the way through. It was unexpected and so sensual she glanced down to make sure steam wasn't rising from her jammies. Nope, no steam. But every inch of the wet material clung to her fore and aft. Oops.

She tried for a normal walk as she went to the closet. But she could feel his gaze cupping each cheek as she moved. Was her butt wiggling? God knew there was enough there to wiggle and jiggle to their own rhythm. Talking about jiggling, she held her shorts and top in front of her chest as she backed toward the bathroom.

"You disappoint me." Something hot and primitive moved in his eyes. "You could almost redeem the whole Kavanagh clan." He thought about that. "Okay, not the whole clan. Maybe two or three."

Gerry couldn't herd her thoughts into one spot long enough to concentrate on them. Who'd tried to destroy her and make it look like an accident? What was she going to do with this luscious but dangerous man standing in her room? She should leave the castle, but that would guarantee she wouldn't have a shot at apprehending the wife killer. Would Conall get the wrong idea if she walked over and ran her fingers over all that wet, gleaming skin?

She reached behind her to feel for the bathroom door. His gaze never reached her face. He had some concentration problems, too. Good. "By the way, how'd you know there was a fire in here?"

"Sometimes the curse tunes me in when a Kavanagh's in danger. It doesn't always work. It worked this time." Conall shrugged. "Something woke me, and I smelled the smoke." He finally met Gerry's gaze. "I'll get dressed. Once you're in your temporary room, we'll talk."

Gerry pushed the door open and slipped into the bathroom. Then she shut the door and flipped the light switch. Temporary room? Didn't Holgarth say there weren't any more empty rooms on the vampire level?

Closing her eyes, she leaned her back against the door. She'd worry about that after her shower. She needed to feel water pouring over her, washing away the smell of burned cloth and the memory of a hard male body. And for just a few minutes she'd stop wondering who wanted to kill her.

Conall dried himself off while he tried to block out how good Gerry had looked. Good? Not a word he'd ever used in the same sentence as "Kavanagh." The only "good" Kavanagh was an old wizened one with one foot in the grave. Right now, though, he had to convince her to accept his protection.

First he called Eric to let him know about the fire and what he planned to do about it. Eric would tell everyone else. Then he pulled on jeans, a T-shirt, and shoes before returning to Gerry's room.

While he waited for her to come out of the bathroom, he took a look at the partially burned candle and then paced a lot. If he hummed to himself, he could block out the sound of the shower and the vivid erotic images that went with it.

She opened the door and walked into the room just as he noticed the plant. "Jeez, Houston looks like shit."

"Houston?" She walked to the couch and sat down.

Conall needed something for his eyes to focus on besides her long bare legs and the thrust of her breasts against the green top she was wearing. Nothing really sexual in the clothes, but on her . . . "The plant. The owner bought him in Houston and thought he looked sort of alpha with the thick stems and big green leaves. Now look at him."

"Yeah, it needs water." She glanced toward the candle. "That wasn't there when I fell asleep at dawn."

"You'd better pack."

"Right." She stood, walked to the closet, and began pulling clothes out to put in her open suitcase. "The door was locked. How did he, she, or . . . it get in?"

He helped her by retrieving the few things she'd left lying around. "Here's the deal about the Castle of Dark Dreams. Lots of paranormal entities stay here. Word has spread that the guys who run it are like them. They figure we'll understand their needs. It's possible that a few of them have powers like Asima."

"So locks mean nothing. Some nonhuman bad guy could appear in my room anytime he wanted to. Gee, I feel really safe." Gerry glanced around to make sure she hadn't forgotten anything before closing her suitcase. "Let's go."

Conall ignored her sarcasm. He picked up Houston and the suitcase. Somehow he didn't think Gerry would want to come back to this room even after the cleaning crew finished with it. He didn't blame her.

Opening the door, he waited for her to pass him. She slipped past and the scent of vanilla trailed her out the door. Free association brought up the words "hunger" and "dessert." Not words he wanted to think about when he thought of any Kavanagh.

As he closed the door, Conall realized that for the first time the name Kavanagh didn't ignite his automatic response of frothing rage. "Follow me."

"Why did you bring the plant?"

"Houston needs someone to care, too."

"How about you?" The first teasing note crept into her voice.

"Not me. My stem and leaves are just fine."

"I'm talking love, O'Rourke." She wasn't going to let it go.

And he wasn't going to satisfy her curiosity. "Houston doesn't need love, he only needs sex."

"You're joking."

Good. He'd distracted her. "I'll explain later." He stopped in front of the huge wooden door, put down the suitcase, and pushed open the door. It made its usual loud grating noise. He flipped the switch just inside the door.

Gerry picked up her suitcase and followed him into the . . . "Dungeon? You're putting me in a *dungeon*? What's the star rating here? Bet you'll lose a few after this."

She peered around at the usual dungeon stuff: rack, iron maiden, whips, chains, and a bunch of other props. Fake sconces and an electric hearth gave the place tons of atmosphere. There were two doors on the opposite wall.

Before he had a chance to explain, the furniture he'd ordered when he called in the fire arrived. He waited while the men set up a bed, night table, lamp, TV, couch, coffee table, and two chairs. They hung a few clothes hangers from the handcuffs attached to the wall.

Gerry watched with open mouth as they left. "Well, isn't this nice. Home sweet dungeon. If the maid doesn't make my bed right, I can chain her to the wall."

"Sit down, Gerry, and let me explain." Good thing he didn't have to work tonight, because this was going to take a while. He sat down and put Houston on the floor beside him.

She perched on the edge of the other chair, but he had the feeling she was ready to bolt.

"I can honestly say this has been the second most surreal night I've ever lived—using the term loosely—through. Guess I shouldn't make assumptions about life though, because the night's not over." She smiled at him, but it was ragged around the edges. "The only night that tops it is the night I was made."

Conall wanted to know about that night, and the fact that he did bothered him. "Once in a while we get too many vampires wanting to stay here. This is the only floor that's light free. So when we run out of vampire rooms, we put the dungeon off limits for the castle fantasies and let someone use it."

"Oh." She looked around.

"There's a bathroom behind the door on the right. The door on the left opens to one of two break rooms for staff. This one's for the nonhumans who work here. You can lock the break room door while you're here because there's another entrance."

She brightened. "Well, then that's okay. Sort of." Her expression said he and everyone else in the castle were so far out there they probably didn't even belong to this galaxy.

He took a deep breath. Time to make his pitch. "Someone tried to kill you tonight. Not Jinx because he doesn't have the power to get past your locked door. It wasn't me because I'm committed to protecting you."

"Whoa, don't cross yourself off the list. Whoever lit the candle was trying to make it look like I just got careless. If this Morrigan couldn't prove it was murder, she'd have to release you from the curse. And I don't think that connecting door would stop you. Sounds like a plan to me."

Her expression said she was turning over possibilities. "Jinx is a thief. He'd know how to pick a lock. But he realizes killing me wouldn't free him, so yes, I agree it wasn't Jinx."

Conall wondered if she could hear him grinding his teeth. "Not Asima, because she doesn't have a motive."

"Hate to interrupt again, but she didn't bust her little kitty butt trying to wake me up."

"Right." This wasn't working. Rather than roar at her, he stood. "I've got to water Houston."

"Water Houston?" She looked bemused. "I must've turned left and the conversation went right, because I've lost it."

He was afraid he'd shout at her, so he didn't answer as he yanked the bathroom door open, filled a glass with water and poured it into Houston's pot.

"So won't he die in here without light?"

"He doesn't live off light. He lives off sexual energy."

"Excuse me?"

"These plants belong to the owner, and they live off the energy generated when guests have sex." He sat down again.

She stared at him blankly.

He couldn't stop his grin. "Houston here has been deprived for a long time. Since he's yours for the duration, guess you have an obligation to him now."

"You're not kidding, are you?" She rubbed between her eyes. "Of course, you're not. A plant that gets off on sexual energy instead of Miracle-Gro." She shook her head. "Makes perfect sense in the Castle of Dark Dreams. Do you know how creepy that sounds? Hey, I feel for Houston, but he'll have to hunker down and hang on to his leaves, because there won't be any sexual energy floating around in here."

Conall didn't think this was the best time to talk about her lifetime protection policy underwritten by Morrigan, but it had to be discussed, especially after the attempt on Gerry's life. "Look, we have to talk about—"

"No talk. My head is going to explode if I have to think about one more thing." She stood. "I'm going for a walk. Alone." She held up her hand as he opened his mouth to speak. "I know. You have to guard me. Just don't get in my way."

As she turned toward the still-open door, Conall heard the sound of flapping wings in the hallway. He stared at the ceiling. Oh, crap.

A huge crow flew into the dungeon, circled a startled Gerry, and landed on the iron maiden.

Conall rubbed the back of his neck. Not that it did any good. No tension relief when the bitch goddess was in the room.

"Hello, Morrigan."

5

"Morrigan?" Gerry stared at the crow.

The crow returned her gaze with beady-eyed intensity.

"What brought you back?" Conall wore no expression.

Gerry thought she understood. No emotion equaled no fun for Morrigan.

Gerry felt enough emotion for both of them. The total insanity of the last two nights washed over her, and she came up sputtering with rage, ready to lash out at someone. And Morrigan was that someone.

"You know, you picked a great form. The old crow is you." She wanted to shriek at the top of her lungs and shake the feathers off the disgusting bird. "Who gave you the right to mess with people's lives?"

Gerry heard Conall stand and then felt his hand on her shoulder. He pulled her back against him, but the press of his hard body did *not* calm her.

"Easy." His voice was low and controlled.

Well, hers was loud and way out of control. "No one deserves to be punished for eight hundred years. And get out of my world. I don't want you manipulating my life just to satisfy your warped need for vengeance."

The huge black bird fluffed up its feathers so it looked even bigger and cawed at her. The little black eyes began to glow red. Urp. Had she said too much? Perhaps she lacked sensitivity. Even evil black birds needed a hug now and then. Nah.

"You will *not* speak to me in that tone of voice, puny vampire."

Wow. Morrigan sounded like a female James Earl Jones. And if Gerry wasn't so mad, she'd laugh at that sound coming from a crow.

Since she'd already ticked off the goddess, she might as well keep on truckin'. "What'll you do, destroy me? Oh, wait. If you do that then you'll have to release Conall from his curse. Wow, you have a situation here, goddess." She couldn't seem to stop running her mouth. A lifelong weakness.

She heard Conall's low curse just before he stepped in front of her.

"She's had a lot of weird stuff happen to her since she hit the castle, Morrigan. We're together, so what's the problem?" His grip on Gerry's arm easily kept her behind him.

Damn, what good was vampire strength if she couldn't get away from one blasted man? "Let me go. I can fight my own battles."

"No." He never took his attention from the crow.

Morrigan looked like she was considering murder and mayhem, but then decided to let the "puny" vampire live for the moment. "What did you mean by, 'What brought you back?' This is my first visit since you began serving Mick Kavanagh."

Conall tensed. "The hell it is. You hopped into my mind right after Mick died to let me know the last Kavanagh was living in Galveston. You told me to get a job at the Castle of Dark Dreams and wait for further instructions. Then last night you showed up in my bathroom, perched on my sink, and said that the Kavanagh would be at Wicked Fantasy. I went. She was. And now we're here."

Morrigan's eyes were doing the red and glowing thing again. Uh-oh. She was not a happy crow. The goddess turned her attention to Gerry. "Why were you at Wicked Fantasy last night?"

"Not that you need to know, but I got an anonymous tip that a thief I was after would be there." Gerry frowned. Coincidence? She didn't think so.

Morrigan didn't think so either. She let out a mental shriek that rattled around in Gerry's head. "Jeez, would you tone it down a little?" It didn't take a rocket scientist to figure this one out. Someone had impersonated Morrigan in order to manipulate them.

Morrigan flapped her wings and made angry crow noises. "Where is this thief?"

"Umm, down the hall. Room three." She wouldn't, would she?

She did. Jinx suddenly appeared in the room wearing nothing but red boxer shorts and a confused expression. "A dungeon? What, you're going to torture me now? I only stole the freakin' ring."

"Be still, puling human." Morrigan cocked her head to get a better angle on Jinx. "You are exceptionally unattractive." She hopped to the back of the nearest chair.

Jinx laughed. Surprisingly, laughter made him almost cute. In a happy-ferret kind of way. "This coming from an ugly black bird? Whatta you do when you're not scaring scarecrows? Oh, and I'm a shape-shifter, not a puling human."

Gerry noticed he wasn't as confident as he sounded. His hands were shaking. "Leave him alone. He doesn't have anything to do with this."

Morrigan ignored her and kept her piercing gaze on

Jinx. "I am Morrigan, Irish goddess of war, destruction, and almost everything worth having power over. Respect me, human, or die."

Jinx swallowed hard. "Got it. Lots of respect coming your way, goddess."

Gerry could feel the anger thrumming through Conall, but he remained silent.

Morrigan studied Jinx like he was tasty roadkill. "Why were you at Wicked Fantasy last night?"

Jinx shrugged. "Got a tip the Bimmel woman would be there wearing a hot rock. Said she tended to get careless with her jewelry. Took her rings off and set them down in places perfect for snatching."

"Who gave you the tip?"

"Anonymous. Didn't know if it was legit but decided to give it a try."

Morrigan nodded. "You may leave."

Jinx didn't wait around to hear more.

Gerry edged out from behind Conall. He didn't try to stop her. His attention was focused on Morrigan.

"Interesting game. Looks like someone is making your moves for you." Conall didn't seem upset by that. "Whoever it is knows about your curse and doesn't give a flip about pissing you off. I'd like to shake their hand."

"You'd better shake it quickly, because when I discover who the guilty party is, I'll scatter their body parts over all of Galveston." Morrigan flew into the air and disappeared out the door.

Gerry shuddered. "Bloodthirsty bitch, isn't she?" God, that was one scary woman.

Conall exhaled deeply. "She has a right to be. She decides who lives and dies on the battlefields. There's no softness or mercy in that goddess."

"Hey, there's *always* someone bigger and badder. I don't believe her Supreme Nastiness is as powerful as she thinks. She's an ancient goddess, ancient as in old and complacent. Can I say, we've come a long way, baby? I don't roll over and play dead every time crow woman caws." Now all she had to do was find this bigger and badder being.

He stared down at her. "Still interested in that walk?"

She nodded. "Yeah. Well, no, but climbing into bed and pulling the covers over my head would be just another notch on the goddess's belt. I let her intimidate me, she wins."

He smiled. And rearranged her internal organs—heart in throat, flip-flopped stomach, and brain hovering somewhere south of her belly button.

Gerry said nothing until they were out of the castle. "So what was my ancestor Sean like? I mean, he must've been something special to bring out all that passion in Morrigan and you." *Who wanted to kill her?*

"Sean could make anyone like him. He had a gift for saying the right thing to stroke egos. He sucked up to Morrigan big-time." Conall shrugged. "In battle he was a stone-cold killer. His men were like army ants. They destroyed every living thing in their path." He looked at her. "If you met him today, you'd think he was a great guy. And as long as you weren't in his way, he'd be fun to hang with."

When she got home she'd pull out the Kavanagh history and reread the family's take on both Sean and Conall. She glanced at his back. "You left your sword in the castle. Bet you feel naked." Oops, wrong choice of words. The word "naked" started an instant replay of how he'd looked with water sluicing over his bare body, gleaming muscles sharply delineated, clutching that great big sword. "See, now you won't be able to protect me." She was trying for teasing, but it came out sounding a little insecure. *Why did someone want her dead?*

A smile touched the corners of that expressive mouth. "I have a knife strapped to my ankle." His smile widened. "Besides, my whole body is a weapon, sweetheart."

"No kidding." And she meant it. "Must be interesting living in the Castle of Dark Dreams. It's a winning concept, combination hotel and semi-authentic castle. Guests get to act out their medieval fantasies and then sleep in a real castle chamber." *Would the killer try again?*

"Yeah, I like it here." He stopped smiling. "And you're avoiding the talk we need to have."

"I'm not avoiding anything." Uh-huh. And he'd believe that. "Where're we headed?"

"I thought I'd give you a taste of one of Live the Fantasy's attractions." He didn't turn to look at her. "You're going to have to let me stay close to you until we figure out where the danger's coming from."

"I can take care of myself." *Uh, no, you can't.* "Well, at least I can take care of myself when I'm awake. It gets a bit problematic when I'm sleeping. Maybe I'll get myself a big junkyard dog. How's that sound?"

He turned those gray eyes on her and the fierceness there backed her up a step. "I'm the only big junkyard dog you'll ever need. Deal with it."

"I don't want you." All right, so there were degrees of wanting. She didn't want him trailing her to the Forever Young Beauty Salon and Spa, ready to lop off Gaston's head if he cut too much off the bottom.

But yeah, a little self-honesty never hurt anyone. She could feel the slide of her fangs every time she thought of him in her bed, or on her floor, or hell, in her closet. Who cared. The place was incidental. Just imagining the hard thrust of his body into hers curled her insides into tight steel coils.

Conall studied her. After maybe a century, she'd get the hang of that expressionless mask other vampires wore so well. Right now, though, he could read every emotion in those green eyes.

They had something in common. He didn't want to be her protector, and she didn't want his protecting. But no matter how hard he denied it, there was lust between them, an ocean of it. He was kicking and flailing away like crazy, but the sex tide was dragging him in deeper and deeper.

He stopped walking outside the Sultan's Palace. "Let's apply logic to this situation."

She grinned up at him. "Logic is good."

"You're a vampire, so you can hold your own from dusk till dawn. But after that? Look what almost happened tonight. Locks will keep out humans, but not beings like Asima. I can make it hard for someone to get to you during the day." He'd have a talk with Eric. The vampire had enough power to throw a mind shield over any door that would keep humans and nonhumans out. Maybe he could teach Gerry how to do that.

"Makes sense." She looked like she was really considering it.

Conall pressed his advantage. "I can help with your job. Sure you have vampire strength and speed, but Jinx almost got to you. If you're hunting nonhumans, some of them will be more powerful than you are. Then what? Morrigan gave me the physical strength to protect you against almost anything."

"You know, it might work." Her expression turned calculating. "I could use you."

Use me, babe. He pushed the thought aside as soon as it surfaced. The part of him that craved using had no working brain cells.

"My boss asked me to stay here for a few more nights. He got a tip that a serial wife killer was in the castle." She frowned. "I'm just supposed to identify and observe, not try to apprehend him. Burke will do the actual takedown. Anyway, it would mean a promotion if I could catch this guy before Burke gets a crack at him. You could help."

"Burke?" A serial killer in the castle? Holgarth would have to get on this fast. Publicity brochures would *not* tempt future guests with promises of good food, comfort-

able beds, exciting fantasies, *and* their very own encounter
with a serial killer.

"My boss doesn't think I'm powerful enough to handle
the really dangerous criminals. He's sending in someone
more experienced. That would be Burke. I'd like to prove
him wrong."

Not good. Sure, Conall craved action, but he didn't
want to spend centuries saving her cute behind from homicidal entities. See, he was mellowing. He could actually
admit that, yes, a Kavanagh behind could be cute.

"I still have a problem, though. I can't sense nonhumans. That'll come with age, but until then . . ."

"You're screwed."

"Yeah."

"I might be able to help with that." Pulling out his cell
phone, he called Brynn. And while he was at it, he mentioned the serial killer. When he finished talking, he guided
Gerry toward a nearby bench. "Brynn, Kim, and Fo will be
here in a few minutes."

"Okay, I know that Brynn is one of your fake brothers,
so I assume Kim is his wife. Who's Fo?"

"Someone who'll be a big help while you're here."
Conall rested his arm across the top of the bench behind
her. He spent the next endless minutes controlling his need
to slide his fingers through the silky length of her hair.

Jeez, it was almost a week before Brynn and Kim
showed up. His forehead was damp with his effort to keep
from touching Gerry. "Took you guys long enough."

Brynn glanced at his watch. "Five minutes?"

"Seemed like it was longer." He didn't meet Gerry's
gaze. "Brynn, Kim, this is Gerry Kavanagh. Gerry, these
are my friends. Brynn is an ex-demon of sensual desire.
Kim's an architect."

Brynn and Kim nodded at Gerry, but there was no
warmth in the greeting.

Gerry met their coolness head-on. "Look, I can tell you

guys don't like me. I get that Conall's told you about the Ka-vanaghs. But this Kavanagh doesn't want someone to serve and protect her forever. None of this is my fault. I have no control over what a psycho goddess does. But since I can't do anything about it right now, I'm trying to make the best of it."

Kim nodded. "Makes sense. Brynn freaked me out when he told me what he was." The glance she sent Brynn said she'd grown to love what he was. "But it wasn't his fault. Ganymede did the damage. I had to deal with it or cut and run."

"Uh, who's going to introduce *me*?" The small voice came from Kim's shirt pocket.

Kim reached into her pocket and pulled out what looked like a camera phone. She flipped it open and turned it so Gerry could see the screen.

Huge purple eyes outlined in neon pink blinked at Gerry. "Hi." The eyes shifted to stare at Conall. "She's not human." The eyes returned to Gerry. "I'm Fo, short for First One. I was created as a demon detector and destroyer, but something happened, and now I'm a sentient being."

Gerry stared at those eyes. "Sentient being?"

"I have a mate, Gabriel, who's like me. We want to cre-ate a little one, so Gabriel gave me one of his microchips." The purple eyes looked excited. "I'm pregnant."

"Pregnant? You're going to create baby cell phones?" Gerry shook her head. "No, that's not what I meant to say."

The purple eyes narrowed before shifting to Kim. "I don't know if I can work with a person so politically in-correct, Kimmie."

Gerry raked her fingers through her hair. "Sorry. I haven't talked to many . . . demon destroyers." Then she seemed to realize what Fo had said. "Work with me?"

Conall gently massaged the back of her neck. Fine, so he had no self-control. He had to touch. "Fo can identify nonhuman entities. If it's a demon, she can even destroy it. And she doesn't have to sleep." Unlike him.

Fo might be able to watch over Gerry when he couldn't stay awake anymore. At least until they found out who'd set the fire.

Gerry nodded. "Handy skills. She could help me find the wife killer."

"Wife killer?" Fo's eyes widened until they filled the whole screen. "Will I be like a kick-ass bounty hunter? I'll get a black case with a skull and crossbones on it. Oooh, I want spikes and piercings." She rolled her eyes toward Kim. "Would there be room for a few scary tattoos?"

Kim sighed. "I doubt it."

Conall looked at Kim. "I'll make sure she's safe."

Kim turned Fo to face her. Conall didn't miss the real concern on Kim's face.

"Don't you think you should discuss this with Gabriel before you make a decision?" Kim ran her finger along the edge of Fo's case.

Fo considered that as Kim turned her screen to face Gerry again. "I suppose he'll want to know." She brightened. "Maybe he can come, too. He's more powerful than I am, but I'm a lot more outgoing."

Brynn grinned. "Translation: Fo never met anyone she didn't love talking to."

Gerry shifted slightly glazed eyes toward Conall.

He nodded. "Fo, talk things over with Gabriel. If everything's a go, we'll start the search for Gerry's serial killer tomorrow night."

"I'll have to let Holgarth know I want to stay until the end of the week and then hope Burke takes his time getting here." Growing anticipation gleamed in Gerry's eyes.

Conall waited until his friends had left before guiding Gerry toward the Sultan's Palace entrance. "Let's have some fun to celebrate our new partnership." The Sultan's Palace was *not* a good idea. He recognized the fact, acknowledged it, and then ignored it.

Once inside, he waited while Gerry stared wide-eyed at everything.

"Wow, I'm impressed." She turned to Conall. "The gold dome, the oriental rugs, the super-plush everything. It looks like a real sultan would live here. So what's the fantasy?"

Conall had already beckoned Sonya over. "Sonya will take you to the harem's quarters."

"Harem's quarters?" Gerry eyed Sonya's wide expanse of bare stomach. "Wait, I don't know if—"

Sonya smiled as she urged Gerry toward a door. "You'll love this. We'll get you some makeup and into an outfit so you'll be ready for the sultan."

"Sultan?" Gerry threw Conall a panicked glance as Sonya led her away.

Conall smiled and waved at her. Then he turned to Ben, who was manning the ticket counter. "Tell Julio to take this next fantasy off. I'll play the sultan." Ignoring Ben's grin, he headed toward the men's costume room.

Gerry glanced around warily. She was comfortable in her job. Chasing bad guys wasn't scary. *This* was scary. Sitting on a thick rug, she was propped up by a mountain of colorful pillows.

With all the eye makeup Sonya had slapped on her, she probably looked like a crazed raccoon. And her clothes? Hah. Clothes covered the body. What she was wearing were strategic pieces of cloth. There was the tiny bra with a playful fringe of beads and bells then nothing until well past her navel. A filmy piece of cloth masquerading as a skirt clung to her lower abdomen with brave tenacity. Go, skirt.

Relax. We're having fun here, right? But for the life of her she couldn't remember ever having even one fantasy about being a member of some sultan's harem. Conall should've asked her opinion.

"Men don't have a clue, do they?" The amused female

voice reminded Gerry that there were three "harem girls" with her.

"About what?" All three women were beautiful and blond with pale eyes she'd seen somewhere before. Where had she seen . . . ?

"About what a woman wants. From your expression, I'd say a man chose this fantasy for you." The woman shrugged. "This is a guy fantasy. I bet he's even arranged to be the sultan."

Gerry smiled. "Probably. And yeah, I don't fit the harem mold. Definitely not soft, sweet, and simpering." But a male harem? Now *that* was a fantasy. "Do you work here all the time?"

They all laughed. "No, we're just filling in for the regulars. They all ate at the same place and came down with food poisoning. Oh, and I'm Tullia." She nodded at the other women. "These are my sisters, Fulvia and Varinia."

Unusual names. "So what will happen next?"

Tullia shrugged. "Your man will come in dressed as the sultan, send us away, and try to seduce you."

Varinia looked contemptuous. "So predictable."

Gerry had her doubts about the seducing part. He was an O'Rourke, and she was still a Kavanagh.

"Didn't I see you last night with Conall?" Fulvia sounded almost gleeful.

"Uh, yeah." She glanced at the door. "He brought me here."

Fulvia leaned close. "Poor you. He can only get women to have sex with him who don't know."

"I'm not going to have sex . . . Know what?"

Varinia shook her head and looked sorrowful. "He roots and grunts on top of a woman like a wild boar digging for turnips."

Well, that was certainly a sensual image.

Tullia chimed in. "He has a foot fetish. Sucks on toes. Sometimes even chews on them." She shuddered. "Gross."

"Foot fetish?" Eww.

Fulvia didn't let her get any further. "And they don't call him the Rocket for nothing."

"The Rocket?"

"Five seconds."

"But that's not even time enough to . . ."

"It is for him." Fulvia looked triumphant. "There's much much more, but we don't have time to tell you."

Varinia smiled. "Why would any woman want to inflict *that* on herself? Personally, we're all virgins."

"Virgins?" Offhand, Gerry couldn't remember the last time she'd seen three virgins in one place at the same time.

Whatever Gerry might've said vanished from her mind as the door to the harem was flung open and the sultan entered.

Conall was big, beautiful, and oozed erotic magic. The robe he wore did nothing to hide the sheer size and power of him. He glanced at the other women. Recognition flashed in his eyes and was gone. "I won't need you tonight, ladies. You may go."

Tullia cast Gerry an I-told-you-so look before silently leaving with her sisters.

Conall sank to the rug beside Gerry. "You look as lovely as a ripe pomegranate, my sweet."

Gerry almost choked on her laughter. "A ripe pomegranate is this big, round red fruit. Was that supposed to be a compliment?"

A smile tipped up the corners of his mouth. His incredibly yummy mouth. "I assumed a sultan would give his chosen woman a regional compliment." He frowned. "Where do pomegranates grow anyway?"

"Got me." As long as he was being playful, Gerry didn't feel threatened. "And what else would a sultan say to his favorite harem girl?"

Suddenly the moment was charged with something hot and intense. "Nothing. If he was a sultan worth his salt, he'd pounce on his chosen pomegranate." The light come-back didn't dispel the thick layer of sexual awareness surrounding them.

"Pouncing is so not sexy." She tried to match his tone. "His chosen pomegranate would probably spit seeds at him."

He studied her, his eyes seeing more than she wanted him to see—her nervousness, her uncertainty. "This isn't an X-rated fantasy. The park gets really cranky if the customers do any consummating during their fun time." Reaching out he flicked the fringe on her bra and listened to the tinkle of the bells. "Just had to do that."

She hated to be the opener of worm cans, but she needed to get the rules straight. "Look, I get that this is a sensual fantasy. I mean, the harem thing was the first hint. Oh, and if you'd asked me, I could've told you a male harem was a much bigger turn-on for me."

Gerry frowned. "Scratch that last comment. No turn-ons needed. But I guess I'm confused. You've made a big deal about how much you hate your curse and the Kavanaghs. And I totally understand. But this?" She swept her arm to encompass the opulent room. "This does *not* say 'I hate everything you represent.' Have I missed something along the way?"

Conall's smile was slow and so potent she figured she'd need a chaser after it.

"Hey, a guy can be conflicted." He lowered his lids so she couldn't see his expression as he drew a sizzling line with one finger along the skin just above the top of her skirt. Her stomach muscles clenched. "I hate Morrigan, all of your ancestors, and the curse. But I'm finding it really tough to hate you."

"My bubbling personality, I assume?"

"Your hot body."

"Jerk."

"And your personality doesn't bubble. It kicks butt and takes no prisoners. Very sexy."

"You're such a sweet-talkin' man."

His gray eyes darkened. "Besides, you're the first Kavanagh who doesn't think the curse makes them a lottery winner."

Gerry sighed. How could she keep her mad? She had no trouble seeing things from his side. They'd just met, so he couldn't admire her for her mind. Especially since she seemed to have lost said mind over the last two nights. Maybe Conall would help her find it.

"So what're we doing here? This hot body isn't feeling a whole lot of erotic vibrations right now."

The darkness left his eyes and something softer took its place. "We can still do the fantasy. Lay back and relax." He shifted a little closer, and as he did so, his robe slipped open.

Her heart did a giant ker-thud. "Um, I think you lost the rest of your costume." All bare. Bare, bare, bare. Ker-thud, ker-thud. Her erotic vibrations were back and thrumming at the speed of sound. She expected a sonic boom at any moment. And one glance between those powerful thighs convinced her that his erotic vibrations had been humming all along.

"I pulled some strings to squeeze this fantasy in. The robe was the only thing left in the costume room."

Did she believe him? No. But he got high marks for creativity. She was suspicious, but since she couldn't stand not knowing what he had planned, she laid back against the pillows. "So what're you going to do?"

"Talk. Just talk."

She frowned. Bummer.

6

Conall made no excuses for himself. He wanted her. Damn.

Eight centuries had taught him a lot about reading what was in women's eyes. She wanted him, too. Hell.

But he couldn't do it. As much as he wanted to wipe away the bitterness of all those years by burying himself deep inside her, he couldn't do that to Gerry. He wouldn't become a user. That would make him like all the Kavanaghs he despised.

Besides, if Gerry and he made love, Morrigan would be pissed off in a major way because he'd enjoyed himself with a Kavanagh. And the bitch goddess took out her anger by killing things. In this case, one of his descendants would die.

So he talked. "Live the fantasy in your mind, Gerry. I'm the sultan, master of everyone and everything. Listen as I tell you all that I'll do to please you."

"I don't know about the master thing." She frowned, evidently not into fantasy mode yet. "And aren't harem girls supposed to please the sultan?"

Talk, talk, talk. He didn't want a friendly chat. He wanted action. He stomped all over that thought. "I'm one of the very few sensitive sultans. So just enjoy it, okay?"

Her smile was sly and knowing. "Frustrated, are we?"

"You bet." Conall rubbed the back of his neck to relieve the tension. "Imagine my mouth on yours—hot, hungry." He lowered himself above her until their lips were mere inches apart.

She slid her tongue across her bottom lip, and the damp sheen of it called to him.

"I'll trace your lips with my tongue, memorizing your taste and texture."

"What will I taste like?" She parted her lips, teasing, inviting.

He resisted. Barely. "You'll taste of . . ." What in his endless memories brought a surge of happiness? "Ireland. The flavor of peat fires on a cold winter night and sea mist rolling in from the Atlantic."

The guy part of his brain said that was a bunch of crap. He didn't talk that way. But the tiny section of his mind that understood what would touch her stood up and applauded. Manipulative? Maybe. He really did love Ireland, but he wouldn't have expressed it in that way.

She reached up to push a strand of hair away from his face. "Go on. I'm riveted."

"I'll cover your mouth with mine, my tongue exploring your warmth and sweet temptation." He fought his growing arousal, because all that blood rushing to harden his body left his brain bloodless. And his bloodless brain made stupid decisions like: *Sex is good, let's do it now.*

Conall watched her breathing quicken, stretching that sexy little bra to the max. Ever hopeful, he waited for it to spring open, spilling her luscious breasts into his waiting hands. He was doomed to disappointment. It was like an eternal taffy pull. The material stretched and stretched and stretched some more. His more violent self suggested he rip the damn thing off.

"Mmm. That sounds good." She wiggled that delicious bottom and arched her back. "More."

Who the hell was the patron saint of self-control? He needed some divine intervention right now.

He kept his hand just above her body as he skimmed the length of all that smooth, soft skin and those man-killer curves. *Don't touch, don't touch, don't touch.* "Next I'll kiss a path over your jaw and down the side of your neck." She was vampire, and he knew what would excite her. "I'll put my mouth over the spot where your life force pulses fast and hard. Then I'll slide my tongue back and forth, back and forth."

Her lips parted in a low moan, and her fangs were fully extended. Conall never thought of vampire fangs as erotic, but on her they were damned hot.

She reached for him, but he stayed just out of reach. "Listen, just listen."

She subsided with a sulky pout on her sensual mouth.

"I'll strip you bare." Just the thought of her exposed body writhing beneath his gaze took his breath away. His brain was going down for sure with no blood or oxygen. He took a deep gulp of air.

"And?" Her eyes were huge, no longer green, but so dark he imagined he could see his hunger reflected in them. She let the human slip away as her vampire nature rose on a wave of sexual excitement.

"First I'll cup your breasts, enjoying the weight and feel of them filling my hands." Conall knew his glance was desperate as he stared at the bra. He wanted to tear it apart with his teeth. "I won't be able to resist sliding my tongue around those mouthwatering nipples. Then I'll nip and flick them with my tongue until they're hard and swollen, so sensitive you'll cry out when I even breathe on them."

He'd forgotten about how fast a vampire could move.

Before he could react, she grabbed a handful of his hair and tried to force his head to her breasts. He fought a battle on two fronts: trying to resist her strength and his own fast-fading self-control.

With a huff of temper, she released him. "Big, ugly, mean tease." She waved her hand at him. "Okay, I take back the ugly."

"I'm suffering, too." No lie. He could probably break bricks with his hard-on. "Want to know what I'll do next?"

He watched her weigh her mad at him against her sexual enjoyment of the fantasy he was weaving. "Yeah, I guess—"

She never got a chance to finish. The booming of a giant gong shattered the moment.

Eyes wide, Gerry jerked to a sitting position. Conall did some inventive cursing.

"Sorry to interrupt, but your fantasy time is up." Varinia stood in the doorway, her gaze fixed on Conall's open robe. "If you want to purchase additional time, you'll have to go to the ticket counter."

Gerry narrowed her eyes as she followed the trajectory of Varinia's yearning glances. Conall couldn't stop his instinctive twinge of triumph.

Gerry reached over and yanked his robe closed. "We've had enough time, thank you."

Conall grinned. She was such a liar.

Varinia heaved a deep sigh. "Sometimes virginity sucks." She turned and left.

"Virginity? What's that about?" He recognized her. She was one of the women he'd seen last night with the guy Sparkle identified as Edge. When had Holgarth hired her?

Gerry ignored his question as he stood and then helped her to her feet. Her gaze skittered away from him. "Speaking of sucks, I just want you to know that I, uh . . . Ahem. I mean, if we ever do this again, not that we will, but if we do . . . Er, do you suck toes or do any mouth-to-feet stuff?"

She stared at one of the exotic tapestries hanging from the wall.

A foot fetish? Who would've thought? Not a turn-on to him. Not that it mattered. There wouldn't be any more virtual seductions. He wasn't sure he'd survive *this* one. Pleasure turned to pain fast when you resisted sex's siren call. "So toe-sucking makes it happen for you?"

Her eyes widened. "No, absolutely not. I'm really really ticklish. I go berserk and hurt people who mess with my feet."

Conall shrugged. "No problem." Why had she mentioned it in the first place?

He didn't overthink the foot thing as they left the palace and walked slowly back toward the castle. Neither one of them had much to say. Good thing, because he was trying to deal with an overexcited body part. He focused on ugly, deflating thoughts: waking up to find Morrigan la Crow in bed with him, trapped with Sparkle in a shoe store, chained to Asima at the opera.

The body part was still plenty ticked, so he thought maybe a drink would calm things down. "Let's stop at Wicked Fantasy."

She nodded but didn't say anything. What was she thinking, and did he want to know?

Once inside the club, they agreed to sit at the bar. Conall didn't need the added intimacy of a table right now.

"Sparkle, Brynn, and Kim are at the bar. Let's sit with them." The most she'd said since leaving the Sultan's Palace. "I don't think I've ever seen a more incredible-looking man than Brynn."

"Demons of sensual desire usually are." Conall had finally found something to quell his cock's enthusiasm. The relief was no relief at all. "It's part of their job description: must be too hot for women to resist." He was jealous—furious, seeing red, and wanting to stomp Brynn into the floor jealous. The realization shocked him to his immortal core.

Gerry plowed on, unaware she'd stirred up thoughts of death and destruction in the man next to her. "Kim's right for him, though. Her red hair with those green eyes are spectacular."

"Your green eyes are prettier." Had that just come from *his* mouth? In eight hundred years he'd never complimented a Kavanagh. No, wait, he'd told Mick's wife he looked good in his coffin. But that was it. God, he needed that drink.

Conall guided them to two stools between Sparkle and Brynn. Relieved, he watched Gerry sit next to Sparkle. He didn't need to listen to the castle's maven of sex lecture him on the stupidity of not making love to Gerry.

Gerry immediately turned to Sparkle. Okay, so she didn't want to talk to him. He could deal. He turned toward Brynn and Kim.

"I don't sense any sexual afterglow, sister. What the hell did you do in the Sultan's Palace?" Sparkle pursed perfectly shaped lips that gleamed moist with a soft, sexy red color.

"How'd you know we went to the Sultan's Palace?" *And why do you care?*

Sparkle glanced across the room. Whatever she saw made her frown. "Someone told me. And I care because I've taken an interest in you and Conall."

Time to ask the question she should've asked when she first suspected Sparkle was in her head. "What are you?"

Sparkle smiled. Not a comforting smile. "Took you long enough to ask. But young vampires rarely have the ability to perceive power in others." She smoothed a finger over her ring.

Gerry stared at the ring. "Hey, isn't that—?"

Sparkle held up her hand. "Please, no lectures. The Bimmel woman would never be able to appreciate something this magnificent."

"But—"

"I simply convinced her that she really wanted me to
have the ring as a thank-you for invigorating her dismal
sex life." She looked righteous. "Which I definitely did. So
it was a fair exchange."

"Okay, back to square one. What are you?"

"I'm a cosmic troublemaker. And I know, you've never
heard of us. But we're some of the most powerful beings in
the universe. Each of us has a particular area of expertise. I've
spent thousands of years spreading sexual . . . bliss throughout the world." She looked like she expected questions.

Gerry wouldn't disappoint. "Let's see if I'm clear on the
concept. You're trying to hook up Conall and me?"

Sparkle smiled. "Of course. You guys are a challenge. I
thrive on challenges."

"Well, don't strain anything, because it's not going to
happen." She pushed aside the memory of her unfortunate
response to Conall the Studly Sultan. When a woman had
been deprived for a certain amount of time, arousal was
only a glance away. Any man would've pushed her happy
button. *Uh-huh, sure.*

Sparkle looked like she was ready to argue, but evidently the someone she'd been watching across the room
decided to join her. A tawny-haired man pushed away from
his table and grabbed the stool next to Sparkle.

He didn't waste time. "We need to talk." No friendly
vibes coming from him.

Since none of the man's anger was directed at her,
Gerry took a good look. Great-looking guy. But then, the
Castle of Dark Dreams had more than its share of hot men.
Thick, sandy-colored hair that shone warm and inviting be-
neath the club's dim lighting combined with a great mouth,
great eyes . . . Eyes. She tried to lean around Sparkle. His
eyes were a strange amber color. The same shade as
Sparkle's eyes. *The same shade as the wife killer's eyes.*

Sparkle didn't make an effort to introduce Gerry, but the
man took matters into his own hands.

"Hi, there. I'm Edge. And you are?"

If Conall hadn't already wowed Gerry with his smile, this guy would've knocked her off her stool. "Gerry. Are you a guest here?"

Her heart pounded at the thought she might've gotten lucky this fast. He looked good enough to be irresistible to most women, and the eye color was right. Too bad the sleeves of his shirt covered his upper arms.

Sparkle's smile was brittle. "Edge works for me. Business before pleasure. We'll get back to our conversation after I take care of this." She turned away from Gerry, effectively shutting her out.

Edge met Gerry's gaze. "I'm Sparkle's *partner*. I don't work for anyone."

Gerry smiled weakly and turned away. She tried to look interested in what Conall was saying. Her enhanced hearing would pick up Sparkle's conversation. She pretended to take a sip of the drink she'd ordered.

"You think you're smart, Stardust, but you're not playing with an amateur here." Edge's voice was a furious whisper.

"Temper, temper." Sparkle sounded amused. "Let me guess. Your challenge is too much for you, and you want to admit defeat. That's okay. I can be gracious in victory."

"You knew Destiny was a shark hunter. When Banan found out, he was ready to tear her apart. She's in her room sharpening her damn harpoon or whatever the hell she uses to kill sharks with." Edge's growl held fury and barely contained violence.

Gerry shivered. She sort of hoped he wasn't her man.

"But see, that's the challenge. If you're worthy to take my place, you need to prove you can win the big games." Sparkle still sounded cheerful. "And what have your demonic helpers been up to?"

Demonic helpers? Gerry frowned. What was that about?

Edge's soft chuckle had nothing to do with good humor. "I bet you're wondering why your happy couple didn't do it in the Sultan's Palace."

"Stay out of my way, Edge, or I'll destroy you." Sparkle was using her serial-killer voice.

Gerry believed her.

"Sparkle, sweet Sparkle, you still don't know what I am. You're just a pawn in the Big Boss's little power game. Don't think you can threaten me. Ever." Without waiting for Sparkle to respond, he left.

Gerry was outta here. Whatever was going on between Edge and Sparkle somehow involved Conall and her. Danger was like a thick fog around her, making Gerry afraid to stick out her hand for fear of something biting it off, because she couldn't see a damned thing. She slipped from her stool and headed for the exit.

Conall caught her just outside the club's entrance. "Where're you going?"

"Back to my room." She kept walking. "To pack and get my behind out of this crazy place."

He matched her stride. "Calm down and tell me what happened."

She didn't say anything as she pounded down the stone steps, shoved past him into the dungeon, and stopped dead. A big black cat crouched on her coffee table with its head buried in a container of Ben & Jerry's ice cream.

Okay, this was the proverbial last straw. "I don't know who or what you are, but get the hell out of my room!"

She welcomed the slide of her fangs. With a screech of fury, she grabbed the lamp, yanked the cord from the wall, and heaved it at the cat with every ounce of her vampire strength. It seemed to bounce off an invisible shield before it reached its target and fell harmlessly to the floor.

The cat didn't even take its head from the container.

Wildly, she looked around for something else to throw. Conall wrapped his arms around her, but she fought him.

"Calm down. That's Ganymede. Throwing stuff won't help." His quiet murmur only infuriated her more.

"Sure it will. It makes me feel great." Gerry broke free and picked up the small TV. She chucked it after the lamp. It didn't come any closer than the lamp had, but it made a satisfying crash as it hit the floor.

Conall winced.

She glared at him. "Put them on my bill."

But at least the cat looked up from its ice cream. It stared at her from amber eyes the same color as Sparkle's and Edge's. Then it carefully licked the ice cream from its mouth with a pink tongue. "You've got a vicious streak, babe. Love that in a woman." The voice was low and husky. Male.

With a sob of near hysteria, she grabbed for the phone and dialed Payton's number with shaking fingers. When he picked up, she didn't even wait for him to speak. "I'm bringing Jinx in. Burke can take over here."

She could hear Payton's huge sigh. "I'm afraid Burke won't be there anytime soon. He has chicken pox. They started popping out last night. You'll have to stay."

"Chicken pox?" As she talked, her fangs retracted and her head cleared a little. "Well, send another agent."

"Sorry, they're all in the middle of important operations. It's you or no one." He sounded impatient. "I realize you're new to the force, but you'll just have to hang in there until I have another agent free. What's happened so far?"

"So far I've interacted with a cosmic troublemaker, a messenger of Bast in cat form, a wizard, two vampires, the Irish goddess Morrigan, an ex-demon of sensual desire, a pregnant cell phone . . ." She glanced at Conall. "And an immortal warrior." Gerry was shouting, but she didn't care. "Now there's a freakin' cat eating ice cream on my coffee table. And, and, and I didn't even buy any ice cream." She held her breath to keep from exploding into tears. A mental breakdown would *not* be good for her career.

"Hmm. Interesting. Do you have any leads on the entity we're hunting?"

"*We're* hunting? I don't see any *we* here. Someone set fire to my bed tonight. Any flames licking around your toes lately? No, I didn't think so."

Payton's sigh grew louder. "I hate to threaten, but if you abandon this assignment, I'll be forced to assume you're not right for the organization. In other words, I'll fire your vampire ass."

Gerry hung up. She raked her fingers through her hair as she turned to Conall. "I forgot to mention the plant that scarfs down sexual energy, but I don't think it would've made any difference to Payton."

Conall sat on the couch and drew her down beside him. "One thing at a time." He met the cat's stare. "What're you doing here, Ganymede?"

Ganymede did a cat stretch and then leaped from the coffee table. He padded over to the plant and sat to study it. "Sparkle sent out an SOS. Said her current project was in danger. So here I am."

Conall frowned. "Project?"

"That would be us. Sparkle told me she was committed to hooking us up." Ganymede? Where had she heard his name before? Oh, yeah. "You're the evil entity that caused Brynn so much trouble."

If a cat could smile, Ganymede was grinning. "Evil entity? That's the nicest thing anyone has said to me in years." He cocked his head to get a different angle on the plant. "Doesn't look like Houston's getting any."

"Like I have time to worry about a plant? Sparkle can take him. He'll be bushy and bright in no time." Gerry was finally calm enough to string a few rational thoughts together, but she was still totally ticked off. "Why're you in my room?"

"Just checking to see if any erotic happenings are going down here. This room is a sexual wasteland. That'll piss

Sparkle off big-time, and she won't be in the mood for a night of sizzling sex. Too bad." He abandoned Houston and padded toward the door. "Oh, I charged the ice cream to your room-service bill."

"Whoa, halt, stop. Get your chubby kitty behind back here." She was over her panic attack. What she wanted were answers. "You have the same color eyes as Sparkle and Edge. Are all of you cosmic troublemakers?"

"Yeah. I'm one of the most powerful beings in the universe. In the bad old days, I spread chaos around the world. But I made the Big Boss nervous. So he said no more death and destruction. Bummer. If I want to have fun now, I have to sneak around behind his back."

"And you're here to do what?" Oh, to have a few hundred years of vampire power under her belt.

Ganymede yawned. "Check out the babes, enjoy a few great meals, and make sure no one gets in Sparkle's way." He paused before leaving the dungeon. "I haven't met this Edge dude. What's he like?"

Gerry knew it was petty revenge, but she couldn't help herself. "He's gorgeous. Tall and built with this dangerous air women love. Gee, I bet he's as powerful as you are."

The cat hissed at her and the whole room shook. With a squeak of alarm, she grabbed the back of the couch. Turning his back to them, he stalked out of the room. The dungeon door slammed shut with enough force to almost rip it off its hinges.

Conall sank onto the couch. "That went well. Look, I know you don't need one more person interfering in your life, but Ganymede will take some of the pressure off. He'll distract Sparkle so she won't have as much time to make our lives hell. And he's the most powerful entity I've ever met, so you want him on your side." He frowned as he thought of something. "Are you leaving?"

She stretched out on the bed and gazed around her. "No. I want to keep my job." God, he must think she was a complete idiot after that last display. For whatever reason, she wanted him to understand.

"I was the victim of a bite-and-run vamp attack. I honestly don't know who turned me, but suddenly my life and my career were over. I tried to explain to my parents, but they're in denial. I'm their 'Goth' daughter to friends." She let her gaze rest on Conall's face—the harsh masculine beauty of it, strength in the line of his mouth and his calm gray eyes. Gerry wondered how many of her ancestors had slept more easily knowing Conall was there. Heaven knows, she would.

"How do you feel about being vampire?"

No one had ever asked her that question. "It's only been two years, and sometimes I forget what I am. I still think like a human. I still get *scared* like a human. Everything that's happened since I got to the castle freaked me out, and I finally just lost it."

Conall nodded. "Hey, I don't blame you. You've met some powerful entities. Fear is a survival instinct. It makes you careful. You'll exist a long time if you know when to back off."

"Thanks for understanding." Right now he was the calm in her storm. "I want to be the one who catches the wife killer, but I have to keep reminding myself that I'm not a twenty-eight-year-old sales rep anymore."

She sighed. Time to stop laying all her fears and insecurities on him. "I like the living-for-centuries concept, but I miss a bunch of things."

"Like?"

He looked interested. Was that part of his curse description: Know everything about the rotten Kavanagh you'll be stuck with? "Pizza, a summer day on the beach, and . . . men." Maybe she should've left that last part off.

"Men?" His lips tipped up in the beginning of a smile.

Loved that smile. "I don't feel comfortable with mortal men anymore. I tried, I really did. When I first became vampire, I didn't know how to control anything. The guy I was going with took me to a sexy movie, and when he made a move on me I bit his neck. No more phone messages from him. Another guy I went out with came on too strong, so I threw him across the room when all I wanted to do was push him away." She shrugged. "And I haven't met that many nonhuman males."

"Until now." His smile widened.

"Yeah." Call her picky, but he was the only one who gave her a serious case of the wants.

Gerry yawned. She was starting to feel a little tired. Dawn mustn't be far away. Maybe as she grew older, it wouldn't affect her this early. "So when are you going back to your room?"

"I'm not." His expression said she'd have to pick him up and throw him out. "I'll sleep on the sofa."

She thought about arguing. Who was she kidding? She needed him. And . . . she sort of liked having him around. "Okay, but once we catch the wife killer and find out who wants me more dead than I already am, I'm turning you loose.

"Turning me loose? Like back to the wild? You still don't understand. You *can't* turn me loose. Neither of us has any say in how the curse works." He hesitated a second before continuing. "And we can't make love."

Her eyelids stopped drooping. "Wow, major buzz kill." She peered at him from under her lashes. "Right, no making love. I got that back in the Sultan's Palace. Only I've always hated dumb stories where he wanted her and she wanted him, but there was this big 'something' keeping them apart. I never did understand why they couldn't just talk about the big 'something' and then make love." She paused to see how he was taking things so far.

"Go on. I'm listening."

"The curse is our big something. If at some point we get past the Great Wall of our last names and want to make love, why not?" She should be all embarrassed by what she'd just said, but she wasn't. He'd wanted her during that fantasy, and lord knew she'd wanted him right back.

He surprised her. "I agree. But it's not only about our feelings. Morrigan is a control freak. If she thought I enjoyed making love with you, she'd punish both of us. Don't think for a minute she has any warm fuzzy feelings for you because you're Sean's descendant. You're just the instrument of my punishment."

"Hmm." She thought about that as she climbed from the bed, grabbed her jammies and headed for the bathroom. By the time she came out, she had a plan. Not for tonight, but for an emergency if the wanting got too much. For both of them. She didn't think she'd share with Conall until he needed to know.

Slipping under the covers, she watched him. He'd picked up the lamp and TV, and now he was checking to see if the TV still worked.

"When will you get some rest?" She scooted farther under the covers.

"When you wake up at dusk, I'll catch some sleep."

She let her lids drift shut. "You know, if you were in *my* harem, I wouldn't start at the top."

"No?" He sounded cautious.

"No. I'd make you lay on your stomach, naked, and then I'd do erotic things to your sexy bottom."

"Hmm."

"I'd massage your luscious butt cheeks like a cat kneading while it thought about bowls of thick sweet cream." She licked her lips.

"Would you purr?"

"Oooh, yeah."

"Then that's good."

She was into it now. "I'd order you to turn over. I'm impatient, what can I say? I'd scrape my teeth over each of your nipples and then slide my tongue past all your scenic wonders until I reached the overlook for the whole panoramic you. Probably I'd pull over. Maybe take a hike to see if the real thing was as spectacular as it looked."

"You're killing me, here."

"I certainly hope so." She smiled. "I'd run my tongue around and around each of your sacs until you moaned for release."

"Would you give it to me?"

She thought about that. "No. I'm in charge. And I'm not done."

"You're a cruel woman." His soft laughter sounded strained.

"Cruel women rule. Okay, back to business. I'd glide the tip of my fingernail—filed to a sharp point because cruel women always have daggers for nails—the length of your cock."

"And?" His voice was a husky murmur.

"And I haven't thought out the rest of it."

He exhaled deeply. "This is payback for the Sultan's Palace, isn't it?"

"Maybe a little."

"More than a little." He got up and headed for the bathroom. "I need a shower."

"Do cold showers really help?" If it worked, maybe she'd try it.

"Not really." He paused in the doorway.

"I meant it. Only a tiny part of that was payback."

"Uh-huh." He closed the bathroom door.

"Houston needed plant food," she explained to the closed door.

7

Gerry opened one eye. Bed not on fire. Goody. She opened the other one. Conall asleep on the couch. Relief. Not the reaction she wanted. Her logical self knew that wanting him to be there when she woke could lead down a dangerous path. But her emotional and sexual self thought he'd be a fine beginning to each evening.

His big body looked all scrunched up on the couch. Some men seemed younger, softer in sleep. Not Conall. He was all coiled power and danger even with his eyes closed. And so tempting he made her clench body parts that hadn't gotten much exercise. Ever. Fine, so she had high standards when it came to her lust objects.

She studied the evidence: TV still on and almost empty coffeepot on the table. He must've lost the battle with sleep sometime during the day. Sort of endearing. Morrigan hadn't given him the ability to stay awake forever, but he'd sure tried.

She crept quietly out of bed. Sleep had helped her. Once again she felt in control. Okay, maybe not completely, but enough to put things in perspective. She had two problems.

One was straightforward. Find and arrest homicidal wife slayer. The second was fuzzy around the edges. Discover who wanted her dead, find out why, and stop them.

She couldn't picture any of the people from her life before the Castle of Dark Dreams hating her enough to move themselves to murder. Sure, she'd arrested a few petty criminals, but she couldn't see anyone connected to them caring enough to stalk her.

So that left someone here. Conall was the only person in the castle with a close connection to her. She'd bet this was about Conall. She just had to figure out how.

Gerry slipped into the bathroom, and when she came out she was dressed for the hunt. Lucky she couldn't see herself in a mirror. If she'd looked into one and asked, "Does this make me look fat?" it would've shattered. She'd morphed into El Blimpo, supersized superhero.

Her hips looked, well, hippy with the four deep pockets of her loose tan pants stuffed with goodies like a sealed plastic bottle of holy water, a wooden stake, a taser, a mini hatchet, and a few extra Securers. Her loose red T-shirt hid her shoulder holster and gun along with the throwing knife suspended between her shoulder blades.

If she ever fell, she'd assassinate herself.

The two pockets in her light jacket held her cell phone and a PDA where she'd stored tons of helpful info for dealing with a variety of entities.

Too bad she couldn't ID any of those entities. She needed her own personal Fo. Hmm, Fo was pregnant . . . How long did it take a baby demon detector to reach employment age?

She hadn't bothered dressing to kill for Jinx. But for a being that had gone through five hundred wives in his search for wedded bliss . . . ? Yeah, she needed all the help she could get. September in Galveston was hot, but she'd sweat for the cause.

Gerry decided to let Conall sleep. He needed his rest.

Besides, he had to work tonight. She'd be fine by herself. She was awake, alert, and loaded for werebear or any other bully being who got in her way.

Before leaving, Gerry tiptoed over to turn off the TV. She reached for the remote. The news was on, so she paused to listen.

"Now for our most unusual story of the day. Live the Fantasy theme park in Galveston was the site of a bizarre robbery. Nola Keady took her diamond bracelet off to show a friend while they shared a few drinks at the Dead Eye Saloon. When she set it on the bar for a few seconds, a thief stole it."

The anchorman smiled into the camera. "What's so bizarre about that? Well, Nola swears she saw a tarantula toting her bracelet away on its back. That's right, a *tarantula*. She tried to catch the thieving arachnid, but it just wasn't Nola's lucky day. So all of you who have plans for spending the weekend in Galveston, don't take off your jewelry, and watch out for those spiders." Wink, wink, nudge, nudge.

Damn it. Jinx.

Gerry turned off the TV, strode from the room, and tripped over Asima. She fell to her knees and found herself nose to nose with the cat. "What the . . . ?"

"A woman should move gracefully. Like a cat. Like me. I'll schedule some lessons." Asima's blue eyes grew larger as she checked out Gerry's clothes. *"Oh, dear. That outfit is a disaster. You look like you should be on a stage somewhere doing something disgusting like . . . rapping."*

Gerry refused to wince. These clothes were all about survival. "I wouldn't have tripped if your arrogant little butt wasn't planted in front of the door. Why?"

"Conall has an affinity for cats. I'm a cat." She did a passable imitation of a cat shrug. *"So I protect him."*

Sounded suspicious to Gerry. "Are you sure that's all?"

Asima gazed at Gerry with innocence oozing from every kitty pore. *"What else would it be?"*

Gerry climbed to her feet. "Am I the only one who sees the irony here? You're protecting Conall, who's protecting me."

Asima looked at her blankly.

"Never mind. Do you always sit outside his door?"

"Only since you came. If someone's trying to kill you, they might hurt Conall, too." Asima looked determined. *"If Conall gets between you and the would-be killer, I'll have to get him out fast."*

"And leave me to the killer?"

Asima blinked at her. *"Why would I possibly care?"*

Gerry sighed. "Right. No caring."

"Oh, I liked all your sexy talk with Conall last night."

"Ohmigod! Tell me you weren't listening at the door."

"I was bored. I listened. No biggy."

Okay, Gerry was outta here. She willed the heat from her face as she walked down to Jinx's room and pounded on his door. She should've stuck a can of Raid in her pocket. He didn't answer, and she didn't have the power to open doors like Holgarth could. She'd eat dirt before asking Asima to do it.

Anyway, Jinx was probably out robbing people in all his sneaky forms. And she couldn't find him. The Securer would tell her if he went out of range, but as long as he stayed within the park, she couldn't get a fix on him. Flawed technology. The Securer needed a mental GPS device.

Gerry was so ticked she was running on steam by the time she reached the castle's great hall. It looked like workers were setting up for the night's fantasies. A long, wooden banquet table dominated the room from a raised platform in front of the massive hearth. Costumed men and women wandered around. People were already buying tickets. She hoped Conall woke up in time.

She searched for Holgarth. Ah, she spied his pointy blue hat at the door. Probably insulting all the customers as they handed over their money. She'd rather not talk to him, but she needed to make sure he woke Conall. Besides, he might give her a hint where she could find Edge.

Gerry took a deep breath, promised herself she wouldn't lose her temper with the wizard, and tapped him on the shoulder.

He turned with his supercilious sneer already in place. "Ah, our intrepid defender of the law has risen." His gaze picked her apart before abandoning her pile of pieces as obviously not worth putting together again.

She squirmed. Gerry hated her automatic response to him.

"One never ceases to marvel at what passes for style today. I might point out that your plethora of deadly weapons is weighing down your pants. Only that rather gruesome T-shirt hides how far they've slipped."

"And you know all this how?" She threw out a few mental curses. He was right. The pants were too big for her, but she'd needed something with a bunch of pockets for her weapons. They didn't have anything in her size. Now only her hip bones held them up. Yay, hip bones.

He shrugged. "They're pooling around your ankles. Of course, that might be perceived as a good thing, because your shoes are . . . Well, let's just say that Sparkle would be appalled."

She clamped her lips shut before something really ugly slipped out. Cute, strappy sandals were a no-no when she was hunting. She couldn't chase bad guys in cute, strappy sandals, and they sure wouldn't do much to hide her ankle knife.

"I know about your weapons because I'm a wizard. Knowing the unknown is a wizardy skill." He paused to turn his "wizardy" tongue on a customer. "A hundred-dollar bill? I haven't looked lately, but perhaps I have BANK tattooed across my forehead? Madam, please tell me you have something smaller. If not, I'll have to take your husband as security until you break this ridiculous bill."

He waited while the woman huffed and puffed, rooted through her purse, and came up with a twenty.

Holgarth smiled coldly. "That was rather painless, wasn't it?"

"I don't know why this place hasn't gone bankrupt with you manning the entrance." Okay, Gerry had to lose the insults and say what she had to say. "Conall is asleep. Someone will probably have to wake him when it's time for the fantasies. And have you seen Edge around anywhere?"

Holgarth touched his chin with one finger and rolled his eyes in mock thought. "Hmm, I wonder where I might find Conall to wake him? In his room? In your room? So many places to look."

"Give me a break. You know damn well where he is. You know everything, right?" The sweet taste of violence tempted her. Gerry wondered if Holgarth did this to everyone.

"Of course I do this to everyone. Sarcasm is my talent, my calling, my destiny if you will." He offered her a huge dramatic sigh. "Never mind. I know where Conall is. And I believe you'll find Edge in Wicked Fantasy." Holgarth turned to offend another customer.

Gerry hurried away just in case he wasn't finished insulting her.

When she entered Wicked Fantasy, she paused to let her eyes adjust to the dimness. It didn't take long to spot Edge. He was sitting at a table with the three sisters Gerry had met in the Sultan's Palace. As she watched, the women got up and left. He was probably interviewing for his next too-rich-to-live wife.

Gerry wound her way across the room and around the small dance floor to his table. Perfect. He was alone and vulnerable. Or as vulnerable as a possible serial killer could be.

"Do you mind if I join you?" Gerry sat in the chair to his right before he could say no. She had to get a look at his arm. Drat, he was wearing a sexy white poet's shirt, open at the neck to expose a great chest. The drat was for the long sleeves.

Edge gazed at her from those spectacular amber eyes and smiled his incredibly sexy smile. Jeez, women would marry him even if he met them at the altar with an ax in one hand and a shotgun in the other. He was that kind of guy.

"Funny, but I was thinking about you, Gerry."

Was he measuring her for wife number 501? This could work for her. "How wonderful." She tried to stare deeply into his eyes, but a pair of angry gray eyes kept getting in the way.

Conall would be totally ticked if he knew what she was doing. Too bad. This was her job. "I would've stopped by sooner, but I had sooo many things to take care of. I had to speak with my family's attorney about my trust fund. I don't understand all that legal junk, so I just sign whatever he shoves in front of me." Did she sound like a bored rich bitch? More to the point, did she sound like a *stupid* one?

"Trust fund?"

"Uh-huh. Of course, I have all the money I need without it, so I don't think about it much. It's tied up until I marry. Isn't that absolutely prehistoric?" She shrugged. "Anyway, if I ever find Mr. Right, we'll share all those cool millions. And if we don't have any kids, he'll inherit what's left if I die." Could she get any more obvious? She giggled. Did her giggle sound suitably dumb?

"Die?"

Was there a flare of interest in his eyes? "Yeah, if I die, he gets it all. But I'll be living and shopping for a long time, so there won't be much left for him to spend." She tried for a flirty laugh.

Was she good at shoveling crap or what?

Edge definitely was into the conversation. "You'll probably need a prenup to protect your fortune in case you guys split."

She widened her eyes to simulate stupid naiveté. "Oh, I'd only marry for love. I mean, if I ask the man I love to sign a prenup, it'll look like I don't believe in his long-term commitment to me." *Gag.*

"Yeah, I can see your point." He upped the wattage in his smile. "You came in with Conall last time. Be careful. I hear he's a violent man when he doesn't get what he wants. I hope you didn't tell *him* about your trust."

For a moment, she allowed herself to wonder about Conall's violent past. She also gave herself permission to be amazed at how much she wanted to know about that past.

"Oh, no. You're the first one I've told." If Edge was as powerful as Payton said, then he'd know she was vampire. "And I think I can take care of Conall if he tries anything." She leaned toward him and smiled, letting him see a little fang. "But sometimes it's tough for a woman who has a hunger for more than . . . the usual."

His expression gave nothing away. "Spell out 'hunger.' "

Gerry didn't want to drag this on any longer than she had to. Besides, she could only spout so much idiocy before it became redundant. Better to make it short and to the point. "Blood and tattoos. I love a man with tattoos. Do you have any?" She hoped he didn't pick up on her eagerness. And if he could read her mind, she hoped he wasn't doing it now.

Edge rolled up his right sleeve. "One."

She gulped. "The grim reaper. Pretty dark symbolism."

"I'm a pretty dark kind of guy."

Hmm. Powerful being, amber eyes, and grim reaper tattoo. Everything fit. She glanced around. It'd be tough taking him down here. Violent guy plus lots of innocent people made for a bad mixture. "Gee, it's crowded in here. Want to go outside and get some fresh air?"

"No." Something that might've been amusement flickered in his eyes.

Okay, on to plan B. Maybe she should've thought of a plan B ahead of time. She'd slap the Securer on him while she came up with one. "No fresh air. Right." She eased her hand into her pants pocket and palmed her tiny electronic leash.

With the Securer in her hand, she reached toward him as if to touch his tattoo. Almost there, almost there. She had that promotion locked up.

Her hand hit what felt like a brick wall about two inches from his arm. Well, maybe not exactly locked up.

Edge put back his head and laughed, really laughed. And if she didn't know what a dirtbag he was, she'd say it was a sexy laugh.

"Good try. You had me going for a while. I was into your lies and the whole I'm-incredibly-dumb act. Didn't jump into your head until the end. Why do you want to 'take me down'?" He leaned back in his chair and crossed his arms over his broad chest.

"For the five hundred wives you've killed." She pressed against the barrier, tried to go around it, and then gave up. "How'd you do that?"

"Power. More power than you want to mess with. *Five hundred wives?*"

A point for her side. He really looked shocked. "You won't get away from me. You run, I'll follow." She studied his expression. He didn't look guilty, but then serial killers rarely did.

"You'll have to show me something worth running from first. Who do you work for?"

She hated this part. Payton had to change the organization's name. "The Paranormal Undercover Field Force." He could take out the word "undercover." The paranormal underworld knew all about them. "We make sure nonhuman entities obey Texas laws." She counted out the seconds until he got it.

"You work for PUFF?" He shook his head. "Sweetheart, if you weren't loaded down with enough weapons to wipe out Galveston, I would *not* believe either that name or your game."

So much for her hidden weapons.

"How'd your organization come up with this thing about five hundred wives?"

She'd blown her cover, so no need to keep anything secret. She was pretty safe inside the club. He wouldn't want to jeopardize his chances of finding a shiny new wife by killing her in front of all these witnesses, some of whom were also powerful entities. And he was evidently secure enough to think she wasn't a danger to him. He'd find out, though, that what she lacked in experience she made up for in stubbornness.

"My boss got an anonymous tip he felt was pretty credible. The person described your eye color and grim reaper tattoo. The tipster said you were a powerful being who'd murdered five hundred wives and that we'd find you at Live the Fantasy."

He looked like he was doing some deep thinking. While he was thinking, Gerry glanced around to see if any help was near enough to signal. Nope. Eric and Brynn had been at the bar a short time ago, but they must've left to do their fantasies. Damn.

"Bitch."

"What?" Startled, Gerry looked back at Edge.

"Not you." He pushed away from the table. "Come outside with me." He didn't look back to see if she was following as he strode toward the door.

You bet she was following. She did a mental inventory of her weapons. Most of them were for hand-to-hand combat. The kind of criminal she'd hunted in her short career with PUFF didn't have her strength or speed. And her fangs were an added plus. If she could get close enough, she could do serious damage. Her chances of getting close to Edge? Not so good.

Once outside the castle, Edge moved into the shadows. Gerry didn't follow him there. That promotion wouldn't do her any good if Payton awarded it posthumously.

"Let's get this trying-to-take-me-down thing out of your system." The white flash of his smile wasn't comforting. "How'd you like to use all of your weapons on me?"

"Uh, is this a trick question?" Even as she asked, she was reaching back for her knife. She'd give it her best shot, but she already had a bad feeling about this.

A few minutes later, her entire arsenal except for her gun, taser, and bottle of holy water lay on the ground in front of Edge. She had a silencer on the gun, so she'd taken a chance that no one would notice her shooting at him. The bullet simply bounced off his invisible shield and joined the knives and hatchet. The taser? Why bother? Nothing got past his damn shield.

"Well, that was pretty futile." Gerry dug in her pocket and pulled out her PDA. She scrolled through her list of entities. "Hmm. No info on how to bash, stab, or mutilate a cosmic troublemaker."

"You still have your holy water and taser." He was openly laughing at her now.

"What the hell." Gerry moved up closer and pressed the taser against his invisible shield. Nothing. Then she used the edge of her T-shirt to unseal the bottle. Didn't know what holy water would do to her and wasn't about to find out. She heaved the liquid at him.

Ever obliging, he lowered his shield so the water could splash over him, wetting his hair and shirt and then trickling down his face. "Oh, the pain, the agony." He smiled as he swept the water from his eyes.

She scowled at him. "Thanks for the bone. You've proven your point. I don't have anything that can touch you."

But she would. She'd do some research on cosmic troublemakers and come back with a new and improved bunch of weapons. She started to walk away and then paused. She turned to look at him. "Did you really kill five hundred wives?"

"I never had a wife." For just a moment, she thought she saw a flicker of emotion. And then it was gone. "But if I did, why would I kill her when there're so many more pleasant ways to get everything I want?"

"Uh-huh. Makes sense." Strangely enough, it did. Wow, major shock. Her intuition said he was telling the truth. Her intuition rarely lied. Besides, if he was the killer, he had enough power to get rid of her like he'd rid himself of all those pesky pool boys and pizza delivery guys. And he was right. She didn't doubt for a minute that most women would hand over all their money and then smile as he drove away with it.

Not me, though. No, she was into immortal warriors. Tall, powerful men with shaggy dark hair, smoky gray eyes, sensual lips, and overprotective tendencies.

"As entertaining as this all has been, I've got to chase down Sparkle."

From Edge's expression, Gerry figured there wouldn't be lots of happy talk when he found her. Well, that wasn't her business. She watched him walk away before focusing on her own worries.

Okay, so now she had three problems. First, how to tell Payton that maybe his tip was wrong. Her proof? Not a damn thing except her intuition. Fat chance that would fly with Payton. So until the boss called her off, she had to keep trying to apprehend Edge.

Second, find the pond scum who was trying to kill her. No clue yet how to do that.

Last, deal with her growing attraction to Conall. Fine, not attraction. Lust. A big, fat honking case of I-want-your-body.

She wasn't sure which of the three was the most dangerous.

Sighing, she headed back into the castle. She'd forgotten a problem. Jinx. She'd go down to the dungeon and nab him when he dragged his loot back to his room.

Gerry had barely stepped into the castle when she saw Conall bearing down on her. He was a rolling thundercloud leaving dark skies in his wake. Whoa, would you look at that costume. He must be playing the Ghost of Christmas Future with that black robe and hood. Scary.

"Where the hell did you go?" *Don't shout.* He shouted. Conall knew his costume plus his fury was cutting a wide swath through the people cluttering the lobby. But he barely noticed them scuttling out of his way.

He stopped in front of her and glared. Armies had fled from that glare.

She sniffed. "Stop shouting. You're frightening the guests."

"Holgarth woke me, and you'd gone." Not unexpected. She wasn't a stay-here kind of woman. He should've found a way to keep awake.

"He said you asked about Edge." That's what pissed him off. Conall didn't try to fool himself. He wasn't angry because she'd put herself in danger. What he felt was raw, primitive jealousy. Over a damn Kavanagh. It was enough to scare the shit out of him.

"I have a job, and Morrigan's curse isn't going to stop me from doing it." She started to push past him.

Damn it, this wasn't about Morrigan. It was about . . . "Wait." He put his hand on her shoulder, not grabbing, not holding. Conall didn't think grabbing or holding would work with this woman. "I have a fantasy to do. Come with me. You can grab a costume, and we can talk while we're waiting for the customer."

"There's nothing to talk about." But she followed him to the costume room.

He wondered why.

Once she was wearing a robe and hood like his, he led her up one of the winding stone steps to a dark landing.

"So what're we supposed to be?" She adjusted her robe and hood.

Conall grinned. She was only about five-three, and the costume was made for a bigger person. The robe swallowed her up and pooled around her feet. Cute. Creepy? Not so much.

"We're evil, demonic entities who wait in darkness to pounce on unsuspecting medieval men and maidens who venture too close."

She nodded. "Cool. So what happens after we grab them?"

He shrugged. "Don't know. Before we can do any wicked stuff, the perfect Prince Brynn rescues them. Eric used to always play the bad guy, but marriage has mellowed him. Now he's the brave warrior who fights the forces of evil with Prince Brynn."

"Playing an evil force is more fun." Gerry tilted her head to gaze up at him. "You know, you look the part. You'd terrify me if I didn't know you were a softy inside."

"Softy?" Not even his worst enemy would've dared throw that insult at him.

She grinned. "Yeah, a big, gooey melted marshmallow. Who else would've thought about saving Houston?"

He ground his teeth. "I'll pull the damned weed out by its skinny roots."

"Oooh, scary." She moved closer while the darkness wrapped them in a false intimacy.

"Woman, you're driving me crazy."

"Mmm, tell me how so I can do it more."

"Mmmph."

"Gee, that was a bit garbled, but I think you slammed my snarky comments and independent attitude."

He could feel the explosion building, pushing up from his stomach, ready to blow away his control. "Wrong."

Only one way to defuse what was coming. "This is what drives me crazy." He pulled her into his arms and lowered his mouth to hers. Tracing her lips with his tongue, he allowed himself to sink into the joy of those sexy lips, their texture and taste—tempting with a hint of something wild and exotic.

"You taste . . . sweet," he murmured against her mouth. He hoped she didn't expect anything more specific, because right now his brain cells were migrating south.

Her chuckle was a soft puff of breath against his lips. "Sweet? I love sweet things"—she nibbled his bottom lip—"with a bit of bite"—she sucked on the fullest part of his lip—"and always creamy."

Godalmighty. Her words ripped him apart. So sensual, so filled with erotic images. He just had to explore the source of those sexy words. When he pressed, she opened her mouth to him.

He met her tongue and tasted his own desire. Sliding into her wet heat he imagined another place—hotter, wetter. He groaned.

She gasped. "I like how you go crazy, O'Rourke."

"Mmm." Reluctantly, he abandoned her mouth. He pushed aside her hood to kiss the sensitive skin behind her ear. "The Castle of Dark Dreams is a place of fantasies. What's your fantasy, lady with a bit of bite?"

"A tree trunk." Her breaths came in small gasps as he pushed her robe open and then lifted the red shirt.

He paused. "A tree trunk? Do I want to hear this?" The sexual haze cleared enough for him to realize what he was looking at. "A shoulder holster?" He slid his hand around to her back. "A knife?"

"Forget the gun and knife. Concentrate on my tree trunk."

How could he concentrate on anything? Her breasts swelled over the top of another of those damn stretchy bras while *his* swelling was getting painful. "I haven't done any tree trunk fantasies lately. Fill me in."

Fill. He wanted to ease into her body, filling her, bringing her more pleasure than any of the men in her past. No. Wrong. He wanted to thrust into her hard, feeling her clench around his cock as he swallowed her gasp with his mouth. And then she'd wrap those gorgeous legs around him while he pumped . . .

"See, this goes back to my childhood. Oh, yesss." She shivered as he slid his tongue over the swell of her breast.

"Your childhood. Right." He wouldn't last past her sixth birthday. With a snarl of frustration, he pulled the bra up to expose her full, ripe breasts with their rosy nipples.

"My brother Will was perfect. He—"

Conall stilled. "Brother? There're more Kavanaghs?"

Gerry had shoved his robe aside and worked her hands under his T-shirt where she was rubbing a heated circle on his chest. "Stepbrother. When my father died, Mom remarried. No more Kavanaghs."

His cock thought the rubbing was way too high. "Got it." He smoothed his palms over her body as he circled one pink nipple with his tongue.

"Put your mouth on me." Her breathing was ragged. "Gotta explain." She wiggled her fingers under the waist of his jeans and shorts, then cupped him.

Explain? Explain what? He couldn't hear past the jackhammer beating of his heart. There was something he was forgetting. Tree trunk. What the hell did he need to do with a tree trunk?

He covered her nipple with his lips and nipped gently before sucking.

"Oh, God, that feels good." She leaned into him and kissed his chest while she slid her fingers around his shaft. "Have to say this fast, because my train of thought is leaving the station. Always wanted to be more perfect than Will."

Well, his train was chugging down the mountain with no brakes. "Tree trunks. Get to the damn tree trunks fast or else it'll be too late." His legs felt shaky and he wanted to drop to his knees, but then she'd have to take her hand from his cock.

"Never let myself fail. I . . ." She moaned as he transferred his attention to her other nipple. "I forgot what I was going to say."

"Put the story on pause and get to the tree trunk." He sucked in his breath, trying to control his need and succeeding, for about another thirty seconds.

"My fantasy. To let someone else win."

Every cell in his body groaned in despair. "The. Tree. Trunk."

She clasped his cock tighter and started the rhythmic up-and-down motion that would bring instant disaster. He put his hand over hers. "Don't."

Gerry looked at him from eyes glazed with arousal. "I want to be chased through a forest by a naked wild savage. I run, but he catches me. I want him, but on my own terms." Her sentences came between quick pants. "He tears off my clothes. Does lots of delicious things to my body with his fingers and tongue. I scream and scream and scream."

She demonstrated her savage's technique by circling the head of his cock with the tip of her fingernail. He shook as he thrust his hips forward, grinding himself into her hand.

Her lips, swollen from his kiss, tipped up in the beginning of a smile, her eyes gleamed hot. "Then he takes me standing up against the trunk of a tree. Thrusting so hard that I can feel the rough bark digging into my bare back." She closed her eyes and slid her tongue over her bottom lip.

Abandoning her nipples, Conall slipped his hand past the waistband of her pants. The waistband didn't put up much resistance. He nudged her legs apart with his knee and then slid his finger back and forth, back and forth over her most sensitive spot. She was moist, hot, and ready.

She clutched at him with her free hand. "My orgasm

spontaneously combusts." Her grip on his cock tightened. They both groaned. "What the hell was I trying to tell you?"

"Beats me." Conall glanced around frantically. A tree trunk. Where the hell was a tree trunk when you had to have one?

He was so lost in his need he almost didn't hear the footsteps. When he did, he withdrew his hand. Then he leaned his forehead against hers, breathing in and out, in and out, trying to regain control. "The customer's coming."

She released him and stepped away, but he didn't miss the tremor of her hand. "That sort of got out of control." Turning away from him, she repaired the damage.

He pulled his robe and hood back into place. Whoever was climbing those steps would get an evil-entity fantasy they could talk about for years. In fact, Brynn and Eric might be too late to save the poor jerk.

Gerry didn't say anything as she turned with him to face the stairway. What was she thinking? He knew what *he* thought.

He'd just fucked up big-time.

8

The footsteps stopped. A woman was silhouetted at the top of the stairs.

"Did I interrupt something?" Sparkle's soft laughter was filled with sly knowledge. "I certainly hope the some-thing was hot and intense. Passion loves dark places."

"What do you want, Sparkle?"

Gerry shivered. She wouldn't care to be on the other side of his sword when Conall used that voice.

"Holgarth said Gerry was up here. I'd like to show her my store, talk a little girl talk." Sparkle swayed over to Conall. Her short black top showed lots of midriff. Her short black skirt showed lots of leg.

Gerry was jealous. She was melting into a puddle of ugly goo inside her clothes. "Sounds like fun." She needed to get away from Conall so she could put her sex drive into neutral before she slammed headfirst into her damn tree trunk. What had she been thinking telling him about *that*?

"She should stay with me."

Gerry sighed. This wasn't getting any easier. "Look, Conall, you have a job to do here. I think I've had all the fantasy I can take tonight."

His sexy mouth set in a stubborn line. "I don't—"

"You can't be in two places at once." He needed to give her some space so she could figure out where this thing with him was going. "I'll be with Sparkle. I'll be fine."

She watched him work it over in his mind.

"You have a choice, O'Rourke. You can give up your job here and follow me around all night—although that is so not going to happen—or you can compromise. I'm not going to take any stupid chances. I'll be careful around dangerous men." Gerry hoped Conall recognized that he was one of the most dangerous men she knew. She glanced at Sparkle. "Or women."

He nodded. "I guess I can't stop you." His expression said he wanted to try.

It was a grudging release, and she took it. "Let's go, Sparkle, and have that talk."

She followed Sparkle. The cosmic troublemaker's candy store was right outside the park. Gerry knew Jinx would feel the pull when she left the park. He'd have to move to compensate for it. Good. He was probably doing something that needed interrupting.

Sparkle led her into the store. Gerry didn't look around. She was too focused on the huge black cat crouched on the counter over a pile of jelly beans.

"Hey, Ganymede." Gerry knew her smile had insincere written all over it.

The cat looked up from his jelly beans. "Had sex with Conall yet? Do it. Soon."

Gerry scowled at the cat. "Anyone ever tell you you're bossy and abrasive?"

"No, but I like it. Sort of classy. Usually it's the same-old, same-old: bastard, son of a bitch. You know, people have no creativity when it comes to insults." He turned his attention to Sparkle. "Hey, babe. Got any cake? I'm in the mood for a chocolate layer treat."

Sparkle gave him a slitty-eyed glare. "Uh, does this look like a bakery? And eat those jelly beans, then get off my counter. The Department of Health will write me a shitload of citations if they catch you up there."

"Hmmph." He scarfed down the remaining jelly beans and leaped from the counter. He padded to the door and looked expectantly at Gerry.

With a huff of impatience, she pulled the door open and then closed it once he was gone.

"Cat hair. I wish he'd choose a hairless breed. No chance of that, though. In human form he's got hair down to his beautiful butt." Sparkle walked around the counter, retrieved a paper towel and absently wiped off the counter. "You know, he can open doors himself, but he just likes people to wait on him."

Gerry had no answer to that. "So what's all this girl talk?"

"Looking at your outfit is like sticking a needle in my eye." Sparkle bent down and lifted a box onto the counter. Rooting around, she piled things on the counter. "Strappy sandals with one-inch heels. Stylish but still comfy enough to run down a werewolf in."

"Gee, that's really generous of you but—"

"Sexy shorts. It's too hot here in September to wear tons of clothes."

"I need lots of clothes because—"

"Flirty top that just skims your waistline and takes the big plunge where it'll do the most good."

Gerry held up her hands. "Okay, time for a reality check. I'm a working girl. I have bad guys to catch. Don't think I'll do it with sexy and flirty."

Sparkle shook her head, her amber eyes sad. "So young, so naive. Sister, women have caught more men with sexy and flirty than with all those weapons you're dragging around with you."

Was there *anyone* who didn't know about her weapons? "But—"

"Here's the bottom line. Once you start hunting big game, you'll be dead before you can reach for that ankle knife." She pointed to the clothes. "Change."

"No." Gerry felt like a mutinous two-year-old.

Sparkle rolled her eyes, and then she stared at Gerry. Her pupils contracted to pinpricks as her eyes began to glow.

Holy crap. The air whipped into a whirlwind around Gerry. Before she could open her mouth to scream, the mini-tornado had sucked up the clothes Sparkle had laid out and . . . *Impossible.* Her own clothes disappeared. Just freakin' disappeared off her body. Everything became a blur as she staggered around the store trying to escape the wind.

Suddenly the air stilled. Gerry pressed her back against the door as she stared down at herself. But running from the store wouldn't change the fact that she was wearing Sparkle's outfit. Her own clothes? She glanced around. Gone. The only things of her own she still wore were her shoes.

Okay, she could handle this. Sure, it pointed out in triplicate what kind of power some of the bad guys she'd be hunting had. And yeah, it sort of highlighted how ineffectual she was. But she'd learn and get stronger. Hopefully sooner than later.

Her weapons lay scattered on the floor along with the sandals Sparkle wanted her to wear. "Why didn't you put the shoes on me?" She didn't bother asking Sparkle how she'd undressed and then redressed her. Wasn't a power Gerry would have anytime soon. Besides, she was too angry to care.

Sparkle pursed her lips. "Shoes are hard. I can't do shoes without knocking you down. Mede's a lot better at this than I am. He doesn't even need the wind."

"Who gave you the right to . . ." Gerry was so mad the words stuck in her throat.

"No one *gives* me anything. I take what I want." Sparkle smiled to soften all that arrogance.

Didn't work. Gerry glanced down again. Her shoes looked ridiculous with her new outfit.

"You're probably thinking about ripping those yummy clothes off your body. I'd consider consequences first. Although a naked run through the park would sure get Conall's attention." Sparkle looked hopeful.

Gerry slid down the door until she was sitting—needed a few minutes of rest to stop shaking—and yanked off her shoes. The mindless act of changing shoes gave her a chance to pull herself together.

"This wasn't just about the clothes." Sparkle played with the glittery bracelet at her wrist.

Diamonds? Probably. She must've convinced another customer that the bracelet was fair exchange for a new and improved sex life. Gerry used the door to steady herself as she stood.

Sparkle walked around the scattered weapons. "I can't believe all this junk. No wonder you looked all bumpy and lumpy. Lethal weapons are good in moderation. They should fit in with the sensual flow of a woman's clothes, though. Oops, I forgot. Your clothes didn't have any sensual flow." She fixed Gerry with a piercing gaze. "Bottom line. Not one of these weapons helped you stop me."

"You made your point. Maybe that means I just have to be more proactive. I'll attack the criminals before they can use their powers. I might not have the skills of an ancient vampire, but I still have preternatural speed."

Sparkle shook her head. "So do they, and a lot more, sister." She glanced at the door. "Edge should be here any minute to watch the shop. Then we can walk for a while, and I can lay some secrets of life on you."

Secrets of life? Gerry didn't have time to think what

that meant before Edge slammed into the shop. Anger vibes rolled off him in waves. He didn't even glance at Gerry.

"We need to get the rules straight, lady." He slapped the countertop so hard Gerry expected the chocolates inside the case to bounce into the air. "You're playing dirty. And while I sort of admire that, it pisses me off. I don't like rumors . . ." Edge seemed to notice Gerry for the first time. He bared his teeth at her. "Want to try and take me down again, sweetheart? If not, get out of here so I can talk to Sparkle."

Gerry stared at him. She'd had one too many people telling her what to do tonight. "Gee, Sparkle said you were the hired help. Kind of uppity for a candy store clerk, aren't you?" Yeah, she had a death wish.

Sparkle yawned. "Cheating is part of the game, Edge. Watch the store while I go for a short walk with Gerry. When I come back we can discuss the 'rules.' Although if you haven't figured out there are no rules, then there's not much I can say." She headed for the door. "The licorice all-sorts are on sale."

Gerry trailed Sparkle from the shop. Wow, tough lady. "Um, how much do you know about Edge?"

"Not much." She seemed to be mad about that. "But I don't want to talk about him. Let's talk about Conall."

"What's to talk about? He's an immortal warrior cursed to follow me around for the rest of my existence. Now it's my curse, too. End of story." Gerry left out a few minor details. Like he was so sexy he made her teeth hurt.

Sparkle strolled past the entrance into Live the Fantasy. No, not strolled. Gerry doubted Sparkle even knew how to "stroll." Every move she made was orchestrated for maximum sexual impact. Men with glazed eyes and gaping mouths littered the path behind them.

"You know, you really need to practice squeezing those old lemons, adding lots of sugar, and stirring up some sexual lemonade with Conall." Sparkle winked at her. "Other-wise the next eight hundred years will be pure hell." She looked thoughtful. "Personally, pure anything doesn't do it for me."

"It's not that simple." Gerry wished it were. Without the curse, they could make hot and crazy love until Houston's branches took over the castle. And once Conall was out of her system, she could forget him. "There're things you don't know about." Like Morrigan killing one of Conall's descendants if she got ticked at him.

Sparkle frowned. "Really? Morrigan would do that? No, forget I asked. Of course she would. She's a goddess."

Damn. Gerry kept forgetting that almost everyone she'd met here could read her mind. Except Conall. Thank God. "I need to ask Eric if he'll teach me how to shield my thoughts."

"It won't do any good. I go where I want to go. And the path inside your head is pretty well worn."

Sparkle looked preoccupied. Not a good thing. A thinking cosmic troublemaker had to be a danger to all humanity.

Suddenly Sparkle brightened. "This isn't a long-term fix, but then we don't need one, do we? When you know you can't stand one more second without Conall's hot, naked body pressed against you, when you think you'll ex-plode unless you feel him deep inside you, when . . ."

"Yes?" The mental images were pushing Gerry to the edge.

"Well, when that happens, contact me and I'll be your lookout." She grinned. "I've never been a lookout before. I'll wear my totally sexy and cool black bodysuit so I'll blend in with the night. Maybe my black nail color so I'll be completely coordinated. I have an incredibly erotic black mask I wear for Mardi Gras. I can't wait."

Gerry wasn't too sure about Sparkle as lookout. "So what will you do if Morrigan shows up?"

Something dark and powerful moved in Sparkle's amber eyes. And for the first time, Gerry realized that this was a being she wouldn't want to tick off.

"Got it." Gerry thought the powers that be in Texas should change all those signs along the highways to: Don't Mess with Texas or Sparkle Stardust.

Sparkle's expression cleared. "Now let's chat about some sensual techniques you can use on Conall. I know ways to drive him wild by just touching—"

"Yoo-hoo! Gerry, wait up." Gerry turned. Fulvia, Tullia, and Varinia were hurrying to catch up. They all wore identical white shorts, white tops, and white shoes. There was something creepy about that.

Sparkle made a rude noise. "Just what we need, the three virgins from hell."

"You know they're virgins?" What was with the "from hell" comment? They'd seemed friendly the last time she met them. Okay, so they were a little fixated on male bashing.

"Oh, we go back a long way." Sparkle smiled as the women caught up. The smile didn't reach her eyes.

"What a coincidence. We're all walking in the same direction." Tullia giggled at her observation. "How do you like my new sandals, Sparkle? My Italian shoemaker's a genius."

Sparkle glanced at the shoes. Gerry had never before seen that much open lust for an inanimate object in a person's eyes. She studied the shoes. Beautiful but impractical. Guess she could describe her lust for Conall with the same words.

"We can all walk together. What fun." Fulvia waved her hands.

Sparkle followed the motion with her eyes. "You do know I'll eventually chop off your hand and take it to the cosmetics department at Dillard's to match that nail color?"

Gerry got the feeling she wasn't kidding.

"Silly. I have someone who mixes the color especially for me." But Fulvia did put her hands behind her back.

Varinia didn't waste time on small talk. "Have you thought over what we said about men, Gerry? Virginity's the way to go. I hear that Conall drinks milk from the carton. Ick."

"Uh, well . . ."

Sparkle grabbed Gerry's arm and pulled her away from Varinia. "Don't listen to her. Think about Conall smoothing his fingers over your bare breasts."

"Yeah, that's a good—"

Tullia edged closer. "He'll never love any woman as much as he loves his sword. There'll always be three in your bed: you, him, and Mr. Sword."

Sparkle's eyes were doing the glowing thing again. "He'll slip his hand between your thighs and then—"

Fulvia jumped into the fray. "He'll ignore you to watch football. He only tunes in to words like 'kill,' 'maim,' 'touchdown,' and 'dinner.' "

Hands on hips, Sparkle stalked the sisters. Gerry backed away from the impending brawl.

"Talk about demonic ditzes. Why would Gerry listen to you when she has me as her guide to sexual ecstasy?"

Demonic? Gerry hadn't a clue what Sparkle was talking about, but this might be her chance to sneak away.

Varinia poked her finger into the middle of Sparkle's chest. "Why would she want advice from a slut?"

Sparkle grabbed the wrist attached to the finger and propelled Varinia over her head. The virgin landed with a splash in a small pond.

Then things got out of control. Gerry sneaked away while Sparkle was screaming, "Hell hags," and trying to rip Tullia's shoes off.

She scuttled around the corner of a building and then sighed when silence settled over her. Free, free, free. The shadow of the building protected her as she decided what to do next. Maybe hunt down Jinx.

"Wow, do you see that catfight out there?" The male voice was familiar.

She turned around to find Dell behind her. His hair was just as red, his smile just as wide, and his eyes just as strange. "Oh, hi. Yeah, they've collected a big crowd. Security should be showing up any minute."

Suddenly, the hunger struck. Bloodlust. Its intensity backed her against the wall. What the . . . ? She shouldn't be feeling it now. But the hunger didn't react to logic. It wanted Dell as fast as she could sink her fangs in him.

No. She wasn't a newbie vamp anymore. She'd control the hunger.

Dell's smile was open and oblivious. "Hey, want to check out a new fantasy? I hear it's powerful stuff."

Gerry took a deep breath. Weird. The hunger was gone. It was like someone had flipped an off switch in her brain. She really needed to talk to Eric or Donna about her feelings. Too bad she didn't have any vampire friends, but vampires weren't a social bunch.

"Yeah, why not?" She needed a few uncomplicated minutes.

She followed Dell around to the back of the building and along a quiet path that went on and on. Was the park this big? She hadn't noticed before.

When the path ended, she stopped and stood blinking. "A French Revolution fantasy? Somehow I don't see that as a big draw. I read *A Tale of Two Cities* in high school. I mean, who'd fantasize about Madame Defarge and her crew?"

She studied the scene. Someone had built a pretty authentic-looking replica of the Bastille. She could see the faces of people inside with their mouths open in silent screams. Creepy. And then there was the guillotine. Now *that* would give a vampire chills.

"Someone who's into horror movies? People have lots of crazy fantasies." He sounded a little excited.

"Different strokes and all that." She followed him into the line for a shot at the guillotine. Personally, this wasn't her fantasy, but yeah, she was a little curious.

"This is so cool." Dell glowed with happiness. "The executioner speaks to each customer while the old biddy over there knits. Then the fake blade falls. How realistic is that?"

Cool if you fantasized about someone cutting your head off. Not for her. She'd rather imagine Conall . . .

"Your turn, Gerry." She looked up to realize Dell had already taken his turn and waited for her on the other side of the platform. Gee, that was quick.

She stepped up and looked at the executioner. He was tall, cadaverous, and his eyes were pale like Dell's. Funny that she'd met so many people with the same unusual eye color. Something about the thought niggled at her, but then she was drawn into what the executioner was saying.

"You've consorted with a man who has the blood of thousands on his hands. For this you will die." He smiled a ghastly smile. "And enjoy it." His voice was deep, hollow, and totally scary. He nodded to the man next to him.

The man said nothing as he pushed Gerry to her knees in front of the guillotine and placed a wooden board over her neck so she couldn't move. Fear arced through her. Wow, this was a little too realistic.

But that's what Live the Fantasy was all about, a fantasy for every taste. Some people liked being scared. Okay, no more fear. She'd seen the people in front of her do this, and they'd left the platform with their heads still attached to their bodies.

She prepared to close her eyes. Even though she'd scoped out the blade—made of thin, flexible rubber with a cutout where a person's neck would be—the whole ritual bothered her. Fine, so she had a vivid imagination. She could picture her head bouncing merrily off the platform to the cheers of the bystanders.

At the last minute, she couldn't close her eyes. She twisted her head to look up at the blade.

She widened her eyes. Holy shit! The blade was the real deal. No cutout, and she could see light reflecting off the metal as the blade started its deadly descent.

Her preternatural speed and strength kicked in. She flung herself backward, taking out the wooden board. The swish of the blade was so close she could feel the breeze it generated. She rolled away from the guillotine and scrambled from the platform.

Once again, someone had almost ended her short vampire existence. She felt the slide of her fangs as she pushed to her feet. First she'd rip out the executioner's throat, and then . . .

She looked around. *Nothing.* Just an empty field. No Bastille, no guillotine, no people. Where had Dell gone? He was the one who'd brought her . . .

The sound of pounding footsteps came nearer and nearer. Someone was in a big hurry to reach her. Hissing, she prepared to protect herself.

For just a moment, when Conall barreled into view still wearing his robe and hood, Gerry thought a mad monk was on the loose. As soon as she recognized him, though, she felt an intense spurt of happiness. She'd dissect that emotion later.

"What happened? Are you okay?" No, not okay. Conall could see the shock in her eyes.

Gerry drew a shaking hand across her forehead. "Tell me that Live the Fantasy has a French Revolution fantasy."

He shook his head. "Wouldn't be a moneymaker."

Her laughter was a little quivery. "Well, a few minutes ago the Bastille and a guillotine were here. Someone tried to chop my head off."

Conall took a calming breath. He glanced around the empty field. "There's never been a fantasy here."

"Someone's messing with my head in more ways than one." She started back toward the castle.

He fell into step beside her. "Tell me what led up to the guillotine."

"Sparkle got into it with the three harem sisters and I sneaked off. I met the guy I told you about on the Pirate Ship fantasy. He told me about this French Revolution thing. I followed him." She shrugged. "And almost lost my head."

"What's this guy's name? What's he look like?" For once, Conall was glad he moved in paranormal circles. Anyone else would've thought Gerry was crazy. Conall knew what possibilities lurked in the dark.

"Dell. No last name. Average height, red hair, light eyes." They used the great hall entrance to the castle instead of walking around to the hotel lobby side. Gerry headed for the stairs to the dungeon. But suddenly she stopped to take a good look at his robe and hood. "Wait. I just realized. How did you turn up at just the right time?"

Okay, this was going to sound dumb. "I was in the middle of a fantasy when I felt you."

"*Felt* me?"

"It was like a psychic scream. Not your *voice*, but something more primal." He glanced away to where Holgarth stood. The wizard glared at him.

"Holgarth's costume is the same as yours." She tried to smile, but there was no humor behind it. "He looks ticked."

"Yeah. He probably took over my fantasy when I ran out. I didn't exactly explain where I was going. He hates it when someone messes with his schedule." She'd sidestepped any comment about his "psychic scream." He didn't blame her.

"Guess I'll go down and see how Jinx is doing." She glanced toward the stairs.

"Tell him I want the bracelet back."

"The bracelet?" Her expression gave nothing away.

"He's the only tarantula I know who's into stealing diamond bracelets."

"I'll get it back for you." Before he could say anything else, she started to walk away.

"Gerry?"

She glanced over her shoulder.

"You look so hot I want to drag you down to the dungeon and lick every inch of your body."

She gave him the first real smile he'd seen since the guillotine incident. "That's Sparkle's outfit calling to you. I think she washed it in pheromones." Then she was gone.

Conall didn't waste any time. He strode over to Holgarth, stripping the robe off as he walked.

"Oh, I'm too excited to express my humble thanks. How wonderful of you to give a few of your precious minutes to your job." Holgarth was at his sarcastic best.

"Hey, you don't need me, wizard. You look like you were made for the part, all scary and creepy."

"Perhaps you'll share why you felt the need to abandon the fantasy right at a crucial moment. I almost had to return the customer's money." He shuddered at the possibility.

"Gerry needed me. From now on, she always comes first. And I won't be doing any more fantasies tonight. Someone tried to kill her again."

Holgarth nodded. Thank God, no more sarcasm. "We'll have to call a meeting of all the entities in the park. This can't go on."

"Right." Conall searched the crowd. "Where's Brynn?"

"In the costume room. He's getting ready for the next fantasy."

Conall was gone before Holgarth even finished. He didn't want to leave Gerry alone too long. No matter how much she bitched at him, he had to do a better job of protecting her. Even though she'd saved herself tonight, next time she might not be so lucky.

His sudden empty feeling when he considered life in the

castle without her surprised him. This was all about the
curse. He was bound to her by Morrigan's order.

Somehow, though, the old bitter mantra didn't seem to
work with Gerry. Yeah, he'd admit he liked her. Okay,
okay, so he wanted to have sex with her. But he refused to
think beyond that. *Couldn't* think beyond that. For both
their sakes.

Once inside the costume room, he didn't waste words
with Brynn. "I need Fo right now."

9

"I crave goat's milk and anchovies, Gabriel. I feel like crying to express my hormonal imbalance, but it's no fun without real tears. Maybe you could work on a real-tears program for the computer." Fo's big purple eyes peeked from one of the twin pouches—one purple and one red—attached to Conall's belt. "Pregnancy is the pits. I'm so glad it's almost over. If I swell any more, I won't fit in my case. How do women suffer through this for nine months?"

Conall grew wary. "Uh, how close to 'almost over'?"

"Oh, it'll be a few days yet." She sounded unsure. "I think."

Great. Just freakin' great. Okay, how to ask the next question. "I've never been around when a demon detector gave birth. How . . . ?" Damn, he was messing this up.

Fo's laughter was a happy trill. "Through my SD card slot, silly."

Conall decided to pass on the question of how Fo got pregnant in the first place. Some things he didn't need to know. "Makes sense." Next tough question. "What if there're complications? Will you need help?"

"What kind of complications could there be?" She didn't sound worried.

Conall shrugged. "Just a thought." Guess popping out a memory card didn't involve much risk. Right now he had other things to worry about. The pouches drew stares. With a demon detector in each pouch, he looked like a man with a kangaroo complex. But he needed Fo and Gabriel. They could root out paranormal entities in the park as well as give him a chance to get some sleep.

It was possible a human had gotten into Gerry's room and lit the candle, but this second attempt on her life was definitely the work of something nonhuman and powerful.

"I'm sending the milk and anchovies right now, beautiful mama." Gabriel's voice seemed too big and deep to be coming from his small case.

Brief pause in conversation. Conall assumed the sending and tasting was in progress.

"Mmmm. Delicious. You take such good care of me, daddypoo."

Conall gritted his teeth. How long could he live with expectant mom and happy dad before barfing? Drawing in a deep breath, he searched for a distraction from the "beautiful mamas" and "daddypoos." "How do you do the taste thing?"

Fo looked up at Conall. "Gabriel's brilliant. He can do anything with a computer." Pride glowed in those big purple eyes.

"I did some upgrades on our PC, and then I developed a few new programs for Fo and me. We're both synchronized with the computer. Now we can taste, smell, and do other human things in our own ways." Gabriel slanted a glance at his love. "I only wish I could give us human bodies." Sadness touched his voice. "But we're just glad we found each other. And we do what we can with what we have."

I envy you. Usually he'd block that kind of thought as soon as it surfaced, but this once he let it simmer. What if he wasn't cursed? What if he could have a real relationship with a woman? Let's get specific. With Gerry.

He firmed his lips along with his resolve and pushed the thought back into the dark corner of his mind where it belonged. If he hadn't escaped the curse in eight centuries, what were his chances now? Right, none.

Besides, if Morrigan released him from the curse, what would he be? At best he'd be mortal with a mortal's short life span. Gerry would go on without him. At worst, he'd turn into a pile of dust, because without the curse he'd be long dead.

And why the hell was he even thinking about this? Gerry and he didn't have anything in common except the curse. Yeah, the lust, too.

His thoughts shifted as he reached the bottom of the stairs. Gerry sat on a chair in front of Jinx's door.

"I know you're in there you sneaky, thieving shifter. Now come out and give me that bracelet. If I have to break down this door, I'll add resisting arrest and whatever it costs me to replace the door to your charges. Oh, and don't think you can wait me out. I'm not leaving."

Conall grinned. She made him smile. Not an easy thing to do. "Your prisoner giving you trouble?"

"From the moment I got this case." She glanced at Fo and Gabriel. "Hi, Fo. And I guess you're Gabriel. Anyone know how to open a door without ripping it off the hinges?"

"I can."

Conall looked down and almost groaned. Asima had followed him. "Anything I can say to make you back off?"

Asima blinked up at him. *"Of course not. As long as you're hanging around this Kavanagh, you're in danger."*

Gerry huffed. "This Kavanagh has a name. And he's immortal. He can't die defending me. Not that I *want* him defending me." She grew thoughtful. "Well, not all the time anyway. He can be a big help apprehending some of the more powerful entities I'll be facing. And maybe I do need someone at my back when I'm out of it during the day." She brightened. "He's not a protector, he's a partner. We'll share the profits when we bring down one of the bad guys."

Conall figured Gerry was way into rationalizing, but at least she was accepting him into her future. That was a good thing.

"Whatever." Asima looked bored. *"Let's get this door open."*

She stared at the door, and it swung open.

"See, that's what I have to learn how to do. Can you teach me?" Gerry didn't look as though she expected a positive answer.

Asima sniffed. *"Perhaps."* Then her gaze turned sly. *"We could exchange favors. You do something for me, and I'll teach you a few things."* Satisfied with that arrangement, she sat and waited to see what would happen.

"Done." Gerry fixed her attention on Jinx's open door. "I'm waiting, Jinx."

He came to the door and yawned as he hooked his thumbs over the top of his jeans. "Crap. Can't a guy get any rest in this damn place? Whatta you want?"

Gerry raised one eyebrow. "The bracelet."

"What brace—"

He didn't get any further. Before Conall could blink, she stood, bent down to grab Jinx's ankles, and then leaped onto the chair.

"Aaagh!" Jinx screeched his outrage as Gerry held him off the floor by his ankles.

Conall muffled his laughter. Fo didn't muffle anything. She shrieked encouragement.

Gerry shook Jinx. Up and down, up and down, until a bracelet and a pair of earrings fell from his pocket. Then she let him drop to the floor, jumped from the chair, and retrieved her loot.

"A bracelet *and* earrings. Busy, weren't you? Don't make me do this again, Jinx." She looked pleased with herself.

Without a word, Jinx stumbled back into his room and slammed the door shut.

Conall picked up the chair as they walked to the dungeon. "I'm impressed. With a few more vampire skills you'll throw terror into the hearts, or whatever passes for hearts, of all evil entities."

Gerry studied his face for sarcasm, and then nodded. "The enhanced strength and speed come in handy, but I'll need a lot more than those to move up the ladder."

"Oooh, a dungeon. I've never been down here before." Fo bubbled with excitement. "Take us out, Conall, so we can see everything."

"Don't overdo it, honey. You need to rest." Gabriel looked at Gerry. "Fo's due in a few days."

"Oh." Gerry looked a little worried. "How will Fo—"

"Through her SD card slot." Conall was becoming an expert on demon detector births.

He took Fo and Gabriel from their pouches and held them up as he circled the dungeon. While he walked he listened to Asima and Gerry.

"Okay, what do you want for helping me, Asima?" Gerry sounded suspicious.

Smart woman.

"I want you to take an interest in cultural events."

"Such as?"

"I have a DVD of Swan Lake. *Watch it with me tomorrow night."*

Conall was never sure what Asima was really feeling because her cat face didn't show emotions well. But he figured she was expecting rejection. The rest of the castle hadn't tuned in and turned on to her brand of entertainment.

Gerry nodded. "I've always loved ballet."

"I never thought I'd find anyone in this castle who appreciated the finer things in life. Come up to my room tomorrow night." Asima didn't try to hide her excitement.

Gerry looked bemused as she watched Asima pad happily from the room. "Do you know she spent last night outside this door? I tripped over her when I left."

That bit of news made Conall uneasy. Of course, everything Asima did made him uneasy. She'd shown up at the castle one day and stayed. No reason. She'd just given everyone her "I'm a messenger of Bast" speech. But she was a powerful being, and no one wanted her gone badly enough to try throwing her out.

"We'll watch TV for a while. Gabriel can get all kinds of channels that no one else can get." Fo peered at Gerry. "When dawn comes we'll be very quiet. Kimmie said she'd hook up our computer in here so we can play games and surf the Web for interesting sexual sites."

"Well, that's . . . nice." Gerry glanced helplessly at Conall.

Conall gave her his don't-ask look.

The TV clicked on. Obviously Gabriel didn't need out-of-date technology like remotes.

"Conall, would you get our cradles from the pouches?" Fo was already engrossed in the program.

Holy shit. Conall stared. *When Computers Go Wild?* "What the hell is this about, Gabriel?" He groped for the cradles.

"It's a video about chips interacting with other chips. Lots of sexy dialogue and erotic graphics."

Conall set the cradles on the coffee table and then put Fo and Gabriel in them without taking his eyes from the screen.

"Not exactly mainstream, is it?" Gerry stared unblinking at the TV.

Gabriel chuckled. "Artificial intelligence has a world all its own. We didn't even know it existed beyond us until I fooled around with our computer. There's a whole alternative artificial intelligence culture out there."

"It's sad though." Fo was in thoughtful mode. "AI fantasies are all about having a human form. We're not very accepting of how we look." She blinked. "Of course, I think Gabriel's form is supremely hot."

"Yo, no one told me about the party." Ganymede padded in and leaped onto the coffee table. "Good thing I thought of refreshments. I ordered a few chips, a few dips, a few . . . Anyway, the goodies are on their way." He glanced at Gerry with those amber eyes that looked so harmless. "I charged it to your account, babe. After all, I'm here to protect you. Gotta keep my strength up while I'm doing all the tough stuff."

Gerry glared as a hotel employee delivered Ganymede's snacks. Conall sucked in his breath. This wasn't going to end well.

"I can't believe this." Gerry flung her hands in the air to emphasize how much she didn't believe it. "I'm a vampire, people. V. A. M. P. I. R. E. Deadly creature of the night. Voracious bloodsucker. I'm fanged, ferocious, and one scary gal. So why do I have a roomful of protectors? I don't need you. Go home." She hissed at them.

Fo never took her eyes from the TV. "Oh, look, Gabriel. The pretty PDA is having a fantasy about being human and . . . Can a man and woman really do that together? I don't think human body parts bend that way. Did you research that position?"

Ganymede tore open a bag of chips with his teeth and then looked at Gerry. "Sure you need protecting. All women need a strong guy to keep them safe. Uh, don't tell Sparkle I said that. How about opening the dip for me, sweet stuff?"

Conall could see Gerry thinking about what kinds of

creative things she could do with that dip. Time to defuse the situation. Without saying anything he nudged her toward the break room door. "Let's talk."

Surprised, she let herself be guided. Once inside, he closed the door and switched on a light.

Gerry felt like her head would explode if she couldn't go back into the dungeon and rip out a few throats. Something else to add to her "unfulfilled wishes" file. "I want everyone gone from my dungeon. I need some downtime to think. I can't concentrate with weird sex on my TV and Ganymede littering my coffee table with popcorn and chips. So if you'll move out of the way, I'll go back in there and kick some ass."

"Relax for a minute." He locked both doors to the room before sinking onto a plush green couch and drawing her down beside him.

Relax? How could she relax when she had so much to do? Discover who wanted her dead. Ride herd on Jinx the Slippery. Find another wife killer in the castle with amber eyes and a grim reaper tattoo so she wouldn't have to go after Edge. And toughest of all? Satisfy her gnawing need to touch and be touched by Conall without Morrigan's vengeance descending on both of them.

Wow, can we say overwhelming? She leaned her head back against the couch and really looked at the break room for the first time. What the . . . ? "Some break room." She ran her fingers over the arm of the couch—smooth, sensual.

Conall watched her from eyes dark with need.

She knew *her* eyes promised she'd do a much more thorough job of touching and smoothing if she got her hands on his body.

"This stuff didn't come from Danny's Discount Furniture Barn." Gerry looked past the designer chairs and tables to the far wall. "The wall looks like one giant screen. What's with that?"

He picked up a small remote from the table beside him and clicked it. The wall became a beach scene complete with wild surf, sun-warmed sand, and the sound of waves crashing on the shore. Amazing, she could actually smell the salt air and feel the sea breeze drifting across her face. This had to be as close to virtual reality as you could get with today's technology.

"I'm totally impressed."

He grinned, and Gerry knew she was in deep doo-doo because his smile actually looked boyish to her. She suspected Conall had *never* had a boyish moment. He probably popped from his mama's womb, picked up his sword, and went forth to do battle wearing diapers and a gorgeous scowl.

"Gabriel did the programming. He's our secret weapon. There's not much he can't do with a computer."

"Hmm. Beautiful, but I don't see any trees. Specifically, no trunks." She slid him a sly glance. "Gotta have trunks."

Excitement flared in his eyes. "Trunks? Sure, I can find you a trunk." His expression said he'd find her a trunk even if he had to gnaw a tree down with his own teeth and drag it into the break room.

His eagerness made her laugh, but beneath the laughter desire stirred. She knew tree trunks and memories of Conall would always be intertwined.

Memories? A sad word, because each day of her existence would be filled with all the things he said and did, tucked away to be taken out when she felt lonely. Yes, even with him always with her, she'd be lonely, because Conall O'Rourke would never let himself feel deeply about a Kavanagh.

Did she want him to feel deeply? Maybe, yes.

He clicked the remote and a scene from the Saguaro National Park in Arizona filled the screen. All cactus and brilliant blue skies.

"Ouch. Saguaros are awesome, but kind of prickly for

what I had in mind." She sighed and snuggled closer as he gave in and put his arm across her shoulders.

The click-clicks became more desperate as scene after scene flashed across the wall. "Where the hell are the forests? Who chose these freakin' scenes?"

Gerry slid her fingers over the top of one muscular thigh—teasing, *hoping*. "They were all shot during the day. Any night scenes?"

Click, click. "No. The vampires use this room the most. They like pretending they're out on a sunny day." Click, click, click!

"So what're we going to do with the mob in my dungeon? Oh, and don't forget the Siamese diva outside the door."

Click, click. "Fo and Gabriel only have to be here when I'm sleeping or if we're hunting paranormal entities. Ganymede's a freeloader. He'll leave when we cut off his food supply. Asima? I don't think anyone except maybe Ganymede or Morrigan could make her go away. But at least she's outside the door." Click! Click! *CLICK!*

Gerry watched the screen anxiously. If a tree trunk didn't appear soon, Conall was going to put his foot through the wall.

"Trees." He sounded like he'd just run a marathon.

But there they were. A forest of glorious trees in fall's brilliant colors. Like Pavlov's pooches, she immediately started salivating for Conall's hot bod. Okay, so she didn't need the trees to do that.

Taking her hand, he dragged her from the couch and over to the left side of the screen where one large maple tree stood, its leaves rustling in the crisp breeze.

"This trunk good enough for you?"

From the heat in his gaze, she didn't think he gave a flip whether the trunk was perfect or not. "Wonderful trunk." She fixed her gaze on those broad shoulders along with the sculpted pecs and abs clearly delineated by his black T-shirt. Down, down her gaze glided to his strong thighs and muscular legs showcased by worn jeans.

Was there any part of this guy that wasn't a savory sensual treat? She had to get him naked to do a more detailed investigation. There must be at least one tiny spot on him that was just ordinary, maybe a mole or an ugly toe. Something.

As he lowered his head to take her mouth, she tangled her fingers in all that thick dark hair. No need for preliminaries. She parted her lips for him and welcomed his tongue, parried his every move as she let his taste of hot male animal carry her to the next level of sexual excitement.

He'd taken an instant leap up two levels if his erection was any indication. She walked her fingers over the bulge. He groaned as he transferred his magic mouth to the swell of her breasts. Sparkle's easy-access top worked perfectly.

Gerry's thoughts became a blur of need, overpowering everything rational, as Conall slipped her top off and then made short work of her bra. He didn't just free her breasts to his touch, he freed everything sexual dammed up since she became vampire. The flood threatened to sweep her into stormy seas with no lighthouse in sight. Oh well. Drowning in sex wasn't a bad way to go.

Before her brain locked the door and took off to party with the sluts living on the ground floor, it gave a shout-out to Sparkle.

"Lookout needed. Now." If Sparkle didn't hear that, Gerry hoped Morrigan was doing her bitch act far, far away. Because Gerry didn't think she'd be able to stop this time.

She leaned back against the screen. Nope, wasn't a tree trunk, but she'd save that fantasy for another time. Gerry didn't need a fantasy when Conall was sliding his tongue across each nipple and then nipping gently before closing his lips over a hard, super-sensitized nub.

He did the suction thing, and her enhanced senses jump-started every nerve in her aroused body. Tiny nerve messengers put on their running shoes and raced to her brain—her brain was still kicked back drinking a wine cooler with the aforementioned sluts—so they could deliver the news. The little guys were so excited all they could say was "Wow, wow, wow." Her brain thought that was pretty cool and went back to party some more.

As each nipple became the power center of her personal universe, she wanted to do her amoeba imitation—absorb him into her body so the pleasure would go on and on and on from the inside out.

"Oooh, Gabriel, that looks like lots of fun. Turn up the volume so I can hear the groans. I wonder what it feels like to get all naked and then kiss and touch until every inch of your body is slick and hot—"

Damn. Gerry tried to block out Fo who was shouting to be heard above the TV. Now, if she could just get Conall's T-shirt off.

He rolled her nipples between his fingers as he sank to his knees and kissed a heated path over her stomach. Whimpering, she grabbed his shirt and pulled.

He obliged by pausing long enough to yank it off and fling it on the floor.

Gerry closed her eyes as she slid her splayed fingers across the wonder that was his muscular back and shoulders. There couldn't possibly be anything more sensual than warm, bare male flesh.

"Yo, Fo and Gabriel. Hot video you got there. Sort of reminds me of what turns Sparkle on. When we visit this island I bought in the Caribbean, I pretend to be a pirate. My wicked lady gets off on pirates. See, my ship sank, but I manage to crawl ashore. Naked. Hey, whatever makes my sweetie happy is okay with me. She meets me on the beach wearing nothing but her whip. Big freakin' whip. She spreads those long, long legs and then—"

Ack! *Focus on Conall—his fingers, his mouth.* Sometime during Ganymede's little sexual trip down memory lane, Conall had rid her of her shorts and panties. Spreading her legs, she assumed Sparkle's position. She didn't have a big whip, though. She'd put it on her shopping list.

"Do you think you could hold that position while I smash a TV and strangle a cosmic troublemaker?" Conall's voice was a low rumble filled with arousal and frustration.

"No." She locked her fingers in his hair to keep him there. "Leave me and you're dead."

His soft laughter prickled across her super-sensitized skin. "And right here is where I want to stay."

He demonstrated exactly where he wanted to stay. Reaching around her hips, he clasped her cheeks in his big hands and massaged them as he drew her closer.

Hey, she understood body language, and her body was screaming, "He's going to put his mouth *there*." The realization dragged a moan from her.

Crash! "Sparkle Stardust is here to protect all those who want to have sex without fear of interruption from vindictive old crows."

"Jeez, babe, you didn't have to break down the door. It was unlocked." Ganymede sounded like he had his mouth stuffed with chips.

"I looove your outfit, Sparkle. Gabriel, can I have one just like it?"

Conall's grip on her behind tightened, and he growled low in his throat. "Where's my sword? I feel a killing spree coming on."

"Easy." She tried to soothe him while her fingers itched to wreak mass destruction on the whole bunch of them. "Where were we?"

"Right here." He put his mouth high on her inner thigh and swirled his tongue over her skin. Warm, wet, and pretty spectacular as coming attractions went.

Gerry was a weak-kneed wuss. She knew that because

the higher Conall's magic tongue slid up her thigh, the more her knees shook.

"I won't be standing much longer." Was that wispy excuse for a voice hers?

"Won't have to." Ignoring her startled squeak, he picked her up and deposited her on a nearby chaise longue. "It's not a tree trunk, but you won't have to worry about bark burn."

"Caw! Caw! Someone get this damn cat off my tail feathers before I donate her gut to some needy stringed instrument." Morrigan?

"You'll be missing more than a tail if you don't leave Conall alone."

"Get lost, Asima. I'm the lookout around here. Hello? See my skintight and very awesome black, kick-butt bodysuit? Notice my black boots with the four-inch heels? Do you have a sexy black mask? I don't think so. Cast envious eyes on my guns and knives. I'm ready to rip a strip from some goddess booty."

"I don't need help from a slut queen to take down this oversized bag of feathers. Go sell some gumdrops, Sparkle. I'm a messenger of Bast. I can do it all."

"Uh, Sparkle? Love your ass, honeybuns, but it's blocking the screen." Ganymede sounded grouchy.

Conall knelt on the floor beside where Gerry sprawled naked on the chaise. He rested his forehead on her tummy and whispered curses she'd never heard before.

Gerry smoothed his hair with trembling fingers. "They will *not* cheat us out of our orgasms. Get naked, O'Rourke."

She half expected him to proclaim that he'd found his self-control hiding under the coffee table, and they had to stop before Morrigan fought her way past Asima and Sparkle.

He didn't. Instead he stood and shucked his shoes, jeans, and briefs.

If she'd really had to breathe to live, Gerry would've been doing the openmouthed guppy gulp. He hadn't lost any of his wow from the first time she'd seen him naked. Conall was all smooth, supple flesh and gleaming muscle.

His erection jutted thick, long, and hard. She wanted to wrap her fingers around it and let his heat melt any misgivings about what was happening in the other room.

She moved over as he knelt beside her. Reaching out, Gerry ran the tip of her finger around the head of his cock. He sucked in his breath.

"Where were we?" His smile was a flash of white teeth.

"We were—"

"Hiss! Meeeow!" Crash!

"She got my tail feathers. I can't freakin' fly without them. I'm about to kill me some cat."

"Useless Irish goddess. Bast is an Egyptian goddess. Only Egyptian deities are worth working for."

"Does no one understand that I have the totally sexy outfit, so I get to do all the killing? Back off, bitch kitty, because Sparkle Stardust is in the house. Mede, I'm busy. Make Asima go away."

"Look, Bat Babe, I'm a war goddess. I'm more powerful than whatever the hell you are. I'll swing you by that red hair and then bounce you off all four walls."

"Yo, asshole, leave my woman alone. You won't be doing any flying without your head, either."

"This is fun, Gabriel. If we had human forms, we could punch things. Oooo, Sparkle just landed a good one."

"I don't know, beautiful mama. If we were crows, we'd have wings and beaks. Look, Morrigan landed on Sparkle's head. Now she's pecking—"

"No, cats have the best forms, cuddle daddy. Asima climbed all the way to the top of the iron maiden. Now she's going to leap—"

"Hell!" Conall flung himself to his feet and strode to the music system in the corner. He rooted through the CDs.

"Damn, no loud bands. Only sounds of nature. Who chose this crappy stuff?"

"Any *loud* sounds of nature?" Something to cover the noise of destruction on the other side of the wall.

"The wind?"

"It'll work. Turn it up all the way."

The wind roared and whistled. Gerry controlled the need to hold on to something.

Conall looked grim as he lay down beside her. "Anyone who interrupts us is dead meat."

10

Primal need drove Conall as he slid his fingers over her breasts, her stomach, and up her inner thighs. Gerry caught his urgency and nipped his shoulder.

He tensed.

"Don't worry. I won't bite you." *Even though I'm really, really tempted.* She sighed. "Hey, if you want to deprive me of the yummiest orgasm of my life, who am I to go all whiny on you. Of course, I don't know for sure if it would be that great, because I've never done the biting-while-making-love thing. But that's what I hear." Was her smile playful and perky enough? "The bite is dessert, though. The main course will fill me up completely, so who needs dessert?" *Memememe.* She'd always been more a sugar than spice kind of woman.

His smile was slow and so sensual she wanted to roll on top of him and ride him into the sunset.

"You can sink your teeth into any part of me you want to, vampire lady."

Something heavy lifted from around her heart. He

wouldn't say that to just any old vampire, would he? "Then why the ohmigod moment when I nipped you?"

"I heard something crash against the wall."

"Oh." Enormous relief.

"Sparkle and Asima are buying us some quality time. Let's make our lovemaking worth a goddess's tail feathers." Scooting down, he knelt between her legs.

"Mmm. Yay for Sparkle and Asima." Should she mention this? Yeah, she should. "Umm, since I haven't been with a man since I became vampire, I'm sort of not sure what will happen. I wouldn't want you to expect calm and controlled, and then have me try to tear your head off with the excitement of it all."

At what point would the danger involved with making love to an inexperienced vampire who might or might not be overcome with bloodlust cancel out any erotic cravings he might have? Gerry steeled herself for that moment. She was tough. She could take the rejection. Maybe.

"Tear my head off? I don't think so. Besides, I don't think that's the body part you'll be concentrating on. And *that* part will do you a lot more good attached to my body."

His soft chuckle shivered its way down her spine and spread to where her brain was still playing the party animal. Her brain was no longer functioning, but her animal instincts were just fine.

"So many body parts, so little time. Right now I'm concentrating on what your mouth can do." She hoped her hunger for him wasn't broadcasting on high volume. It sure was turned up as high as it could go for her.

"Smart lady." He slipped his hands beneath her bottom and lifted her. Then he put his mouth on her *there*.

Heat. The pressure of his lips. *There* spasmed in gleeful anticipation. Gerry wrapped her legs around his neck. No way was he getting away from her.

And when he slid his tongue across the nub of flesh that

was so ready, so sensitive that she could barely *think* about him touching her, she screamed and then tried to muffle the sound with her hand.

Wait. She could hear heavy objects bouncing off walls in the other room, so a few shrieks from her wouldn't even register over there.

Conall flicked his tongue back and forth over the nub. Then while she moaned her appreciation, he slid his tongue inside her.

She gasped, arching her back, trying to squirm closer, as he dipped in and out, in and out. "Not enough. *More.*" Her thoughts didn't go beyond two-word sentences expressing great need.

He got the picture, because he lowered her to the chaise, reached for his jeans, and then fumbled in the pocket with fingers that trembled just a little. Trembling was good, because it meant he was involved and not just trying to please her. She hoped some of that involvement was emotional. It sure was for her.

Gerry knew her laughter held an edge of hysteria to it. No way would she last more than the minute it took him to rip open the foil package, put on the protection, and once again kneel between her legs.

"I've never wanted anything this much since Mom introduced me to ice cream when I was three." This was a thousand times more intense, but it had some of the same elements—primitive hunger and unreasoning lust for fulfillment. The mature Gerry felt a brief connection with her inner child.

The rumble of his laughter was a sexy promise that he'd be the hot fudge on her sundae of life. A bit more exciting than the bowl of vanilla ice cream Mom had put in front of her so many years ago. Then as well as now, though, she still wanted to get her fingers in it and stir it up.

Something thudded against the wall. A hurry-up warning.

Once again, he lifted her hips, pressing the head of his cock against the lips that were already wet and more than ready to gobble him up.

She welcomed the slide of her fangs, the explosion of her senses. Conall's eyes darkened with emotion Gerry suspected he'd held in check for eight centuries. Something in those eyes suggested he might lose his precious control this time. A woman could hope. This wouldn't be a quiet joining on her part.

And then he thrust into her. Deeply. Completely. She cried out at the delicious friction, the sense of being stretched and filled.

Gerry rose to meet him as he buried his cock in her body. Then he stilled. Reaching beneath her, she cupped his balls—caressing, raking her nails lightly over them. He threw back his head and groaned. Pain or pleasure? What they were sharing was a little of both.

He moved, sliding his cock out and then plunging back into her, faster and faster. With each thrust she groaned her pleasure. The heaviness, the building pressure gathered momentum, tumbling her end over end toward screaming completion.

Gerry clenched around his cock, dragging a gasp from him. His muscles tightened as his rhythm became a blur, his breathing a harsh rasp.

She'd arrived at her orgasmic tipping point, that moment when she leaped into space and hoped to hell the bungee cord didn't break.

Reaching up, she wrapped her arms around him, pulling him close. She pressed her mouth to his throat where his pulse beat a drumroll of life. This wasn't a feeding feeling. It was a holy-wow-I-don't-know-if-I'll-survive-this feeling. Maybe the head-ripping-off thing wasn't so far-fetched.

Still she hesitated. Every one of her multitude of roiling emotions shrieked that this was getting damn personal, and she'd better think before she bit.

"Bite me, Gerry. Now. Or it'll be too late. Trust me on this." Each word seemed forced between clenched teeth.

Closing her eyes, she drew in his scent—hot, aroused male and the essence of *him*. Never to be duplicated, never to be forgotten.

She sank her fangs into him.

The explosion of pleasure was so intense she could only whimper as the waves washed over her. Conall made guttural sounds of sexual excitement as he pumped into her so hard she expected the chaise to collapse.

She drank from him as her orgasm took her, that moment out of time and space when she couldn't move, but hung frozen as spasm after spasm shook her. Gerry clenched tightly around him one last time.

As she lifted her mouth from his neck, she savored the diminishing tremors, that feeling of complete fulfillment. And she wondered if she'd ever feel this way with someone else. Gerry didn't think she could ever feel *more*. Jeez, more would kill her. Again.

The world resumed spinning on its axis, the haze of passion lifted. The euphoria remained.

"That was . . . amazing." She slid her tongue across the puncture wounds in his neck and watched them disappear.

Was she afraid to meet his gaze, to try to read his emotions? You bet. Just call her Cluck Cluck Meow, the proud daughter of Daddy Chicken Heart and Mommy Fraidy Cat.

She couldn't remember. Had he shouted? Did his high match hers? This was major need-to-know stuff.

When she finally worked up the courage to slide her gaze to his face, he lay with eyes closed. Uh-oh.

"That was off-the-charts fantastic. I never saw that coming." He didn't sound too thrilled with his revelation. "I don't have a clue how the hell I'll give up what we just shared."

Another crash from the next room reminded them they couldn't lay around basking in a sexual afterglow.

Gerry thought about what Conall had said as he helped her up and they quickly dressed. Then she opened her mouth to ask why they had to give it up, why they couldn't keep dodging . . .

With a crack of splintering wood, the reason crashed through the door.

Morrigan had found them.

"Hah! I caught you. The cat and the red-haired harlot thought they could stop me." She walked toward them on her crow feet and then hopped onto a low coffee table.

Conall figured the cat and harlot had done a good job of stopping her tail feathers.

"My wrath is great, and your punishment will be terrible." The all-powerful goddess twitched her tail, minus feathers.

Conall fought back laughter. It was tough buying into the all-powerful goddess thing when said goddess was walking around with a bare bird ass.

"Uh, we were just looking at magazines. So magazine reading ticks you off?" Gerry was trying to look innocent as she flipped through the latest pro wrestling monthly.

She was cute when she lied. Uh-oh. Dangerous thought. Conall could justify the sex. He'd lusted after Gerry until visions of her body consumed every blasted moment. How could a man function in that state? So he'd done something about it. Now he was cured. He could go back to a normal Kavanagh-versus-O'Rourke relationship, which was no relationship at all. Couldn't he? Sure he could.

The crow cocked her head and peered at them from beady eyes that still glowed red after her recent battle. "You had sex. Admit it and I'll spare you."

"Sorry, Morrigan. No sex. We fear your power too much to chance it." His pride took a hit every time he had to say things like that. He'd love to drop-kick her self-important little self into the Gulf. Each time he felt the urge, though, he reminded himself of her power. She was a scary proposition.

He felt the first push of her mind, and he pushed back. He might not have any real powers other than his strength, but he'd learned to protect his thoughts from prying entities. She wouldn't discover anything from inside his head.

Conall glanced at Gerry. He hoped she wasn't thinking about their lovemaking, because Morrigan would go to her next. Well, maybe he wanted her to be thinking about it a little. In code of course.

Morrigan's gaze shifted to Gerry, but after a few seconds she harrumphed and hopped down off the coffee table. "I'll catch you another time." She started to walk toward the door.

"Aren't you going to change into your true goddess form and disappear or whatever goddesses do? Or at least fly away?" Gerry seemed really interested.

"You'd like it if I disappeared, wouldn't you?" Morrigan was one bitchy bird.

"She asked a simple question, Morrigan. And she didn't do anything for you to get all bent out of shape about. Just give her a damn answer." Conall frowned. Was he experiencing a protective moment? One not connected to the curse? For a Kavanagh? Not likely. This was his normal instinct to lash out at the goddess, nothing more. He felt better after getting that settled.

Morrigan continued walking toward the door on her crow feet. "I can't change back to my true form when my animal form is damaged. I have to wait until my feathers grow back. Luckily, my goddess powers will restore my feathers in a few days." She glared at Gerry. "Until then, I can't change and I can't fly. So I'll just hang around the castle seeing what I can see." She cast Conall a meaningful glare.

Bemused, Gerry watched Morrigan leave the room. "A tailless crow will be walking the castle halls. Will Holgarth put up Warning-Crow Crossing signs? What about bird droppings? How will Holgarth explain those to guests?"

"What were you thinking?" The question exploded from Conall.

"What?"

"When Morrigan was trying to get into your head? You felt her, didn't you?" What the hell did it matter? She could've been thinking about her next meal for all he cared. *Yeah, way to lie to yourself, pal.*

Gerry stared at him blankly. And then wicked understanding lifted the corners of her sexy mouth. "I was thinking about tree trunks—big, thick, hard tree trunks with lots of sap."

"Trunks. Great." His relief didn't make any sense at all. He was pretty sure that was code, though. He *wanted* it to be code.

Conall returned to the dungeon with Gerry in time to catch Morrigan's behind disappearing into the hallway. He'd love to see Holgarth's face when the goddess made her entrance into the great hall where his precious fantasies were in full swing.

Ganymede still sat staring at the TV. He glanced at Fo and Gabriel. "Too bad you little guys don't have arms and legs. If you did you could do what those people on the screen are doing." He watched the action for another few seconds. "Guess you'd need mouths, too. Couldn't have much fun without mouths."

Sparkle stood glaring at her thumbnail. Then she transferred her glare to Gerry and Conall. It looked like Morrigan had tried to nest in her hair. "Tell me you did it like it's never been done before. Tell me it was a freaking light show. I broke my thumbnail on that bitch, so it better have been worth it."

Asima looked cool, regal, and untouched perched atop the iron maiden. *"I did my part to keep you safe, Conall. I leaped onto Morrigan while she was trying to peck a hole in Sparkle's head. The goddess was calling up her power to make Sparkle disappear forever when I struck."* Long pause. *"I was tempted to let it happen."*

"Bitch." The comment was halfhearted because Sparkle's attention was focused on her broken nail.

"But in the end I succeeded in pulling out the rest of the goddess's tail feathers. She's grounded because of my courage and quick thinking." Asima was one smug kitty. *"And as much as she wanted to destroy me, she couldn't. Bast protects me. Have I mentioned that Bast is a more superior goddess?"*

Fo looked impressed. "You were very brave. When you leaped at Morrigan, you almost fell. But your reflexes were so fast you were able to dig your claws into Sparkle to save yourself."

"Bitch." Sparkle was now holding the broken nail up to the light the better to assess damage.

"Gimme a break, will you." Ganymede tore his attention away from the sex act being performed on TV long enough to comment. "No one was in danger. I could've taken Morrigan down during a commercial break and still had time to get some ice cream." He cast Gerry an accusing stare. "If someone *had* any ice cream. I like Ben & Jerry's. All flavors. If I'm gonna protect you, I gotta eat."

Conall couldn't let that pass. "*I'm* here to protect her."

But Gerry had the magic words. "No more food. I don't eat, so I won't be getting ice cream anytime soon. And no chips, cookies, or candy. I don't get an expense account on this job, so don't charge any more treats to my bill."

"No goodies?" Ganymede widened his amber eyes. "You're right, Conall. You can protect her. I'm going where the food is." He stood, leaped from the coffee table, and headed toward the door. "I'll be in the candy store when you finish here, babe." He flicked his tail at Sparkle and exited, leaving his empty bags and tons of crumbs behind.

"Now that I've saved the day, I'll go back to guard-cat duty outside the door. I'll intercept any evildoers trying to reach you, Conall." Asima didn't have a modest bone in her Siamese body.

"Yeah. Thanks." What else could he say? She *had* helped. But why the hell was she so fixated on *him*?

She slanted her cat gaze at Gerry. *"Don't forget our bargain.* Swan Lake, *my room, tomorrow night."* Then she padded after Ganymede. The door swung shut behind her.

Conall breathed a little easier once she was gone. Two down, three more to go. He'd changed his mind about having Fo and Gabriel stick around. Gerry needed some downtime. With him. *Only* with him.

"We don't want to keep you guys tied up." Conall aimed his smile at Fo and Gabriel who were watching the unfolding drama with open fascination. "You probably have stuff you have to do."

"No." Fo stared at him with wide purple eyes. "We want to see you make love. The TV is interesting, but we'd like to be involved in the emotion of a live performance."

"Uh, making love is sort of private, Fo." Gerry cast a desperate glance in Conall's direction.

"Why is it private?" Fo slid her gaze to the screen. "Those humans don't mind."

Hell, he'd never known how to handle Fo's questions.

Sparkle galloped to the rescue. "Here's the deal, Fo. A man can't get it up if he's nervous. You'd make Conall nervous because he's not used to someone watching."

His male pride might not survive Sparkle's help.

"Get it up? Get what up? Is something sleeping? I'm not familiar with that idiom." Fo's gaze shifted to Gabriel. "Have you ever heard—"

"Well, how was the sex?" Gabriel didn't talk much, but when he did, he got right to the point.

Silence fell. Sparkle's gaze returned to her broken nail, but both ears were wide open.

Gerry stared at Conall, and there was something in her expression that warned him his relationship with this Kavanagh would never be the same.

"It was worth a goddess's tail feathers."

And that would be his measuring stick for all future lovemaking with Gerry Kavanagh.

Gerry glanced away, and he sensed she hadn't meant to put so many unspoken words into that one sentence.

He had no time to ponder those unspoken words because Holgarth appeared at the door. His pointed hat rested somewhere left of center, a sure sign he was pissed.

"An emergency has occurred." Holgarth would've used the same tone to tell them a comet was zeroing in on the castle, and they'd all be dead in five minutes.

Conall had a feeling he knew what the "emergency" was. "You've seen Morrigan."

"*Everyone* has seen Morrigan, and heard her as well. She's telling the customers what's on her mind and theirs, too. I tried to impress upon her the need for circumspection, but my powers aren't strong enough to stop her. I actually had to refund *money*." Holgarth loved money. Hated giving it back. Ever. To anyone.

"I've called in our substitutes to take over tonight's fantasies while we deal with this situation." From his expression, Holgarth felt the black plague would be preferable to this "situation." Dead people didn't ask for their money back. "And since we'll be discussing Morrigan, we can also ruminate over the attempts on Gerry's life, understandable though they may be."

"Hey, did anyone ever tell you you're a vile old man?" Gerry wasn't taking any more crap from this arrogant, self-important, bombastic—

"You *must* include sarcastic in your list. I'll be so disappointed if you don't." Holgarth offered her a thin-lipped smile.

"Yeah, that, too. And stay out of my mind." How did you insult someone who refused to be insulted?

Gerry gave up the attempt in favor of something more productive. "Where will we meet?"

"Back off, Holgarth." Conall glowered at the wizard before glancing at Gerry. "There's a conference room next to the restaurant in the lobby."

Holgarth's lips thinned a little more. "Be careful where you give your affection, warrior." Then with a dramatic swirl of his robe, he disappeared in a cloud of smoke.

"Damn show-off." Conall turned to Gerry. "Feel intimidated yet?"

"By Holgarth?" She thought about the question. "Nope. Not feeling any overwhelming need to bow until my nose touches the pointed toes of his little blue slippers."

"Too bad. He wasted all that energy for nothing. As he gets older, it takes more of his power to do simple magic. He should've taken the stairs like everyone else." Conall smiled. "It would make the old guy feel good if you said a few words about how amazed you were with his disappearing act."

Gerry raised one brow. "And I'd want to make him feel good, why?"

"Because you're kind? Because Holgarth gets a kick out of complaining and insulting everyone, but he'd put his life on the line to save any of us."

"Even a Kavanagh?"

"Maybe not an ordinary Kavanagh, but you? Yes." He studied her with those gray eyes she suspected saw too much of what she wasn't ready for him to see. "I think he'd go to the mat for you."

What could she say to that? "Let's get to this meeting before Holgarth recharges his insult machine. If we walk in late, he'll be off and running."

"I've got to make an appointment with my manicurist before I go to the meeting." Sparkle glanced at Fo and Gabriel. "I'll take you guys with me. We'll go to the meeting together."

Thank you, Sparkle. Gerry owed the cosmic trouble-maker a new bottle of nail color.

"Manicurist?" Conall looked confused. "It's after midnight, Sparkle."

"I go to Forever Young Beauty Salon and Spa on the Strand. Stella stays open all night. She's a vamp with centuries of experience making female entities of every kind gorgeous. Stella can make anything look good." She studied Gerry. "I'll make an appointment for you."

"But I don't want to leave." Fo looked mutinous. "I want to see—"

With a long-suffering sigh, Sparkle picked up Fo and Gabriel along with their pouches and left.

What remained behind was a very sexy immortal warrior and the elephant in the room disguised as the memory of their shared lovemaking.

Conall met her stare with a direct one of his own. "Tonight was incredible, but I can't do my duty if I'm busy thinking about the next time we'll be together, or how we'll fly under Morrigan's radar, so—"

"Finish that 'so' and I'll be tempted to make sure you'll never 'get it up' again." It was time to bring everything out into the open, be upfront with him, lay all her cards on the table, collect a few more idioms for Fo. "We're going to be together for a long time. No way will I spend centuries in silent lust for you. I'm an instant-gratification kind of woman. I see, I want, I take. I mean, assuming that you want, too." Okay, that sounded lame.

"I want. And I wasn't going to make an excuse why we can't be together again. But I do think we need to find somewhere Morrigan and our army of protectors won't look."

She brightened. "Oh, in that case, I'll start looking for—" Her cell phone rang. Payton.

Her boss was to the point. No, he hadn't found anyone to track down the serial wife killer. Yes, he expected her to bring him in. And no, he didn't want to hear any nonsense about this guy at the castle not being the right one. Catch him. Now. Sigh.

"Your boss?"

"Yeah."

"Anything I can help with?"

"Maybe." She wouldn't let him spend the rest of his existence as her immortal bodyguard, but she could be okay with him as a partner. "Payton is convinced Edge is a serial wife killer. Edge fits the description Payton has. I don't think Edge is our guy, but what I think doesn't matter. So how do we pull it off?"

"We don't."

"Gee, that's a great idea. Why didn't I think of it?" Partner, hah!

"Neither one of us has the power to make a cosmic troublemaker do anything. Edge has to want to go with you."

"Like that's going to happen." She could wave goodbye to her promotion.

Conall shrugged. "Offer him incentives."

"Yeah, how about, 'If you let me take you to jail, Edge, I'll include a gift certificate to the cell-décor store of your choice. That'll work."

He grinned. "We'll think of something. Let's get to that meeting before Holgarth comes looking for us."

As Gerry followed Conall up the winding steps from the dungeon to the great hall, she thought she caught a glimpse of Dell in the shadows.

Dell. He was the key to the last attempt on her life. She'd bring that up at the meeting.

And after the meeting? Maybe some time alone with Conall? A woman could hope and dream of tree trunks.

II

Gerry glanced down the long table. The meeting room next to the restaurant was packed. Most of the nonhuman entities she'd met so far, plus a few she hadn't, were crowded around the table. Only Ganymede, Sparkle, Fo, and Gabriel seemed to be missing.

Holgarth stood at the head of the table, gavel in hand. Figured. He had to be in charge.

Conall sat next to her, his arm resting across the top of her chair. As much as she wanted to believe she was a big bad vampire who didn't need a man's comfort, she wouldn't mind if he dropped his arm across her shoulders instead.

Edge sat across from her. He grinned, and every woman in the room took a collective gulp of air, whether they needed it or not.

"Thought of a way to bring me to justice yet?" His gaze slid to Conall. Assessing. Then he nodded. "Hope we won't be tangling, O'Rourke."

Gerry frowned. "I'm the one you should worry about."

It was okay for her to secretly want a little male comfort, but in her professional role, others needed to see her as a force to be reckoned with. "I might not be able to match your power, but I'm top-notch when it comes to sneakiness and trickery."

"I'll keep that in mind."

He didn't smile when he said it, but she'd just bet he was laughing inside. Or maybe that was only her insecurity speaking.

"We might be able to work out a deal, Edge. You go with me to get booked—let's face it, you'll be able to get out anytime you want—and I'll owe you a favor to be collected at the time and place of your choice. You'll save yourself a hassle if you go with me, because if I fail, they'll just send someone more annoying to bug you." A dangerous bargain, but she really wanted that promotion.

Conall dropped his arm from her chair and leaned across the table toward Edge. "I'll negotiate what can and can't be considered a reasonable favor."

"Hey, O Great Buttinski. My deal, my right to negotiate."

Conall leaned back in his chair, tension charging the air around his powerful body. A lifetime with this man would always be a push-pull of power. But as she added centuries of experience to her vampire skills, perhaps he'd learn to accept that she could look out for herself.

A lifetime with this man. The enormity of that thought almost brought her to her knees. What would it be like to wake up every night to his face, his body . . . ? *His love?* No, that wasn't a place she was ready to go to yet. The whole curse thing would always play counterpoint to any real emotions between them. You didn't fall in love with your "duty."

"More annoying? Is that possible?" But Edge looked like he was really considering her offer.

Hope made Gerry reckless. "I'll be there to plead your case. I mean, someone has obviously set you up. We'll track down that anonymous tip and expose the liar behind it." Okay, so she wasn't sure he was innocent, but she was pretty sure. And that was good enough for her right now.

Edge nodded. "Fine, you have a deal. But first I have something I have to take care of here. And you have to find out who or what wants you dead. When everything's wrapped up, we'll take a trip to your jail. I won't stay long, just long enough to get a few laughs."

Winner, winner, winner. Triumph made her giddy. And if she suspected Edge had his own agenda in agreeing to go with her, she chose to ignore it. She glanced at Conall. "You were right about offering him the right incentive. Thanks. This proves that everything doesn't always have to come down to who can beat the crap out of the opposition."

"Maybe." Conall looked like he was second-guessing his own advice.

She never found out what else Conall might've said because the missing members of the nonhuman conclave finally made an entrance.

Holgarth watched with narrowed eyes as Ganymede padded around the table to the only empty chair and then waited for Sparkle to sit down before leaping onto her lap. She set Fo and Gabriel on the table and then looked around. Her gaze froze when she spotted Edge.

"I thought you were watching Sweet Indulgence."

He shrugged. "I got bored, so here I am. It's late. You won't sell many chocolate creams now anyway. I put up the closed sign."

A low growl filled the room and everyone's attention fixed on Ganymede. The cat had put his front paws on the table and was glaring at Edge. His ears were flat against his head and his tail was fluffed up to fighting size. "Finis."

"Ganymede." Edge's reply was a low rumble of warning.

"You guys know each other?" Sparkle actually forgot to check her nails. "And what's this Finis stuff?"

Ganymede's gaze never wavered from Edge. "His real

name is Finis, The End. He's the cosmic troublemaker in charge of death."

Without warning, massive power filled the room, power that shook the walls and pressed everyone back in their seats with the g-forces of a fighter jet taking off. If Ganymede and Edge were having a virtual arm-wrestling match, it was a draw.

The silence was complete.

Then everyone started talking at once.

"I can't believe it." Sparkle half rose from her seat, putting Ganymede in danger of tumbling to the floor. "Why would the Big Boss send me one of the most powerful troublemakers in existence to mentor? I hate it when people don't tell me things."

Edge smiled grimly. "Ganymede and I have something in common. We're both powerful enough to worry the Big Boss. He doesn't want any competition for top-dog status. So Ganymede got his wrist slapped—no more messing with the universe—and I'm stuck handing out bags of gumdrops."

"Oooh, Gabriel." Fo's purple eyes filled her whole screen. "Maybe he could give us two bodies he doesn't need so we could try to transfer our essences to them."

"Death?" Horrible possibilities jockeyed for position in Gerry's thoughts. "So you get to choose who dies? Do you personally bump people off? Fascinating job." Not. "Oh, and do we call you Finis or Edge?"

"Edge. Finis sounds too . . . final. Edge seems like a kind of guy you could have fun with." His gaze said she could call him anytime she was ready for fun.

Conall's expression said fun with Edge wasn't an option.

Jealous? A possibility. The thought gave her a warm, fuzzy feeling.

Edge glanced at both of them. "Too bad." He looked amused. "Anyway, I'm not in charge of all deaths. That belongs to a higher power. I'm a specialist. I bargain for human lives."

"Huh?" Maybe she didn't want to know this.

"I bargain with people for their lives. Say I see someone whose life intrigues me. I offer them an upgrade in the here-after. I won't bore you with all the after-death possibilities, but if the person likes what they hear, I take over his or her life and the lucky individual gets to move on. Everyone's happy."

Gerry wasn't sure she bought all that, but now wasn't the time to ask for details.

Holgarth brought his gavel down so hard the table jumped. "This meeting will not degenerate into mindless babbling. I demand silence."

And surprisingly, he got it.

He straightened his pointed hat and muttered to himself before speaking. "First, we'll discuss the goddess Morri-gan, who even as we speak is creating havoc throughout the castle. She threatened to peck out the eyes of a cus-tomer who suggested she was a special effect created through the wonder of technology." Pain filled his gaze. "The customer demanded his money back."

"I could eat her." This helpful offer from Banan, the man someone had pointed out as a wereshark.

"She's too powerful for you, Banan." Conall sounded positive about that.

"Morrigan will be taken care of." Asima spoke for the first time. *"I've sent for Bast."*

This brought another pregnant silence.

"Just what we need, another goddess."

Conall's soft whisper next to Gerry's ear shivered down her spine.

"If she can distract Morrigan, it'll be worth putting up with her." Maybe. When she got the chance, Gerry would ask Asima why she felt the need to call in her big gun.

"And when will Bast arrive?" Holgarth was so eager he forgot to be sarcastic.

Asima curled her tail around her elegant body before answering. *"Bast said she would come when she would come. I might add that the goddess is inscrutable."*

Holgarth's mouth turned down in a sour expression. Conall smiled. The wizard was all about schedules. He didn't work in the abstract. What he wanted was the exact hour, minute, and second of Bast's arrival.

Time to steer the discussion in another direction. "What about the attempts on Gerry's life? We're talking about something with lots of power. That French Revolution fantasy was as real as the ones Eric creates. Real and deadly."

Eric nodded. "I've been vampire as long as you've been immortal. This is either an ancient entity or a being who gets his power from another." He thought for a minute. "A demon comes to mind. He could get his power from the supreme Big Bad and pass it on."

"Anyone seen any demons lately?" Sparkle put her finger to her jaw in fake thought. "Wait. I have. The demonic vestal virgins have been playing in the park. Hmm. Now I wonder why they're here?" She cast a sly glance in Edge's direction.

Edge sent Sparkle a silent snarl. "I called them forth. I had a job for them to do."

"And that would be?"

Conall figured Sparkle already knew, but she wanted to see Edge squirm.

Edge shrugged. "I'll tell all, if you will, too."

Sparkle chose not to.

"How do you ID a demon? Horns? Red suit with forked tail?" Gerry leaned forward.

"Pale, almost colorless eyes, unless they've possessed a human's body. Red glowing eyes when they're excited." Brynn smiled at Gerry. "I thought I was a demon of sensual desire for centuries, so I'm the ultimate authority on demons. Did lots of research. Never figured out why I couldn't do the glowing eyes thing."

"Pale eyes? I think I've met Sparkle's vestal virgins. All blond. All wear white. All think men are useless pieces of . . . Well, useless, anyway."

"Did they threaten you?" Conall's gaze sharpened.

"No. They just pointed out the advantages of virginity." She grinned. "I didn't listen too well." Then she grew serious. "Wait. I met someone else with those same eyes." Excited, she turned to Conall. "Remember the red-haired guy I told you about? The one on the pirate ship with me? He was the same one who pointed me toward the French Revolution fantasy."

"I'll find him, and then I'll send him back to hell." Conall knew it wouldn't be that easy. Demons never were. But the demonic dirtbag wasn't getting another crack at Gerry.

And this had nothing to do with the protection clause in his hated contract with Morrigan. This was all about a need to protect the woman he'd just made love with, and intended to make love with again. *And again, and again, and again?* He wasn't ready to commit to that yet, because with the commitment came an admittance of other things.

"It would be logical to find out a motive before destroying the demon." Gabriel blinked his huge red eyes. "He might be doing the will of a master."

"We don't have definite proof that this demon . . ." Holgarth glanced at Gerry. "What's his name?"

"Dell."

"We don't have proof that Dell is the guilty party or even *is* a demon. He might simply be a human with pale eyes. It would be foolish to jump to conclusions. We could be sued for wrongful death by the demon's estate. The owner of the park frowns on lawsuits of any kind." There spoke Holgarth the lawyer.

"Whoever that is." Conall grumbled his annoyance. Holgarth always invoked this mysterious owner to justify whatever blasted decision he wanted everyone to accept.

"Know, wizard, that if anything happens to Gerry because of your fear of a lawsuit, all your spells will not keep me from you." Whenever he grew angry or upset, Conall reverted to his old speech patterns, the ones he used as a warrior. Nothing would happen to Gerry. He wouldn't allow it.

Beside him, Gerry sighed. "There's only one solution. I have to die."

All the breath whooshed from him. *"No!"* It was a primal shout of denial.

"Not really die. At least I hope not." Her gaze softened on him. "Pretend to die. When the killer makes his next attempt, I'll play dead. Once he thinks he's succeeded, maybe he'll reveal the reason why he wanted me out of the way."

"Excellent idea." Holgarth.

"Rotten idea." Conall.

"We'll need a plan with safeguards in place." Gabriel.

"Can I destroy the demon?" Fo.

"I'll wear my hot demon-hunter outfit." Sparkle.

"Oh, hell. Will this cut into my TV time? Count me out if I'm in the middle of a bowl of ice cream." Ganymede.

"Destiny tried to harpoon me today, so I took a chunk out of her boat. She's a babe, but she's got some serious issues with sharks." Banan.

Everyone stared at him.

"Here's my plan. Anyone can jump in with an idea." Gerry got down to the business of catching a demon.

An hour later, Gerry's eyes were narrow slits of fury, and Conall figured his face was red with rage. The room had emptied of everyone but them a long time ago.

"You can't go out in the dark by yourself. You'll be easy pickings for the likes of the demon."

"You're such a primitive, Irish sexist. If I were a male vampire you wouldn't say that. You'd just warn me to be careful. Okay, I'll be careful."

"Like you were when the guillotine almost separated your head from your body?"

"I didn't suspect Dell then. I'm on to him now."

Conall used his strongest argument, the one she wouldn't be able to refute. "If this whole thing is about me, then the demon knows about the curse. He'll expect me to be protecting you from another attack. It'll look suspicious if you're out by yourself."

Gerry thought about that. "Fine, so you can come along."

He'd be generous in triumph. "That's a wise decision."

"But stay far enough away so he can make some kind of attempt."

He'd be understanding, kind . . . "What? That's idiocy."

"I'll take Fo with me. I'll make loud comments to her about hating someone following me around and how smart I was to sneak away from you. Dell might see you trailing me, but he'll figure he can kill me and still escape from you. Fo will make sure I stay alive until you arrive."

Hardheaded. Conall knew he wouldn't get a better deal by arguing. But he'd decide how far behind he'd stay. Maybe he wouldn't even stay behind. Maybe he'd scout ahead.

"So when are you going for your walk?" Did he sound a little sulky? Warriors didn't sulk, but this woman drove him to act in ways he'd never acted before.

"Now sounds good. In a few hours it'll be dawn." She headed for the door. "I'll find Fo. Go get your sword. I know you feel naked without it. Meet you outside."

He fetched his sword and then strode through the great hall and out the door. Would she try to sneak away from him? He hoped not. After a few tense minutes, she joined him.

Fo peered from her purple pouch. "I'll keep Gerry safe. I'll warn her when the demon is near, and I'll turn him into a pile of ash if I have to." She looked pretty excited about the pile of ash part.

Gerry glanced around before speaking loudly. "Damn. I forgot my key. Would you run back to get it for me, Conall?"

Disgruntled, he stepped back into the castle and made a show of going to the dungeon. When he went outside again, Gerry was disappearing into the darkness. He followed quickly.

He could hear her talking to Fo, but she seemed to be drawing away from him. Blasted woman, she was doing that on purpose. He was fast, but if she used her preternatural speed, he'd have trouble keeping close to her. And in the time it would take him to catch up, disaster might strike.

He knew he should trust her abilities more. He knew she could hold her own with the demon if he played fair. But he wouldn't. The fire and the guillotine proved he was a backdoor killer—sly and stealthy. He wouldn't give her a chance to defeat him in open battle.

And just as Conall broke into a full-out run, he heard the screams. Fo!

A blast of adrenaline sent him pounding down the path, his breaths coming in huge gulps, his rage and fears living things inside him. The bastard wouldn't get his woman. He drew his sword as he ran, swinging it above his head as he shouted a battle cry the world hadn't heard for eight centuries.

He came to a skidding stop in front of the Cock Crows at Dawn, the official brothel of the Wild West attraction. He expected . . . Conall wasn't sure. Fighting, blood, death? All he saw was a small crowd gathered around someone. Without worrying about what anyone would think of his drawn sword, he pushed his way through the people.

Gerry crouched in the center, cradling Fo in her hands.

"Are you and Fo okay? Did the bastard hurt you? Where is he?"

Gerry looked up at him, panic in her gaze. "I didn't see Dell."

"Then why—?"

"Fo's in labor, Conall. The baby's coming, and I don't know what to do."

Conall gulped. He would've welcomed a dozen demons instead of this. They had to get Fo back to the castle as fast as possible. He glanced around at the crowd. "Fo's the lady's sister. Her mom left a message that Fo's in labor." He nodded at Gerry. "She's trying to call the hospital, but her cell phone won't work. Can't say I blame her for getting a little upset. I'll loan her my phone, and everything will be fine." That was about as much damage control as he had time for.

Murmurs of sympathy came from the crowd, and then everyone wandered away.

"Let's get moving." Conall reached for Fo.

"No, no, no!" Fo had a loud voice for her small form. "I need to give birth right now. If I don't, I'm afraid I'll shut down forever. The stress on my system will be too much. That's what Gabriel said. He knows about these things. Help me." The last was a pitiful wail.

Where did Gabriel get his info? Conall didn't think you'd get many hits if you Googled "sentient machine births."

"I don't know anything about electronics." Gerry turned Fo over and peered into her card slot. "It seems to be stuck up there."

"Ouch, ooooh, owie!" Fo wasn't suffering in silence.

Gerry made female sounds of comfort.

"How bad is the pain?" Knowing Fo's love of drama, Conall wanted to pin down how bad things were with the demon detector.

"I'm not in pain, but those seemed to be appropriate human sounds for giving birth." Fo stared at him from wide purple eyes.

If the situation wasn't so desperate, Conall would've smiled. Fo never lost sight of her goal—to be human in every possible way.

"Can your system correct the problem?" He figured not, but he'd hang on to hope until the last possible moment.

"No. I'm having a breech birth. Do something." Her voice grew even louder. "Save my baby!"

People started to stare again. Gerry grinned weakly at them. "Sorry. My cell phone. It's broken. I'm really attached to it. It's like a baby to me."

She drew a few strange looks, but people kept moving.

They weren't going to reach the castle in time. Conall had to do something now. "Let's see." When Gerry handed Fo to him, he studied the problem. "The chip's wedged in there." He rooted around in his pocket. Keys. He pulled them out. A small thin key that unlocked his safety-deposit box might just fit into the opening.

"Hurry. I'm about to crash!" Fo's voice was fading in and out.

Hell. "Hang in there, Fo." He worked the key into the narrow slot, then poked and prodded until there was a sudden click and the small chip popped out.

"You saved my baby! You saved my baby!"

While Fo sobbed, Conall stood helplessly holding Fo in one hand and the tiny chip in the other. Gerry rode to his rescue.

"I'll take Fo. You hold on to her baby."

Something warm and tentative touched him. Gerry accepted Fo as a sentient being along with her very real human emotions. Not many people would do that. But then Gerry was special.

Once Gerry had Fo, they hurried toward the castle. Conall closed his fingers gently around the chip and only fleetingly thought about the bizarre nature of the whole thing.

"Is it a boy or a girl?" Fo sounded weak but joyful.

Conall looked. "Haven't a clue, Fo." No tiny penis to tell the tale.

They entered the castle almost at a run. While Gerry spread the news, Conall took Fo and her baby into the privacy of the conference room. He set her on the table and placed the chip on top of her where she could see it.

Fo's big purple eyes filled with wonder. "It's a girl." She turned her gaze on Conall. "You saved her, so I'm going to name her after you."

Conall didn't have a chance to react before an excited crowd filled the room. Kim brought Gabriel to the table and set him in his cradle so he could see mother and child.

"She's beautiful, Fo. She looks just like you." Gabriel's voice was hoarse with emotion.

Conall didn't see the similarity, but then what did he know about mothers and babies?

Fo rolled her eyes so she could see Kim. "You're a grandma, Kimmie. Grandmas babysit, don't they?"

"I guess so." Kim sounded uncertain.

Conall figured Kim wasn't quite clear on the concept. Computer chips didn't need diaper changes.

"We'll get our baby a spectacular case and then choose the color of her eyes. They have to be unique because she's so incredible. She's the firstborn of two sentient machines." Gabriel's eyes glowed with pride.

Fo frowned. She was into the whole human experience and didn't like anyone reminding her of her electronic roots.

As everyone pushed forward to congratulate the new parents, Conall and Gerry made their way toward the door.

Gerry grinned. "You did good, warrior. You were sympathetic, caring, and came through when Fo needed you. I like that in a man."

"I've faced barbarian hordes with less fear than—"

"Conall, Gerry, don't leave." Fo's cry rose above the general uproar.

"Guess we don't get to sneak away." Resignedly, Conall walked back to the table with Gerry beside him.

"Gabriel and I have an announcement." Fo had recovered from childbirth in record time. "Since Conall's courage and quick thinking saved me and our child, Gabriel and I are naming her Conalla in honor of him."

There was applause all around along with one voice, it sounded like Ganymede's, that asked, "Isn't that a cooking oil?"

"You're thinking of canola oil, sweetie." Sparkle's voice.

Then there was silence. Conall glanced around. Everyone was looking at him expectantly. Damn. He was supposed to say something? What? He looked at Gerry and she gave him a thumbs-up.

Here went nothing. "Conalla is beautiful." She was the most beautiful small black square he'd ever seen. "I'm sure she'll have her mother's love of life and her dad's curiosity about all things. And I'm proud that Fo and Gabriel named her after me." No doubt his namesake would cause him no end of trouble somewhere down the line, just as her mother had on many occasions. But for now, he'd celebrate her birth.

When Gerry and he finally escaped, they returned to the dungeon. Dawn was close, so they decided to put off the search for Dell. She headed for the shower, but he didn't follow her. The same way he wouldn't join her when she crawled into bed. No matter how much he wanted to curl his body around her while she slept.

Conall had lots of thinking to do. And not just about how to find the bastard stalking her.

He clearly remembered thinking of Gerry as "his woman" while charging to her rescue. His woman? Those two words carried a lot of weight and would require some deep soul-searching tonight. And Conall O'Rourke hadn't corresponded with his soul in a very long time.

12

"Wake up. Rise to a new, sensual décor, sister. I need to fin-ish sexing up this dismal excuse for a dungeon and then get back to my store before Edge gives away all my candy just for spite. Men can be petty, don't you think?"

Clatter, bang.

"I mean, so I let it slip that he was conspiring with a few demonic vestal virgins. What's the big deal?"

Crash, boom.

"Yes, his demon partnership does make one wonder if he's behind the attempts on your life, but who am I to men-tion that?"

Bump, click.

"Are you awake yet? The sun has set, time for all crea-tures of the night to do their things. And their main thing should be having superior sex."

Kerplunk, swish.

"Oh, and tell Jinx the next time he tries to lift my fave earrings, I'll disconnect his tail—or whatever other appendages he's sporting—from the rest of his miserable little body."

Slam.

Sparkle? Gerry opened one eye. The other one popped open all on its own when she saw what Sparkle had done. "You've got to be kidding."

"Good, you're up. And I never kid about sex." She finished hanging red velvet drapes across the back wall of the dungeon. "There. Turns cold and gray into hot and happening. If sex had color and texture, it'd be red velvet."

"What the . . . ?" Gerry sat up and looked around. "The place looks like a bordello."

"Exactly. A first-rate cathouse." Sparkle paused to study the painting on the wall over the iron maiden—a man and woman tangled in white sheets and red-hot passion. Then she walked over to straighten it. "Whoever first called a bordello a cathouse had it right—a place that's all slinky and sly and sexy."

"Where's the furniture?" Okay, there was furniture, sort of.

"The stuff you had here was vintage motel cheap. I don't know where Conall dug it up. Now this furniture oozes sensual invitation." She slid her hand across the back of a silky black chaise longue. "Big enough for two."

"Yes, well—" It was almost worth shutting her mouth just to see Conall's face when he walked in here.

"Don't argue. It won't do any good. I borrowed this big round couch from the Cock Crows at Dawn. They won't miss it. Don't the erotic possibilities just scream at you?"

Nope, no screaming going on, except for her sense of good taste, which was shrieking over the red velvet couch that matched the red velvet drapes, accented by the black silk chaise longue.

Luckily, Sparkle didn't wait for her to answer. "I've left an assortment of interesting oils on the table along with a candle to heat them. Rub them in. Everywhere." She rolled her eyes up in her head as she contemplated the oily event.

"Slide the hot oil over Conall's glorious chest and totally awesome abs. Then sit back and admire all that glistening male flesh."

"I don't think—"

"You don't have to think, you have me to do that for you. I've also left a variety of spreadable sweets—chocolate syrup, honey, and caramel topping. Lather them on, then lick them off."

"We'll be sticky messes." Why was Sparkle doing this, and how would she stop her?

Sparkle narrowed her gaze on Gerry. "You're supposed to lose yourself in the passion of the moment. Take a shower together afterward, for heaven's sake. Do I have to tell you everything?"

"You're not subtle, are you?" Jeez, all she needed was a madam at the door welcoming clients.

"Subtle? Subtle never won any wars, sister. Men think about sex every seven seconds, so we give them the visuals, the scents, the textures of sex, and thought becomes action. Simple."

"Cold." Where were the emotions in Sparkle's formula?

Sparkle shrugged. "I only deal with the physical pleasure part. That's yummy enough for me. You supply the warm fuzzies."

"The bed looks the same." An island of normal floating in a sea of sex.

"Not quite. I replaced the mattress while you were sleeping. Good thing you sleep like the dead, because I kind of bounced you off the floor when I moved you. But now when passion rises, and you fling yourselves onto the bed, erotic scents will drive you and Conall to unexplored sensual heights."

"I'm afraid of heights." Oops, a Freudian slip. She carefully climbed from the bed, making sure she didn't trigger the mattress's sensual scent-o-meter. Where was Conall when she needed him? Wait. Where *was* Conall?

"You wore *that* to bed?" Sparkle's eyes widened. She sounded like she was choking on the horror of Gerry's cotton jammies.

"Uh, yeah." Gerry glanced down. Yep, same old jammies. "They're comfy."

"Burn them."

"What?"

Sparkle did some eye-rolling. "It's about your erotic image. You look like a cute bunny, all soft and sweet. Can we say prey? A vampire's supposed to be sexy and sleek. Predator. So lose those . . . things. I'll bring you something appropriate."

She narrowed her eyes to slits of concentration. "Now we start with your face. Makeup. Men like dramatic. Sure, they say they like the natural look, but they really don't. I bet Cleopatra never got up in the morning and said, 'Gee, I think I'll skip the eyeliner today and let Antony see the real me.' Uh-uh. Didn't happen."

Dazed, Gerry watched Sparkle open a makeup case that looked as big as a steamer trunk. Oh, wow. "Where's Conall?" Fat lot of protecting he was doing.

"He's sleeping outside the door. He worried about leaving you, but I told him you'd be safe with me." Her smile was pure evil. "I lied."

Uh-oh.

"I promised I'd wake him up when I finished. Lucky me, there was no sign of Asima cluttering up the doorway. She has this thing about 'elegance.' Boring bitch. If she knew I was here, she'd be here, too, putting in her snooty two cents on everything."

"Why're you doing this?" Something Edge had said at the meeting poked at Gerry's suspicions.

"Umm, because sex is the greatest thing in the universe, and I'm the sorceress of all things sensual? Guess that's about it." Sparkle sounded playful, but her amber eyes looked wary.

"Okay, I get all that. Maybe it's just me, but I had the feeling back in the conference room that there was something going on between you and Edge."

Sparkle showed her innocent face. "The conference room? Hmm. That's all a little hazy now."

Gerry sighed. "You can tell me, or Edge can tell me. He's pretty up front about things. And I get the impression he'll blab all day if he thinks it'll tick you off."

"No big deal. Just a little friendly wager." She played with one dangly silver earring.

"Anything to do with Conall and me?"

"Sort of. I bet that I could hook up Conall and you before he could get Banan the wereshark and Destiny the shark hunter together. I'm doing better." Sparkle looked thoughtful. "You guys have already done it once, right? Banan's batting zero so far." She gripped her bottom lip between perfect white teeth and then released it. The wet shine was wasted on Gerry. "This room, and the new you, will blast Edge out of the water. He'll never catch up."

Gerry hoped the steam coming from her ears didn't fog up any mirrors. Wait. No mirrors. "Well, the old me is throwing you out on your sexy ass."

Sparkle widened her eyes. "*Moi?* Why would I want to leave when we haven't discussed makeup or cool clothes or—"

"Out."

"Or the tree trunk. I—"

"How'd you know about the tree trunk?" Gerry revved her anger up another notch.

"I went shopping in your mind." Sparkle's smile was all about sly satisfaction. "I came home with lots of bargains."

"Out!" Gerry felt the slide of her fangs as she hissed at Sparkle.

"You're right. We'll save all that for another session. Enjoy the bed." She closed her makeup case and dragged it to the door.

Gerry watched her leave. Did Sparkle *have* to put sexual invitation into every sway of her hips? She thought about Conall. Would Sparkle teach *her* how to do it?

As Sparkle closed the door behind her, Gerry started to sink onto the bed. Then she remembered the erotic scents. No sense in wasting all those sexy smells when she was the only one there to appreciate them.

Sparkle would wake Conall and then they'd go out searching for—

The click of the lock startled her. Someone had just locked Conall out. How? She was the only one in the room. Before she could react, Dell materialized beside the door.

"Hi there. Thought I'd drop in to see if tonight was a good night for you to die. It's good for me if it's good for you."

His friendly smile took none of the chill from his words. His eyes glowed red. They matched the drapes and couch. If she came out the other end of this alive, she'd give Holgarth first-person proof of Dell's demonic nature.

Her fangs were still out, so she was ready to rumble. "Before I tear your demon head off . . . No, maybe ripping out your heart would be more satisfying. Hmm, what's the status on your heart? Have one? Anyway, before I rip off some body part, I have two questions."

Dell raised one brow. "More feisty than I expected. Good. Ask away, but make it quick. I have to kill you before Conall realizes something's wrong and smashes through the door."

"I'm guessing you know we're on to you. That's why you're taking this chance. How'd you find out?"

He shrugged, and Gerry noticed the powerful width of his shoulders for the first time. When she'd first seen him, she'd thought he looked like her uncle Ray. Sure, some of their facial features might be similar, but even in old pictures you could see a soul in her uncle's eyes. Dell's easygoing personality had blinded her to a lot of things.

"You talked about me at your meeting. I listened at the door. I would've joined you—invisible of course—but a few in the group were powerful enough to sense my presence. Since you outted me, I thought I'd better get it over with." While he talked, he silently stalked her.

She moved so the bed was between them. "Why do you want me dead?"

He laughed. "Nothing personal, darling. You just need to die so something else can happen."

Without warning, he flung himself across the bed at her. A wave of scents filled the air as he landed heavily on the mattress.

"What the hell?" He stared down. "I have this uncontrollable urge to have sex with the bed." Then he sneezed.

Gerry wasn't going to miss an opportunity. She threw herself on top of him and sank her fangs into the back of his neck. She shook him like a dog. Woof.

A heavy weight thudded against the door, and Conall exploded through it, sword in hand.

With a final "Damn," Dell broke free and disappeared.

"Well, hell." Gerry pushed herself from the bed. "I was kicking major demon ass, and he just disappeared on me. We've got to come up with a way to stop him from going poof."

"Did he hurt you?" Conall dropped his sword while he ran his hands over her body.

"That feels really good, O'Rourke, but shouldn't you be asking if I hurt *him*?" She tried not to show her disappointment when his pat down stopped. "Did you get a look at him?"

"No. You were blocking my view. He disappeared before I could check him out."

He pressed those sexy Irish lips together, and she'd guess he wanted to comment on the battle he'd seen. Probably wanted to say she should've let loose with a few girlish squeals and allowed Dell to chase her around the dungeon until the big, strong warrior rescued her.

Suddenly, he grinned. "You were giving him a butt whooping, vampire lady. Couldn't have done better myself."

An emotion she could only describe as a deep yearning tugged at her chest. Not heartburn. "Thanks."

Then Conall was all business. "Did he give a reason for the attack?"

Gerry frowned. "He said it wasn't personal. I had to die so something else could happen." She absently brushed a few strands of hair from his face, a gesture Conall found oddly sensual. But then everything she did lately turned him on.

He sniffed. "The room smells different. It makes me . . ." Hard. No, not an appropriate reaction in the middle of life and death stuff.

"Sparkle's shot at driving us crazy with lust. She made a bet with Edge that she could hook us up faster than he could get Banan and Destiny together. We're winning one to zip. She wants to run up the score."

"Figures." He pushed Sparkle and the scents to the edge of his consciousness. "So why a direct attack now?"

"Our meeting convinced him to act. He listened at the door. And since we already suspected him, he decided to move on me."

"Okay, so now we have the key. What would happen if you die?" Morrigan. But Conall didn't have a chance to stroll down that obvious path as Asima stepped over the destroyed door.

"Did I miss something? Holgarth will boil you in bitter words when he sees that door. What—" She blinked and looked around. *"Sparkle's been here. Only the queen of bad taste could've conjured such a horror in the name of sex. Is there no low that woman won't sink to? Someone should tell her that red velvet is* not *a fashion statement. We can fix this. First we'll get rid of—"*

"Dell attacked Gerry while I was sleeping on the other side of that door." He hoped Asima got the message that an attack on Gerry was more important than an attack of red velvet.

He scanned the room, for the first time getting the full impact of Sparkle's work. She was one scary woman.

"Oh." Asima looked alarmed. She padded around him. *"He didn't touch you, did he? I don't see any obvious wounds."*

Conall snapped. "What the hell is it with you? *I* wasn't attacked. Gerry was. While I was asleep on the job. Don't you feel *anything*? How about a little guilt? Weren't you the one who was going to stand guard outside the door?"

"Guilt? Maybe." She avoided his stare. *"A small fluttering, perhaps. But Gerry's not my . . . Umm, anyway, no one was injured."*

"I'm not your what, Asima?" Gerry hunkered down in front of the cat.

Said cat yawned.

"You're not her job." Conall couldn't avoid that conclusion anymore when the proof was shoved in his face on a regular basis. "You work for Bast, so I guess you're protecting me on the goddess's order, right?"

"I couldn't say."

"Why would Bast care?" He crouched down beside Gerry and Asima.

"I'm not free to discuss this." She looked around the room again. *"Will you be going out soon?"*

"Maybe. Why?" Conall didn't like the gleam in her eyes.

"Hmm?" She dragged her attention from the velvet drapes. *"Oh, I just want to make sure I'm here to accompany you."* Her gaze slid back to the drapes.

"Isn't this the night I watch *Swan Lake* with you?" Gerry didn't sound too pumped about it.

"Oh, yes." Asima's blue eyes lit with excitement. *"The red velvet made me forget. I've invited a few other messengers of Bast to join us. We'll have a party. Get dressed now. I'll wait for you."*

Gerry nodded. "Sure. Sounds like fun." She smiled at
Conall. "We'll talk as soon as I get back. Dell won't make
another attempt while I'm with Asima. The two of us
would take him apart."

Conall tended to agree, but he couldn't let her escape
without a warning. "Don't underestimate him. He's a
demon. If he can disappear, he can do other things. He
didn't realize you were one tough lady. He won't come at
you directly next time. Make sure you're never alone."

He was thinking about his words a short time later as he
hunted down his friends. Even though he knew Asima had
enough power to take care of a dozen demons, he still worried about Gerry. And his worry was mixed with other
emotions he never thought he'd feel for any Kavanagh.
What to do about them? He'd face them, but not until
Gerry and he had taken out the demon.

Luck was with him. Holgarth, Eric, and Brynn were all
standing together at the entrance to the great hall while the
fantasies went on without them. They stopped talking as he
approached.

"We have a problem." Holgarth's grim expression
hinted that the problem involved loss of money. "Jinx has
stolen a ruby brooch from one guest and a diamond toe
ring from another. And even my gift for creating plausible
lies fails when confronted with a hysterical guest claiming
a snake robbed her. Either Gerry stops him or I will. The
reputation of the castle is at stake."

Conall figured they could all hear him grinding his
teeth. If Jinx was smart, he'd slither into some crack and
stay there for the duration, because if Conall found him
now, he'd twist the thieving serpent into a pretzel.

"We'll take care of him." We? A limited partnership?
How limited? And would he remain on equal footing with
his "partner" when they butted heads and Gerry realized
she was really the boss?

"I should hope so." Holgarth sniffed.

"Later."

"Later is *not* acceptable."

Eric made an impatient sound. "Give it a break, wizard. I think Conall has more important news for us."

Relieved, Conall forgot to be pissed that the vampire was rooting around in his head. "The demon attacked Gerry while she was alone in the dungeon for a few minutes. When I broke down the door, he disappeared. I didn't get a look at him."

"Regrettable, of course, but we need to discuss Jinx and lost revenue first." Holgarth wouldn't let it go. "And did you mention a broken door? Dungeon doors cost—"

"Don't push me, wizard." The words came out as a low rasp of warning. "Gerry comes first. Always. Anything happens to her while you're counting coins and I'll bring this castle down around your money-grubbing head."

Holgarth shut up.

Brynn put his hand on Conall's shoulder. "What can we do?"

Conall forced his muscles to relax. These were his friends. Wouldn't do any good to unload on them. "Gerry was holding her own with the demon when I broke in, so he probably won't take the direct approach again. Problem is, he can disappear." He glanced at Holgarth. "Anything you can do about that?"

"Perhaps." He pursed his thin lips while straightening his damn pointed hat. "I'll need to borrow some power from all of you, but I should be able to keep him from dematerializing while he's in the castle. That means, of course, that Gerry can't leave the building."

Conall nodded. "That'll be a big help. Do it."

Holgarth held up one thin hand. "Wait. Not so fast, my immortal friend. I'll need to tap into a deep well of concentration. And how can I possibly concentrate when Jinx is on my mind?" The gaze he sent Conall was filled with sly triumph.

Conall surrendered to the inevitable. "Okay, what do you want?"

"I want you to find Jinx and keep him under surveillance at all times."

"Yeah, yeah. Done." Holgarth was a human thumbscrew, squeezing painful compliance from his victims. Conall would worry about what he'd agreed to later.

Holgarth allowed himself a tight smile to celebrate his victory. "Come with me. I'll need all of you." As he motioned them outside, he threw out orders that everyone be kept away from the door leading to the courtyard. Once in the courtyard, he turned to face the two gargoyles guarding the entrance to the great hall.

Conall made eye contact with Eric and Brynn. They'd all seen what he could do with those gargoyles.

Now that serious stuff was about to happen, Holgarth shed his snarkiness and got down to business. "I'll draw energy from all of you to merge with mine. Then I'll wake the Guardians of the Castle. Do you give your energy freely?"

"We do." They gave the ritualistic response as one.

Holgarth nodded before raising his arms to the two grotesque stone heads with their bulging eyes and fanged mouths stretched wide in silent screams.

As the wizard began to chant in an old language, Conall felt a sudden draining of his strength. Only pride kept him erect. If the demon appeared right now, they'd all be easy pickings. Silently, he hurried Holgarth along.

When Holgarth reached the grand finale, he switched to English. Conall suspected it was for effect, but he'd forgive the wizard his love of drama if the chant worked.

"Guardians of the Castle, awaken." A flash of lightning streaked across the clear sky followed by booming thunder that shook the ground.

Conall was pretty sure even stone faces couldn't sleep through that. He just hoped they weren't grouchy before they had their first cup of coffee.

"Only those in corporeal form may enter the castle. Any who attempt to dematerialize within these walls will fail." He waved his arms around, and the lightning and thunder did their things again. "Awaken and do my will."

"At least he got rid of that dumb wand." Eric sounded amused. "He doesn't need props."

No kidding. No matter how big a pain in the ass Holgarth was, Conall never doubted his power.

"Maybe he should exempt everyone on our side." Brynn winced as another round of thunder echoed across the courtyard. "We might need a sudden appearance by one of the good guys."

"Too late." Conall sucked in his breath as he riveted his attention on the twin faces.

Low rumbling growls rolled from the gaping mouths. The growls grew to roars that made Eric cover his ears. "Jeez, tone it down. That level of noise is a killer for those of us with sensitive hearing."

Holgarth cast him a dismissive glance.

"You'll scare the customers. They'll want their money back." Brynn knew how to argue in Holgarth's language.

The wizard spread his arms wide. "Watch silently, Guardians of the Castle."

The roars died, but the bulging eyes glowed yellow in the darkness.

Holgarth wilted right before Conall's eyes. He sat down on the pathway and took off his pointed hat to rake his fingers through his gray hair. "That kind of ritual takes a lot more out of me than it used to."

"Yeah, we know." Conall's legs still felt rubbery.

"Wouldn't it have made more sense to just ban all demons from the castle?" Eric rubbed his ringing ears.

"Gerry can't stay in the castle forever. It's best if we lure him here where we can meet him on our terms, in a place he can't escape from by disappearing." Conall clenched his fist around the anticipation of making mush of Dell.

Eric nodded. "Gotcha." He stared into the night. "Got to go. Donna and I have some vampy things to do in the dark." And then he was gone.

Brynn slapped Conall on the back. "Go take care of your woman. Oh, and if you need Fo, give a shout. Of course, be prepared to cart Conalla along, too. Might be interesting. Fo's baby demon detector has an intriguing skill." He grew serious. "Okay, so it's kind of scary, too."

Conall watched Brynn walk away. "She's not my woman." Who was he trying to convince? If it was himself, he was doing a piss-poor job of it. He didn't get to puzzle over Gerry's status in his life for long, though, because Holgarth interrupted his thoughts.

"I assume you're pondering where to find Jinx. And I'm positive you intend to track him down right now, because you're a man of your word." The wizard climbed to his feet and dusted himself off. Then he centered his pointed hat on his head, thereby returning his universe to its normal position.

"Sure. I'll get right on it." Not. He'd spend a few minutes looking for the shifter, not find him, and then head for Asima's room.

"Excellent. I believe I saw Jinx slip into the great hall just before I awakened the Guardians. And if I'm not mistaken, at this very moment he's hiding his ill-gotten goods in a crack in the battlements. If you hurry, you'll catch him."

"Thanks." Well, hell. Conall jerked the door open so hard it bounced against the wall with a booming crash. He strode across the great hall as panicked customers scurried out of his path and stomped up the winding stairs till he reached the door leading to the battlements.

Sure enough, Jinx was crouched over a small package he was stuffing into a crack in the wall. With a muffled curse, Conall crossed the distance between them in a few strides and hoisted Jinx into the air by the scruff of his thieving neck.

Jinx squeaked his alarm. "Jeez, watch the shirt. It's the only clean one I have left. Does the castle have laundry facilities?"

"You won't need a clean shirt if you're dead."

"Got a point there." Jinx peered fearfully over the wall. It was a long way down.

"I'll take that package from you and then you come with me."

"And if I don't want to go with you?"

Conall stretched his arm out until Jinx was dangling over empty space. "Do you bounce?"

Jinx gulped. "Okay, okay. You and me, we're a team."

Conall drew in a deep breath and resisted the urge to let go. He set Jinx down, retrieved the package, and then stuffed it in his jeans pocket. "Follow me."

He didn't look behind him as he dropped the stolen jewelry off at the registration desk and then headed for Asima's room. Conall could hear Jinx running to keep up. What was he going to do with this guy trailing around after him? He'd better think of something fast, because no way was Jinx moving into the dungeon with Gerry and him.

When he reached Asima's door, he knocked. He was still busy turning over the problem of Jinx in his mind when the door swung open. As music swelled around him, he stepped inside.

And froze.

Cats. Lots of cats. All dancing. And in the middle of the dancing cats was Gerry. She whirled and twirled to the music, and her laughter swept Jinx from his mind.

"Whoa, mama! Are those cats wearing diamond collars?"

"Looks like it." Conall was vaguely aware of Jinx edging around him into the room, but his attention was only for Gerry.

He'd seen so many shades of her emotions, but this was the first time he'd watched her taking lighthearted joy in the moment. As she twirled, her long dark hair floated around her and those green Irish eyes sparkled. In his mind, he didn't see the jeans and top she wore. His imagination painted her in a short red dress that swirled above her knees, exposing a smooth expanse of thigh. Maybe he'd buy her that dress.

"Dance with me, O'Rourke." She swayed over to him and tugged at his hand.

Okay, this was weird. There had to be at least ten cats in the room, all on their hind legs, all keeping time to the music from the ballet on the DVD. Asima was in the midst of them, her blue Siamese eyes slitted in ecstasy.

"I can't dance." And he was damn glad he couldn't if it meant pirouetting around the room on his toes with a bunch of cats.

"I'll teach you." She gave him no choice as she wrapped her arms around him and moved to the music.

Conall found that he couldn't resist putting his arms around her when she was this close. Swaying with her, he drew her close. "This I can do, but nothing fancy or I'm outta here."

Her laughter was warm against his chest. "You really never danced? Not even when you were young? What did you do for fun?"

He frowned, trying to remember. "It was so long ago. All I recall is training for battle from morning to evening. Childhood wasn't a carefree time back then."

"I'm sorry."

She hugged him close, and he gave himself over to the sensation of her body pressed against his, heat building at all the important pressure points.

Conall shrugged. "Eight centuries ago it was the way of life."

"Would you go back to Ireland if you were free of the curse?" Her arms slipped to around his waist, and she laid her head against his chest.

"Why?" Since all the cats were bopping to their personal rhythm and not paying any attention to him, he allowed himself to put his lips on her hair and then run the silky strands through his fingers.

"Oh, I don't know. Closure?" She sighed and burrowed closer.

"Would you go with me?" He stopped moving. He'd asked something important here, but he wasn't quite sure what it was. Maybe it wasn't the question itself, but how he'd phrased it, as if he was free of the curse and could go where he pleased.

"Yes." She met his gaze.

He had the feeling they were talking in code again, but he was enjoying their closeness too much to bother pulling out his decoder ring. Shutting his eyes, he gave himself to his senses—the slide of her breasts over his chest, the brush of her thighs against his cock, the scent of citrus from whatever shampoo she used.

"If you could do anything you wanted, what would it be?"

With eyes still closed, he savored her voice, all husky and sexy. It rubbed against nerve endings that came alive to the stimulus, demanded more of everything.

"Um, Conall?"

He opened his eyes. "Huh? Oh. What would I do?" *Lay you down on this rug and bury myself deep inside you.* "I don't know. It doesn't matter anyway."

"Sure it does. Tell me." She wasn't going to give it up.

"I'd play in the NFL." There, he'd told her. Now maybe he could get back to enjoying all the close contact.

"Why?"

Conall drew in a deep breath of patience. He didn't want to talk about himself, about things that could never happen in his life. But she wasn't going to let it alone. "Sometimes I miss the battlefield. Not the killing, but the physical challenge."

"And?" She looked rapt, completely tuned into his admission.

It made him uneasy. He wasn't comfortable letting anyone slip beyond his surface thoughts. But this was Gerry, and for her he'd do a little elaborating.

"I love watching football, and I'd make a good player. I honed my skills on a real battlefield. If you don't run fast or hit people hard enough there, you die."

"Why didn't you ever try out?" Her fingers crept under his shirt and massaged a searing circle on his back.

"Couldn't. I had other obligations."

She nodded. "The curse." Her fingers slipped to the edge of his jeans and wiggled underneath the material until she cupped his cheeks. "So do it now. I'll come and cheer."

She squeezed and he groaned.

"Of course, you could only play for about ten years, and then you'd have to retire before anyone noticed you didn't age."

Conall never found out where her clever fingers would go next because without warning the door was flung open and Morrigan stood there in her bare-butt crow form. Crap.

Ten pairs of kitty eyes lit with interest.

"Forget it, girls. I'm one bird that's off limits." Her beady stare focused on Conall and Gerry. "Any sex going on here? Don't think you can sneak off to someone else's room to do it." She glanced around. "Let me guess. More messengers of Bast. Does the goddess know all her help is partying on company time?" She narrowed her gaze. "Diamond collars? Bast is overpaying all of you. Leather collars and minimum wage, that's all any of you're worth."

That opinion was met with hisses and growls.

Oblivious, Morrigan rattled on. "Talking about collars, I just saw a snake slithering down the hallway with one of them. Any of you lose an extra you packed?"

"Ooomph! Ugh!" When the stampede for the door cleared, Morrigan was flat on the floor with a scattering of black feathers around her. "Damn. I can't afford to lose any more feathers." She looked around the catless room. "Guess the party's over."

Conall clenched his fists, imagining he was squeezing the life from Jinx. "I'll kill him."

Gerry put her hand on his arm. "I'd help you, but I have to take him back to face trial. Right now we have to get to him before the cats do."

He knew his smile spoke of his hopes for an evil outcome for the shifter. "We'll walk slowly."

"No, we won't." She tugged at him. "Those cats will eat him alive if they catch him."

"I'll go with you." Morrigan seemed energized at the possibility of a bloody end to Jinx.

Reluctantly, Conall followed Gerry out the door. This keeping-Jinx-with-him promise wasn't going to work. He needed to find someone with paranormal power who'd be willing to take over the job, someone who could bind Jinx to him.

But who'd be stupid enough to do that? Maybe someone who needed what Gerry and he could offer. And that would be . . . He'd have to think it through.

"Slow down. Crows' feet take tiny steps." Morrigan sounded cranky. "I hope you guys realize that I'm on top of everything. You can't hide from me. It didn't work the first time, so give up on looking for a hidey hole where you can have sex. I've kept Conall miserable for eight hundred years, and the misery isn't going to end anytime soon."

"Yeah, we get that, goddess." He glanced down at her. One well-placed stomp would make up for a lot of those years. Problem was, Morrigan was immortal, so all he'd do was piss her off.

"I don't have anything personal against you, Gerry. But you're going to have to restrain your lust for him. It's doable."

Gerry's expression said she'd be open to some stomping, too. "How?"

"I noticed the demonic vestal virgins wandering around. Talk to them. When they're finished, you won't want Conall anywhere near you."

"Been there, done that. Didn't work." Gerry kept scanning the hall. Probably looking for any sign of a snake's tail sticking out from a crack.

Personally, he was hoping for the sound of mortal combat followed closely by cat voices raised in shouts of triumph.

"Who called the virgins from hell?" Morrigan was chatty tonight. "Most have found they're more trouble than they're worth."

"Edge." Conall answered absently as he headed for the stairs.

Edge. He stopped walking. He grinned.

"I don't sense any bloodshed." Morrigan turned around. "This is boring. Remember, I'll be watching." And she walked away.

"What're you so happy about?" Gerry followed him as he picked up his pace.

"First we find Jinx, and if the cats have left anything worth saving, we take him to Edge."

13

"Any idea where Jinx might head?" Conall didn't slow his pace.

Gerry trotted to keep up. "The great hall."

"Why?" Not willing to wait for the elevator, he took the stairs.

"The more people around, the easier it is to lose pursuers."

They entered the great hall to chaos. Cats everywhere. Confused customers. Puffing castle workers chasing cats. Lesson learned? Cats run faster. And in the middle of the mess, Holgarth.

The wizard glared at them. "I don't know how, but you're responsible for this. Do something."

"Hell." Conall worked his way over to where Asima was leaning against the leg of one of the kilt-wearing actors who took part in the fantasies. She was peering upward.

Gerry joined Conall. "I don't think you'll find the snake under that kilt, Asima."

Startled, the guy moved away.

Asima shifted her attention to Gerry. "Snakes hide in unexpected places."

Conall made an impatient noise. "Look, call off your cats. I promise I'll get the collar back to you."

Asima offered him a regal nod. "I'll expect it by morning. And you might suggest that the snake keep a low profile until all the girls have left. They don't have my forgiving nature."

Conall and Gerry waited only long enough to see Asima and friends head back to her room. They escaped the castle just as Holgarth bore down on them.

Gerry breathed in the warm night air before turning to Conall. "Since Sparkle's out and about spreading her special brand of sexual cheer, I'd guess that Edge is taking care of Sweet Indulgence."

He nodded. "The store's just outside the park's entrance. It's a nice night. Let's walk."

"You said you wanted to find Jinx first. Oh, and why do you have to talk to Edge?" Everything had happened so fast that she didn't question what he was doing. Not good. Her career in sales had taught her that winners always knew the what and why of everything around them. She was fast losing touch with both.

He shrugged. "Jinx could be anywhere in the park by now. I don't think he'll stay in the castle. The messengers of Bast are powerful enough to sense him there. And Edge can solve one of my problems."

Gerry pushed aside her continuing worries about Dell and her job so she could focus on the night and the man walking beside her. "Problem?"

He didn't get a chance to answer, because as they took a shortcut through the employee parking lot, Conall stopped to peer into a car.

"What?" Gerry was just getting into the walk—the feeling of rightness in having this special man beside her, the sensual awareness that arced between them, the total relaxation of knowing she was safe with him and . . . No, wouldn't touch the L word. But cared for? Maybe. It could happen.

"My car."

Surprise, surprise. Somehow she'd expected a Hummer, all hulking and macho. What he had was an ordinary midsize. Guess he didn't need a car to prove his manhood.

He yanked the door open. "There's a naked low-life shifter in the backseat." Conall pulled Jinx out of the car.

Unrepentant, Jinx grinned up at him. "Good thing you keep this blanket in your car. It wasn't safe to go back to Asima's room to get my clothes." He sighed. "You're gonna make me give back that collar, aren't you? You know, if you'd let me keep something, I might lay off for a while." He shrugged. "Or not. I got mouths to feed. Talking of mouths, any chance of making a fast-food run?"

Conall held out his hand and waited until Jinx dropped the collar into it. Then he slammed the car door shut and motioned Jinx to follow him. He didn't speak.

Jinx glanced at Gerry. "He always this grouchy?"

"Guess you bring out his inner bear." Gerry tried to ignore the stares they were getting as Jinx trailed them wrapped in a blue blanket. "How'd you know that was Conall's car?"

"I didn't. When I hit the parking lot, I took human form so I could move faster and look in windows. His was the first car with something inside I could use to cover myself. I thought I'd wait until no one was around, then slip back to my room. Bad luck I chose his car."

They reached Sweet Indulgence, and Conall held the door open for her. When Jinx hesitated, Conall yanked him inside.

Edge was leaning on the display case looking bored. The cosmic troublemaker might not be her choice in men, but no woman could ignore how yummily delicious and sensually dangerous he was. He brightened when they walked in. "I was just thinking about you guys." He grinned. "And how to derail your love train."

The word "love" hung in the air, and Gerry looked away from it. So tempting, so fraught with dangling supercharged wires to singe her heart if she ran into them.

"Before she went off for her night of scheming and manipulating, Sparkle told me she'd blabbed about our bet. Part of her scheming involves keeping me trapped here so I can't work on Banan and Destiny." His smile faded. "Not much happening on that front."

There *was* a lot happening on Gerry's front. Usually she'd stand with eyes closed as she sniffed the mouthwatering scent of the forbidden—chocolate. But with Edge and Conall so close together, she chose instead to do a little comparison shopping. And not for chocolate-covered nuts.

It didn't take her long to choose. Conall's presence filled the store. His sleeveless T-shirt showcased his tanned, muscular arms and powerful shoulders. His gray eyes tracked Jinx's every movement. Even with Finis, alias Edge, alias Mr. Death, in the room, Conall's whole package still shouted "top of the food chain" loud and clear.

"How much do you want to win this bet?" Conall narrowed his gaze as Jinx's attention turned to the diamond stud in Edge's ear.

"A lot." Edge's expression grew speculative. "If she wins, she gets to mentor me. She'd love the power trip." Speculative slid into deadly. "That wouldn't be healthy for either of us. If I win, she'll be so glad to see my back I bet she won't even whine to the Big Boss when I take off." Speculative returned. "You look like someone with a deal to make."

Deal? Gerry didn't know anything about a deal. And she liked to be kept inside the loop when deals went down that might impact her.

Conall nodded. "Holgarth did a favor for me tonight. In return, he made me promise to keep an eye on Jinx twenty-four-seven. Can't do that."

"What favor?" See, this is what Gerry hated. Playing catch-up.

"Holgarth awakened the Guardians of the Castle. Those are the gargoyles beside the great hall door. They'll make sure Dell won't be able to disappear the next time we meet."

Okay, that was good. At another time, she'd want to know how Holgarth activated the gargoyles, but right now she had too many more important things on her mind. Like why Conall didn't fill her in first. Where was the partnership, the planning together, the sharing of ideas?

"So you want me to make sure Jinx doesn't sneak off with any more jewelry. It's doable. I can bind him to me." Edge's gaze shifted to Jinx. "And don't even think about my diamond stud, shifter. I don't play nice."

"Hey, I'm just looking. How many carats?" The avaricious gleam was back in Jinx's eyes.

"Not enough to make it worth your life."

Jinx nodded his understanding.

Edge turned his attention back to Conall. "If I watch him, I'll want a few favors in return."

"Jinx is my responsibility, so maybe you should be dealing with me, Edge." She was pretty sure this wasn't an equal opportunity partnership.

The gleam in Edge's eyes said he heard the irritation in her voice and was hoping for a show of open hostility. "So who's the decision maker here?"

"Me." Gerry and Conall answered together.

Gerry glared at Conall, but he fought off the negative vibes she zapped at him. "What do you want?" He kept his attention on Edge.

"I want Gerry and you to talk to Banan and Destiny. Convince them that sex between them would set Galveston on fire."

For the first time, Conall looked at Gerry for her opinion. Too late. She was totally ticked. "Sex isn't everything. Consideration for your partner's feelings and mutual respect are way up on my list." She hoped her stare let Conall know he was at the bottom of her personal list.

Conall exhaled impatiently as he turned back to Edge. "What else?"

"No sex with each other until I win." His smile was a mocking twist of his lips. "That shouldn't take long if you do your job with my couple."

Conall looked pained but nodded. "Okay."

Gerry wasn't about to do any nodding. "No sex? No one dictates that part of my life." She wasn't above compromising, though. "I guess we could talk to Banan and Destiny."

Edge raised one expressive brow. "A difference of opinion?"

Conall finally gave her his full attention. "We need to do this. Without Holgarth's help, the demon could appear anywhere, take you out, and then just disappear."

"Oh, so this is about me? Who would've guessed? I sure would've liked to be part of the planning committee." Gerry heard her sarcastic-bitch voice, but just couldn't stop herself. She met Edge's amused gaze and then looked away. "I bet Sparkle would keep an eye on Jinx if she knew Edge was trying to make a deal with us."

"Yeah, Sparkle has a fantastic jewelry collection." Jinx gave everyone his happy-ferret grin. "And she's not as touchy as this guy."

Conall firmed his lips. "Sparkle has too many other agendas. Besides, he's freaking death. Who'll be more ruthless?"

"Damn straight." Edge looked pleased.

"Sparkle, for one, if she finds out about the no-sex clause in this agreement." Another thought occurred to Gerry. "Maybe you think a woman can't be ruthless." Gerry's latent feminist genes rose to the occasion. "Horse poop. If Jinx crossed Sparkle, she'd crush him with one hand while she put on her mascara with the other. Then she'd slip on her favorite pair of Manolo Blahnik stilettos before strolling across his lifeless body to get to her earrings." Fine, so that was a little extreme. But right now she was truly ticked.

His face was all angry male. "Morrigan says I have to protect you, so consider yourself protected." He looked back at Edge. "We accept your terms." Then to Jinx. "Stay with him until we come to get you."

"Uh-uh. No terms accepted. Wasn't there a serve clause in that curse? Someone who serves does *not* make the decisions. I think—"

"Typical Kavanagh." With that muttered condemnation, Conall slammed from the store.

"Assertive women are sexy." Edge looked interested.

"Forget it." She followed Conall into the night.

Playing the "serve" card had been cheap. Her only excuse? He was being such a . . . She sighed. Okay, so there was no excuse.

Once outside, she looked around. Conall was nowhere in sight. Luckily, the area was well lit, so she didn't feel uneasy about the dark. But she was alone. What if Dell—

She only had an instant to register the wooden spear whizzing toward her before Conall sprang in front of her and plucked it out of the air.

"Well, that was exciting." Gerry clenched her fists to stop the shaking. "You gotta give Dell credit, he's an opportunist." *Calm.* She was an officer of the law, always cool under fire. At least that's what the police manual said. "Actually, I could've used my preternatural speed to throw myself out of the way." If she could've gotten her brain into preternatural thinking mode. "Talking of preternatural speed, you don't have it. So how'd you grab that spear out of the air?" She finally gave up and allowed herself to shake.

"I've had eight hundred years to hone my reflexes." Conall broke the spear like a matchstick and then flung the two pieces away. "And I know you can take care of yourself."

She could see his admission didn't come easily.

"But I couldn't take a chance. I acted." His expression said he hated justifying what he did.

"Thanks." The strain between them made her uncomfortable. She rushed into speech to fill the awkward silence. "Where was Dell? I didn't see him."

"He dematerialized as soon as he'd flung the spear. He couldn't do that inside the castle now."

Left unsaid was that she'd better stay inside the castle until they sent Dell back to hell. That made sense. She hated to admit it, but maybe she owed Holgarth a kind word. Gag.

"I apologize for reminding you that serving is part of the curse." The attack and his awesome save had cooled some of her anger at Conall. "And I'm not a typical Kavanagh. At least not from what you've told me of your life."

"Guess not. No Kavanagh ever apologized to me for anything."

He met her gaze, but she couldn't read his emotions. Time for a subject change. "Do you think Dell is still hanging around?" The thought of an invisible demon hovering at her back gave her chills.

"No. Once he knew he'd failed, he'd be out of here. Dell might be able to dematerialize and appear somewhere else, but I don't know how long he can remain invisible if he stays in one spot." Clasping her hand, he started toward the castle. "If we're going to fool the demon into thinking you're dead, it won't be in this kind of setting. We need a good plan that allows us to control all the variables."

Talk about stating the obvious. "No kidding."

Conall didn't look comfortable talking about her pretend death, and she sure didn't like listening. "I've had enough excitement for the night. We can talk to Banan and Destiny tomorrow. Let's go back to the dungeon." She had to take a poke at him, though. "Where we definitely *won't* have sex."

He growled low in his throat, and she smiled. Conall O'Rourke would rue the night he made that agreement with Edge. She made her plans as they walked.

Once inside the castle, she waited while he delivered the collar to Asima and placated Holgarth. When they walked into the dungeon, Sparkle's sensual décor was a blast of sexual heat.

Amused, Gerry watched him try to ignore the red velvet and black silk as he walked into the bathroom. While she waited for him to come out, she studied the paintings Sparkle had hung on the walls. Interesting. Explicit. And she was sure Sparkle had pulled a few of them from Wicked Fantasy's walls.

He emerged a few seconds later with a glass. "I have to water Houston."

Houston was a mess. He was little more than a few dried twigs. "Too bad we were in the other room when we released all our sexual energy. Guess I need to cheer him up again." Did she look concerned enough?

Conall instantly went on high alert. He remembered how she'd cheered the plant up last time. After her little sexy chat, both he and Houston had grown new wood.

"I get what you're planning. You figure you'll talk sexy, and I'll break the promise we made to Edge."

"*We* made? I don't remember agreeing to anything." Her smile was as insincere as she could make it. "And who said anything about talking sexy? Hmm, I seem to remember Sparkle saying something about a tree trunk just before she left." Gerry widened her eyes in mock surprise. "Well, look over here in the corner." Flipping on the switch for the corner lights, she spread her arms wide. "Ta-dah! A tree trunk. No, it's the whole tree."

"Sparkle does it in style. A gold palm tree. Great." Hell.

"Oooh, I love palm trees." She wrapped her arms around the tree. "They're thin, trim, and perfect to dance with."

Conall had a feeling he knew what was coming. "Cover your eyes, Houston." And him? He'd watch. This would be a test of his no-sex promise to Edge. Bring on the pain.

Gerry stretched, raking her fingernails as high as she could reach on the trunk. "Meow." She glanced over her shoulder at him and smiled a sneaky feline smile.

Her breasts lifted, full and tempting under the snug top she wore beneath her open shirt.

Distractions. He needed *lots* of distractions. "The last Kavanagh I served was too cheap to hire a cook, so he made me fix his meals. His favorite was liver and onions." Conall riveted his attention on Houston. "God, I hated cooking."

"Did someone mess with the air in here? I'm feeling soooo hot." She let the shirt slip from her shoulders and from there to the floor.

Her sleeveless top clung to every fascinating curve of her breasts and stomach. He could see this from the corners of his eyes even as he concentrated on Houston.

"A few centuries back I had to protect a Kavanagh who was so paranoid he made me taste all his food before he'd eat it. The dumbass forgot I was immortal. So the poisoned pudding tasted fine to me. Killed him."

"Tree trunks are so yummy to cuddle up next to." She pursed her sensual lips in mock thought. "But it really has to be skin against bark to get all the sexy sensations. Of course, I'd rather do this with a hot guy." She glanced around, letting her gaze skim across him. "Nope, no hot guys around. Well, palm tree and I will carry on."

"Had one Kavanagh who owned a bar. He made me the bouncer. Friday night was my favorite. Lots of drunken brawls. I could work off some of my aggression." He wiped his suddenly damp palms on his jeans.

Dragging out the torture, she slowly pulled her top over her head and dropped it on top of her shirt. "There, that's better." She turned to wiggle her cute little bottom against the trunk. Her breasts bobbed in time to the wiggling, threatening to pop right out of the tiny piece of material masquerading as a bra. How could something so little hold so much?

His breathing was starting to sound raspy, and he forgot about Houston. "The first Kavanagh I served after slicing and dicing Sean made me build his house. I knew squat about building houses. It fell on top of him. Morrigan couldn't blame me. I'd warned him."

"If there were a hot guy in the house—which there isn't—I'd have to get rid of everything keeping me from full bare-body contact." She slid her tongue over her top lip and then her bottom one as she considered her options.

The sweet sheen of those lips took him right out of his game plan. He couldn't think of one more thing to tell her about all those damn Kavanaghs he'd served.

She shrugged. "Oh, what the hey. I'll pretend." She turned her back to him. "Would you unhook my bra?"

A direct challenge. He could play it safe and tell her to do it herself. But admit it, this was the first thing a Kavanagh had ever asked of him that he really wanted to do. Besides, he was strong enough to handle anything she threw at him. He swept his gaze across her smooth, creamy back. He drew in a deep breath of courage. Anything except maybe her lacey white bra.

Before he could think it to death, he moved behind her and reached for the bra. His knuckles skimmed her back as he took care of the hooks. Her tremor reached all the way to his cock and wrapped relentless fingers around it. Not good. He stepped away.

She turned to face him, and the heated flush of her cheeks proved she was way into her own fantasy. He felt better immediately. Suffering alone was no fun.

Gerry looked like she wanted to say something, but in the end she just dropped the bra to the floor.

There were times when words weren't necessary. This was one of them. Her breasts thrust high and full, the pink nipples hardening to delicious little nubs beneath his gaze. All he wanted to do was kneel in front of her while she leaned forward so those ripe nipples would fall into his mouth.

She turned away and obviously found her voice hiding in the blasted tree trunk. "We can't leave a job half done, can we?" With her back to him, she kicked off her sandals and unbuttoned her jeans. As they pooled around her feet, she stepped out of them.

Whoever said that white was a virginal color had never seen Gerry in her white panties. The silky material cupped her perfect round behind. Hooking her thumbs under the top of the panties, she wiggled out of them and kicked them aside. Then like a car salesman lovingly running his hand across the hood of the little sports beauty with the big engine he was trying to sell, she reached behind her and slid her fingers over both gorgeous cheeks.

Edge? Promise? There was something he was supposed to remember about a promise to Edge. Whatever it was, it was gone.

Gerry wrapped one arm and one long, long leg around the tree and twirled around it to face Conall. "It's amazing how many things a palm tree is good . . ." Her voice trailed away as her gaze glided the length of his body.

His body told no lies. He reached to unfasten his jeans before the pressure cut off the blood supply to his . . . brain.

She remained still for way too long. And then she sighed. Laying her forehead against the tree trunk, she closed her eyes. "If I keep going, we'll end up making love, won't we?" She didn't wait for him to respond. "If Morrigan pops in while we're making love, you're royally screwed. And this would be the logical place for her to check." Straightening, she walked over to retrieve the robe that lay across her bed.

He decided against interrupting her while she was on a roll. Besides, he was too busy trying to explain the situation to a body part that did *not* understand why the action was on hold.

"I can be a selfish witch. All I was thinking about was how ticked I was because you didn't include me in the decision making. I didn't think through the consequences." She smiled. "And I *really* didn't want to stop making love with you. That first time was a great coming-attractions demonstration."

"I see."

"And since I'm feeling all humble and chastened—which might never happen again—I may as well tell you how sorry I am that my ancestors were such jerks."

He glanced away so she wouldn't see the emotion he knew filled his eyes. All those long centuries, no one had given a flip how he felt.

"I should've told you my plans. My only excuse is that you're the first Kavanagh who didn't expect me to do it all. I'm not used to anyone wanting to help." Conall figured she'd recognize the apology. He wasn't good at them because he'd made it a point of pride never to say he was sorry to the hated men who'd controlled his life.

She nodded and started to slip into the robe.

"Morrigan will only get pissed if we're actually making love." Boy, he must have a thing for suffering. "If I'm just watching you, she won't do much except threaten."

Gerry's lips lifted in a wicked smile. "*Can* you just watch?"

Conall shook his head. "Woman, you have no idea what strength O'Rourke men have." Lowering himself to the couch, he spread his legs to allow for expansion. "Let's see what you can do with that tree."

"I learned how to pole dance before I became vampire.

I hope I remember everything." Her smile widened. "Or maybe you should hope I don't."

Dropping her robe, she pressed her back against the tree, her hair a long shimmering fall of black silk. She arched her back, her breasts gleaming in the dim wall-sconce light. Spreading her legs, she leaned forward to slide her fingers up her inner thigh. Her hair fell around her face, hiding her expression.

She was *woman*—mysterious, sensual.

Conall sneaked a glance at the still partly filled glass of water he'd used for Houston. He might have to toss the rest of it over Houston and himself to keep them from going up in flames.

Gerry's laughter was a light ripple of amusement. Wrapping her lithe and lush body around the tree, she ran her hands over the rough surface.

Conall felt each stroke of her fingers as a sizzling slide of pure erotic sensation—across his chest, circling his stomach, and teasing the length of his overexcited cock.

The space between them vibrated with so much sexual tension he expected to hear a sonic boom when it snapped.

Her naked body glistened damply as she slid down the trunk to crouch at its base. Then she opened her thighs—tempting, inviting.

And all the gods help him, he rose to go to her. Standing above her, he spread his legs so she could have a clear view of what she did to him.

She gazed up at him from eyes hot with passion. Reaching out, she finished unfastening his jeans. He helped her by shoving them, along with his briefs, down his hips until his cock sprang free.

Clenching his fists at his sides, he forced himself to remain still, to not reach for her, when all he wanted to do was touch and taste every inch of her warm, smooth skin.

She, on the other hand, felt no compunction about reaching for him. The light scrape of her fingernail over the head of his cock dragged a groan from him. He was so big, so hard, that it didn't feel like he'd fit in his skin much longer. Something had to give.

Leaning forward she replaced her fingernail with her lips, her tongue, her teeth. Nipping gently, she worked up and down the length of him before closing her lips over the head.

The slide of her fangs along the most sensitive body part he owned added something new to the sensations he was feeling. Fear. Yes, he trusted her, but there was the primitive part of his brain that refused to feel safe. The fear was like adding hot pepper to the sexual recipe. It intensified everything and came close to pushing him to orgasm.

He'd reached his personal limit. He had to touch her.

Sensing his shift from passive to active, she released him and leaned back to look up at him. The cool air sliding across his cock, still warm and wet from her mouth, startled him.

What startled him even more was the sound of feline screeches and yowls drawing closer and closer to the closed door.

Damn.

Gerry stared at him from wide eyes. "Someone's killing a cat."

"No. Asima's singing." Conall straightened and then raked his fingers through his hair.

A minute ago, Morrigan and his promise to Edge hadn't even been a blip on his memory's radar. All he'd wanted was to make love with Gerry. Only Asima's cat voice raised in song could've stopped dead what probably would've been the greatest orgasm he or Gerry would ever have.

He growled low in his throat as he turned toward the door. "Dead kitty."

Conall was aware of Gerry scrambling into her robe as the door swung open and Asima padded into the dungeon.

"Everything turned out well. Everyone had a lovely time. There were a few who said they would've enjoyed ripping a certain shape-shifter into tiny pieces, but all in all, the night was a success." She leaped onto the coffee table to stare at them. *"My, we look a little disheveled. Did I interrupt anything?"*

Gerry lifted her lips to show her fangs.

"Hmm. I'll take that as a yes." She glanced around the room. *"If Sparkle's horrendous attempt at interior design raised your lust level, please don't tell me. Anyway, I just wanted to let you know I'll be guarding the door while you guys sleep."* She jumped from the table and padded back toward the door. *"I'll be unflagging in my vigilance. Of course, I might allow myself a few short cat naps. Very short. Nothing will get by me."* Then she left. The door swung shut behind her.

He dropped onto the couch, and Gerry joined him.

"That could've been Morrigan." He clasped her hand.

"We should thank Asima for stopping us." She squeezed his hand.

"I still hate her."

"Yeah."

14

Gerry wakened the next evening to a sense of unfinished business. With eyes closed, she allowed herself to adjust to life's small noises—the soft hum of the air conditioner and the sound of the TV turned down low.

What was that smell? It made her want to . . . Then she remembered. She'd slept on Sparkle's bed of sensual scents. Too bad when Gerry hit her nightly off button it was instant nothing. A few erotic dreams would've made sure she didn't wake up cranky.

Yep, cranky thoughts front and center. She hadn't seduced Conall. Asima had done her best impression of a bucket of ice cubes and put their lovemaking into the crisper until further notice.

And once she got past that biggie, there were still the problems of Dell, Morrigan, and the deal Conall had made with Edge. Oh, and gee, she'd almost forgotten she had a job. Payton wasn't a patient man.

"If you're finished gnawing on all our problems, you can open your eyes so we can begin to solve some of them."

Conall's deep, sexy voice spread warmth all the way to her toes. She curled them in anticipation of another night spent with him. For just a moment, she celebrated the fact that he'd be with her for the rest of her existence. Then shame rolled over her. He'd stay because he couldn't leave, and she had no way of freeing him.

She opened her eyes.

He sprawled across the couch, dwarfing it with his large frame. "There's some good news. No reports of stolen jewelry."

"Way to go, Edge." She stretched and enjoyed the way his gaze followed every movement. "How'd you know I was awake and thinking about our problems?"

"I sense when you're awake, even if you don't move. Can't explain it." He switched off the TV and then walked to her bed. He sat down beside her. "And you get this sexy little crease between your eyes when you're worried."

"A crease between my eyes is sexy?" He had on a short robe and his hair was still damp from his shower. Gerry wanted to slide her fingers up his muscular thigh and right under that robe to see what she could find. She nixed the idea. If she found what she expected, they'd be off and running again. Too frustrating with Asima, the ice cube queen, right outside their door.

"Lady, everything about you is sexy." His wicked grin said he knew what she'd been thinking.

"So what happened after I fell asleep?" When dawn caught her, she conked out no matter what was going on. If she was in the middle of making love with Conall? *That* would keep her awake. They'd experiment sometime—she thought of Morrigan—or not. Color her depressed.

"I went up and brought down Fo, Gabriel, and Conalla. They watched videos until I woke up." He glanced away. "The kid's kinda cute. She liked me."

Was there a female alive who wouldn't like him? Gerry

didn't think so. Oh, and she couldn't forget the dead. All the dead women she knew would think he was pretty hot.

He quickly jumped to the next subject. "We have to bring Morrigan in on our plan to trap Dell."

Awww. He was embarrassed because he'd admitted to thinking Fo's baby was cute. How endearing was that? She'd like to . . . "What did you say about Morrigan?"

"I've been thinking about motive while I was waiting for you to wake up. If the demon got to you, and I had nothing to do with it, Morrigan would have to release me from the curse."

She nodded. "I guess you'd be an ordinary human again." *Not* ordinary. Hook an extra onto the ordinary, and maybe you'd be close. "Doesn't the thought tempt you?"

Conall's gaze darkened. "Not that way. Never that way."

His words warmed her from the inside out.

"That must be what Dell wants. Didn't he say you had to die so something else could happen?" Conall stood and began to pace.

"Yeah." She splayed her palm over the spot where he'd been sitting and soaked in the heat that still remained from his body. Pitiful that even small warm crumbs excited her. "So what do you think happens as soon as you become human?"

He shrugged. "Right now I'm immortal. Not so easy to kill. Demon versus human makes it a little more one-sided. Nothing else makes sense. But why?"

"Maybe you have a friend somewhere who just wants you free of the curse. Have you considered that?"

Conall didn't even pause to think. "For eight hundred years I've fought and killed enemies of the Kavanaghs. When I wasn't fighting for them, I served them in other ways. I never had time to make friends."

His comment wasn't a plea for sympathy; it was simply a statement of fact.

That made Gerry unutterably sad. "You've never seen him. Maybe you know him. He sure knows you. Or maybe someone powerful needed a demon to do his dirty work."

"Could be. I've pissed off a few people over the centuries."

"So what about Morrigan? Why does she have to be in on this?" Gerry hated dealing with the goddess.

"Dell has to believe it's all real. He won't buy the act if he doesn't see that Morrigan accepts your death. He'll want proof that I'm human again. Morrigan gives legitimacy to the whole thing."

He stopped pacing and flung himself down on the couch again. The robe rode high on his thighs, and she knew if she slid down on the bed a little more she might be able to see . . .

She lifted her gaze to meet his. He grinned. "Concentrate."

"I am." On many things. Multitasking was her gift. "I suppose we'll have to meet with Morrigan before we hunt down Banan and Destiny." She'd hook those two up even if she had to drag them kicking and screaming to the bed.

He nodded.

She sighed.

"Dress and then let's do it." Conall rose to grab some clean clothes he'd flung over the chair. "I got some things from my room before I went to bed."

"That couch doesn't look too comfortable. Can't you get another bed in here?"

"I didn't sleep on the couch."

She flicked a quick glance to the other side of her bed. Extra pillow with head indentation. Uh-oh. "Isn't this going to make resisting temptation a little tough?"

"Sweetheart, it's lights out as soon as your head hits that pillow. You have no temptation to worry about." His grin was wry. "I suffered enough for both of us. But I

couldn't sleep all scrunched up on that couch. Not that I
did much sleeping tucked up next to you."

"What did you sleep in?" This was important stuff. She
needed to know.

"Briefs. Had to stay decent for the kid." He grinned.
"Otherwise . . ."

"I get it, I get it." Oh boy. Now the mental image of his
almost-naked body resting next to her all day would haunt
her night. "We have to take care of Banan and Destiny fast
and then find a spot safe from Morrigan. Once she gets her
tail feathers back, maybe she'll get bored and leave."

Frustration darkened his eyes. "How long can we live
like that? Can you see us in a hundred years? Two hundred? Still sneaking around behind the goddess's back?"
He turned away from her.

"Maybe we'll just be friends by then." Did she believe
that? No. But if saying it made things easier for him, hey,
she could give him the words.

Conall looked back at her. He'd replaced the frustration
with a savagery that had her thinking about pulling the
covers over her head.

"Friends?" Bitter laughter. "Friendship is too bland a
word to describe anything I'd ever feel for a Kavanagh. I'd
use high-impact words like hate and . . ." He shook his
head like he was trying to clear it. "Forget it."

Gerry didn't want to forget it. She had to know what the
missing word was in that sentence. But now wasn't the
time to bug him about it. She scrambled out of bed,
grabbed her clothes, and headed for the bathroom.

She came out a short while later dressed in a cotton skirt
and camisole. And yeah, she was trying for the flirty girly
look. So? She didn't have to dress like a member of PUFF
every day.

Conall had just come in the door. He stopped and
stared. Then he gave her a slow sexy smile that made her

wish she had more than one flirty girly outfit. "You're beautiful. Always."

Gerry blinked. How could those few words light her up inside? Jeez, she must look like one of those carved pumpkins people put candles in at Halloween.

Since she didn't know what to say, she resorted to a question. "What were you doing?"

"Asima's still camped outside the door. I told her to find Morrigan and tell her we wanted to talk."

Gerry frowned. "Do you think she'll listen to—"

A force flung the door open so hard it bounced off the wall where it hung drunkenly from one hinge. Holgarth would have to fix it. Again.

Gerry looked up, expecting at least a seven-foot mountain of muscle to be standing in the doorway. Nothing. She looked down. Morrigan, still pretty much tailless, stood there. Asima hovered behind her.

Conall looked past the goddess to Asima. "What the hell did you tell her?"

Asima yawned, a study in feline boredom. *"That I'd heard sounds of passion coming from the dungeon. I told her if she hurried she'd catch you in the act."* She slid a sly glance at Morrigan. *"Conall's a fast finisher. Too bad for you."*

The goddess fluffed up her feathers and walked into the room. "Just wait until I get my feathers all back. You'll be hiding somewhere you think is safe, hoppin' and boppin' toward an ultrafine orgasm, and poof, I'll be there." She opened her beak wide and tried out a chorus of "I'll Be There" before taking her usual perch on the coffee table. Everyone winced. "But I'm in a good mood tonight, so I won't bore you with the gory details of your punishment." She turned her beady gaze toward her tail. "My tail feathers are growing back."

Everyone leaned in to take a look. Sure enough, little feathers were sprouting from her bare behind. Conall

didn't know whether to cheer or curse. That's because he
didn't know how the return of her tail feathers would affect
Gerry and him.

"We need to talk." Conall wanted to get this over with.
"A demon is trying to kill Gerry."

Morrigan cocked her head to stare at them from bright
black eyes. "Why?"

Score one for the goddess. She got right to the point.

Gerry moved closer. "He said I had to die so something
else could happen. If I die, you'll release Conall from the
curse. Once he's not immortal anymore, he'll be a lot easier to kill."

"Who wants you dead, O'Rourke?"

Conall could see interest gleaming in those eyes. She
must be getting bored walking around the castle threatening guests and driving Holgarth crazy.

"That's what we want to find out. We'll set a trap and
invite the demon in. If he thinks Gerry's dead and you've
canceled the curse, he'll make his move on me. But we
need you to pretend to make me human so he'll think it's
all legit."

The goddess wiggled her bare ass in frustration. "If I
had my tail feathers I could whack the demon in a nanosecond by just thinking about it. Now I can only do the small
stuff—opening doors, pissing off wizards, and . . ." She
glanced back at her tail again before casting a sly glance
Conall's way. "Ending curses."

"Uh, goddess, will you leave when your feathers are all
back?" Gerry sounded hopeful.

Conall could've told her the goddess lived to disappoint.

"Definitely. I've had enough of this place." Morrigan
hopped to the floor and headed for the door. "But I'll always keep an eye on you, warrior. You'll never know when
I'm going to pop up." She paused in the doorway. "Count
me in on your plan. Call when you need me and—"

"I know, you'll be there." They all listened in pained silence to a final chorus by Morrigan of "I'll Be There." Conall thought she and Asima should team up and record a few songs. They could title the CD *Tunes to Drill Teeth By.*

"I used to like that song." Gerry evidently didn't think much of the goddess's chances on *American Idol.*

"I don't trust Morrigan. Once a bitch, always a bitch." Asima had put Morrigan firmly in the can't-be-redeemed column of her personal spreadsheet. *"Protecting you guys is exhausting. I think I'll take a break for a while. Bast will fix everything when she gets here."*

"And that will be when?" Gerry sounded like she didn't believe it would happen anytime soon.

"When she gets here, of course." Asima stared at the door hanging drunkenly from one hinge. *"Morrigan enjoys making a dramatic entrance."* She padded into the hallway, tail waving gracefully.

"Holgarth's going to have a hissy fit over the door, isn't he?" Gerry raised her hand. "No, don't bother answering that. Can we hunt down Banan and Destiny now?"

He grinned. "Impatient?"

"You bet. The faster they embrace their inner lust, the faster we'll be rid of at least one problem." She glanced pointedly at his robe. "Get dressed."

Conall could do that. And get some of his own back while he was at it. He untied his robe and shrugged out of it. Ignoring her gasp, he walked over to his clothes. Her gaze seared a path down the middle of his back and fixed on his ass.

"I thought you said you wore briefs." Her voice was raw, hungry.

His cock wanted equal attention, so Conall turned to face her. She didn't meet his gaze. *Her* gaze had better things to do.

"To bed, not after my shower." He rubbed his hand across his chest.

Her gaze slid up to follow the motion. "We don't really have to find Banan right now. We could sit around and talk for a while."

"About what?" He'd never make a sexual tease. A tease was cool and calm, always under control. His cock didn't know the meaning of cool around Gerry. It was threatening to run away from home if he didn't give it what it wanted.

"I don't know." She moved closer. "Maybe about how much I want to close my fingers around your shaft and slide them up and down, up and down, up—" She closed her eyes and gripped her lower lip between her teeth.

Hell. This wouldn't work. Forget about payback. Reluctantly, he reached for his clothes. "We need to get started on Banan and Destiny fast, because I don't have much self-control where you're concerned."

Gerry opened her eyes and stared at him. "Right back at you." She looked away while he pulled on jeans and a T-shirt. "I've been wondering. Okay, so we have a huge attraction going on. But beyond that, does my being a Kavanagh still bother you?"

Conall stilled. He was tuned in to Gerry, so he sensed the tension thrumming through her. This question was important to her. *It's important to you, too, pal.* "When I look at you, touch you, I only think about the woman I . . . care about." *Cop-out, O'Rourke.* But was it? Was he ready to think in terms of love? He didn't know, so probably he *wasn't* ready. "I don't think about being with you as a bad thing, so that's different from what I felt about all the other Kavanaghs. I don't feel trapped by you, only Morrigan. So, no, I guess it doesn't bother me." Surprised, he realized he'd told the truth.

She looked back at him, and what he saw in her eyes made his mouth go dry and his heart pound out a drumroll of excitement. Then she smiled. "Finished dressing?"

He looked down. "Yeah, let's find Banan and Destiny." He'd think about her eyes later.

Gerry thought this was a beautiful night to be on the beach. And if everything around her wasn't so crazy, she might even enjoy it.

"Do males and females often fight before mating? Is that an accepted ritual?" Fo looked up from her pouch hanging at Gerry's waist. "How long will they argue before having sex? Will I get to observe the mating?" Excitement crept into Fo's voice.

Gerry was getting a headache from Fo's never-ending questions. But Conall had figured that since they were leaving the castle, they'd better take extra protection with them. Fo was it. Not only could she sense Dell even if he wasn't visible, she could turn him into a small pile of ash. Perfect.

"No, it's not an accepted ritual." Gerry sighed. "And no, you can't watch them mate." Probably because it wasn't going to happen. How had Edge let himself get roped into trying to hook up these two?

"Goo-goo, ga-ga." Conalla thought Banan and Destiny would never get it on either.

Gerry smiled down at Fo's baby. She was tucked into her dad's pouch. Conalla had a pink case and big rainbow eyes. Fo and Gabriel had outdone themselves in making their baby a beautiful sentient machine.

"Damn it. Calm down and take a freaking minute to listen to each other." Conall was still trying to make something happen between Banan and Destiny, but Gerry heard the temper simmering in his voice.

Personally, Gerry thought Destiny should close her mouth long enough to take a good look at the guy standing opposite her. Banan was spectacular. Wearing only khaki shorts, he was a stroll down every woman's candy aisle. With long pale hair that should've looked washed out but instead seemed to flow with all the colors in the spectrum, and eyes so dark she couldn't see his pupils, he was memorable on every level.

Banan was the reason they were all standing around on a Galveston beach in the dark. He'd decided he was going to reveal his unique . . . gift to Destiny. Gerry didn't think that was a good idea, but who was going to stop him?

"She hunts sharks. I think she needs to rethink her motivation for killing every shark she can find." Mr. Great White reached for the button on his shorts.

Uh-oh. This wasn't heading in a good direction. Gerry covered Conalla's screen.

Destiny glared at Banan. Gerry thought he could do worse. Ms. Shark Hunter had a tumble of brown hair, big hazel eyes, and a curvy body. Why didn't he just shut up about his alter ego and seduce her on this nice warm beach instead? Once they were into each other, she'd be more receptive to his unique qualities. Besides, if he thought being a wereshark was a sticking point in their relationship, he should try on an ancient curse for size.

"A shark killed my brother. Now I take out as many of the cold bastards as I can find." Destiny seemed to think that was all the justification she needed. "And it's not as if they're helpless. One of them bit a chunk out of my boat the other day." She narrowed her eyes in thought. "That was so strange. A great white. I didn't expect to find one here, but suddenly there it was. No way did I think it could do that much damage to my boat."

"*It?* Where do you get off—"

Conall interrupted before Banan's anger could explode. "Let's look at your logic, Destiny. So that means if an airline pilot killed your brother, you'd be hunting the friendly skies now."

She flushed. "That's different."

"Don't bother trying to reason with her. It won't work. She needs to see what she's trying to kill." Banan dropped his shorts along with his briefs and walked toward the water. He looked over his shoulder. "Follow me if you have the guts."

Conall cursed softly even as Gerry kept her hand over Conalla's eyes.

Fo's purple eyes widened to fill her whole screen. "Look at his ass. I've compared hundreds of butt cheeks online, but those are two of the best I've seen. He doesn't have an erection, so I can't do a comparison check on his penis." She sounded bummed out about that.

Gerry sent a warning glance her way. "Conalla can hear you."

Fo seemed puzzled. "Gabriel and I gave her all our knowledge, so she's familiar with the human body. You don't have to cover her eyes."

No way was Gerry taking her hand away from Conalla's eyes. She was still old-fashioned enough to equate baby with innocent.

Destiny's shocked expression turned to concern. "What the hell is he doing? That great white is still out there somewhere." She glanced around as if expecting her spear to materialize beside her on the sand. Nothing. Then she cast Conall a speculative glance. "You have a sword strapped to your back. Your business. I'm not going to pry. But how about loaning it to me so I can go in and save his stupid ass?" Something in her eyes said she thought his stupid ass was mighty fine and well worth saving.

Conall shook his head. "You don't need to go in after him. Banan can take care of himself."

No kidding. Gerry stared out at the Gulf where moonlight shining on the water lent it a magical quality. False advertising. Twenty feet and 4,000 pounds of killing machine lurked beneath the water's glittering surface.

Destiny looked disbelieving.

"Look, if he gets in trouble, I'll go in after him myself." Translation: Conall wasn't handing over his weapon so

Destiny could hack away at Banan. But he'd underesti-
mated Destiny's determination.

"I can't see Banan anymore." Glancing around the
beach, she strode over to pick up a tire iron half covered
with sand. Without a backward glance, Destiny hefted the
tire iron, kicked off her sandals, and walked fully clothed
into the surf.

"Where the hell did that come from?" Conall looked
outraged. "What's a tire iron doing on the beach?" Troubled, he watched Destiny wade out almost to her chest.

"They'll be okay. Banan won't get near enough for her
to tag him." Gerry hoped. "He wants to change back to
human form in front of her. Don't ask me why. Me? I think
it's dumb. And we didn't get a chance to work on the ro-
mance angle."

"Banan assumes partial shark nature when he changes.
She's ticked him off. I hope he holds on to his temper."

Gerry stared with Conall. She hadn't thought about that.
The theme from *Jaws* played a sinister background to her
vivid imagination.

Conall waded into the surf a few feet and then stopped.
Gerry stayed just at the water's edge.

"I can't go in to help. Fo and Conalla would be in danger." Gerry peered into the darkness. The beginnings of
fear wrapped her in chilling tentacles. This whole idea was
dangerous. They should've tried harder to talk Banan out
of it.

"There's Banan." Conall pointed, his voice tight with
tension.

Sure enough, Gerry saw the shark's fin break the surface and glide toward Destiny. She held her breath as Destiny scanned the water looking for Banan. Gerry saw the
exact moment Destiny spotted the shark's fin.

"Hey, how's it going?" Brynn's voice swung both Gerry
and Conall around. "Gabriel finished his work, so I told

him I'd take him to Fo and Conalla. Holgarth told me you
were here." He glanced at the water. "What's happening?"

An explosion of sound answered his question. Struck
silent, everyone riveted their attention on the unfolding
drama.

A short distance from Destiny a giant conical snout
broke the surface. Even from where they stood, Gerry
could see the shark's open mouth. Ohmigod, Banan made
Little Red's big bad wolf look like a toothless old crone.

Destiny screamed at the shark and swung the tire iron.
"What'd you do with Banan, you ugly son of a bitch?"

Gerry exhaled in relief when she missed.

"What . . . ?" Brynn gaped.

"Banan." Conall moved farther into the water.

"A lover's spat." Gerry handed Fo and Conalla to Brynn.

Distracted, Brynn took the pouches with Fo and
Conalla in them. "I don't think Banan liked the 'ugly son
of a bitch' comment."

Evidently anger made Banan careless because he drew
a little too close to Destiny. She clipped him across his
nose.

"Uh-oh." Conall charged into the water toward the two.

Just as Conall reached them, the water erupted into a
maelstrom. Gerry couldn't see anything. Only one thought
registered. *Conall*.

He wouldn't use his sword to protect himself from either Banan or Destiny. No way did he need to get between
a steamed great white and a really angry woman wielding
a tire iron. But he would, because he was a warrior and
that's what warriors did.

Slogging through the waves to reach Conall would take
precious seconds she couldn't spare. Gerry focused, pic-
tured herself levitating, and willed it to reality. Savagely,
she shoved aside reason that said she'd never tried this before, that she'd go splat into the water long before she
reached Conall. No. She *wouldn't* fail.

And as she rose into the air and skimmed above the water to where the battle raged, she forced any twinge of doubt from her mind. She could do this. With all the splashing she couldn't make out exactly what was happening.

Then she saw Banan's massive body breach the surface. She didn't hesitate. Diving, she landed on the shark's back. Clinging like cat hair, she shouted at Banan. Where *were* a shark's ears? "Change, dumbass, before you hurt someone." She freed one hand long enough to punch him on the top of his head. "If she clocks you with that tire iron, you'll be walking around with a dent in your head for a week."

Banan changed.

And Gerry found herself piggybacking on a naked man. Destiny froze with her tire iron in mid-swing and Conall stood staring.

Oh, boy. Gerry grinned weakly and offered them a finger wave. "Hi." She slid from Banan's back.

Destiny's breaths came in huge gulps. "Banan? The shark?" Her eyes widened to the size of saucers and then they rolled up into her head as she keeled over.

"Damn." Banan caught her before she went under and lifted her into his arms.

Gerry blinked and looked down. Holy cripe, the water was up to her chin. And then Conall was beside her. "Don't you dare pick me up. PUFF officers leave the water under their own power." Actually, she was afraid if he touched her she'd fall apart.

He only nodded. "You flew. How? You're too new to have that power."

She shrugged. "I concentrated real hard, and suddenly I had liftoff." Gerry had to tread water to make her way to shore while Warrior Guy strode along as easily as he'd walk across a parking lot.

"Why?" His eyes were silver in the moonlight. "Why didn't you stay safely on shore?"

"I thought you might need help." *I couldn't stand the thought of you getting hurt.* And with that realization came her personal aha moment. The slippery slope with love at the bottom? Well, she was a human toboggan heading for the L word at the speed of sound. She just hoped she wouldn't wipe out on one of the tricky curves.

15

"You're a *wereshark*?" Destiny sat on the dungeon's couch staring unblinkingly at Banan. She was wearing a change of clothes Conall had gotten from her room.

Banan nodded. "I knew you'd have to see me in shark form before you'd believe me."

"I . . ." She rubbed her hand across her forehead. "Yeah, I guess. I'm *so* not ready to deal with this. I always thought all that paranormal stuff was crap."

Banan watched her, his eyes dark with emotion. "Well, believe it now."

She looked brittle enough to shatter into a million screaming pieces. "For God's sake, why would you show me what you are? You made it clear how much you hated what I did. I was okay with that. I could hate you right back for being so judgmental when you didn't know where I was coming from. Why not leave it like that?"

Conall thought Banan looked like he wanted to reach out to touch her. Wisely, he kept his hands to himself. Destiny's emotions were raw and volatile right now.

Banan didn't seem to have an answer for that. Not good. Conall needed to move things in the right direction.

"Banan wanted honesty between you guys." Okay, now what? "He wanted the chance to explain what it's like looking through the eyes of your enemy. You know, to promote understanding between species and all that. Right, Banan?" Would she buy it? Not a chance.

"Uh, yeah." Banan seemed a little puzzled, but he nodded dutifully.

"So talk. And why'd you put your damn secret in *my* hands?" Destiny's eyes glittered with unshed tears.

Thank God, Gerry grabbed the ball and ran with it, because Conall was out of words. "He put the secret in your hands because he cares for you, Destiny."

Conall watched Destiny digest that revelation. Her eyes softened. "Really?"

"Yeah." Banan had finally said something useful.

"Why don't you guys go up to Banan's room and talk things over?" Gerry's smile was tense, but triumph gleamed in her eyes.

Banan reached out to clasp Destiny's hand. She didn't jerk it away. He turned to Conall. "I don't know why you bothered to help tonight, but thanks."

"Hey, no problem." They were home free. Things had gone a lot better than he could've expected.

"We did it because we were trying to hook you guys up."

No. Gerry didn't just open her mouth and blow everything. Conall stared at her, as speechless as Banan had been a minute ago.

"I don't understand." Destiny didn't look like she could take another revelation tonight.

"I know, I know, you think I'm dumb for telling them." Gerry met Conall's glare. "But Banan decided honesty had to come first or else everything that came after would be built on a lie. Nothing lasts long on a weak foundation. He was right."

Who cared about foundations? They weren't building a freaking fortress. This was about throwing up a shack that would last the few days it took to trap a demon. Then the damn thing could fall down. "There'll be consequences."

Gerry shrugged. "Aren't there always?" She turned her attention back to Banan and Destiny. "Sparkle Stardust and Edge made a friendly bet."

Hadn't looked too friendly to Conall.

"Edge bet Sparkle that he could hook up you guys before she could get Conall and me together." Gerry glanced at Conall. He scowled. "We needed a favor from Edge. He said he'd help us if we'd help him." She lifted her hands. "So here we are."

Banan nodded. "Now everything makes sense. He's come down to the beach a few times to talk about how sexy Destiny was and how great we'd be together."

"Same here." Destiny didn't seem too upset about it.

Banan grinned. "I'll have a talk with Edge tomorrow. Meanwhile, Destiny and I have some things to work out." If he wanted to know more about the how and why of the bet, Banan was too into Destiny to ask.

Destiny still looked in shock, but she didn't seem able to tear her gaze from Banan. "Maybe Edge will still win that bet."

Conall let silence build as they watched Banan and Destiny leave. He waited until Banan shut their new door softly behind him before turning to pierce Gerry with a stare he hoped told her how pissed off he was. "I assume you had a good reason for that amazing moment."

Anger flared in her eyes. "No. It was completely spontaneous. Maybe, though, I've finally had enough of watching people being manipulated. Could be that I wanted to give Banan and Destiny back a little control over their lives." She rubbed the crease between her eyes. "Since we don't seem to be having much luck getting any for ourselves."

Conall refused to recognize the twinge he felt as guilt. So he'd done his own share of manipulating by strong-arming Gerry into letting him move in with her. It was for her own good. And he didn't have a choice when it came to serving and protecting. It was a by-product of the curse.

As she stared at him, her expression said she knew what he was thinking. Some of the anger drained from her. "Not you. You're doing what you have to do." She rose from her chair to pace between the iron maiden and the rack. "We have so many entities pulling our strings I don't know why they don't get them tangled up." She shrugged. "I saw a chance to strike back in a small way, so I did it."

He hated to remind her of this, but . . . "If you make Edge too mad, he might back out of his agreement to let you cart him off to jail."

Her eyes widened. "Oh, no. I forgot."

Raking his fingers through his hair, he tried to let go of some of his tension. "Feels like the walls are closing in. Want to go up to the battlements with me?"

She shook her head. "You reminded me that I have a job. I need to e-mail a report to Payton. I'll come up when I'm finished."

He opened his mouth to say he wouldn't leave her alone.

She made a shooing motion. "I won't be alone. I'll call Kim right now to ask if Fo can visit for a while. We left Brynn standing on the beach with Fo, Gabriel, and Conalla. I'll tell Kim what happened so she can pass it on to Brynn."

Conall waited while she made the call and only left when Kim was finally sitting on the couch with both Fo and Conalla.

Asima was curled up outside the door. He grinned. Sleeping on the job. Good. He wouldn't have her trailing after him. But he didn't escape everyone's notice. As he climbed the winding stairs up to the battlements, Morrigan joined him.

He looked down at her, blinked, and looked again. Then for the first time in 800 years, he almost laughed at her. "What the hell is that—"

"I'll do the talking, O'Rourke. I don't see any protecting going on here." She hopped up a few steps ahead of him.

"Kim and Fo are with Gerry." Conall stopped and leaned closer. "What's that on your ass?"

"A wig." Her crow eyes glowed red. "If you laugh I'll torture you for untold centuries."

"Been there, done that, goddess. Why the wig?" He bit his lip and tried to swallow his laughter. The wig was long and trailed behind her. She looked like she was wearing one of those Shih Tzu dogs on her butt.

"An idiot who works in the castle compared me to a plucked chicken."

Uh-oh.

"His ass is now covered with an itchy, burning, disgusting rash. He won't be sitting down anytime soon."

Conall nodded. "So what do you want?"

She flapped her wings at him. "I'm not done talking about my tail. Find something that'll keep the damn wig on. I've tried double-sided tape, glue—"

"Staples?"

"We are not amused." Morrigan almost vibrated with temper. "If I didn't want you to continue suffering, I'd have destroyed you centuries ago, warrior."

Conall wished he could cut her strings and wrap them around her scrawny neck.

"Now get me something to keep—"

A sudden breeze blew down the stairs as if someone had opened the door to the battlements. It lifted Morrigan's wig and dropped it on the step beside him. He picked it up, prepared to put it back on the goddess's butt.

"Hey, your feathers are almost all grown back." He stared. "I don't remember some of them being white."

"Put the damn wig back on."

He plopped it on her behind and then straightened. "Old age catching up with you, goddess?"

"You did *not* see those white feathers. You will *never* speak of them to anyone." She twisted her head to make sure the wig covered the offending feathers. "Sparkle Stardust is a bitch, but she takes care of herself. I'll make an appointment with her hairdresser. A good color job will fix everything."

Conall would pay to see the expression on the unlucky hairdresser's face. "Anything else you need?"

"I've decided to give you and the Kavanagh female one night of sex."

After eight centuries, Morrigan had finally said something to shock him. "Why?" He wouldn't pretend he wasn't interested. Conall just hoped she didn't know how desperate that interest was.

"I've spent days trying to find out who impersonated me. If I'd had all my tail feathers, I could've appeared in my true form and scared the shit out of everyone in this cursed place. All I've been able to do, though, is listen at some doors and read a few puny human minds." If a crow had teeth, she'd be grinding them. "You know everyone here. They'll tell you things."

"And?" He guessed what was coming.

"You'll track down the pretender and in return I'll give you your night." She wiggled her butt. "My revenge will be horrific."

"So I can make love to Gerry after I give you a name." Where should he start looking? The odds were against him earning that night with Gerry.

Morrigan cocked her head to study him. "Make love to her tonight or tomorrow night or whenever you want. But it'd better be just one night."

"Aren't you afraid I'll take my reward and not give you what you want?"

Her eyes shone in the dim stairwell. "You'll come through. You know that if you try to mess with me I'll punish some unsuspecting descendant of yours. Your conscience is a weakness. Too bad for you."

Bitch.

"That's why I liked Sean so much. He was like me. His conscience was never an issue. Sean wouldn't care who I hurt as long as he got what he wanted." She sighed. "I thought of him as a son. So much potential for greatness."

And I killed his ass. Even after all these years, the thought still gave him satisfaction. He turned and continued climbing the stairs. She didn't follow.

As he stepped out onto the walkway, he was busy planning how he'd find the person who impersonated Morrigan.

"Beautiful night, isn't it?"

Startled, Conall turned toward the woman's voice. Well, so much for being alone. The three demonic vestal virgins stood smiling at him. "Yeah, nice night." Maybe they'd leave.

Instead they moved closer. All three of them were gorgeous, but they creeped him out. Blond hair, pale eyes, white dresses . . . "Did you ever think about buying some red dresses?"

They studied him a little too long. One of them finally answered. "I'm Tullia, and these are my sisters Fulvia and Varinia. We'd never wear red. It's a carnal color."

Personally, he thought a little carnality would do these women a lot of good. He glanced over the wall at the people leaving the castle after their fantasies. It must be nice not to have demons cluttering up your life.

"We noticed that you've been with Gerry a lot."

This from Fulvia, although Conall wasn't sure. They looked interchangeable. "Uh-huh." If he didn't encourage them, would they go away?

Varinia chimed in. "Ordinarily we wouldn't intrude, but

we think you should know some things about Gerry." She glanced at her sisters for confirmation. They nodded their agreement. "She's fixated on her body."

"And that's a bad thing?" So was he. It gave Gerry and him something in common.

"She'll whine about her cellulite." Varinia gave him a so-there look.

"Cellulite?"

"And when she goes to the store? She'll come home with a beer brand you hate because it was on sale," Tullia chimed in.

Conall frowned. Not buy his favorite brand? This could get ugly. It wouldn't be a deal-breaker, though.

Fulvia delivered what she probably thought was the knockout punch. "Picture this. Houston Texans. Behind by six points. Need a win to get in the playoffs. One minute left on the clock. Fourth and goal for the Texans. And . . ." She smiled with wicked glee. "Gerry grabs the remote, presses the mute button, and plants herself in front of the TV screen because she wants to discuss your relationship. When you growl at her, she asks what you're thinking. Do you tell her?"

"No. I pick her up and move her away from the screen. I don't see that as a problem."

"Argh." Fulvia's eyes glowed red, and she bared her teeth at him.

Conall exhaled wearily. "Look, I get that you don't want Gerry and me together, but there's nothing you can do to stop it. Maybe you should trot on back to hell."

"You know we're demons?" This from Varinia.

"Yeah. And you failed. Gerry and I have already made love."

The three sisters looked at each other, then they looked at Conall.

"Does anyone remember what sex feels like? I don't."

"What do we have to look forward to when we go back? Just another thousand years of freakin' chastity."

"He has a good body, and I bet his cock is very large."

"What do we have to lose?"

"What have all those centuries of virginity gotten us? No fun, and we still get PMS."

Conall didn't bother trying to put a name to each comment. The overriding message was clear. It looked as though he'd be fighting demons sooner than he'd expected.

They rushed him. His innate unwillingness to hurt a woman disappeared fast as all three flung themselves on him at once. He went down beneath the assault. Damn, he'd forgotten that they might look like women, but they had demonic strength.

Conall fought the clawed fingers that ripped his clothes from him. He managed to hold on to his briefs. Barely. Three pairs of glowing red eyes stared down at him. He had no trouble reading the sexual hunger stored up over centuries in them. The sisters smiled at him, exposing pointed demon teeth. In their excitement, they were losing their human forms.

"This isn't going to work. No matter what you want, it's not going to happen without my cooperation." He grunted as one of them threw herself across his chest while the other two tried to yank off his briefs.

Conall heaved himself to a sitting position and then to his feet dragging the three virgins with him. He fought them back and forth around the walkway. This would teach him to take his sword everywhere. When he'd thought about battling demons, fighting for his virtue was *not* what he'd had in mind.

Gerry hit the key that would send her message winging its way across cyberspace to Payton. A really short message. Yes, she still had Jinx. Yes, she had the alleged serial wife killer. And, no, she didn't know when she'd be leaving the Castle of Dark Dreams. Payton wouldn't be happy with her short report, but his happiness wasn't at the top of her priority list right now.

Shutting down her laptop, she looked at Kim, Fo, and Conalla. "Done. I appreciate you staying with me."

"Always feel free. That's what friends are for. And thanks for filling me in on what happened at the beach. Brynn will want to know the whole story." Kim tucked Fo and Conalla back in their pouches and stood to leave.

Gerry joined them. Friends. She leaned forward to give Kim a spontaneous hug. "Thanks. I'm at that in-between stage. Too weird for my old friends and too new for any vampire friends."

Fo peered up at Gerry. "Conalla wants to tell you something." Her tone suggested it wasn't a good something.

"Conalla?" Gerry would need an interpreter. She hadn't taken goo-goos and ga-gas as her second language. She stared into Conalla's rainbow eyes.

"You must tell Conall he will never be free of Morrigan's curse."

There was something creepy about that very adult message of doom delivered in a little-girl voice.

"What happened to the baby talk?" Gerry looked at Fo. "And how does she know this?"

Conalla answered both questions. "Baby talk is the expected form of communication for newborn humans, so I conformed to what would make those around me feel comfortable. But when I receive a vision of what will be, I must abandon that form of speech so everyone will understand me." She looked at Fo. "Did I do what was right, Mother?"

"Yes." But Fo's purple eyes looked sad.

Kim sighed. "Conalla has a gift. It manifested right after she was born. She sees future events. So far, they've all centered around family or friends. We're so afraid what would happen if her ability became known. But Conall is special to her, so we gave permission for her to give Conall her message." Kim tried to smile but failed. "He'll probably wish she'd kept her vision to herself."

Gerry looked back at Conalla. "Why tell me? Why not go directly to Conall?" She didn't want to be the one to watch despair fill his eyes. No, that was a cowardly thought.

Conalla stared at her from unblinking rainbow eyes. "Because you are the most important person in his life. You must choose the right moment to tell him."

Gerry could only nod while her heart bled for Conall. Her only hope was that Conalla's vision was the result of a malfunction that needed tech intervention.

But Kim wasn't finished. "One of the first things Conalla told us was that Fo mustn't be present at the final confrontation between Conall and the demon or she'll be destroyed." Kim looked torn. "I know Fo's the logical one to destroy the demon, but we can't take a chance."

"No problem." Liar. It was a huge problem. "We'll come up with a plan." On the positive side, they didn't *have* a plan yet, so it wasn't as if they'd depended on Fo and now everything would fall apart. It was just that a demon destroyer would've made things a lot easier.

"I'd better go up and see what Conall's doing." Gerry tried to look cheery, but from Kim's expression she figured she wasn't fooling anyone.

"I'll go up with you."

"Don't bother. Asima's outside the door. I'll be safe with her." *Probably.* Gerry watched as Kim left. Should she tell Conall about Conalla's prediction? Could she justify depriving him of all hope? After all, it would happen whether she told him or not.

One good thing, the prediction suggested they'd spend a long time together. So that must mean Dell wouldn't destroy Conall or her.

Gerry gave herself a mental shake. The prediction could

mean nothing, just the product of a child's imagination. Even if said child was a sentient machine.

Staring at the floor, Gerry worried over this new problem as she headed out the door to join Conall . . . and slammed into a cart pushed by Sparkle Stardust.

"Good. We caught you before you could run off."

"Uh." Gerry stared at the clothes and shoes piled high on the cart along with the ever-popular makeup case. Atop the pile, Ganymede lounged with one black paw hooked around a bag of gingersnaps.

"Hey, babe. Sparkle's here to work her magic on you. I'm the muscle. No one will interfere while I'm around."

Sparkle translated. "What he means is that he tagged along because your TV has more channels."

Gerry tried to look regretful. "Look, I'd love to stick around, because there's nothing I love more than trying on tons of clothes and stuffing my feet into dozens of shoes. But I promised I'd join Conall on the battlements."

"I totally know where you're coming from, sister. After all, the more time you spend with your immortal hot bod, the more chance there is for sex and more sex. I mean, you can try on clothes anytime." She smiled. "I noticed that Asima the Anal isn't outside your door. Must've taken a kitty-litter break."

Sparkle seemed pretty cheerful, so the castle's sex diva mustn't know that Gerry had blabbed about the bet to Banan and Destiny. Good. She couldn't handle a ticked-off cosmic troublemaker right now. "Thanks for understanding."

Sparkle shrugged. "Hey, we're flexible. Aren't we, sweetie?" She glanced at Ganymede, who'd already settled himself on the couch with the remote beside him.

"Sure." He didn't glance their way.

"That's why we'll go up with you to meet Conall. Won't we, sweetie?" Sparkle cast Ganymede a pointed stare, which he completely missed because he was already channel surfing.

"Sure." Pregnant pause. Ganymede turned his amber gaze on Sparkle. "We? Why do I have to go?" He was in full whiny-child mode.

Sparkle's sunny mood was picking up a cloud cover. "Because you're the big bad protector in this group, *sweetie*."

"I don't want to." He wouldn't meet Sparkle's gaze.

"Then I guess *I* don't want to cook that roast tonight. Oh, and I'll probably forget to bake that apple pie. Maybe I'll even accidentally throw out the ice cream I bought."

"You're a cruel woman." But he got his behind off the couch. "Besides, you don't cook. You'll just have some restaurant deliver it."

Sparkle narrowed her eyes to angry slits.

"Okay, okay, I'll come with you." He mumbled his way all the way up the stairs to the battlements.

Gerry followed in Sparkle's and Ganymede's wake wondering what she'd done in a previous life to deserve this. But all self-pity disappeared as she stepped onto the walkway atop the curtain wall. She froze and then blinked to make sure she wasn't hallucinating.

Yep, Conall was down to his briefs as he struggled with the demonic vestal virgins. The virgins didn't look too chaste and pure right now. Their hair stuck out in every direction. Their dresses were torn and dirty. And their eyes glowed with a bright red fervor. All of that fervor seemed focused on getting Conall's briefs off.

"Whoa, babe, I'm glad you dragged my ass up here. Looks like Conall's holding his own with those three hot demons." Ganymede circled the combatants yelling encouragement to Conall.

Sparkle almost bounced with excitement. "We have to help Conall. I'll take the demon with the handmade Italian shoes." She flung herself into the fray.

Gerry watched in disbelief as one the demons grabbed Conall's crotch. Who the hell did she think she was? Rage painted a red film across Gerry's vision. She welcomed the slide of her fangs, the surge of adrenaline as she raced to Conall's rescue.

"Mine!" Gerry grabbed Fulvia, or maybe it was Varinia, by her blond hair and dragged her off Conall.

Then she kicked Tullia, or maybe it was Fulvia, away from his leg. "Mine!" Good thing she'd gone for girly tonight because these sandals had a nice pointy toe. Great for kicking demon butt.

Talking of butt, Gerry threw herself on the bitch that was trying to dig her nails into Conall's luscious ass cheeks. "Mine!" Drawing back her fist, Gerry socked her. Damn, that felt good.

Gerry was just hitting her stride. She hissed her fury as she looked around for someone to sink her fangs into.

"Yo! Everyone stop now." Ganymede's booming command startled Gerry. She paused to look at him. Everyone else did, too.

"This is great, and I hate to make you guys quit, but I hear sirens. Someone called the cops." Ganymede had leaped onto the battlements and was peering into the darkness. "I don't like to step in when everything's even, three against three, but I've gotta come down on the side of my sweet tart."

Then he turned to face them. Gerry gasped. The easygoing good-old-boy black cat was gone. What had taken his place was something else entirely. Oh, the cat form was still there, but his eyes . . .

Thousands of years of wicked power looked out of those eyes. Power that made Gerry gasp for the breath she no longer needed. He was way beyond scary. Her mind might reject that scariness ratio, but the echoes of primitive ancestors reaching back to the beginning of time recognized Ganymede, and feared him.

Ganymede's gaze slid over them until it focused on the three sisters. Then they were simply gone. No muss, no fuss, just gone.

"Where'd they go?" Conall pulled on his jeans as he kept track of the police cars entering the park now.

"Probably somewhere in a South American rain forest. Could be as far south as the Antarctic, though." He leaped from the wall, and when he turned his gaze on Gerry, he was once again the entity she'd thought she knew.

"All that power. You never gave a hint. Why?" The germ of an idea was forming in Gerry's mind. "I mean, I know Edge said you were powerful, but you just didn't look the part."

Sly amusement moved in Ganymede's eyes. "I don't have to advertise, babe. Anyone who sees me in action once remembers. And those who don't know about me?" He offered her a cat shrug. "Too bad for them."

Conall pulled his torn T-shirt over his head. "The cops just went into the castle. We need to move it." He waved them toward the stairs.

They clattered down the spiral steps and when Gerry peeked into the great hall on her way to the dungeon, she saw Holgarth waving his arms as police officers argued with him. The wizard had given them time to get out of Dodge. Gerry felt almost kindly toward him. Almost.

Once safe in the dungeon with the door closed, Gerry sank onto the couch. Conall sat beside her. Ganymede leaped onto the coffee table. Conall picked up the cookies and remote the cat had left on the couch and put them next to him.

Sparkle took her hand from behind her back and waved a pair of cool shoes in the air. "Got them. I ripped these hand-made Italian cuties off that bitch Tullia's feet. The little old man who made them put his name inside." She was almost dancing in place. "I wanted to tear one of Fulvia's finger-nails off so I could match the color, but she was too slippery for me. Oh, well, the shoes were the most important."

Everyone stared silently at her.

"What?"

Gerry sighed and looked at Conall. "What happened?"

His thick hair was tousled and he still had the gleam of battle in those gorgeous gray eyes. "They were waiting for me when I got there. First they tried to discourage me from making love to you." For the first time humor crept into his voice. He looked at her and smiled. "They told me some scary things about you, lady. We'll have to talk about beer brands and who controls the remote. Oh, and I don't give a damn about your cellulite."

Cellulite? She opened her mouth to remind him she was a vampire. Vampires didn't have cellulite. Did they? Maybe they did. See, this was the kind of vampire trivia she needed to know.

Gerry shook her head to clear it. Forget the cellulite. Right now something else was more important. "Ganymede, we need your help."

Ganymede glanced away from the TV. "I don't come cheap, babe."

16

Conall made an impatient noise. "Look, we need to stop this demon. We can't predict when he'll strike again, but we can make sure he fails. Then we need to send his ass back to hell."

"Yeah, I'm listening." Ganymede bit into a gingersnap.

"Holgarth activated the gargoyles, so Dell can't dematerialize while he's in the castle. That's a point for our side." Conall couldn't read Ganymede's expression.

"You'll need a lot more than that." Crunch, crunch. "The demon can off Gerry in lots of different ways." Crunch, crunch.

"We have to work out a plan." Gerry reached over and pulled the cookie bag away from Ganymede. "And the cookie crunching is driving me crazy."

"No one takes away my cookies." Ganymede's amber eyes narrowed to angry slits.

"Okay, kiddies, time to refocus." Sparkle slipped off her own shoes and put on her spoils of war.

Conall rushed into speech before hostilities escalated.

"We need a team. Ganymede, you just showed that you can handle demons. What could you do if you had a shot at Dell?"

Ganymede speared Gerry with a death stare. Sighing, she returned his cookies.

"Get someone who can open a portal to hell, and I can send the demon back through it. Can't destroy it, though. The Big Boss won't let me kill anything anymore. Bastard." He eyed the cookies. "I don't know many beings with both the power and the knowledge to open a portal." Giving in, Ganymede dragged another cookie from the package with his paw.

Conall's patience was wearing thin. "Who?"

Ganymede bit into the cookie. "Finis, aka Edge. When your job is dealing in death, you better know how to open a few portals." Crunch, crunch. "Neither of us is a team player, though. We create as we go along." Crunch, crunch.

Gerry wore a pained expression as she glanced at Conall. "Isn't that crunching driving you nuts?"

Conall shrugged. "Not so much." He wondered what their chances were of getting any help from Edge after he discovered they'd told Banan and Destiny about the bet.

"That's because you don't have enhanced hearing. Each crunch is like a clap of thunder." She frowned. "Fine, so maybe not quite like thunder." Focusing on Ganymede, she gave him her don't-mess-with-a-vampire stare. "So what do you want in return for helping us?"

"Don't know if I *can* help you. I'm a busy guy." Ganymede yawned. "Depends on what night you need me. See, on Sunday night I watch football, drink beer, and eat pretzels. On Monday night I watch the SCI FI Channel and eat ice cream. On—"

"On Saturday night—tonight, cuddlebunny—you help Conall and Gerry catch a demon or you'll be eating bread crumbs and drinking tap water." Sparkle turned her foot one way and then the other as she admired her new shoes.

"This demon is distracting them from their lovemaking. I can't win the bet if they don't have sex. And losing isn't an option."

Ganymede looked like he was gauging how serious Sparkle was about the bread crumbs. "Okay, count me in." He turned his bad temper on Gerry. "But you'd better buy ice cream for me. Lots. Ben & Jerry's. All flavors." Muttering a few curses under his breath, he returned to his gingersnaps.

Conall caught Gerry's glance, and she gave him a thumbs-up.

Sparkle looked up from her shoes. "That means you'll have Edge to open the portal and Ganymede to send Dell through it. What else will you need?"

Edge wasn't a sure bet, but Conall didn't mention that to Sparkle. He wondered what her reaction would be when she found out what Gerry and he had down. Because she *would* find out. Nothing got by Sparkle.

"We can't just put Gerry out there as bait without some protection, but on the other hand, Dell might not make a try for her if he sees any of us hovering." Conall looked at Gerry for her ideas.

She shrugged and lobbed the ball back at him. "Haven't a clue."

"Eric specializes in sexual fantasies." Sparkle didn't meet anyone's gaze. She was once again fixated on her newest treasure.

Gerry frowned. "What does that have to do with anything?"

"Eric. I should've thought of him." Conall tended to let Sparkle's joy in all things shallow make him forget how really smart she was. He reached for his cell phone. "I'll call and ask him to drop by as soon as his last fantasy is done."

"Not until you explain what Eric has to do with protecting me." Gerry crossed her arms over her chest, the international symbol for unyielding determination.

Conall sat on his impatience. "Eric can create false re-
alities. He can make people see what he wants them to see.
That means he could make Dell think you're vulnerable to
attack when you really aren't."

Gerry nodded. "Gotcha. Sort of." She looked thoughtful
as he called Eric.

Sparkle glanced at her cart still loaded down with
clothes. "I'll bring these back later." She scooped
Ganymede and his bag of cookies off the coffee table and
plunked them on top of the pile. She pushed the cart
toward the door. "You won't have time to go through them
now. But tonight we'll pick out something sizzling and
sexy for you to wear. If you're going to be center stage,
you may as well look like the star."

Gerry put up her hand to stop Sparkle. "Oh, I almost
forgot. Morrigan wants Conall to find the person who impersonated her. Any ideas?"

"Not that I'd share with Crow Woman."

"Too bad. As a reward, the goddess said we could make
love for one night. I bet if Conall had a name to give her,
he could talk her into a few more nights." Gerry widened
her eyes as if a thought had just occurred to her. "Wow, if
we had permission to make love for three or four nights,
you'd probably win your bet."

Sparkle's eyes gleamed with sudden interest. "Yeah?
Hmm. Well, you know I hate to rat out anyone, but I seem
to remember seeing Asima changing into a crow. Don't tell
Asima I said that. She gets all homicidal about every little
thing."

"Thanks." Gerry didn't look convinced.

"Morrigan sent me an e-mail—guess she didn't have
the guts to show up in person—asking for the name of my
hairdresser. She didn't explain why, but no way was I
going to ruin my relationship with Stella by sending
Creepy Crow to her." Sparkle's smile was so wicked it
made Gerry shiver. "I pointed her toward Happening Hair.

They specialize in the unusual, and you don't get more un-usual than Morrigan." Sparkle offered a finger wave as she left.

Conall waited until Sparkle and Ganymede were gone before looking at Gerry. "Think there's any truth in what she said about Asima?"

Gerry shrugged. "Who knows. Sparkle can't stand Asima or Morrigan, so she'd love to see them trying to kill each other. And I can't see Asima wanting to bring us to-gether. She's all about protecting you."

Another possibility made him frown. "We still don't know if Dell is working on his own or for someone else. If Asima brought you here and then you died, I'd be released from Morrigan's curse. For whatever reason, Bast cares about what happens to me, so if Asima engineered my freedom, it'd raise her stock with Bast."

"I don't know. That seems kind of convoluted. Asima strikes me as pretty straightforward. If she knew who I was ahead of time, why even bring me here? She could've killed me and made it look like I died on the job." Gerry sighed. "I guess we'll just have to wait until we get our hands on Dell."

"I know you described Dell before, but is there anything else you remember that you didn't tell me?"

She got that cute crease between her eyes that signaled deep thought. "Nothing that I . . . Wait. When I first saw Dell on the pirate ship, I thought he sort of reminded me of my uncle Ray. It was just a passing thought, and I guess the only reason it occurred to me was because they both had red hair."

Conall's inner radar went off with flashing lights and screaming sirens. Incoming revelation. But it was still not close enough to eyeball. He'd roll it around in his mind until he made a connection.

Someone knocked on the door, and Gerry glanced at her watch. "Must be Eric. The fantasies end at four o'clock.

It's amazing that some people wander around the park until dawn."

Conall opened the door and Eric strode past him. The vampire settled into a chair while Conall returned to the couch. "What's up?"

"We need a favor." Gerry looked a little uneasy.

She was probably wondering what price Eric would demand for his help. Conall knew Eric didn't attach strings to his friendship.

"*Two* favors." Conall caught Gerry's surprised glance from the corner of his eyes.

"Ask away." Eric yawned, reminding Conall that they needed to wrap up plans for tonight before dawn.

Unable to sit still any longer, Gerry got up and walked over to Houston. The plant would need a two-week orgy to restore it to bold and bushy. She'd love to accommodate the poor guy, but she didn't see it happening anytime soon. But one night would do for now.

She turned to look at Eric. "Sparkle mentioned that you can alter the appearance of reality."

Eric nodded. "Go ahead."

"We're going to try to trap Dell tonight. We hope Edge will agree to open a portal to hell, and Ganymede has agreed to cast the demon through the portal." She stroked one of Houston's poor scraggly leaves. So deprived. Gerry knew exactly how he felt.

Conall picked up where she'd left off. "I don't think Dell will make a try for her if he sees a bunch of would-be rescuers hanging around. But she can't be left open to a sneak attack. And that's what it'll be because he knows Gerry can put a hurting on him if he comes out into the open."

"I guess you want me to create a reality where she's an open target." Eric didn't even blink.

Gerry wondered what it would take to upset Eric. Maybe she didn't want to know. "I'd like to be in the room, but not where Dell sees me. When he attacks, it'll look like I'm dead. Morrigan has agreed to show up and pretend to release Conall from the curse. Dell will think it's all legit."

"And then?"

Conall's expression turned coldly dangerous. "Then he'll attack me. After all, I'll be a weak human, easy for a demon to kill. And I won't be immortal anymore. The odds will all be in his favor."

At which point, Edge and Ganymede could do their things and Dell would be gone forever. She hoped. Their plan was still a little too sketchy for her, built on the assumption that everything would run smoothly. Nothing had run smoothly since she stepped into the Castle of Dark Dreams.

"Sounds like a reasonable plan. Let's hope the demon falls for it. You wanted a second favor?"

"Yeah." Conall cast a quick glance her way and grinned. "Morrigan has given Gerry and me one night to make love."

Gerry cringed. Did he have to tell everyone?

"Tonight we go to war. We want the lovemaking that comes before it to be memorable."

Memorable. Such a bland word for what Conall and she would share. Gerry knew what Conall had left unsaid. If they didn't win the battle with Dell, if Morrigan never gave them another night, this might be all they had. No, she refused to believe there wouldn't be centuries of nights together.

Conall met Eric's gaze. "You did a fantasy for Brynn and Kim. They've never stopped talking about it. I'd owe you big time if you'd do one for Gerry and me." He took a deep breath. "I don't have any special fantasy in mind, but Gerry does." Conall looked expectantly at her.

Oh, no. Gerry couldn't tell Eric about her fantasy. The words just wouldn't come out of her mouth.

Eric didn't say anything, he just stared at her. Then a

smile touched his mouth, and Gerry was once again reminded what a beautiful man he was.

"You don't have to tell me. I already know. Hope you don't mind me slipping into your thoughts." Eric leaned his head back against the chair and stared at the ceiling. "Tree trunks. Interesting fantasy. Sometimes, though, we don't really want what we think we want." He shifted his gaze to Gerry. "I'll come to the dungeon right after I rise. We'll do it then." Standing, he walked to the door. "I feel the dawn, and Donna's probably wondering where I am. See you guys tonight."

Gerry waited until he'd closed the door behind him. Then she turned to Conall. "How is this all going to work out? There're so many intangibles. And what about the hotel guests? Won't we be putting them in danger?"

He pushed to his feet and pulled off his shirt. "We need everything to look normal or else Dell will know it's a trap. But he's not interested in anyone except you and me. So unless they get in his way, bystanders should be safe."

Gerry tried to ignore the play of muscles across his bare back as she worried the problem like a favorite chew toy. "How can we be sure?"

He turned to face her. "We won't know until we talk to Edge. If he won't work with us, we don't have a plan. If he's okay with everything, we'll see what we can do to make sure there's no collateral damage."

She nodded. Sleep tugged at her, turning her thoughts fuzzy. No use trying to think anymore. Anything she came up with this close to dawn would probably be useless. "You need sleep. Do we have to drag Fo down here to play lookout for us?"

"I should've asked Eric to put a mind shield over our door. The bad part about the shield is it stops all traffic until he removes it. I wouldn't be able to get out until sunset." He reached for the button on his jeans and then paused. "I'll get Asima in here. Let her earn her money from Bast."

Gerry wasn't sure she liked that idea. "But what if she's—"

"She's not. I think you're right. If she wanted you dead, she would've taken care of it before this. Besides, even if she wanted to hurt you, she wouldn't do it now."

Gerry admired the pure maleness of his stride as he headed for the door. "What's going to stop her?"

Glancing over his shoulder, he grinned at her. "Me. I'll be sleeping in bed with you. And to make sure you're completely safe, I'll just wrap myself around you."

How absolutely delicious. The crappy part? She wouldn't be able to enjoy one single minute of it. Sleeping like the dead sucked lemons.

17

Noise. Lots of noise. She tried to calculate the amount of energy it would take to put her pillow over her head. Nah, too hard. She'd have to lift her arm.

"I think this silky purple top, black leather pants, and silver metallic stilettos say kick-ass-but-sexy heroine. Why is she still asleep? The sun set fifteen minutes ago." Sparkle.

"Wake her up, O'Rourke. We had a deal, and she broke it. So I have a special delivery for her." Edge.

"Where does she keep her jewelry? Does she have any good pieces?" Jinx.

"You know, I have this great fantasy worked out for you and Gerry, but you have to lose the audience first." Eric.

Gerry might've opted to keep her eyes closed all night if she hadn't remembered that lovemaking with Conall was on the schedule. Surrendering to the inevitable, she opened them . . . and gazed up at a circle of faces.

"Goody, you're awake." Sparkle's amber eyes gleamed with excitement. "I brought you this totally sensual outfit for tonight." She paused. "Try not to get any blood on it."

"I had a visit from Banan and Destiny this morning." Edge's expression suggested that begging for her life would do no good. "They told me about your little confession."

"What confession?"

Edge ignored Sparkle's question. "Normally, I would've just killed you, but since they seemed pretty happy with each other, I may let it slide." He offered her a tight smile. "But I feel completely justified in returning your . . . friend."

"Hi." Jinx grinned his happy-ferret grin at her. "I'm glad I'm back with you guys. Edge wasn't any fun. I couldn't find the dude's jewelry stash. That's major frustration for a professional like me. Where do you keep *your* stuff?"

Conall smiled down at her. "I figured you'd want them to take their shots right away and then I could kick them all out."

"Hello? Sparkle Stardust standing right here while Edge ignores her question. This irritates me. I am *so* not fun when I'm pissed." She made ugly eyes at Edge. "What confession?"

Edge's gaze darkened as he stared back at Sparkle. "I'll tell you later. And don't threaten me, lady." The sharp, angry points of power from both troublemakers jabbed at everyone in the room.

Gerry groaned. Her brain was wide awake now and busy making a list of all the things that would, should, or might happen tonight. So much to worry about when all she wanted to do was make love with Conall.

"Edge, we need to talk." Conall's comment snapped the dangerous tension building between Edge and Sparkle.

"Pay attention, sister. I've left your outfit for tonight on the chair and the rest of the clothes hanging on the handcuffs. Check out your choices for sensual sleepwear, because those jammies you have on now would qualify as nightmare-wear." Sparkle gave Gerry a speculative glance and Edge a furious one before slamming from the room.

Gerry didn't want to be anywhere around when those two sat down for their friendly chat. Thank heaven Edge hadn't blurted everything out here. She couldn't take a full-blown battle before she even got out of bed.

Next, Conall turned his attention to Jinx. "You. Go to your room. Do. Not. Leave."

"Sure, sure."

Conall might scare Jinx, but Gerry knew the shifter wouldn't be able to control his larcenous impulses for long.

Gerry admitted that Conall had handled things better than she would have. She'd have gotten into it with Edge about returning Jinx and probably ruined any chance of convincing him to help tonight. And yelling at Jinx would've had no effect besides raising her blood pressure. Oops, no blood pressure.

Her admission sort of surprised Gerry. She was starting to relax with Conall, not always thinking she had to do everything. It was nice to be able to share responsibilities. This boded well for their partnership.

As Gerry climbed from the bed, she glanced longingly at the indentation of Conall's head on the pillow beside her. From now on, maybe he could go to bed a little before dawn and then climb back into bed right after sunset so she could get that great feeling of falling asleep and waking up with her man.

From now on? Reality check. She was assuming a lot if she thought he'd want to fall asleep and wake up with her for longer than it took her to check out of the castle. He'd be forced to go wherever she chose to take him. And if she decided to tell him about Conalla's prediction? No, she wouldn't be his favorite vampire.

Grabbing Sparkle's new outfit, she hurried into the bathroom. Hey, she was no dummy. Her last girlie outfit was a hit with Conall, so she'd see what reaction this one got.

When she finally emerged, she was tugging at the tiny piece of silky material Sparkle had laughingly called a top. Nope, no way was there enough to cover up her tummy. And the stilettos were incredible-looking, but she'd have to kick them off to do any serious running.

Okay, so she'd stay positive. Dell would fall into their hands like an overripe apple with worm still in residence. No pursuing required.

Eric was busy on his PDA, Edge was studying the iron maiden, and Conall was looking at her.

"What can I say?" Conall's gaze was gray smoke backed by hot flame.

Something joyous and giddy bubbled inside her where only worry and fear should be. "Don't say anything. Just keep looking at me that way."

Edge turned to Conall and Gerry. "Talk. I have to get back to that damn candy store. I'm looking forward to a serious discussion with Sparkle about who's on top."

Gerry gathered her courage and jumped right in. "We need another favor." No use working up to it gradually.

He raised one tawny brow. "And the other favors I've granted have worked out so well for me."

She chose to remain calm in the face of whatever snarkiness he flung her way. "You're right. And I'm sorry for that. But you did say Banan and Destiny were happy with each other. Conall and I were the ones who brought them together. So technically we helped you."

Edge thought about that and then nodded. "What do you want?"

"We're working up a plan to trap the demon tonight and then send him home. Ganymede recommended you for the job of portal-to-hell opener. Do you want all the details now?"

He shook his head. "Don't need to know. Just tell me

when and where to show up. Scratch the where. There's only one place in the castle where a portal can be opened, the hearth in the great hall."

Conall frowned. "Tonight's the Vampire Ball. The great hall will be crowded with humans."

"Cancel it." Edge, a man of few words.

"If things don't look normal, Dell will suspect a trap." Argh! So many details to worry about. Fine, so Gerry wanted all the planning over so Conall and she could be alone.

Eric joined the conversation. "We can cancel it and still make things look normal. I'll call in some favors." His smile was all wicked anticipation. "I'll contact a few vampires I know. Tonight, the great hall will be filled with the real deal. Vampires love a battle between good and evil. Sure, they don't always know which side to root for, but that won't get in the way of their fun." He grew thoughtful. "It would make it easier for me if I let them in on what's going down, but with that many vampires, one of them might accidentally give things away. Besides, I don't trust all of them. Someone might tip off the demon."

Conall still seemed uncertain.

Eric looked like he was mentally rubbing his hands together. "The reality I create will blow everyone away. I can make the vampires appear human to the demon so he doesn't get nervous. Gerry can stand in front of the hearth while I make it look like Conall's talking to Holgarth, Brynn, and me on the other side of the great hall. I'm counting on Dell figuring he has her trapped between him and the fireplace. All he has to do is wait until her back is to him and then stake her. I'm betting on his ego being big enough for him to think he can kill her and still get away."

Gerry's head was beginning to spin. Not a comforting sensation. "Okay, break it down for me. Where will everyone *really* be?"

For the first time, Eric looked uneasy. "This is the tough

part. Conall and the rest of us will be in the crowd surrounding you. We'll only be a few feet away."

"Uh-huh. Sounds good. But where will *I* be?"

"Umm . . ."

"Umm" was not good. From long experience, Gerry
knew that any sentence starting with "umm" would end
badly for her.

"Manipulating the minds of two people is no problem.
But this time you're asking me to work with a roomful of
mostly nonhumans. I can't let any of the vampires in the
hall see what Dell's doing because they might scare him
off. So I have to change all those perceptions at exactly the
right moment for this to work." He met Gerry's gaze. "The
only way I can pull this off is if I save you till last. You'll
be standing exactly where Dell sees you standing. But just
as the demon is ready to strike, I'll switch all my concentration to the two of you. He'll miss you."

"Uh-huh."

"But not by much."

"Ooookay." Gerry glanced at Conall. Here's where he'd
jump in to nix the "not by much" part. She already had her
mouth open to refute his argument.

He met her gaze and remained silent. Nothing in his expression revealed his emotions.

"Thank you." She smiled at him. He trusted her to make
the right decision. Without him. Probably one of the hardest things he'd ever done.

She looked back at Eric. "What time?"

"That's up to you." What Eric didn't say was it depended on how long she and Conall wanted for their
fantasy.

Try forever. "Let's go for two a.m."

Edge looked impatient. He wasn't a detail type guy. "I
have the time and place. I'll be there." Without further
comment, he left.

Conall finally spoke. "I don't want Dell sent back to

hell until I know what his game is. He could still be working for someone else. Can we do that without endangering Gerry more than she already is?"

Eric nodded. "Once he thinks he's killed Gerry, we'll surround him before he can escape. Since he can't disappear, he'll be trapped. Morrigan will make her appearance and declare Gerry officially dead and you human again. If we assume this is what the demon's been waiting for, he should jump at the chance to battle you."

"Battle Conall?" Had she missed something? Conall fighting a demon wasn't acceptable.

When had she grown so protective of him? A few days ago, the plan would've sounded fine to her. He was immortal, for heaven's sake. But now? Everything inside her tightened at even the suggestion he might get hurt. Why? *You know why. Self-deceit is not an admirable character trait.*

"Uh, maybe it's just me, but I can't seem to remember when the Conall-battling-demon decision was made." She tried to look bland, definitely *not* freaked out. Conall had just let her make her own decision, so she'd have to do the same for him. Damn.

Eric smiled. "I have a few years on you, Gerry. That means I can rise a little before sunset. Conall and I talked while we waited for you to wake up."

"Oh." It didn't sound like a gracious, approving "oh." It sounded like an I-can't-believe-you-did-this "oh." So she wasn't a great actress. Sue her.

Conall exhaled deeply and raked his fingers through his hair. "Understand why I have to do this. I'm a warrior. You can dress me up in jeans and a T-shirt, but the heart of me still lives in my ancient roots. I need to personally defeat this thing that's almost taken your life."

Uh-oh. He was going all medieval on her. "Isn't that being a little self-indulgent? I don't want you putting yourself in danger for me." *Not when I love you.* The thought came so easily, so naturally. And it rang so true.

His stare was all hard alpha male. "I allowed you to choose. Do the same for me."

He had her. She couldn't refuse him. "How do you see the battle playing out?"

"I'll back the demon into the hearth, Edge will open the portal, and Ganymede will fling Dell into hell. Then Edge will close the portal."

Then what? She didn't have the courage to look beyond the battle.

So Gerry forced herself to relax and concentrate on what would come before the battle. "Fantasy time!" Jeez, she sounded ten years old again. Only then it was, "Disney World time!" But it was still all about the fantasy.

"Why don't you guys get comfortable on the bed." Eric leaned against the door and crossed his arms over his broad chest.

Conall didn't hesitate. He flung himself onto the bed and folded his hands behind his head. "This better be good, Eric. I've had to listen to Brynn bragging on you until I thought my ears would start bleeding. You have a lot to live up to."

"Hey, I'm good." Eric looked expectantly at Gerry.

Gerry joined Conall on the bed, but she wasn't quite as confident as he was. "We could always just make love the old-fashioned way. This bed is nice." She patted it. "Soft, comfy. A making-love bed."

"Getting cold feet, Kavanagh?" Conall grinned at her.

Actually, yes. Nerves made her hands and feet cold and clammy. "I want to believe this is going to be a defining moment in my sexual life, but I can't help having doubts. Logic tells me it can't be that good."

"Be prepared to say good-bye to logic." Eric captured her gaze. "I took a look into your mind, Gerry. I slipped right on past your surface thoughts and the fantasy you *said* you wanted. I went deeper and found something else altogether."

She frowned. "Hope you had a good time rattling around in there."

Eric grinned. "The mind never ceases to amaze me. Oh, and thank Conall for your fantasy. What I found in your subconscious would never be *his* favorite fantasy. But when I told him about it, he didn't hesitate. He wanted you to have the fantasy that burned brightest for *you*."

Horrified, she stared at Eric. "You told him what was in my subconscious?"

"Sure did. You'll be living it in a few minutes anyway." He was unrepentant.

If she had the nerve, she'd ask Eric to tell her what he'd found in her mind, because she hadn't a clue. But then he'd say it out loud. Total embarrassment.

Puzzled, Gerry watched Eric straighten and open the door. "I don't get it. Is that all there is?"

"Pretty much." He looked amused. "Every time I met your gaze tonight, I was imprinting the fantasy in your mind. Once I leave, all you have to do is relax, close your eyes, and it'll come."

Gerry didn't think so. She could never fall asleep on Christmas Eve when she was a kid because she knew Santa was coming. This was sort of the same concept. "Will we have any free will, or have you scripted everything?"

Eric held up his hands. "It'll unfold the way you want it to. All I do is put you in the situation and give you the belief that it's all real. The rest is up to you."

Gerry glanced at Conall. "You buy into this?"

"Donna, Brynn, and Kim all said Eric's fantasy was one of the highlights of their sexual lives, so I guess, yes, I do buy into it."

"Okay, I can do this." She rubbed her clammy hands on the sheet. "Don't we have to get undressed?"

Eric shrugged. "It's your call. It won't make any difference to the fantasy." He glanced into the hallway. "Asima's asleep out here. Do you want me to shield both your doors? Wouldn't want any interruption right at the best part."

Conall nodded. "Sounds good. And would you shield Jinx's door, too? I don't want to come out of the fantasy to find he's lifted Holgarth's sorcerer's ring."

"Call me when you want the shield gone." Eric gave the iron maiden a friendly swat as he passed it. "Ah, the good old days, when death was still creative." Winking at Gerry, he left.

"Wow, I can't believe Eric's power." Why was she talking about Eric's power? Why didn't she just close her eyes and relax. Because her eyes were glued wide open, that's why.

"You won't lose control during the fantasy, vampire lady."

She frowned. "Of course I will. I mean, that's been my sexual fantasy forever. Being chased through the woods by this savage."

"And you've been lying to yourself."

Gerry blinked. "Is that what Eric saw?"

"Yep."

"It's *my* mind. Why didn't I know?"

"You wanted to believe your version. You wanted to believe you could be different from what you were because . . ."

"Wanting to be in control and being supercompetitive was okay for my brother, but I always got the feeling Mom and Dad didn't approve of me being the same way. It wasn't 'feminine.' So I figured I could at least live down to my parents' expectations in my fantasy."

Something seemed to pop inside her, and suddenly she felt free. Finally, she understood.

Conall reached across to clasp her hand. "A strong woman is sexy. She needs a strong man to match wits with, though. Otherwise boredom will set in, and she'll run amok raising bloody hell."

"Run amok? Bloody hell?" She smiled. Sometimes in the midst of his contemporary speech patterns, Conall would throw in phrases that reminded her of his long past. "And you know this because?"

"I just know."

"That's an Asima answer." Laughing, she closed her eyes and at last let herself relax.

When nothing immediately happened, she didn't know whether to go limp with relief or be really disappointed. But she'd give it another few minutes and then . . .

18

Suddenly, Satona opened her eyes. What was she doing just lying around? Tonight was the annual Mate-Hunting celebration. It was the one night of the year when a female vampire who was ready to claim a mate could go into the Sensual Forest and hunt down one of the savage males that lurked there.

Of course, the aforementioned savage males weren't vampires, so they didn't have much chance of escaping once one of the Sisters of the Night picked up their trail.

Even though the Sisters could've claimed any of the many males living outside the forest, the males who called the forest home were so potent, so totally sexual, that every Sister wanted one for herself.

Well, tonight was her night. Satona climbed from her bed, carefully readied herself, and then left her house. The other members of her sisterhood waited for her.

"Oooh, I love the sparkly champagne tint you used on your nipples, Satona. Very sexy." Meerit almost thrummed with excitement.

"The champagne thong that matches your nipples is sooo sensual. I wish I'd thought of it." Tahira twirled for all to admire her naked perfection. "I'm just me tonight."

Satona laughed. "And that'll be much more than any male can handle." The ten Sisters surrounding her were either naked like Tahira, or wore a bare minimum like Satona. She'd chosen to tint her nipples and wear a thong because she thought a few subtle accessories made her body sexier.

She glanced up. "A full moon. The hunting will be good tonight." The darkness called to her. Even if Satona hadn't been a vampire, she'd love the night—its shadowed secrets, its danger. She shivered in anticipation.

Chiva held up her hand. "It's time, Sisters. May you all achieve orgasms so powerful you'll have to sleep for three straight days."

With shouting and laughter, the Sisters of the Night swept into the Sensual Forest.

Once among the trees, everyone separated. Satona became one with the forest, a stealthy shadow stalking her prey. An unskilled female wouldn't catch a forest male. But she was one of the sisterhood's greatest hunters. A male would be hers tonight.

It didn't take her long to pick up a trail. She found proof of his passing, a discarded ticket stub for one of the ritualistic male events called football. Satona moved faster now, gaining on her prey. There, she spotted a further sign of his passing, a tab from a metal container that held a forest male's favorite drink, beer.

She'd never tasted beer, but since the forest males were a primitive species, she assumed their beverages would be bitter and nothing a Sister of the Night would enjoy.

Satona thought of the smooth muscular neck of the male she hunted, and the hot blood pumping beneath his skin. She peeled back her lips to expose her fangs. Now *there* was a drink worth sampling.

Startled, she realized the male had led her into the heart of the Sensual Forest, where the magical trees grew. A Sister was allowed to hunt in the Sensual Forest only once in her life, so Satona knew she'd have only this one chance to experience what older vampires only whispered of.

She quickened her pace. The male she hunted was fast and clever, but he didn't have her enhanced senses or her preternatural speed.

Suddenly, she burst into a small clearing dominated by one enormous tree. She stared, awed. Its massive trunk, thick branches, and gold-tipped leaves proclaimed that this was the storied Tree of Eternal Pleasure.

Satona gasped. Few even from the sisterhood had ever seen this tree. But it was the male standing in front of the tree that held her complete attention.

He was all a forest male should be. With feet planted wide and eyes narrowed in defiance, he was six feet plus of naked, muscular, male animal.

Forest males who'd been captured and brought back to be the mates of other Sisters rarely spoke. Satona thought this was an admirable characteristic. Vampire males had an opinion on everything.

So she wasn't surprised when he said nothing. His low warning growl warned her off. A challenge. Yes! She wouldn't want a mate who whimpered and cowered. Of course, she'd have to be in control, but she also needed a male who didn't fear her.

Satona knew her smile was sensual, promising that he'd enjoy being her mate. All males desired the Sisters of the Night for their erotic knowledge and insatiable sexual appetites. Lucky male.

The lucky male didn't look like he appreciated the honor she was about to bestow on him. Oh well, it wouldn't be any fun if he groveled at her feet. She smiled with wicked anticipation. Anything he did with her body wouldn't be aimed at her feet.

She inched toward him, watching his eyes for a hint of when he'd launch himself at her. Lord, he was magnificent close up.

His bared body gleamed in the moonlight, a play of light and shadow in the darkness. His broad chest rose and fell, proof of the strong heart pumping all that glorious blood through him. He had the sculpted pecs and washboard abs all forest males had, but he somehow seemed bigger, more impressive here in his natural habitat.

She slid her gaze past his chest and stomach to admire his thighs, all powerful muscle and sinew. His legs had the strength needed to run for miles. It spoke much of his courage that he chose to make his stand here instead of forcing her to chase him until he dropped from exhaustion.

"Who are you?" His voice was a harsh rasp of anger.

"Satona." Deliberately, she shifted her gaze to his sexual organs. If she could breathe, she'd be gulping for air. She'd seen male vampires naked, but none of them came close to *this*. Even though the male was not sexually excited yet, his shaft showed promise of huge size. And his sacs hung large and heavy between his thighs.

She would've asked his name, but it wasn't his name she hunted tonight. Only his body mattered, and all the pleasure it would give her over the years until she discarded it for the body of a male vampire. Because the Sisters of the Night could only keep their beautiful savages for ten years. Those ten years were their pleasure years. When their time was up, they had to do their duty by mating with one of their own kind.

"You're a Sister of the Night. Only your sisterhood would dare stalk their mate to the very center of the Sensual Forest." He narrowed gray eyes that shone silver in the moonlight and tightened his sexy lips into a stubborn line. "Your hunt is useless. I don't wish to be your pleasure mate."

She'd throw out a few incentives, although Satona

hoped he'd reject them. She looked forward to a battle. "I have a big-screen TV and an endless supply of beer." The beer was a lie, but how hard would it be to find some? "You can watch primitive sporting events such as football and NASCAR." When he wasn't sharing his yummy body with her.

He raised one dark brow. "You think to bribe me? The sisterhood wants forest males only for sex."

She frowned. "Is something wrong with that?"

"I'll choose my own mate."

He turned his back to her, prepared to walk away. Satona lost precious seconds admiring the smooth play of muscles in his back and the firm perfection of his butt cheeks. She'd been truly blessed in finding him.

None of the other Sisters would come even close to capturing a male like the one who was walking away from her. *Walking away?* No. Reaching for her power, she gathered it to her, and then flung it outward.

With a startled yell, the male was flung face-first against the Tree of Eternal Pleasure and held there, spread-eagled.

Mine, all mine. Ten years wouldn't be nearly enough to explore all the sexual possibilities with him. She wouldn't hold him against the tree for long, though. After all, males had fragile egos. She didn't want him to feel completely powerless, even though he was.

"If you promise to stay, I'll release you." Perhaps not just yet, though. "But first I'd like to touch you." She wisely didn't ask his permission.

Surprisingly, he laughed. "Go ahead, touch me."

Strange. Where was the anger, the threats? Satona decided not to think the whole thing to death.

Moving up behind him, she ran her palms across the warm, smooth expanse of his back. If she didn't know better, she'd almost believe she felt a light tingling in them. "You have a wonderful back. I look forward to snuggling up to it on a cold winter day."

"What do you know about the Tree of Eternal Pleasure?"

Satona frowned. What did that have to do with anything? "Not much. I know it sits at the very center of the Sensual Forest. And there are legends hinting of its magical powers. Only a few have ever even seen it."

She wasn't interested in the Tree right now. For some reason, she felt a little dizzy. She was vampire. Vampires didn't feel dizzy or experience any other human weaknesses. It was probably just the excitement of capturing her very own pleasure mate.

But as the dizziness increased, she slid to her knees. That was okay, because now she was in a perfect position to glide her fingers over his butt, that firm and deliciously masculine monument to sin and temptation. Forcing herself to ignore her wooziness, she squeezed each cheek just to make sure they weren't the products of clever implants. No, they were as real as her growing desire.

He clenched his buttocks, and she smiled. Leaning forward, she kissed each luscious cheek.

"Do you feel a strangeness, vampire woman?" His husky voice was so sexy it banished her dizziness for a moment.

"I'll be fine." Well, maybe.

The unusual physical sensation made her uneasy. Perhaps it was this place. Over the centuries, a few of the sisterhood had never returned from the forest. It was so rare that no one thought too much about it. Satona thought of it now. She needed to leave the forest with her mate.

"I'm going to release you, and then we'll leave the forest. Don't try to flee because I can stop you with my mind. Once we reach my home, you'll realize how fortunate you were to be chosen." She struggled to her feet, trying to keep from swaying.

"Maybe the Tree doesn't want you to leave." The husky

voice she'd thought was so sexy a few minutes ago now took on a sinister tone.

"I don't think I have to ask the Tree's permission." As a new wave of dizziness hit her, she fell against his back and reached around him to brace her hands against the Tree's trunk.

As soon as her palms touched the bark, she got a sinking feeling. *A sinking-into-the-tree feeling.* What the . . . ?

Absolute horror froze her vocal cords as the Tree of Eternal Pleasure slowly absorbed them. It was like falling in slow motion with nothing to support her, nothing to break her fall. But she didn't fall. The male wrapped his arms around her as they drifted in a sea of white nothing.

"The Tree has chosen us." He sounded surprised.

Not as surprised as she was. "What do you mean? Where are we? How do we get back?"

"We're one with the Tree now. Later it'll give us a choice." He sounded in awe of this kidnapping Tree.

"I'll make my choice now instead of later." Frantically, she looked around but saw only the endless white. "Tree." She felt stupid talking to a tree. "Send me home right now or . . ." No immediate threats came to mind.

"The Tree doesn't react to threats." She thought she heard laughter in his voice. "It'll give us a choice when it's finished with us."

Finished with us? She had a gruesome mental picture of the giant tree turning them into liquid plant food. Fear crawled up her spine. What good did it do her to be a powerful vampire now?

"Don't you feel it? The Tree is speaking to us."

"What's it saying?" She hoped it was apologizing for detaining them unnecessarily.

Then *she* felt it, too. If this was the Tree's language, it was one of sensation and emotion. No words were needed.

Satona's fear drifted away as she became acutely aware

of the male who still held her—the sensual texture of his skin wherever it touched her body, his scent of deep forests and dark nights, and a need to merge with every particle of his powerful life force.

Against her mind's express command, she turned her face into his chest and slid her tongue across his warm flesh. His taste unleashed a sexual hunger so strong it would've brought her to her knees if she'd had something to kneel on.

He groaned as he lowered his head to take her mouth. She caught his sexy lower lip between her teeth and tugged. When she released him, he traced her lips with his tongue before transferring his attention to the rest of her mouth. She matched his passion, silently demanding, begging. As her need grew, she welcomed the slide of her fangs. He acknowledged that need by touching the tip of each fang with his tongue.

They rolled in the white nothing that seemed suddenly filled with phantom fingers that slid along their skin, each touch increasing their hunger for each other.

He abandoned her mouth and floated lower until he could mold her breasts with his large hands.

And then he dipped his head to capture her nipple between his lips. He scraped his teeth lightly across the hard nub before drawing it into his mouth where he teased it with his magic tongue.

Somewhere during his magic tongue demonstration he slipped off her thong. She barely noted its disappearance into the whiteness.

Satona buried her fingers in his long dark hair to anchor herself. She was afraid if she didn't, she'd float away into the white nothing never to feel his mouth on her again. Throwing back her head, she moaned her pleasure.

Her moan echoed in the stillness and returned to her in faint whispers of erotic pleasure. It seemed they floated in a cocoon that fed their passion, their hunger for each other.

Once he'd teased both nipples to screaming points of sensitivity, she slid down his body, eager to prove that her tongue was no less magic than his. She flicked each male nipple until he made inarticulate sounds of pleasure. Then she used the tip of her tongue to draw lines of sizzling temptation over his chest and stomach, all intersecting at her point of final destination.

She nudged his thighs apart, and as he spread his legs she clenched around desire so powerful she had to bite her lip to keep from screaming.

The white nothing swirled around them, agitated ripples fanning out from their bodies. It seemed almost to pulse in time to the pounding of her heart. Heart? She had no heart. But it was as if the whiteness remembered what it had once been like, the excitement, the living joy of it.

Satona skimmed her fingers along his inner thighs, memorizing the sensory thrill of hard muscle beneath warm, smooth skin. Then she put her mouth on each of his sacs, stretched tight now by his arousal. The tactile connection between them dragged a gasp from him.

As she transferred her attention to his cock, she could almost hear the battering of her common sense against the closed door of her mind. Nothing mattered now except what they were doing. She'd let her common sense out later.

"Stay with me, Sister of the Night. Forever." The male's fevered murmur was a siren call, one she didn't understand.

What she did understand were the things she wanted to do with his body. Satona trailed her fingers along the impressive length of his cock before measuring its thickness by pressing it between her breasts. It filled up the space nicely. The tales told about the sexual organs of the forest males were true. She sighed her satisfaction.

Then she circled the head with her tongue before covering it with her lips. And as she slid her mouth over his shaft, he moved his hips in the beginning of the instinctual thrust-and-retreat rhythm of sex.

Her own sexual excitement was starting to spiral out of control as she tightened her lips around him and glided up and down, up and down. The Sisters of the Night knew all there was to know about a male's pleasure, and Satona used those skills now with her teeth, tongue, and fingers.

With a muttered curse, the male clasped her shoulders, forcing her to release him. But before she could question him, he'd drifted to between her legs and brought her to his mouth.

Oooh, yes. She wanted this. And as his warm breath touched her, she opened herself to whatever he chose to do. What he chose to do was to use his tongue to flick and tease the most sensitive sexual spot on her body until she writhed with her need for release.

Satona grabbed his hair and yanked. "I don't care what other things you have on your list of ways to drive a female crazy, skip to the last one *right now*."

His soft laughter shivered along every one of her nerve endings. "My exact thought, but we have a problem."

Problem? No, there could absolutely *not* be a problem. If he didn't fill her within the next thirty seconds, she'd explode into a million shards of sexually frustrated female.

"We have nothing to brace ourselves against."

She looked wildly around. Nothing, just the ever-present whiteness. Sure, the male could pull her to him and enter her, but where would the thrusting, plunging, and all the other movements that guaranteed a spectacular orgasm come from if she couldn't brace herself against something?

Well, the Tree of Eternal Pleasure had gotten them into this, so it could just provide the necessities. "Tree, we need a trunk here."

She felt it against her back and buttocks, the solid roughness of tree bark. Satona arched her back, reveling in the joyous freedom of her body naked to the male's gaze.

"Now . . ." She stared into his gray eyes and frowned. There was something she should remember. Then she smiled. "*Now*, Conall."

Heat flared in his gaze as he reached around her to clasp her cheeks in his large hands. Easily, he lifted her and eased her onto his erection. And as he braced his hands against the trunk, she wrapped her arms and legs around him.

He froze as she slowly let her body sink onto his cock, taking his hard length into her, focusing every bit of her concentration on the feel of him stretching and filling her.

She could feel his arms trembling from the strain of trying to remain still. Leaning into his chest, she whispered the magic words. "Let's stuff all this empty space with so much passion it'll ooze from the tree's leaves." Then she spoke his name. A name she shouldn't know, but did. A name that somehow was very important to her. "Conall."

Without answering her, he began to move. Pressing her back against the bark, he slid almost out of her and then thrust back in. And as he moved into the rhythm of sex, she used his shoulders to brace herself.

She felt the familiar pressure building, the delicious heaviness along with a damp readiness that signaled her orgasm was close. But something was different.

"Do you feel it?" His voice was harsh and raw, his breathing labored. "Nothing has ever been like this before. It's as if whatever is coming will blow me apart." He closed his eyes. "The Tree is talking to me."

In another time and place, Satona would've thrown Conall back because of obvious mental deficiencies. But she was feeling it, too. Something beyond them was whispering in words that had no language, that was made up of the senses and emotions.

The white nothingness was suddenly alive with emotion, with sound, taste, and scent. It seeped into them, became part of them. Satona felt such love for Conall that tears streamed down her face. The sound of his heartbeat was a drumbeat of anticipation, his scent driving her into an aroused frenzy, and as she nuzzled his neck, she knew she'd never survive if she couldn't taste him.

"For eight hundred years I've waited. I wait no longer."

His sensual rumble vibrated in her soul. And, yes, in this place and with this male, she refused to believe she didn't have a soul. No one could feel as she was feeling who didn't have one.

"Drink from me, Satona."

He buried himself deep inside her one last time, and at the same moment she sank her fangs into his neck. He shuddered as the erotic rush of his life force flooded her, and then he stiffened as his orgasm slammed into him.

Her control snapped. Closing her eyes, she let go, and the most powerful spasm of pleasure she'd ever felt shook her. The force of her release froze her in place, unable to scream, unable to do anything except *feel*. Wave after wave of unspeakable sexual ecstasy washed over her.

And after the waves had died to ripples, she felt weak and shaky. Gradually, she realized they weren't surrounded by the white nothingness anymore. They stood at the fork of a forest road, and only Conall's arms kept her upright.

"There has never been anything like we just shared." He didn't look at her as he spoke, but instead stared down the road that branched off to the left.

Satona was still too shaken to talk about what they'd experienced. But at least her brain was finally functioning. "Where are we?"

He shrugged. "I don't know. But the Tree is giving us a choice."

"I don't understand." How long had the Tree held them? She had to be out of the Sensual Forest by dawn.

Conall still didn't look at her. "The right path will take you out of the Sensual Forest. The left path will take you to a new place, one where nothing will be as you remember. But the Tree promises it will be a world of happiness. The Tree of Eternal Pleasure only offers the left path to a very few during each lifetime."

Now she knew what had happened to those of the sisterhood who'd never returned from the forest. "So the Tree expects us to trot on down the left path with no guarantees except what it offers. My common sense is alive and well and says this sounds like a gigantic scam." She spun in a circle. "Tree, could you elaborate a little on what's at the end of the road? It's tough to see around that bend."

The forest remained eerily silent.

Frustrated, she stared at Conall. "The Tree evidently talked to you at length. What's down the left road?"

He smiled. "Definitely not at length. I don't know any more than what I told you, but the Tree wants us to go."

"I don't trust trees with unknown agendas." "The Road Not Taken." A poem she remembered from her past. Something about taking the road less traveled and it making all the difference. Satona shook her head. Where had that thought come from?

Releasing her, Conall turned toward the left road. "Come with me."

"Are you crazy?" Horrified, she watched him start to walk away. Her common sense was free and making up for lost time. "We don't know where it goes. We don't have any clothes." He kept walking. "I can make you come with me."

His laughter echoed back to her. "Only in your world, Satona. This is the Tree's world." He was disappearing around that blasted bend in the road.

She teetered on the edge of all her tomorrows. Reason couldn't explain what was happening.

Suddenly she was running. As she rounded the curve in the road, she found him waiting for her.

She stopped, breathing hard. "You knew."

He shook his head. "No, but I hoped."

"I love you." She took his hand, and they walked into the future.

What had they seen as they traveled that road? Where had they sought shelter to escape the dawn? These things should be clear in her mind. She pondered why they weren't as she lay with eyes still closed.

"Gerry. It's over."

Conall's voice. But who was Gerry, and what was over?

"Open your eyes."

Something in his voice made her nervous. But nothing bad had happened in the forest. She'd remember, wouldn't she?

"We're back."

Back from where? And was that regret she heard in his voice?

"Satona is gone, Gerry." His voice was gentler than she'd ever heard it before.

Gerry. Working on the theory that what she didn't see couldn't affect her, she squeezed her eyes more tightly shut. It didn't work, though, because she remembered who Gerry was.

Opening her eyes, Gerry turned her head to look at Conall. "We never saw what was at the end of the road." And damn it, she had tears in her eyes. She blinked as fast as she could to hold back the flood.

"That's not the way it was supposed to happen." He looked troubled.

"How was it supposed to happen? I thought Eric said it could go in any direction we wanted it to go." She was back in the real world now . . . Funny, but Satona felt more real than Gerry right now.

Conall rubbed his hand across his bare chest, and she followed the motion. His chest was the world's eighth wonder in any reality. "Wait, we're naked." The tangled sheet told its own tale.

He grinned. "*That* part was real."

She frowned. Her back felt irritated. "What's wrong with my back?" Gerry rolled over so he could look.

"It's red and scraped in a few spots." He touched one of the scraped places.

"Bark burn." She swallowed hard.

"I think Eric is scarier than I ever imagined." His quiet voice said a lot about his respect for his friend's power.

"So explain what you thought would happen." It couldn't possibly be any better than what they'd experienced.

"It was supposed to be pretty straight up. You chase me, you get me, you seduce me, and then you take me back to be your pleasure mate."

"You were going to let me have the control Eric and you thought I wanted." The control she *had* wanted. But something had sent the fantasy spiraling off in a different direction.

He nodded. "Suddenly there were all those unexpected layers. We were supposed to make love against the *outside* of the tree. End of fantasy." Conall looked thoughtful. "And you weren't supposed to remember my name."

"You didn't recognize *me*." Fine, so she was a little hurt by that.

"Not your name, but I remembered *you*." He glanced away. "I think I said something about you staying with me."

Okay, now she felt better. Gerry smiled, because she remembered *exactly* what he'd said. *Stay with me, Sister of the Night. Forever.*

She felt energized as she climbed from the bed. They'd kick some demon butt and then come back here to analyze the fantasy. Conall would hate it, but she liked analyzing things, especially when Conall O'Rourke was involved.

Gerry was humming happily in the shower when she re-membered.

Ohmigod. The warm water spilling over her didn't even begin to touch the cold shock of realization.

Satona's last words to Conall.

"I love you."

19

Gerry had said she loved him. *Him. Conall.* Not some anonymous forest male. His surge of happiness warmed a part of him frozen and alone for 800 years. This was his personal tipping point.

In a matter of moments, he'd shed his love-will-never-work attitude and replaced it with I'll-make-it-happen. He'd chosen not to share her shower and all the accompanying pleasure because, as he'd done before every battle he'd ever fought, he needed to plan.

While he thought things out, he put the clothes back on that he'd flung off during the fantasy. Funny he didn't remember shucking his clothes. Then he sat on the couch and waited for Gerry.

When she finally emerged, one look at her face told him she'd remembered. So he stood and got right to the point. "Do you love me?"

Conall didn't know what he'd expected, maybe a little eye-contact avoidance. What he *hadn't* planned for was an in-your-face attack.

"I don't believe you. Of course I love you. I've tossed out so many clues it's amazing you didn't trip over them." She tied her robe shut with angry jerks. "And I said so during the fantasy."

He held up his hands. "Okay, just making sure."

Her anger slid into uncertainty. "So, how do you feel about me?" She glanced away. "I'm not trying to put you on the spot, and I'll understand if you don't want to—"

"Stop. Don't say another word until I get this out."

Gerry looked startled, but she stopped talking.

"I love you, Gerry Kavanagh." The ease of the words surprised him. The truth behind them didn't surprise him at all.

Other than emotion flooding her eyes, she didn't react. He didn't blame her. Hell, a few days ago he'd hated all things Kavanagh. Now? His need for her was so raw and intense it felt like something was ripping him apart inside. You didn't have to be a shifter to own a beast, because his was roaring and clawing its way to the surface at even the thought of anyone but him touching Gerry.

"And you've said these words how many times before?" She raised one sexy brow, but hope lived in her eyes.

One part of him resented that she'd question his love, while the other part of him applauded her caution. He tried for a thoughtful expression. "Once."

"Oh?" Her smile looked forced.

"To my horse. I told him I loved him after he got me through a tough battle." There'd been so many battles, and so many times he'd thought about the relief of resting forever. But it had never happened. And now he was glad.

She didn't fling herself at him but moved quietly into his embrace. "I want you forever, Conall O'Rourke, even if you told your horse you loved him."

He covered her mouth in a deep, drugging kiss. When he finally raised his head, she asked the question he'd known was coming.

"If you have descendants, then I guess you were married. I'd like to know about that time in your life." Left unsaid was, "Didn't you say the words to *her*?"

"There was caring and children, but not love. It was a time when marriage didn't require love. Marriages were built around expediency. In my case, it was the need to bind two families for the good of both. Two armies can protect a lot better than one."

She nodded. "I don't need details. Whether they were good or bad memories, don't feel you have to revisit them for me. I understand that some things should stay personal."

"Thanks." He appreciated her gift, because he could see curiosity burning in her eyes.

Conall returned to the couch and pulled her down beside him. Tucking her into his side, he told her his plan. "I don't think I can get Morrigan to release me from the curse, but I might be able to get a concession from her. She has to agree to let us make love."

"Damn straight." Gerry looked militant. "We're not going to spend the rest of our days making love while we listen for the flapping of wings."

"That's why we have to talk to Asima as soon as I take my shower."

"Asima?" Gerry rose to walk over to the bed, where she began picking up her clothes from the floor. She glanced at Houston. "Hey, look at our boy. Leaves sprouting all over the place."

He sensed her nervousness. The last of the fantasy's euphoria had drained away leaving only the solid facts of their coming battle with both Morrigan and the demon.

"Asima represents Bast. For whatever reason, Bast wants me kept safe. So we're going to pressure Asima to hurry Bast's arrival. Maybe Bast can do a little arm-twisting—or in this case wing-twisting—to make Morrigan ease up on her lovemaking ban." He hated doing this, because asking for help rubbed his face in his own inability to help himself.

Clothes in hand, she walked over and stopped in front of him. "I recognize that expression, O'Rourke, because I've worn it myself. If I was only a few centuries older, I could do some of the cool things Eric can do. If I only had a little more experience, I could take on bigger cases. If my fangs were only a little longer, I could be the biggest badass in Texas."

He couldn't help it, he grinned. She made him feel good. And she was right. He'd work with what he had. "Call Eric while I'm in the shower. He has to remove the shield. Then we'll talk to Asima."

If Gerry had been in there with him, his shower would've emptied the castle's hot water supply. She wasn't, so he made it quick. He pulled on jeans and a sleeveless T-shirt. His battle gear was a lot different from the old days. Only his sword stayed the same.

When he came out of the bathroom, Eric was standing in the open doorway. But his friend was simply a blur on the edge of Conall's field of vision. Gerry took his breath away. "Wow, you heat up that outfit. Lady, you make it hard to concentrate on business."

Her love for him was there in her smile. "Beaded camisole, Sparkle. Really short black skirt, Sparkle. Nosebleed stilettos, Sparkle. My happiness, you."

Eric coughed. "I guess the fantasy worked for you guys."

Gerry flung her arms around Eric and hugged him. "It was life-altering. Thank you."

"What you can do with your mind blows everyone else out of the water, Eric. I'll pass on the hug, though."

Eric grinned and then glanced at his watch. "It's almost time. We've closed the great hall to everyone except the vampires, us, and hopefully, Dell. Gerry, we've set up cameras outside of all the entrances to the great hall.

We've moved the long banquet table to the side so the path to the hearth is clear. You'll be standing in front of the fireplace. I want you to keep your eye on the monitors we've set up behind the table. When you see Dell approaching one of the doors, signal me so I can catch him before he enters the hall."

"What if he's disguised? He won't want Gerry spotting him before he reaches her." Conall wasn't smiling now. The reality of her danger landed squarely on his shoulders. He almost buckled under its weight.

"I'll recognize him." Her grim expression must mirror his. "I told you he looks a little like Uncle Ray."

Suddenly, it was there, an emotional punch in the gut. Conall finally made the connection he'd sensed when she'd first mentioned Dell's resemblance to her uncle. He rubbed a hand across his forehead. It couldn't be, but it was. No one needed to know, though. The knowing didn't change anything. This was his battle.

"Ganymede and Edge are already in place. Ganymede's hitting the buffet table and Edge is hitting the brandy. Both seem happy for now. Oh, and I took the shield from Jinx's door. I use some of my power to maintain his shield, and I'll need every bit of power I can get tonight. I just hope he's too scared of you to steal anything right away." Eric turned to leave. "Here comes Asima. I think she was glad to get some downtime."

Conall walked to the door. "Thanks for everything, Eric. I owe you." He watched Eric leave as he waited for Asima to reach him. "We need to talk for a few minutes, Asima."

"I know about your plan to fight the demon. I'm exhausted from listening at your door to get all the details. And I absolutely forbid it. Bast wouldn't want me to allow you to do this." Asima padded into the dungeon, tail waving elegantly in the air.

Gerry moved to Conall's side as she narrowed her gaze

on the cat. "This has to happen, Asima. If you really want to help Conall, you can contact Bast and tell her he needs her in exactly . . ." She looked at the clock. "One hour."

For the first time, Asima looked unsure of herself. *"I don't understand. I can remove Conall from harm's way if he's in danger. Bast is a busy goddess. I don't know if she's free tonight."*

Gerry was losing her patience. Fast. "Look, you already said Bast would be here. Eventually. Well, tell her to move her schedule up a little."

Asima looked scandalized. *"No one tells Bast to—"*

Argh! No more nice vampire. Gerry crouched down until she was eye to eye with Asima. She showed a little fang to let the cat know she was seriously ticked off. "Conall and I love each other." She held up her hand to stop any comments. "Deal with it."

Asima hissed her unwillingness to "deal with it."

Gerry ignored Asima's opinion. "But Morrigan won't let us make love. I know you don't care about me, so let's just say this makes Conall really unhappy. Now, I think your employer *wants* him to be happy. So if she gets here in one hour, she can catch Morrigan in the great hall and discuss the situation."

Asima looked at her from those big blue eyes, and Gerry wished she knew what was going on inside the cat's head.

"I'll contact the goddess." She turned and left, her tail waving a little less elegantly.

Conall looked worried. "If Asima listened at the door, Dell could, too. He might know the whole plan."

"I don't think so. There've been too many powerful entities in and out of here for him to take a chance at our door. Besides, Asima has been outside for most of the time. If someone spotted him, he couldn't disappear, and he wouldn't want to get trapped in this hallway. He hasn't had much luck killing me, so I bet he's being a little more careful now."

Conall reached out and pulled her to him. "There're too many what-ifs in this plan, but we have to take the chance." He stroked his finger along her jaw. "But know this, vampire lady, nothing or no one will hurt you. I promise."

And she believed him. He wouldn't want her going all teary-eyed over him, so she smiled brightly as she stood on tiptoe to kiss his cheek. "I'll have your back, too, partner."

A short time later as they climbed the stairs to the great hall, she made a silent vow that no dirtbag demon would get in the way of the love they'd just found.

Gerry shifted from foot to foot, trying to ease the pain of Sparkle's sexy shoes. Sparkle had stopped by to chat for a minute so things would look natural.

"Great outfit choice for your big night. I mean, if you have to get staked, go out with good hair and killer clothes. You have a chipped nail. If I knew the shade, I could take care of it for you."

"Thanks, but I'll live with it." Gerry hoped. "I haven't seen Morrigan lately. If she doesn't show up on time, our plan is dead." *Dead.* Not a good word choice.

"I think she went to Happening Hair this afternoon. Haven't seen her since." Sparkle's smile was all wicked anticipation. "She'll come out a changed bird. Well, at least her feathers will."

Sparkle wandered away, leaving Gerry staring at the buffet table. Which was dumb because she couldn't eat anything on it. She couldn't drink whatever was in the glass she was holding, either. But she had to keep her attention on the monitors tucked behind the table so she wouldn't miss Dell if he made an appearance.

On a positive note, she felt great since making love with Conall. Before that, she'd been thinking about searching out a dinner donor. She smiled. Not now. He was a human energy bar.

"Don't look at me."

Startled at Eric's voice in her head, she resisted the urge to turn around.

"Remember, if you see Dell, don't say anything out loud and don't look toward any of the doors. I'm in your mind, so I'll see what you see. Then I'll take it from there. Make sure you face the hearth so he thinks he's sneaking up on you. Just as he's about to strike, I'll release the minds of everyone else so I can use all my power to shift his perspective about two feet to your right."

Gerry swallowed hard. Two feet, twenty-four inches. Didn't sound like much room for error.

Eric's laughter calmed her. *"Don't worry. I'm good. When Morrigan comes in, she'll see the you Dell's seeing. Yeah, I know she's in on the plot, but it'll help her act natural if she has a body to look at."*

"Then what?" Oops, a few vampires noticed her talking to herself.

"Once Dell thinks you're dead, I'll let him see everyone as they really are. You're the only one I'll still want hidden. He has to believe you're dead and Conall's human."

"You're scary." She remembered to say it in her mind this time.

"When you have as many centuries on you as I do, you'll be scary, too."

Yeah, but that would be too late to help Conall if he needed her tonight.

"You can't try to help him. No one can. His wish, and we'll all honor it."

Eric's words chilled her from the inside out.

"I don't make those kinds of promises." If she saw someone hurting the man she loved, she'd try to tear that someone's throat out. Injured male pride wouldn't stop her.

Eric didn't respond, so she figured they understood each other.

"Please try not to inflict any damage on the great hall."

Holgarth's hat was perfectly centered on his head, signaling that he felt things were reasonably under control. "If you must bleed, do make sure it doesn't splatter. It's difficult to remove from some fabrics."

Gerry sighed. Her night was complete. "And you're here why?"

"I'm taking my turn chatting with you so things will look normal on the off chance the demon has any cohorts, which I seriously doubt. Only archdemons seem able to mobilize their minions into a fighting force." The wizard frowned at the buffet spread out on the banquet table. "My God, Ganymede's stomach is a black hole. He's the only one who's touched the food, and it's half gone."

"Yes, well I hope he's storing up all that energy to heave Dell through the portal." She shifted her gaze to the next monitor and froze.

A figure in a hooded cloak was approaching the outer door of the great hall. It slowed as it approached the two guardian gargoyles. The cowl hid its face, but Gerry had enhanced vision, and for once she was damn glad of it. She could just make out the features. Yep, he looked a lot like Uncle Ray.

"Eric?"

"I see him. Face the hearth and don't turn around no matter what." A moment's silence, and then his soft murmur. *"Trust me."*

Holgarth must've recognized what was happening, because he put his hand on her arm. "We'll clean up the blood as long as it's demon blood." All his usual mockery was gone. "You belong to the Castle of Dark Dreams now. Be safe, Gerry Kavanagh." He gazed at her from eyes old in power and wisdom. Then he turned and left.

Just before she swung to face the fireplace, Gerry looked for Conall. He stood along with Brynn, Kim, Donna, Edge, Sparkle, and even Banan and Destiny in a semicircle at the edge of the crowd of vampire revelers.

Ganymede crouched on the buffet table behind a leafy cen-
terpiece. Eric, Asima, and Morrigan were missing. She allowed herself a moment's worry over the goddess's
absence before focusing all her attention on Conall.

He looked poised to break free of Brynn's restraining
hand and drag her from the great hall to someplace he considered safe.

She shook her head and smiled at him. Gerry hoped
Conall saw the love and confidence in her eyes. Okay, so
the confidence was a big, fat fake, but the love was as real
as it got.

Conall relaxed marginally, but his jaw was still in lock-
down as he fought his need to do *something. Now.* He concentrated on slowing his breathing, his pounding heart, and
his doomsday imagination.

Gerry and he had some of the most powerful entities
Conall knew on their side. He had to believe Eric wouldn't
let anything happen to her. Conall just couldn't get it out of
his head, though, that keeping her safe was *his* job.

He didn't turn around to look at the door, but after 800
years Conall was sensitive enough to feel the sudden psychic hum from the more powerful entities around him. The
demon was in the hall.

Endless seconds stretched into forever, and then a
hooded and cloaked figure slipped past him. The mad-
monk look wasn't unusual on the night of the Vampire
Ball. Guests interpreted the vampire look in strange ways.

The demon paused a short distance from Gerry and
glanced across the hall, where Eric's manipulation of reality had convinced him Conall was.

Conall still couldn't see the face inside the hood, but he
knew. He hoped his smile looked as savage as he felt. *I
don't know the how or why, but it doesn't matter. It'll end
the same way it did 800 years ago, with you in hell.* He
gathered himself, wanting to launch himself across the
short distance separating them.

"Don't." Brynn's warning brought a little sanity back to him.

Conall had to let this play out, trust everyone to know their parts. He watched the demon reach beneath his cloak and slide out a stake. The spirits of all his warrior ancestors shouted for him to strike the creature down that threatened his woman.

He clenched his fists, digging his nails into his palms, welcoming the pain. The battles he'd fought were easy compared to this. *This* was the hardest thing he'd ever done—watching and doing nothing.

Drawing in a harsh breath, he unclenched his fists. She'd want him to have confidence in her, to trust her ability to do this, and because he loved her, he forced back his need for instant violence. She'd never know what that control cost him.

The demon edged closer and raised his stake. And as the stake started its deadly downward arc, Conall felt a slight shift in his reality. He blinked away the sensation, and when he looked again, Gerry lay on the floor, a stake sticking out of the left side of her back.

Only the sight of the real Gerry standing frozen a few feet from the demon kept him from roaring his agony. As quickly as he looked back at the image of the dead Gerry, it was gone. The demon was crouched over an empty spot on the floor.

Uneasy murmurs rose from everyone in the hall as Eric allowed them to see the reality of what was happening. Eric stood off to the side. He stared at the crowd and they suddenly stilled. Conall didn't need anyone to tell him Eric had spread the word mentally.

Now that Eric didn't need to expend his power on anyone else, he focused all his attention on the demon. Conall knew exactly how potent that attention could be.

The demon rose from his crouch and slowly scanned the entities that formed a semicircle around him. His gaze froze on Conall and only an angry hiss revealed his shock that he was trapped. Then he flung back his hood to glare at Conall.

"Hello, Sean. Let me guess, hell couldn't hold you." Conall wished he'd gotten a look at Sean sooner, but then Sean had made sure he didn't.

His old enemy's face was the same, but not. The short hair changed his look a little, and the pale eyes that were changing to glowing red even as Conall watched sure added a new touch. It was Gerry's description of Dell's pale eyes that had thrown him off. Eight hundred years ago, Sean had the same green eyes as Gerry. Evidently hell faded them out a little.

Sean ignored everyone but Conall. "I've waited eight hundred years for this, O'Rourke. The devil liked my vengeful attitude so he raised me to demon status. Then I spent the next eight centuries killing off my descendants." He frowned. "They were all like me, fucking everything in sight. There were so many I never thought I'd get rid of them all." His frown vanished, and he smiled. He glanced down at the spot where he was seeing Gerry's image. "Now the last one is gone."

"And?" Where the hell was Morrigan? A quick glance at Gerry caught her horrified expression. He didn't blame her. She'd never known Sean, so she wouldn't understand the kind of evil that would drive someone to kill those of his own blood.

"Morrigan will release you from your curse. You should thank me." His eyes glowed red with hate. "Well, maybe not. Because once you're human again, we can finish our battle." Sean glanced at the menacing faces surrounding him. "Unless you intend to let your friends do your fighting for you."

Sean understood him. He knew Conall's pride wouldn't let him hide behind someone else.

"They won't interfere." Conall refused to look at Gerry.

Seeing her fear for him would weaken his will. And he needed to do this for Gerry—who could be lying dead on the floor—for himself, and for all those dead Kavanaghs who'd died because of Sean's hatred of him.

"Call Morrigan." Sean's eagerness for his death lived in his narrowed eyes, his bared teeth.

As if on cue, the sound of chanting along with the blare of a boom box with the bass turned up so high the floor vibrated filled the great hall.

"I'm the goddess, bow down." Boom, boom, thump, thump of the bass.

Every vampire in the room covered their ears. The rap rhythm set on high volume had to be hell on enhanced hearing.

"She's the goddess, she's the goddess." A chorus of voices with more bass thumping.

"Yo, I'm lean, I'm mean, I'm the goddess, bow down." Boom, boom, thump, thump.

Conall winced. Talk about bad rhyming.

"She's the goddess, she's the goddess." The chorus voices got louder along with the bass.

Everyone's gaze riveted on Morrigan as she finally entered the great hall. One of the visiting vampires shouted to be heard above the bass, "Hey, this is a lot more fun than trolling the clubs for dinner."

Conall sucked in his breath and then exhaled on a huff of disbelief. Morrigan's tail feathers were dyed different shades of red, blue, purple, and green. The feathers on top of her head were the same colors and stuck up straight in the air. She had glitter sprinkled along the length of her wings.

"I decide who lives or dies. Stay outta my way if you're wise." She didn't deign to look left or right as a path opened for her.

"She's the goddess, she's the goddess." Boom, boom, thump, thump. Morrigan's chorus of five crows followed behind her.

"I gotta do what I gotta do. Get in my way and I'll make you pay." She stopped in front of the spot where Sean thought Gerry's body lay.

"She's the goddess. She's the goddess." Boom, boom, thump, thump.

"Oh, for all that's sane, I can't stand this." Holgarth's voice somewhere in the crowd.

"Wow, Happening Hair really outdid themselves this time. Looks like she's living the moment." Sparkle sounded somewhere between amused and awed.

Morrigan circled the body Eric had made sure only Sean and she could see. "She's dead. That's what I said. She's dead."

"She's dead, she's dead." Boom, boom, thump, thump. At least they'd changed up the chorus a little.

"I . . ." Morrigan glanced up at Sean. She stilled.

Conall didn't like the feel of that stillness. Morrigan obviously had just realized who the demon was. Sean had been her favorite, but 800 years was a long time.

"Hello, Morrigan." For a moment, Sean's eyes lost their red glow and a smile touched his lips. "You always could make an entrance. I'm looking forward to seeing you in your true form again. I've missed you."

And Conall got a glimpse of the man he'd once known, the one who hid his viciousness under a surface layer of humor and charm.

The goddess finally looked away from Sean. "I remove my curse from Conall O'Rourke. He's as he was eight hundred years ago." The shock of seeing Sean had taken her right out of her rapping-crow persona.

Conall took a deep breath. He felt different. But he *shouldn't* feel different. Morrigan was simply supposed to say the words so Sean would think he'd have an easy kill. Trying to ignore his budding suspicion, Conall pulled his sword from his back scabbard.

Sean threw off his cloak and drew his own sword.

"A tux? So, is your return-to-hell party a formal affair?" Conall knew his smile didn't reach his eyes.

Sean's smile was a mere baring of his teeth. "I've developed a sense of style over the centuries. You're still the same savage you were eight hundred years ago." He flung himself at Conall.

The force of Sean's attack drove Conall back even as he realized what that strange feeling had been. *You're in a world of shit, O'Rourke.* The bitch goddess had double-crossed him.

He was really human. And unless he came up with something fast, he was soon to be really dead.

20

Morrigan and Sean had been lovers. A man might not recognize the signs, but a woman always would. It was there in the way Morrigan had said his name and the expression on Sean's face when he'd spoken to her. Gerry figured that could only be bad news for Conall.

And as he crossed swords with Sean, her worst fears were realized. Conall was a powerful man, but Sean beat back Conall's attacks with ease while the demon slowly forced him to retreat.

She watched horrified as Sean's sword sliced across Conall's arm, drawing first blood.

"Doesn't seem too fair, does it? Morrigan knew a human couldn't take out a demon." Ganymede plunked his ample bottom on the toe of her shoe. "Makes you want to cheat right back at her. Too bad the rest of us promised Conall we wouldn't interfere." He peered up at her from sly amber eyes. "Did *you* promise?"

"No." Rage heated her blood. She felt the slide of her fangs.

"There you go." Ganymede sounded as though everything was perfectly clear now. "I'd say a human and a newbie vampire against one demon makes things pretty even." He glanced at the buffet. "I'm in love. I want to marry the cheesecake."

"What about Morrigan?" If Gerry had the power, Morrigan would be a dead goddess. She winced when Sean drew blood again, but this time Conall sliced across the demon's stomach, drawing a scream of fury from him.

"I'll pad on over to the goddess and sit beside her for a while. I guarantee she won't meddle in the battle." Ganymede stood and stretched. "I promised not to help Conall fight the demon. I never said I wouldn't sit next to Morrigan and jam her power cells for a little while."

Gerry didn't even see Ganymede leave as she crouched and began to stalk Sean. The babble of vampire voices rose higher and higher. Probably betting on the winner. Too bad they didn't know a wild card was about to mess up their bets.

She was so close now she could hear what Conall and Sean were saying. Sean never noticed her. Eric must still be in the demon's mind.

Sean's eyes glowed with bloodlust and triumph. "This is the way it should've ended eight hundred years ago. I've had all those years to think about how it would feel when I killed you. I could've just shot you, but the sword is more personal. Now I get to look into your eyes as you die."

"What happens if you fail, Sean?" Conall's words came in hard pants.

"I can't fail. I'm a demon, stupid. Poke me full of holes, but I won't die. Sure, it'll put a hurting on me, but I'll survive. One of my demonic perks." He swung his sword and then laughed as Conall stumbled back.

"No, I mean what'll happen if you don't kill me?" Conall wasn't swinging his sword with enough strength to force Sean to retreat toward the hearth.

"Isn't going to happen. But if it did, I'd still be okay as long as I didn't go back to hell. Haven't been back since I got sprung as a demon. If I go back, I won't be let out again. I was supposed to check in five hundred years ago. The devil gets pissed when his demons mess with his schedule. Lucky for me, I'm not high enough on the ladder of evil to warrant a search party." He was so busy talking that he let Conall slip under his guard.

Conall thrust hard, driving his sword into Sean's chest.

"Well, shit, that hurt." Sean glanced at the wound and then up at Conall. "Give it up, O'Rourke. All you're doing is making me madder."

Gerry watched the demon almost drive Conall to his knees with a blow. She could see Conall's fatigue, the growing heaviness of his sword arm. Time to go into action.

She glanced at Eric. He nodded. Okay, Mr. Sulfur Breath would be able to see her now. Time for the undead to rise and kick some demon ass. She launched herself at Sean.

The demon saw her at the last minute and leaped back in time to avoid the worst of her strike. She did leave two painful puncture wounds in his sword arm, though. Reminders of what a vampire's fangs could do.

Sean's eyes widened as he realized she wasn't dead, but he recovered nicely. "So now you need a woman to help you fight. You've gotten soft, O'Rourke." For all his sneering, he looked wary.

Gerry didn't glance at Conall. He was bound to be ticked at her interfering. She could almost hear the sound of crumbling ego as she moved in on Sean.

"Conall and I are partners. We work together. I'd say this makes things a little more even. You're a coward, Great-times-ten-Granddaddy. You didn't have the guts to fight Conall when he was immortal. You're the rotten apple on my family tree, and it's time someone knocked you off your branch." She chanced a quick glance toward Conall. "Sorry, this is a family thing."

Surprisingly, she didn't read outrage or anger in Conall's expression. Nothing but grim determination.

She timed her next attack to follow right after Conall swung his sword. It was like a one-two punch.

"What's your point, vampire bitch? You can't kill me. Even if I don't get your man this time, I'll get him when you aren't around." He backed up a few more steps.

Just keep on moving toward the fireplace, you bastard. "Maybe it's about making you look like crap in front of all these people."

Gerry was so busy talking she misjudged her distance from Sean, and he got her in the shoulder with the tip of his sword. Owie, owie, ouch. Good thing Conall was the warrior in the family, because she didn't do pain well.

When he saw the blood welling from her shoulder, Conall roared his rage and charged Sean, driving the demon back until he stood right in front of the open hearth. Now all they had to do was make Sean take that last step.

Sean wasn't into last steps. Fifteen minutes later, he was still going strong. "Tired, Conall? You're human now. You can't go on forever. And when you fall over from exhaustion, I'll knock your vampire bitch aside and skewer you. Her fangs can't compete with my sword."

Conall didn't waste his breath in answering him. Gerry had enhanced everything, but Sean was right. If the demon wasn't armed, she'd have a chance, but he was an experienced swordsman. What to do? Her thoughts ran in panicked circles.

That's when she saw Jinx. He was wiggling his way across the mantel above the fireplace. A ruby ring circled his little green body. In a few seconds he'd be directly behind Sean and about a foot above the demon.

She locked gazes with the snake. A silent understanding passed between them.

Unfortunately, she took her attention off Sean just long enough for him to drive his blade deep into her thigh. The pain doubled her over.

Conall shouted his fury as he swung his sword with berserker rage. At the same time, Jinx dropped onto Sean's head.

Sean wasn't a snake person. Cursing, he lowered his sword arm and reached for the snake. Jinx being Jinx, he bit Sean's finger and held on.

Sean flapped his hand trying to make Jinx let go at the same time he stumbled back into the fireplace to avoid Conall's sword.

Before Sean could recover, Edge chanted the words that would open the portal to hell.

Gerry saw everything happen through a haze of pain. Jinx released the demon's finger, slipped to the floor, and slithered away. He'd lost the ring.

Suddenly, a bloodred vortex formed beneath Sean. Sounds of chaos rose from deep within the vortex. The demon screamed as he realized what was happening. The force of the vortex held him in place, though, when he tried to scramble out of the fireplace.

Ganymede didn't need any chanting. He crouched in front of the hearth and simply stared at Sean. As he met Ganymede's gaze, the demon's eyes widened in terror. Then the vortex sucked him down. His panicked shriek echoed distantly and then was gone.

Edge once again chanted, and the vortex disappeared.

Everyone in the great hall was silent for the moment it took to realize what had happened. Then everyone started talking at once.

Conall knelt in front of Gerry. "What can I do? Do you need Eric or Donna?" Fear for her shadowed his gaze.

Good. As long as he was worried about her, he wouldn't be working up a mad at her for interfering. "No. I'm fine. I'm already healing. It just really hurt." Fine, so she was a wuss. "We still have a loose end to tie up."

The loose end flapped her wings, rose into the air, and landed in front of them. Evidently Operation Tail Feathers was complete. "I'm reinstating the curse I removed. Consider yourself recursed, O'Rourke. I didn't even get a chance to reminisce about old times with Sean."

Gerry glared at Morrigan. "You can't do that, you double-crossing old bitch."

"Of course I can. I'm a goddess." The crow's eyes gleamed with satisfaction. "If you weren't such an insignificant nothing, I'd curse you, too. But you're not worth the effort."

Conall seemed too involved with checking Gerry's body for wounds to understand the full horror of what Morrigan had done.

The hall had grown strangely still. Gerry was so wrapped up in hating Morrigan she hadn't noticed. She did now. Following everyone's gaze, she stared at the suit of armor that stood at the entrance to the great hall.

A cat sat atop the armor. Sleek and elegant, her spotted coat gleamed smoke-colored in the dim lighting. She watched them from almond-shaped, pale green eyes outlined in jet black.

Asima leaped onto the buffet table to mentally broadcast her exciting news. *"Bast, protector of cats and women, patron of sensual pleasure and secrets, and a superior goddess in every way"*—she shot Morrigan a vindictive glare—*"has honored you with her presence."*

Morrigan huffed. "Big deal."

Gerry met Conall's gaze. He hid his emotions behind an expressionless mask. Well, she didn't care who saw the hope in her eyes. Could Bast force Morrigan to release Conall from the curse?

Bast leaped from the armor and seemed to flow toward them, all sinuous grace.

"Yo, beautiful mama, you make me forget my cheesecake." High praise from Ganymede.

"You won't be forgetting it for long when I shove your leering face into it." Sparkle making her intentions clear.

When Bast reached Conall, she looked up at him. "I've come to you in my cat form, Conall. Do you remember me?"

Conall's heartbeat quickened. So much of what he'd experienced during eight centuries had faded from his memory. But yes, he did remember this cat. "Egypt. Near the Nile. A lion."

Bast nodded, clearly pleased. "You came upon a lion you thought was threatening me. Ignoring danger to yourself, you picked me up and escaped from the lion. That was a brave thing to do."

Conall shook his head. "Not so brave. I was immortal. That was my only trip to Egypt. The Kavanaghs I protected didn't wander far from home." His lips tipped up at the memory. "You made my visit memorable."

"The lion was my sister, the goddess Sekhmet, and we were having a sibling disagreement. I wasn't really in danger, but that didn't lessen my appreciation for your act. You showed a caring nature, so I took an interest in your history." She cast Morrigan an enigmatic glance.

Morrigan cocked her head. "What?"

"I don't like to interfere in the curses of other deities, but I think eight hundred years is long enough for any human to suffer. I want you to release Conall." She cast Morrigan a dismissive look. "Oh, and you really need to find another hairdresser."

"No. My curse, my decision." Morrigan wore her stubborn-crow face.

Bast sighed. "I so hoped you'd see reason." Without warning, the elegant and possibly even gentle goddess morphed into Evil Cat. Eyes glowing, she bared her teeth in a snarl. Her low growl echoed to the farthest corners of the great hall.

Then the lights went out, throwing the hall into complete blackness. Gerry's childhood fear of the dark chose that moment to manifest at its panicky best. Chaos reigned in the great hall. The vampires seemed to know what was coming, because they stampeded for the exits. With everyone around her shoving and screaming, she got turned around. For a few frantic moments, she felt like she was lost in the hell Sean had just returned to. Terror clogged her throat even as she tried to convince herself that vampires weren't afraid of the dark.

Then she felt someone wrap his arms around her. Gerry didn't need him to speak. She recognized the warm comfort of his hard body, his familiar scent that promised safety. Wrapping her arms around Conall, she hung on.

Conall held her close. No matter what happened here, he'd made his decision. Morrigan could huff and puff until she keeled over from hyperventilation. He wasn't giving up what he had with Gerry. They'd find a way to make a life together no matter how much Morrigan tried to interfere. The goddess could issue thou-shalt-nots until she ran out of breath, but he and Gerry would find ways around her attempts to make their lives miserable.

"Hang on to me, sweetheart. Things are about to get ugly." He moved Gerry as far away from the two goddesses as he could without actually leaving the hall. This was all about their future, so they needed to stay.

"What's going to happen?"

"Bast and Morrigan are going to mix it up. We're the Bast cheering section." He ran his hands up and down her back to soothe her. Conall wouldn't admit it, but he probably needed some soothing, too. This was the closest he'd gotten to freedom in eight centuries. "Oh, and thanks for helping me out, partner."

She was silent for about two beats, proof that he'd surprised her. "Partners always have each others' backs. Morrigan cheated. Cheaters shouldn't be allowed to win."

Conall didn't get a chance to comment on that because he felt a furry body rub against his leg.

"This is so exciting. I haven't seen Bast battle another

deity in over five hundred years." Asima's voice vibrated with excitement.

No matter how much he'd gag on the words—because she'd been a real pain in the ass—he owed Asima a thank-you. "Look, we haven't always agreed on stuff, but I want you to know I appreciate everything you did to try to keep me safe."

"Thank you." Asima sounded prim. *"You were a very difficult man."*

"Amen." Gerry's agreement.

Then silence fell over the great hall. The last vampire had fled, slamming the door behind him. Conall assumed his friends still remained somewhere in the darkness.

The first warning of what was to come touched him. Static electricity, like what you felt before lightning struck, skimmed over his skin, raising goose bumps in its wake. He tightened his grip on Gerry.

Even though Conall thought he was prepared, he wasn't. An explosion of light and sound drove him back against the wall behind him. He felt Gerry shudder in his arms.

In the flashes of light, he saw the goddesses struggling. They'd grown to fifty times their original size. They moved so fast that all he could see was a blur of teeth, claws, and beak. The booms and crashes from their power made him afraid for his eardrums.

Then came the wind. It whirled and swirled, threatening to pick Gerry and him up and then fling them into the high reaches of the hall's ceiling. Planting his feet, he pressed himself against the wall, trying to anchor himself and Gerry. At some point he was aware she'd pulled one arm from around him to hang on to a column.

Gerry leaned her head back to look up at him. Her hair whipped around her face. She shouted, "My God, did I really have the nerve to yell at Morrigan? I didn't have a clue about her power. Remind me to keep my mouth shut around goddesses from now on."

Then as quickly as it started, it ended. The wind died, the light-and-sound show was over, and the electricity came back on.

Dazed, Conall and Gerry gazed around them. Furniture was reduced to kindling and food from the banquet table decorated the walls and even the ceiling. The few windows close to the ceiling were all blown out.

His friends were scattered around the room. They all looked as shocked as he felt. Except for Ganymede. He gazed at Bast with adoring eyes. "You're one scary witch, babe. Love that in a woman."

Sparkle was busy smoothing down her hair and checking her nails for chips. She paused for a moment to cast Ganymede a glance that promised lots of payback when they were alone. Poor Ganymede.

The goddesses had returned to their normal animal sizes. Conall wasn't sure where the damage from Morrigan's visit to Happening Hair ended and her battle with Bast began. But she was one sad-looking bird. Tail feathers all gone again. Conall refused to think about the implications of *that*.

Bast, on the other hand, looked untouched. She used one elegant paw to wash her face. Then she gazed at Conall.

"Morrigan has graciously agreed to release you from her curse. You'll be human again, and she will never again interfere in your life." She waited for his response.

Gerry looked up at him with love and happiness, along with a shine of tears, in her eyes. "*Your freedom.* After all those centuries you can do what you want." Her joy was all for him, with no thoughts about how it would affect her.

He loved her even more for that. "No."

Conall could feel the stunned response of everyone around him. Gerry reached up to run her fingers along his jaw. "Conall?" Confusion swam in her eyes.

Raking his fingers through his hair, he explained. "I

want to keep the curse. I love Gerry, and I want to be around to serve and protect her and our descendants. A human life span is too short now that I've finally found her." He looked at Morrigan. "But I want you to stay out of our business. We go where we want and do what we want. Understand?"

Morrigan sniffed. "I suppose. Of course, now that the kitty goddess has pulled out all my tail feathers again, I'll have to stick around until new ones grow in. But I'll find ways to amuse myself."

There was a collective groan from everyone in the room.

Morrigan brightened. "There'll be a wedding. I can help plan it. My friends from Happening Hair would be glad to offer their services."

"Over my dead and unaccessorized body. I'll take care of the clothes and hair for the bride." Sparkle sounded close to violence.

Asima looked at Bast. *"I believe I have some vacation time coming. Could I take it now? Someone with good taste needs to guide the bride away from them."* She glared at Morrigan and Sparkle.

Conall grimaced. They were all in cart-before-horse mode. He stared at Gerry. Here went the whole rest of his life. "Will you marry me, Gerry Kavanagh?"

She stood on tiptoe and kissed him. "Try and stop me, Conall O'Rourke."

While their friends whistled and cheered, he clasped Gerry's hand and turned to Bast.

"I appreciate what you've done for Gerry and me tonight, goddess." Conall smiled at Bast even as Gerry and he backed toward the stairs leading to the dungeon. "To honor you, I promise we'll always have a cat in our house."

Bast nodded. "A wonderful honor. And you're wise to leave. The battle has drawn the attention of your police. Even now they're preparing to batter down the doors I sealed shut before Morrigan and I settled our . . . differences." Without further comment, she disappeared into the great hall's shadows, an ordinary cat to any human who saw her.

Conall and Gerry didn't stop running until they were safely back in the dungeon. Laughing, she threw herself onto the bed, releasing its sensual scent. He could tell Sparkle neither of them needed a smelly bed to put them in an erotic mood.

Reaching up, she dragged him down beside her. "So what do we do now?"

"Make love. I'll talk to Eric. Wouldn't you like to know what was at the end of that left path?"

She slapped at him. "No, I mean for the rest of our lives."

Puzzled, he shrugged. "Make love." Then he thought about it. "Yeah, we'll have to let Sparkle, Morrigan, and Asima mess with our wedding. I'd like to kick Morrigan out, but I can be a little generous because if it weren't for her I never would've found you."

She rolled over, and he caught her to him. "I released Jinx from the Securer. We came to an agreement during the fight with Sean. If he helped us, I'd release him. But I somehow don't think Jinx will stay out of trouble long, so we'll be tracking him down again soon."

We. One of his favorite words now. They'd work at PUFF together. He frowned. Someone had to change that name.

"I have to leave for just a few days, and when I come back we'll plan our wedding."

Only one word registered. "Leave?"

"Edge promised me he'd go with me to jail. It'll mean a promotion. Of course, he shouldn't have any trouble proving he's innocent. If they don't believe him?" She shrugged. "Payton doesn't have any way to hold a being with his power."

"I'll go with you."

She met his gaze. "As much as I want to be near you, I need to do this alone. Sure, I know that staying close to me is part of the curse, but Morrigan doesn't have the power to enforce it anymore. Probably other Kavanaghs would just order you to stay here, but that's not what love's about. So I'm asking you to please let me do this myself."

"Whatever's best for you. Don't stay away long, though." A week ago, he would've demanded she let him keep her safe. He'd grown a lot in that week.

She slipped her fingers under his T-shirt. "We're all icky. Why don't we take a shower? Together."

"Mmm. Great minds think alike."

"I guarantee it isn't our minds doing the thinking now." Laughing, she dragged him off the bed and into the bathroom.

She'd only been gone for three days, but Conall felt like her trip had lasted for weeks. Besides missing Gerry, he'd had to field all the congratulations, ribbings, and general pain-in-the-ass suggestions from everyone. Sparkle and Asima were driving him crazy with wedding stuff. What the hell did he know about that crap? Morrigan had the good sense to stay away from him, but he knew she was manipulating behind the scenes.

But now Gerry was home. When he finally released her from his arms, she drew him down on the couch.

"Lots of good and some weird news." She rubbed her fingers along his inner thigh.

He sucked in his breath and tried to concentrate on her news.

"Once we got to the prison, Edge called in the favor I owed him. He asked me to arrange a one-on-one meeting with Payton." She shook her head in wonder. "Payton never came out of that room. When Edge came out, he said he'd arranged a buyout for my boss. Payton moved on to a new plane." Her expression said she suspected the new plane began and ended with a *d*. "And before Payton left, he appointed Edge the new boss. When I left, Edge was working on a different name for the organization. He was having trouble, though. If you can think of three words with initials that spell BAD, call him."

"So that's the weird news. Let's hear the good." With her hand still working its magic on his thigh, Conall knew she could easily see *his* good news.

"Edge gave me my promotion, and he assigned me to Galveston. So we won't have to leave the island or our friends."

Conall couldn't keep his hands off her anymore. He pulled her into his arms and covered her mouth with his. Long minutes later, he released her with only one word in mind. "Bed." Okay, two—bed and sex.

As he carried her to the bed, she ran her fingers through his hair. "Any news on the wedding front?"

He dropped her on the bed. "Yep. Sparkle says we're getting married at Wicked Fantasy. What do you think?"

She nodded even as she pulled at his shirt. "Wicked Fantasy is our place of beginnings. We met there, so it seems sort of right that we start our married life there, too."

His thought patterns were starting to scramble like they always did when she was close. "Are we finished talking?"

"Gee, I don't know. I thought maybe we'd talk about our relationship for a while." She laughed at his horrified expression, but her smile slowly faded. "I have one more thing to tell you. I wasn't going to say anything, but I don't want our life together to start with secrets."

Okay, this was going to be bad. But Conall couldn't think of much that would dent his happiness.

"Conalla told me when we were planning our trap for Sean that you'd never be free of the curse." She glanced away. "I chose not to tell you. I didn't want you to feel hopeless."

He tipped her face toward him. "Conalla saw it right, but she only got part of the picture. And you were right. I would've felt bad. A curse is only a curse, though, when you don't want it. I look forward to centuries of serving and protecting you, vampire lady."

She was into some serious stripping now, so he let everything go but his need for her. Forever.

"Oh, I talked to Eric. We're about to take a trip back to the Sensual Forest. We'll see what's down our personal Yellow Brick Road."

And they did.

Epilogue

"I've known lots of wicked women, babe, but you're the wickedest of them all. Evil and sexy. What's not to love?" Ganymede sprawled across the top of the display case in direct defiance of all health inspectors. "None of them ever suspected." He glanced around. "Where'd the death dude go?"

"Edge went away. I don't know where. I don't *care* where. Just as long as he doesn't come back." Sparkle studied the chocolate display she'd set up in the center of the store. Everything began and ended with chocolate in Sweet Indulgence. She might eat a whole box tonight to celebrate the completion of her master plan.

Ganymede pursued his main point. "How do you keep track of all these people you mess with? We're talking thousands over the centuries. I picture you with this giant Rolodex where you keep millions of names."

Sparkle was okay with a little bragging. Settling onto the high stool behind the counter, she leaned her elbows on the top of the case. "No Rolodex, Mede. It's all up here." She tapped her forehead. "I followed the lives of Eric,

Brynn, and Conall for centuries until I was ready to rewrite their destinies."

"Why them?" Mede must be interested. He hadn't made a move on the candy yet.

She shrugged. "Why not? I just choose people who catch my interest, people with serious emotional issues. Hey, I love the drama." Sparkle sighed her pleasure. The feel of a plan successfully completed was like slipping naked into a warm bath.

"So when I sensed the guys were ready, I bought Live the Fantasy and offered them jobs in the Castle of Dark Dreams. Once they were in place, I went after the women I'd chosen for them, women who were wrong for them on so many levels, but perfect for them when it came to sex. Instant lust plus instant conflict equaled fun for Sparkle Stardust."

"And all the other stuff?"

"I called Donna's show with tales of vampires in the Castle of Dark Dreams. I had Holgarth offer Kim the job of architect for the castle. And I supplied the anonymous tips that brought Gerry and Jinx here. Oh, and I masqueraded as Morrigan to warn Conall the last Kavanagh would be at Wicked Fantasy." *It was all me, me, me.*

"So what happens now, babe?" Mede looked hopeful.

"Oh, I don't know. Maybe after the wedding we could make a quick run to our exotic island, you could take your golden-god form, and we could get naked for about a week." Hot sex on hot sands. The perfect wind down to a hard job well done.

"After that?" She knew her smile was filled with wicked anticipation. "I have a certain vampire in mind that needs my help."

She turned wide, innocent eyes toward Mede. "Did I ever mention that I love this job?"